Advance Praise for *Foreign and Domestic*

"*Foreign and Domestic* delivers . . . absolutely fantastic! It captures the pulse-pounding intensity of *Lone Survivor* and wraps it in a brilliant, cutting-edge plot that will keep you on the edge of your seat . . . Tata *truly* is the new Tom Clancy. Turn off your phone, lock your doors, and jump into the phenomenal new book that *everyone* is going to be talking about."
—**Brad Thor,** #1 *New York Times* bestselling author of *Black List*

"Tata writes with a gripping and a gritty authority rooted in his matchless real-life experience, combining a taut narrative with an inside look at the frontiers of transnational terrorism. The result is so compelling that the pages seem to turn themselves."
—**Richard North Patterson,** #1 *New York Times* bestselling author of *In the Name of Honor*

"General Tata's story mixes high-threat combat with an intriguing and surprising mystery. . . . Vivid and complex characters make this a fascinating read."
—**Larry Bond,** *New York Times* bestselling author of *Exit Plan*

"Grabs you and doesn't let go . . . Written by a man who's 'been there,' this vibrant thriller will take you to places as frightening as the darkest secrets behind tomorrow's headlines . . . bound to be a breakout book for a gifted storyteller who served his country as splendidly as he writes!"
—**Ralph Peters,** *New York Times* bestselling author of *Lines of Fire*

FOREIGN AND DOMESTIC

A. J. TATA

PINNACLE BOOKS
Kensington Publishing Corp.
www.kensingtonbooks.com

Kensington Publishing Corp.
119 West 40th Street
New York, NY 10018

All Kensington titles, imprints, and distributed lines are available at special quantity discounts for bulk purchases for sales promotions, premiums, fund-raising, educational, or institutional use.
Special book excerpts or customized printings can also be created to fit specific needs. For details, write or phone the office of the Kensington special sales manager: Kensington Publishing Corp., 119 West 40th Street, New York, NY 10018, attn: Special Sales Department; phone 1-800-221-2647.

PINNACLE BOOKS and the Pinnacle logo are Reg. U.S. Pat. & TM Off.

ISBN-13: 978-0-7860-3540-3
ISBN-10: 0-7860-3540-4

First printing: March 2015

10 9 8 7 6 5 4 3 2

Printed in the United States of America

First electronic edition: March 2015

ISBN-13: 978-0-7860-3541-0
ISBN-10: 0-7860-3541-2

For my beautiful wife, Jodi, as always.

MILITARY OATH OF ENLISTMENT

I do solemnly swear that I will support and defend the Constitution of the United States against all enemies, **foreign and domestic**.

Chapter 1

The generals had labeled the mission "Kill or Capture."

Though Captain Jake Mahegan refused to consider anything but capturing the target.

With one hundred mph winds whipping across Mahegan's face, he was running through the checklist in his mind: insert, infiltrate, over-watch, assault, capture, collect, and extract.

Mahegan knew his men were fatigued from days of continuous operations. They couldn't afford any mistakes this morning. He felt the mix of emotions that came with knowing they were close to snaring the biggest prize since Bin Laden: The American Taliban, the one man who had posed the gravest threat to United States security since Army aviators and Navy SEALs had killed Osama. Concern for his troops gnawed at the adrenaline-honed edges of excitement. Mission focus was tempered with empathy for his men.

This morning's target was a bomb maker and security expert named Commander Hoxha, who would lead them to The American Taliban.

Mahegan and what remained of his unit were flying in on the wing seats of an MH-6 Little Bird aircraft to raid Hoxha's compound. Doubling as both expert bomb maker and the primary protection arm for The American Taliban, Hoxha had weathered wars in the Balkans, Iraq, and Afghanistan. Mahegan's review of Hoxha's dossier told him this could be the toughest mission he'd ever faced.

No mistakes.

The generals gave Mahegan this mission because they were on a timeline for withdrawal and he was the best. From the start of his special operations career, his Delta Force peers had called him the "Million-Dollar Man." The other twenty-nine of the thirty candidates in his Delta selection class had washed out. Each selection session cost the Army one million dollars.

For a year, Mahegan's outfit was casualty-free with impressive scalp counts of sixty-nine Taliban and al-Qaeda commanders. The better and more consistently he'd performed, the more Mahegan's legend had begun to take on mythical status within the military.

But that had mysteriously changed two months ago. A twenty-man unit had been whittled to eleven men over the past eight weeks, during which they had conducted twenty-two missions. The pace had been relentless and Mahegan knew his team was sucking gas.

The brass, however, had insisted on this early morning mission. They had told him that the President wanted The American Taliban captured before the final troops withdrew. His senior officers directed him to press ahead based on what they called "actionable intelligence." Translated to Mahegan and his men: They were on their third night with no sleep as they kept pressure on the enemy like a football team blitzing on every play with the added threat that their lives were at stake.

In the two helicopters, Mahegan's team whipped through canyons so tight the rotor blades appeared to be sparking off the granite spires of the Hindu Kush Mountains. Through his night-vision goggles, Mahegan could see the static electricity produced by the rotors painting a glowing trail, like a time-lapse photo. The helicopters, called Little Birds, were nothing more than a light wind through the valleys. Two canvas bench seats on either side were supporting him and his three teammates with a similarly configured one in trail.

As a backup extraction plan, Mahegan had his protégé, Sergeant Wesley Colgate, leading a two-vehicle convoy from the ground a couple of miles away. The lead vehicle carried Colgate and two more of their Delta Force teammates. In the trailing Humvee was a contract document and detainee exploitation team, known as Docex, from private military contractor Copperhead, Inc. Mahegan had fought Copperhead's inclusion, but the generals had insisted.

The Task Force 160th pilots skillfully flared the aircraft and touched down into the landing zone at a twenty-degree angle like dragonflies alighting on grass blades.

"Blue," Mahegan said into the mouthpiece connected to a satellite radio on his back, giving the code word for a successful offload in the landing zone. He expected no reply, and received none, as they were minimizing radio communications. The two helicopters lifted quietly out of the valley and returned to the base camp several miles away in Asadabad.

It was nearly 0400, about three hours before sunrise.

As always, as on every single mission it seemed, the fog settled into the valley as if the helicopters had it in tow. He considered Colgate and his two vehicles a few miles away. Moving quickly through the rocky landing zone, Mahegan found the path to their target area.

"Red," he said, as they passed the ridge to be used by the support team. He watched through his night-vision goggles as Tony "Al" Pucino and his three warriors from the trail helicopter silently chose their support-by-fire positions.

Moving toward the objective, Mahegan noted the jagged terrain and ran the remainder of the checklist through his mind: assault, capture, collect, and extract. Eyeing the darkened trail above the Kunar River a half mile to the west, he paused. His instincts were telling him it would be better to walk away from this objective than to have Colgate risk the bomb-laden path to the terrorists' compound.

Registering that thought, Mahegan knelt and adjusted his night-vision goggles. He spotted the enemy security forces milling around. They were not alert. To Mahegan, they looked like a bunch of green-shaded sleepy avatars. The offset landing zone had kept their infiltration undetected. They were good to go.

Mahegan gave the signal; they had rehearsed the assault briefly in the compound a few hours ago. From over fifty meters away, he put his silenced M4 carbine's infrared laser on the forehead of the guard nearest the door, pulsed it twice, which was the cue to the rest of the team, and then drilled him through the skull. He heard the muffled coughs of his teammates' weapons and saw the other guards fall to the ground, like marionettes with cut strings. Motioning to his assault team, he led them along a defile that emptied directly into the back gate of Commander Hoxha's adobe compound. With a shove of his massive frame against the wooden back door of the open compound, Mahegan breached the back wall just as the target was yanking his tactical vest up around his shoulders and reaching for his AK-74. Mahegan knew questioning Hoxha was key to the ultimate mission, so he shot him in the thigh, being careful to miss the femoral artery. Hoxha fell in the middle of the open courtyard between the gate and the back door. Several goats bleated and ran, bells around their necks clanging loudly.

"Target down," he said. "Status."

"Team One good," Pucino reported.

"Move to the objective. Help with SSE," Mahegan directed to Pucino. Not only had they come to capture Hoxha, but Sensitive Site Exploitation usually garnered the most valuable intelligence through analysis of SIM cards, computer hard drives, and maps.

He led the assault team into the courtyard and Patch, one of his tobacco-chewing teammates from Austin, Texas, strapped the terrorist's hands behind his back using plastic flex-cuffs. Two more men were already making a sweep through the compound, stuffing kit bags full of cell phones, computer hard drives, and generally anything that might be used to kill American forces or provide a clue as to The American Taliban's location. Mahegan's agenda included searching for something called an MVX-90, a top-secret American-made transmitter-receiver he believed had fallen into enemy possession.

Mahegan pulled out a picture and a red lens flashlight to confirm he'd shot the right man. He felt no particular emotion, but simply checked another box when he confirmed they indeed had Commander Hoxha, the leader of The American Taliban's security ring.

With the fog crawling into the narrow canyons, Ma-

hegan confirmed his instinct to call off the Little Birds
and Colgate's team. They were walking out.

With the terrorist flex-cuffed in front of him and the
place smelling like burned goat shit, he radioed Colgate, "We are coming to you. Do not move. Acknowledge, over."

"Roger." He recognized Colgate's voice.

On the heels of Colgate's reply, Pucino radioed,
"Team One at checkpoint alpha." This was good news
to Mahegan. Pucino's team had completed their portion of the sensitive site exploitation and was now securing the road that provided for their egress toward
Colgate's vehicles.

Mahegan checked off in his mind the myriad tasks
to come. They were in the intelligence collection
phase. He entered the adobe hut, saw his men zipping
their kit bags, and then moved outside where Patch was
guarding Hoxha.

He heard Hoxha speaking in Pashtun at about the
same time he noticed a small light shining through the
white pocket of his *payraan tumbaan*, the outer garment.

Mahegan thought, *Cell phone*.

He also thought, *Voice command*. Like an iPhone
Siri.

"Patch, shut him up!"

He went for the cell phone in the outer garment,
while Patch stuffed a rag in the prisoner's mouth, tying
it off behind his head. Fumbling with the pockets, Mahegan grabbed the smartphone, but saw the device had
made a call.

His first thought was that the adobe hut was rigged
with explosives. He pushed the end button to stop the
call and wondered if he had prevented whatever the
phone was supposed to trigger. He smashed the phone

into a nearby rock, knowing the SIM card would likely be undamaged and still valuable.

"Everyone inside, get out of the house! All outside, get down! Now!" he said to his men in a hoarse whisper. Mahegan landed on top of the bomb maker, crushing him beneath his 6'4", 230-pound frame. He saw Patch and two others digging into the dirt, wondering. Patch silently mouthed the letters, "WTF?"

A few seconds later, he heard an explosion beneath the house as the rest of his team came pouring out of the back door.

"There was a tunnel. Put a thermite in it," Sergeant O'Malley, from southeast Chicago, said.

"Roger," Mahegan replied. A thermite grenade would have only stunned anyone in the tunnel, but Mahegan didn't want to risk going back inside. Two minutes passed with no further activity.

Mahegan stood, pocketed the crushed smartphone, lifted the terrorist onto his back, and said to his team, "Follow me."

Colgate

About ten minutes before Mahegan said, "We are coming to you," Colgate was getting eager. He inched his way forward from the rally point along the raging waters of the Kunar River, assuming the worst when he noticed the weather would most likely prevent aircraft from conducting the extraction.

Colgate kept easing forward, pulling the contractors along behind him. The trail they were on was rocky, filled with potholes. It made the Rubicon Trail look like the Autobahn. His gloved hands gripped the steering wheel, sensing the tires on the Ground Mobility Vehicle pushing dirt into the raging waters fifty meters below as he crept toward his mentor.

He and Chayton Mahegan had been together in combat for two years now. To Colgate, Mahegan was a brave warrior, a throwback to his Native American heritage. Chayton and Mahegan were Iroquois names for "falcon" and "wolf," and Colgate had no doubt Mahegan possessed the ferocity of both predators.

He was proud to be one of Mahegan's Quiet Professionals. Colgate adhered to his boss's motto: "Keep your mouth shut and let your actions do the talking." After two months as Ranger buddies and then being one class apart in Delta selection, Colgate and Mahegan had bonded. Combat had made them closer, like brothers.

Colgate was a big man, a former college running back for Norfolk State University. He had almost made the big time. As a walk-on for the Washington Redskins, he had been cut the last day and enlisted a few hours later. After basic training, he was assigned to the Rangers and graduated Ranger school with Mahegan as his Ranger buddy. They got the same Ranger tab tattoo on their left shoulders and Colgate later made sergeant.

Now, Colgate flexed his left arm, thinking about the Ranger tab tattoo. He inched the vehicles closer. Not all the way, but closer, expecting the call. He was Plan B. Then Mahegan called: "We are coming to you. Do not move. Acknowledge, over."

"Roger," Colgate replied. But on the single-lane dirt road with a drop to the violent river beside him, he couldn't turn around. He was committed. He had to continue.

He heard a dull thud in the distance, like a grenade, and stopped momentarily. But he had to find somewhere to turn around, so he continued toward the objective. He leaned forward straining to see through his own goggles.

His gunner was getting nervous. "Colgate, I can't see jack, buddy," he said through the VIC-5 internal communications radio set. "No place to turn around. We better hold up."

But Colgate had state-of-the-art jammers that could detect buried mines and roadside bombs better than cats could find mice. He had passive finders and active jammers. He had a heads-up display and wide-angle night vision that made it seem he was watching high-definition TV as he drove. He could see thermal out to thirty meters in front of his vehicle and he was scanning every radio frequency every second with a jammer so powerful he figured they were sterilizing the men in every village they passed. To Colgate, this vehicle was like the Terminator on steroids. He was good to go and so he kept going. Besides, he couldn't even Y-turn where they were without tumbling into the river. He considered calling Mahegan to tell him he had already committed, but knew his friend was busy.

Then he heard Holmesly say, "Hey, man, big-ass rock pile in the road!"

Never a good sign, the rock pile loomed large in the HD viewer. Colgate slowed his vehicle and noticed through his goggles that they had crossed an infrared beam. He knew it was too late and muttered, "Oh shit."

Then he heard his radio come to life. It was Mahegan's voice. "Colgate—"

Mahegan

As Mahegan led his team single file down the road away from the village they had just raided, he stopped. He heard the GMVs moving not too far away, which was not good, not part of the plan.

He pressed his radio transmit button and said, "Colgate—"

A fireball erupted through the night mist. The billowing flame hung in the distance, a demonic mask sneering at Mahegan and his men. Shrapnel sizzled through the air with a torturous wail. Mahegan felt the pain of burning metal embedded into his left deltoid.

The shock wave knocked all eight of them down, plus the terrorist Mahegan was carrying. Hoxha, bound and gagged, was getting up to one knee. The fireball had momentarily destroyed Mahegan's night vision, but he could see enough to tell that the prisoner was standing, squaring off with him. Mahegan calculated Hoxha's options. Run toward the wreckage? Jump into the river rapids with hands bound? Scale the cliffs to the east? Or move back toward his compound?

The fireball receded but still flickered brightly about one hundred meters away. The shadows of the jagged rocks were black ghosts dancing in ritual celebration of more foreign blood spilled in this impossible land.

Mahegan ignored the burning and bleeding in his left deltoid as he fumbled for the weapon hanging from a D-ring on his outer tactical vest. A secondary explosion sent another fireball into the sky, probably the ammunition from Colgate's GMV, he thought. The second blast gave the terrorist more time, but Mahegan still had him in his field of vision. Instead of choosing the three options away from him, Hoxha ran directly at him.

Hoxha faked one way as if he were a football running back and then attempted to get past Mahegan. Mahegan thought about Colgate and the casualties his team had suffered over the last two months. Then a flywheel broke free in his mind.

"Impulsive and aggressive," the Delta Force psychiatrist had said.

Mahegan figured, this time, the man was correct.

He cocked his elbow with his right hand on the telescoping stock of his M4 carbine and his left hand on the hand guard and weapon's accessory rail. He stepped forward with his left foot and propelled the leading edge of the butt-stock forward toward the terrorist's torso. He rotated his upper body and extended his right arm, locking his right elbow as he connected with Hoxha. His aim was high, or Hoxha ducked, and the weapon caught him across the face. The claw of the butt-stock connected with the man's temple. Hoxha crumpled to the ground, dead.

Mahegan saw the flesh and brain matter hanging off the end of his weapon and knew he had unleashed mortal fury onto the prisoner. He sprinted one hundred meters to Colgate's vehicle and found what he'd suspected: burning bodies. He reached in through the fire, his own shoulder burning from the shrapnel, and pulled at Colgate. All he got was charred skin coming off in his hands. He grabbed for Colgate's upper body and wrenched him out of the GMV, placing him on the ground. Patch and O'Malley were crawling over the burnt windshield to grab Coleseed. No one could find the gunner, Holmesly.

"Search away from the vehicle. He probably got thrown into the river. We'll have to search downstream," Mahegan said. Inside, he was a raging storm. Three more of his men were dead.

Eight left.

He stared momentarily at the trail vehicle in the distance, undamaged, with its crew of Copperhead, Inc. contractors standing stunned and motionless in the eerie darkness. Turning back to the burning vehicle, he only cared about piecing back together the bits of Colgate so that he could make him whole again. He was furious. He wondered how all the jammers, scanners, and thermal equipment had failed to defeat a homemade bomb in Nuristan Province, Afghanistan. In fact, there was only one way it could have happened and Mahegan refused to believe what he suspected.

As he stood over Colgate's remains, the charred flesh and the horrific grimace seared onto his face, he asked him, "Why, buddy?"

Pucino approached and said, "I don't know why, but I do know how, boss."

Mahegan, towering over the Italian soldier from Boston, looked down at the box in Pucino's hand.

"An empty MVX-90 box. From the bomb maker's hut. Made in the Research Triangle Park of North Carolina. Several more in there, unused," Pucino said.

Mahegan internalized this information. This was the only device that could have guided an electronic trigger signal past the jammers in Colgate's vehicle. And it had come from the U.S. of A.

The raging storm that had been building inside him for two months, ever since he had lost his first soldier in combat, finally unleashed. Mahegan howled with a primal ferocity that roared through the distant canyons, the valleys echoing with his anguish. Then he turned toward the Copperhead, Inc. private military contractors and stared at them, wondering why they were on the mission at all.

Chapter 2

Mahegan knew he was being watched. After a year of drifting in eastern North Carolina, he had finally been found.

Which wasn't all bad.

The black Ford F-150 pickup truck had driven past his rented above-garage apartment on Roanoke Island one too many times. Mahegan had noticed the unusually clean exterior of the vehicle the first time. Here in the Outer Banks of North Carolina, a shiny, waxed truck was as obvious as a gelled playboy among seafaring watermen. The second and last drive-by, a day later, coupled with a slightest tap of the brakes, confirmed that either the Department of Homeland Security or the Department of Defense had located him.

He kept to his routine.

At five a.m. on a typically warm September morning, he ducked out of the Queen Anne's Revenge, a guesthouse owned by Outer Banks proprietor Sam Midgett, and walked along Old Wharf Road of Roanoke Island. Mahegan slid around the fence that blocked the pavement a hundred meters from Croatan Sound, and found Midgett's twelve-foot duck-hunting boat. Pausing to listen to the bullfrogs and inhale the brackish odor, he shoved off through the low marshes, pushing through the reeds. A small white-tail deer darted past him, splashing through the knee-deep water. Stepping into the boat, he used the paddle to get some momentum and then he was in the deeper water of the sound, which was to the western side of the island. About one hundred meters out was an orange channel marker. He reached it, pulled a half hitch through a rusty cleat on the buoy, kicked off his mocs, and dove into the black water.

The sun was about an hour from cresting over the horizon of the Atlantic Ocean less than half a mile to his rear. He pulled with broad-shouldered strokes, the lightning-bolt scar from the shrapnel of Colgate's vehicle explosion screaming with every rotation. The doctors had removed the embedded metal from just beneath his Ranger tab tattoo on his left deltoid and had told him to swim for rehab.

So he swam. Every day.

He preferred swimming this way, in the darkness. Alone, he was able to rehash the botched mission and its aftermath. And here he was also able to evade the vigilance of the Homeland Security noose that was tightening around him. He let his mind drift again, from being watched now to what had come before.

He latched on to the moment he had turned in his papers to resign his commission as a military officer. His teammates had written seven too-similar statements about how Mahegan had thwarted an escape attempt by the clever terrorist who used the bomb blast as a diversion. The Army Inspector General had balked at the carbon-copy testimony of his teammates.

"What my team says is essentially true. But I let my emotions take over," he told his commander, Major General Bob Savage. "Colgate was dead. Hoxha may have given us something useful on Adham. Hoxha *did* try to escape, but he was still cuffed and gagged. I killed him. I failed. And we're no closer to Adham than before. It's that simple."

Mullah Adham was the nom de guerre of The American Taliban. Actually, Adham was an American citizen in his mid-twenties from Iowa named Adam Wilhoyt who had gone native with al-Qaeda.

General Savage nodded, trying to persuade him not to resign, but Mahegan never wavered.

"I could drive on like this never happened, but without my integrity, what do I have?" Mahegan said. Savage stared at the captain like a seasoned poker player.

"You know it was an MVX-90 that killed Colgate, Holmesly, and Coleseed. And I'm sure you have thought this, but once Hoxha was able to make that call to activate the trigger on the bomb, all you had to do was initiate a radio call to trigger the blast. Only the MVX-90, US manufactured and tested, could allow our radio signals, which operate on a very specific bandwidth, past all of the jammers that were operating."

Of course, it was all he could think about. He had technically killed his own men. In order to simultaneously jam enemy trigger signals and communicate to friendly forces, the American Army had developed the MVX-90. The device left discreet, protected gaps in the radio spectrum so that friendly communications could enter and exit while still searching for ill-intended incoming signals to block. The only way to find those gaps and know how to program a trigger device on the American frequency, Mahegan knew, was for the enemy to have an MVX-90 operating in the area. Effectively, it was like finding a programmer's back door into a software operating system.

A flash burst in his mind from the fateful radio call: *"Colgate—"*

Running his hand across his face, Mahegan said, "I know I killed them, sir."

After a moment, Savage responded. "Your radio did. Not you." Reacting to Mahegan's silent stare, he continued. "And whoever gave them the MVX-90."

Mahegan looked up at his commander and said, "I have an idea."

He explained as Savage listened, sometimes nodding and sometimes frowning.

"I have a different thought," Savage said.

Mahegan listened to his commanding officer, who pushed the papers toward him across the gray metal desk in Bagram Air Base. Mahegan looked down, shook his head, and pushed the papers back at his general.

"I've got to do this my way, sir," he said.

Savage nodded, saying, "You always do, Jake. But if you stay over here in the sandbox you can get your revenge for Colgate . . . and the rest of your team."

Mahegan grimaced. "You know what they say about revenge, sir."

"What?"

"It's all in the anticipation. The thing itself is a pain."

"Twain," Savage had replied. "Since we're discussing authors, then we might as well state the obvious: You can't go home again. You ought to take me up on my offer."

"I'll think about it, sir. Like I said, it's got to be done my way. And maybe there's another way to do it." Mahegan paused, and then said, "Thomas Wolfe, by the way."

"Roger. And that means you know what I'm talking about. You go back to America, especially with Homeland Security all over your ass, and nothing will look the same. You'll be blacklisted by that new moron they have running the nut farm at DHS and this list of vets she says are threats to society. You've gotten some press over this thing, too. And, Jake, General Bream, the Army Inspector General, is sniffing all around this faster than a blue tick coonhound. He's an ass hamster of the highest magnitude and wants to be Army Chief of Staff. They are calling him the 'Chief of Integrity' or some such bullshit. If you go back, he will be gunning for you."

Mahegan shrugged. "Got a fair amount of that kind over here, too. I'll be okay."

"He's putting on his best indignant performance for the press. He's going for a dishonorable discharge, you know."

Actually, no. This was news to him. Bad news. He had fought with honor, risking his life for his fellow Americans and his teammates. Endless days and nights with no sleep, little food, and unspeakable danger.

"Didn't know that, sir." Mahegan looked away at the maps of Afghanistan on the plywood walls, reminders of firefights, combat parachute jumps, and helicopter raids everywhere.

"Don't sweat it for now, Jake. Cross that bridge when we get to it. Your team covered for you."

"They didn't cover for me, sir. They reported what happened."

Savage waved off Mahegan's statement and continued his sales pitch for Mahegan to stay in the Army.

"For the record, you belong here, with us, doing this," Savage said, pointing his finger at the maps. "This is your home. I took you in despite your psych evaluation, Jake. That counts for something."

Mahegan nodded, recalling how the Army psychiatrist had identified Mahegan's sometimes "impulsive, aggressive behavior," and recommended against inclusion in the elite force. Savage had stood firm and the "million-dollar man" was born. Oddly, Delta Force *had* been Mahegan's home, and he had left all that he loved.

"I just need time, sir," he told Savage. "Then, maybe I can do what you suggest."

Now, this morning, pulling hard through the black water, he wondered whether or not he should have accepted Savage's deal. The general had been right. Someone was looking for him and General Bream was gunning for a dishonorable discharge. He tried to push the black pickup truck and the Inspector General out of his mind.

His broad shoulders and powerful legs propelled him through the sound. After a shark incident while swimming off Wilmington's fabled Frying Pan Shoals, Mahegan was determined to appear dominant in the water. He swam with purpose, as if he were the apex predator, some kind of savage beast on the prowl.

His mind drifted from Colgate to The American Taliban, Mullah Adham, to his shoulder and to Martin Strel, who owned the world record for the longest continuous swim. Before beginning his swimming rehab, Mahegan had researched the sport. Strel swam 312 miles in the Danube River in 84 hours. Mahegan did the math. He was doing 5 miles max each way. Strel had cruised at a sustained rate of 3.7 miles an hour. Mahegan was doing something less than that, but not by much. Plus, Strel had a helping current while he was going cross-current. The tide was either coming in or going out, which was always perpendicular to his axis of advance. Mahegan knew he wasn't doing the miles all at once, of course.

He swam that way for an hour and a half until, on a downward stroke, his hand hit sand, touching the small beach of the mainland of North Carolina. He pulled himself up, strode through the knee-deep water, and sat on the jutting spit of land that was the easternmost point of the Alligator River National Wildlife Refuge.

He sat about twenty meters back from the water, facing east, and watched the dawn appear over the Atlantic Ocean, Outer Banks barrier islands, and Roanoke Island. The sun cast an orange streak along the spreading vee of his swimming wake. The water rippled outward, inviting the coming day. The vee eventually disappeared, and he wondered about his life path. What was left in his wake so far? What more would there be? Would his trail simply blend back into the environment with no remaining signature?

As Mahegan stared at his diminishing path, he felt welcoming eyes surround him from behind.

He smiled. They had learned to come to him, or perhaps he to them.

The red wolves crept from their Alligator River refuge and joined Mahegan as he watched the sun and wondered about life. Mahegan had researched the terrain of Dare County Mainland, and among other valuable lessons, he learned that at one time there had been only sixteen red wolves left in the United States. The National Wildlife Refuge had tried an experimental repopulation program by placing a few of the sixteen in Alligator River National Park. Fierce hunters, the red wolves began to thrive on the abundant wildlife in the remote national park.

They traveled in family packs of adults and cubs. Mahegan turned and saw a youngster lying in some saw grass, staring at him. The pup looked more like a red fox than a wolf.

Mahegan felt a comfort here, removed from even the sparsely populated Roanoke Island. Drifting up the Outer Banks of North Carolina for a year, he had worked the odd job for a couple of weeks before moving on. He was a deckhand on a fishing boat out of Wilmington, a bouncer at a bar in Beaufort, and part of a landscaping crew in Hatteras. Remaining obscure was paramount.

But a year was enough. The one-year anniversary of his failed mission in Nuristan Province was tomorrow, and he was at the end of this particular trail.

Plus, they had found him. He needed solitude to finalize his plans. Today.

The first part of his plan, if he could call it that, was to borrow his new landlord's pickup truck, drive up to Arlington National Cemetery, and visit the gravesites of Colgate and the rest of his men who had been killed in action.

The second part was, well, complicated.

He stood and turned slowly, facing west. He counted the faces poking through the reeds and tall grass. Eight. Just like the remaining members of his team.

They seemed to be staring at his arm, where the scar that looked like a lightning-bolt welt ran from his left shoulder to his elbow. Mahegan suspected that somewhere deep down in the psyches of these animals, they knew the threat to their species. Sixteen left. Just as families passed stories from generation to generation, these red wolves, Mahegan was certain, were passing the story of their near extinction to their offspring.

One of the wolves circled past him. He didn't know,

but perhaps his kinship with these animals had something to do with being backed into a corner, the very essence of their being whittled to the core. Would they survive or evaporate into thin air? He closed his eyes, becoming certain of his connection with these predators. He relaxed and let his mind drift outward to them, and then opened his eyes. They had slipped silently into the bush, Mahegan catching the flipping tail of the pup.

He turned, waded into the sound, and began swimming.

As he glided into the water that was now showing some chop from a southerly wind, a distant, but enormous explosion shook the water around his body.

He stopped, stood in the chest-deep sound only twenty meters offshore, and turned toward the mushroom cloud fueled by a large plume of smoke billowing upward like a miniature nuclear blast. He gauged the distance to be about ten miles away at a two-hundred-degree azimuth, southwest, in the center of Dare County Bombing Range.

Picturing the source of the burst cloud, Mahegan thought, *That's about right*. More than a year ago the Department of Defense had closed Dare County Bombing Range, which oddly enough sat in the middle of the Alligator River Wildlife Refuge. In an attempt to appease a shunned contractor, the DoD had given the dirty job of clearing the bomb detritus to the private military contractor Copperhead, Inc.

As he began swimming back to Roanoke Island, Mahegan suddenly felt better about his decision regarding Savage's offer.

Chapter 3

Fort Brackett, South Carolina

While Mahegan was stepping into Croatan Sound for his early morning swim, about 350 miles from Roanoke Island, a man named Chikatilo watched his two-man construction crew outside the front gate of Fort Brackett, South Carolina. They had been working for several hours under the glare of high-intensity spotlights. The workmen wore orange-and-yellow striped vests and had placed diamond-shaped signs along the road that read FINES DOUBLED FOR SPEEDING. One of them even held the reversible STOP and SLOW sign, though it wasn't really needed.

Chikatilo looked at his smartphone and saw the Twitter direct message:

@TuffChik . . . Road construction looks good!

Chikatilo and his crew were ghosts. Though he didn't look to be of Afghan descent, he was. He had blond hair and blue eyes, a by-product of the Soviet invasion of Afghanistan in the late 1980s. Born in Bamian, Afghanistan, he attended the University of Colorado in a preparatory step to eventually ascend into Afghan politics, like his father, who was the governor of Bamian Province. The success of the 9/11 attacks had stoked his militant fervor and his father, a moderate, had cast him out of peaceful Bamian like spoiled seed.

Like any good jihadist, he had found a way to infiltrate the enemy and had secured a job as an interpreter based upon the bona fides of his father, whom the American Army had never questioned about his son. His tour with the Americans had led him to Mullah Adham, who had anointed him "Prizrak Chikatilo"—*prizrak* meaning ghost in Russian. Then The American Taliban had made Chikatilo a ghost and named him the leader of all of the ghost prisoners.

Chikatilo had just two ghosts with him. He watched a big, muscled guy he'd named Bundy lean his hardened abs into a jackhammer that was spitting chunks of curb concrete in all directions. Bundy was wearing safety glasses and a work belt with tools. Chikatilo looked professional in his construction hat with the big letters BOSS stenciled across the top. He stared at his team for a minute and then let his eyes drift toward the military police gate at Fort Brackett, South Carolina, home of the US Army's largest training base.

It was near five a.m. As the jackhammer cleared away the curved six-foot chunk of curb, the crew began emplacing prefabricated, Styrofoam, shaped replicas of the curb. Manson, the second man in Chikatilo's crew, wore an orange vest and white construction hat. He handled his two three-foot sections of curb gingerly and placed them side by side. They fit nearly perfectly, though he brushed some curb dust away from the crevices to achieve a snug fit.

Their construction truck was parked along the lane where, when vehicles slowed to have their identification checked at the military police checkpoint, they would be stopped directly in front of the construction site. Chikatilo tugged down on his hard hat and hitched up his pants as a military police vehicle cruised slowly toward them. They were on the civilian side of the gate about one hundred meters away from the guards.

Chikatilo had picked this location because it was off the military installation, yet also that magic spot where traffic in the mornings backed up as the guards fell victim to math issues. Too many cars were trying to pass through too few gates in too short of a time. Accordingly, the lines were sometimes a quarter mile long across the four entry lanes. Worse than the Lincoln Tunnel in Manhattan, Chikatilo thought.

A military police officer pulled up next to him and smiled.

"Y'all going to be finished before long? In about an hour the entire city is going to be waiting to pass through right there," he said, pointing at the four stalls where security guards checked identification. Chikatilo noticed the dashboard lights gave the man's face an eerie glow, so he wasn't too worried about the MP remembering much about his own face.

"We're about done, officer," Chikatilo said. He knew the man in the car wasn't a commissioned officer, but he wasn't about to cause trouble or draw attention to himself. As a ghost, he'd been careful to look the part of an American construction worker, wearing a long ponytail clip-on hanging out of the back of his BOSS helmet, a gold veneer cap covering his right incisor, and a large *"Mom"* tattoo on his forearm. His safety glasses distorted his eyes and the brown contacts disguised his blue eyes.

"Good. Don't want no unnecessary backups," the military policeman said.

"No worries, officer," Chikatilo said, reaching his hand out for a shake so he could show the full breadth of the tattoo. He saw the man glance at his arm and then reach his hand out of the window to give him a shake. As he clasped the man's hand, Chikatilo looked into the cruiser and saw the radio in the passenger seat. He recognized the state-of-the-art Harris RF-7700V series handheld radio that was pressed to talk, chat-enabled, and able to transmit photos.

"Hey, is that a Harris radio?"

"Sure is. Best we got. Can even text on this puppy." The MP held up the dark green device not much bigger than a remote control.

All Chikatilo cared about was that the Harris radio operated in the 30–108 MHz range, confirming his intelligence that the range he needed was what the installation military police used. The Army would be blocking all other radio signals to protect against remote detonated explosives at the gate, just as in combat. Which meant that the only signals that could be sent and received here would be within that spectrum and most likely attributed to one of the military police-operated Harris radios.

"Have a nice morning, now, y'hear," the man called out to him as he nudged the gas pedal and slowly turned back toward the gate.

"Same to you, officer."

Chikatilo turned and saw that Bundy and Manson were staring at him, apparently done with their work.

Once the police cruiser was out of earshot, Chikatilo said, "Rig the bitch."

Rig the bitch really meant connect the battery wires to the MVX-90, the programmer's back door into US military communications. When armed by a call from Chikatilo's cell phone, the MVX-90 would recognize the next radio transmission within the 30–108 MHz bandwidth as "friendly" and allow it to proceed to its intended target, the bomb. Once activated, a passive infrared device would pulse an invisible light across the road. When a vehicle crossed the beam, the passive infrared device would ignite the blasting caps in the twenty explosively formed penetrators they had just installed in the faux curbstone.

The copper discs would turn to a nearly molten form, enough to transition from concave to convex and become a hardening fist of alchemy heading straight for twenty different targets at the speed of seven thousand feet per second. The blast was intended to maim and kill as many soldiers and family members as possible at the main gate.

Bundy and Manson looked at him when they were done and nodded.

"Camera set and ready?"

Bundy, the Iraqi, nodded and said, *"Inshallah."* God *willing*.

Chikatilo had them secure a small wireless camera that could be monitored from the mobile command post inside the white work vehicle in which they traveled. When he was satisfied that the target area was sufficiently populated, he would call the small cell phone lying in the grass underneath some leaves. The cell phone was connected to the MVX-90 receiver inside the faux curbstone by a thin copper wire no bigger than a speaker wire for a stereo.

"Let's move."

The two men nodded. One was from Iraq and the other from Afghanistan. The Iraqi was an excellent electrician, while the Afghan made the best homemade explosives Chikatilo had ever seen.

They understood most of what Chikatilo said to

them and of course they understood "Rig the Bitch," because they had rehearsed it a hundred times. Where necessary, Chikatilo easily rotated between his native Pashtun tongue or his passable Arabic.

Chikatilo packed up his troops in their utility van and slowly pulled away into the early morning dawn that beckoned just over the horizon. He drove about a mile up the road and turned onto a side street. Slamming the van into park, he turned around and watched Manson, the one from Afghanistan, strip off his construction uniform and shave his body. The man held a Koran for a moment and spread his palms upward as he canted his supplications. Done, Manson strapped rows of C4 explosives packed with one-penny nails and wood screws around his midsection. He then donned khaki pants, running shoes, and a Hawaiian shirt. He looked like an average Middle Eastern American trying to fit into Western culture.

He had begun to connect the detonator when Chikatilo reached out and said, "Whoa, buddy. Rig *that* bitch up when you get there."

Manson grinned, understanding.

"You know the route, right? Don't forget this." Chikatilo held up a second cell phone, pressed dial, let it ring once, and then hung up. He then made a cradle with his arms, as if he were holding an infant. "Get close to children and women."

Manson, the Afghan, nodded. They had rehearsed this part, too. He grabbed the cell phone and pocketed it, then hugged Bundy, the Iraqi, before jumping out of the double back doors of the van. Chikatilo gave him a few minutes to get moving, confirmed he was heading in the right direction, and then pulled onto I-20 heading east before turning north on I-95.

He parked the van at a rest stop on I-95 about forty

miles away from the base and watched the remote camera's image through the Wi-Fi/satellite uplink. He saw
the traffic creep along through the panorama of the
camera. He tilted the toggle and zoomed in, catching a
few officer stickers on the passes. Those were blue, enlisted were red, and civilians were green. He slewed the
camera to the left and saw the line of cars growing. He
slewed to the right and saw the security guards taking
identification tags, scanning them in bar code scanners, and handing them back. The line had slowed to a
crawl, giving Chikatilo the opportunity to study the
faces in the cars. He saw mostly men, but also several
women and children. He was thankful that there were
schools and day care centers on the base. Everything
was moving according to plan. Now was the time.

Chikatilo picked up one of many disposable cell
phones, dialed the number, and listened as the receiving phone began to ring. He zoomed the camera onto
the phone in the ditch beneath the leaves and saw the
red light flashing in a gap in the detritus they had purposely left behind. He zoomed in to the tiny passive infrared switch and saw that it had properly activated as
indicated by the dull green light on the back, which he
could see through the tiny hole he had carved through
the Styrofoam curb. There was a similar hole on the
other side of the Styrofoam that would soon be pulsing
an infrared beam.

The key now was to get the military police at the
gate to make a radio call, which would begin the cycle.

Chikatilo next dialed the military police station at
Fort Brackett and said, "I can't say who I am, but you've
got something really bad about to happen at the main
gate. I'm watching it now and people are going to die.
Remember the sniper who shot at an entire brigade formation or the guy who shot all those people at Ziti's

restaurant? Well, this is bigger. You need to lock the main gate down now!"

He heard some scrambling in the background and a new voice came on the line, asking, "Who is this?"

"I'm telling you, man. Some serious shit is about to go down if you don't get some dogs and military police and first-aid teams out to the main gate. You are not prepared for this."

"Stand by," the voice said. Chikatilo heard the man pick up something, which thudded on the desk once, and then heard some more voices in the background. Then he heard a small beep indicating the man in the police station had pressed the transmit button of a secure radio, probably a Harris and most definitely in the 30–108 MHz range. Push to talk.

"Guardian six, this is Guardian one six," the voice said.

Chikatilo turned his attention to the camera, which showed the passive infrared switch was now glowing a bright green. The MVX-90 had done its job. He hung up the cell phone and panned the camera out so that he could see more cars still stacking up.

There was a bored young man with the high-and-tight haircut of a paratrooper driving a Ford Focus directly in line with the lethal curbstone. He looked ahead, mouthed something that Chikatilo thought looked like, "This sucks," and then looked to the right. The soldier's car was completely stopped and perhaps three feet from the now pulsating infrared switch. Nothing was moving. Then the young man stared hard at the curbstone. It occurred to Chikatilo that a lot of the men and women in the traffic jam at the front gate had been on three or four tours in Iraq and Afghanistan and knew what these bombs looked like.

The young man yanked up the parking brake on his

car, eyes wide, and stepped out of his vehicle and started screaming. Chikatilo couldn't tell what he was saying, but he guessed it was something like, "Nobody move!" He was holding his arms up and walking to the rear of the formation of cars, away from the curbstone. Chikatilo saw a female soldier in uniform with two children in child car seats, both in the back. The soldier turned her head and braked hard.

For a moment he worried that the male soldier would stop the mission, but then someone in the other lane flipped him off and nudged forward. The car broke the invisible beam, and suddenly the camera picture was lost in an explosion that a few seconds later he and Bundy actually heard at the rest stop forty miles away.

Chikatilo continued to watch the bedlam as fuel tanks on cars exploded. Copper plates traveling seven thousand feet per second through thin-skinned vehicles, mangled bodies, and tore off limbs. Survivors began screaming for medics.

Chikatilo resisted calling Manson, who should be waiting on the opposite side of the chaos from where the bomb had exploded. It took exactly fourteen minutes and thirty-two seconds for the first ambulance to get to the scene. Chikatilo timed the response. He had predicted fifteen to twenty minutes. All of this was important for the future missions.

Manson's instructions were to wait until he had a crowd of over thirty people gawking at the scene. Soon, another three ambulances arrived and the throng of do-gooders trying to yank the injured from their vehicles grew dramatically.

Chikatilo watched as Manson, in his blue jeans and Hawaiian shirt, jogged to the largest mass of people near the main gate. He was running as if he wanted desperately to help. No one turned in his direction, as they were all fixated on the death and destruction to their front. Cars were smoldering, tires were smoking, and fires were burning. *People were burning.* Chikatilo watched on the display monitor as Manson became the single best guided missile ever.

Manson waded into the middle of the crowd, pushing and shoving his way to the absolute center of the mass as if he were a doctor who could heal all that had been broken. He found a mother holding a baby, screaming with an outstretched arm, perhaps looking at the molten ruins of another child. Manson put his arm around the grief-stricken mother holding the wailing baby.

Then he detonated himself.

For a second time the screen went gray with smoke and debris flying in a fury of destruction.

Chikatilo nodded, looked at Bundy, and said, "You're up next, buddy."

Chapter 4

Unknown location

From his lair in Iraq or Afghanistan, or wherever his Internet protocol put him today, The American Taliban, Mullah Adham, watched the high-definition video uplinks of the attacks on Fort Brackett.

"Take that, bitch," Adham whispered to no one in particular.

He sat cross-legged on a prayer mat as he absently tugged at his dark beard. He backed up the video and replayed it again, like a football coach watching postgame film. He saw as the camera had zoomed on the flashing green light of the MVX-90, then as the soldier had exited his own car, screaming for everyone to stop.

He paused the tape as he watched the young soldier duck when the explosion coughed outward from the curbstone. In successive frames, Adham kept his eyes focused on the soldier. He noticed a black object, an explosively formed penetrator, spit straight from the curbstone toward him and cut him in half as it moved at supersonic speed.

"Yes," he whispered to himself.

He replayed it again, this time watching as a copper plate exploded through the car with the female solider and her two children.

"Sweet," he whispered.

Adham, born Adam Wilhoyt, was raised in Davenport, Iowa, by his mother, whom he loved. He had no memory, until recently, of his father.

As usual, he was alone in his Spartan warren. Adham kept two pictures on the wall of his hut, not that he needed reminders of his transition from normal kid to The American Taliban.

One was a magazine photo of Ned Lieberstein, the FBI agent who had led the raid on his childhood home's basement in Davenport. Lieberstein had been tracking his, Adam Wilhoyt's, massive online game called *Monument Hunter*. The purpose of the game had been to find the quickest routes to famous American landmarks such as Mount Rushmore or the Jefferson Memorial and defend them from attack by the other players. Meanwhile, the other online gamers, not having arrived first to establish a defense, could choose to team with the attacking force or the defending force. Battles were being waged online for the survival of American landmarks. Adam Wilhoyt had written the code and placed it on the Internet to the delight of hundreds of thousands of users. It was an untapped goldmine.

Apparently, though, virtual monument hunting was illegal. Wilhoyt's mother had unwittingly let the FBI into their home, and Adham recalled the SWAT team spilling down into the basement where he was sitting amid all of his computers and servers chewing up terabytes of information. Lieberstein had paraded him in

handcuffs out of his house, along the sidewalk in front
of the peering neighbors and into the waiting van, its
blue lights flashing like spotlights, highlighting his
embarrassment.

He was tried as a juvenile, spent a year doing community service, and ultimately graduated from high
school by earning a GED.

In his school program, he actually started falling for
a girl, Elizabeth Carlsen, a blond-haired, blue-eyed Scan-
dinavian girl who was a research assistant at the library. She shared his interest in computers. They had
met at the library, the only place the FBI allowed him
to use a computer.

Without any compelling reason, one day about eighteen months after his arrest, he conducted a Google
search on Lieberstein. He learned that the FBI agent
had retired to Malibu, California, where he was marketing an online game called *Shrine Seekers*, which was
essentially the Adam Wilhoyt code, and making millions. Lieberstein's minor code modification had somehow circumvented the court's ruling against Wilhoyt
and had flooded the gaming market.

Something had flipped inside him that day. His government had screwed him out of a fortune. But it was
more than that. His country, in the form of a bureaucrat
named Lieberstein, had betrayed him, taken his dignity, isolated his mother, and stolen a year from his
young life—an eternity—that he wouldn't get back. He
was not going to be the sucker his fellow citizens were
by letting their government screw them over without
ever standing up to it. *Don't tread on me, bitch!*

While he worked out a plan, he found a job developing websites during the first day at the library, moved
into his own apartment, and bought enough equipment

to improve his hacking skills, riding electrons through forbidden mazes of security in the Pentagon, the FBI, the NSA, and anywhere he wanted to go. He dated Elizabeth long enough to fall in love before she had to move "somewhere down East."

What he learned was that his country was corrupt at every level. Not only had they screwed him, but also they were giving the shaft to Joe Six-pack every day. One day he hacked into al-Qaeda and saw it was the same bullshit with different players. Then he hacked a few large private military contractors where he learned that more state secrets were held in the servers of those companies than in the Pentagon.

His confused twenty-year-old mind had seen too much. Like a child watching his parents fight, he saw the machinery of nations and corporations struggling for survival. What he learned was that with the Internet, one person could do what one country could do. He also figured out that the rule of law only applied when the law wanted it to.

If his country was going to be at war, then so would he. But he wanted to be *somebody*. He checked out Nietzsche from the library and thought he could be the Beast with Red Cheeks. He studied Camus, reflecting on the notions of absurdity and nothingness. Delusions of grandeur dancing in his mind, Adam then sought a different perspective. He tried contacting his father before he made his decision, but the man would have nothing to do with him. That act of omission led him to make the biggest decision of his life: He bought a plane ticket to Islamabad, Pakistan, and began to live a life of minimalism. He sought the fame that Nietzsche said he needed and felt the nothingness that Camus promised.

From there, he began floating between madrassas, where he was called "Amriki." The American. After a year, it was The American Taliban. Because of his size, over six feet tall, he learned to survive as the fittest in the madrassa. With his Internet and newfound mechanical skills, he became valuable to his suspicious new friends. His IQ hovering above 170, he learned to negotiate with his would-be adversaries. Adham convinced the tribal leaders in Western Pakistan, the Quetta Shura, that he could be of value and showed them a homemade video where he taunted the American government.

The elders liked what they saw, especially that Amriki had worked to learn Arabic and Pashtun. His words floated effortlessly between the languages. He even taught various bomb makers the skills necessary to remotely view and detonate roadside bombs. With the right equipment, the triggerman could be one hundred yards or ten thousand miles away.

The al-Qaeda and Taliban elders were impressed.

In less than a year, he had catapulted himself from a juvenile delinquent in America to a person of immense worth in the enemy's camp. He thrived on that feeling of value. He had brilliantly subjugated himself to al-Qaeda, knowing that their leaders were just as useless as the leaders in America and just as frustrated; *and* he had risen to prominence. It would have been impossible in America.

The doctrine didn't matter; the power was the intoxicating drug.

After his first taped message to America, pronouncing himself as Mullah Adham, The American Taliban, al-Qaeda and Taliban forces saw increased funding from the diaspora. Mullah Adham was a sensation. With each performance, his sandbox grew and soon he was doing live streaming Internet performances, bouncing Internet signals around the globe. The senior leadership of al-Qaeda and the Taliban were thrilled, viewing him as a strategic combat multiplier.

And like that moment in the library after Google-searching Lieberstein, Adham had another moment. A squad of Delta Force commandos had nearly killed him when he was visiting his friend, Commander Hoxha. If not for the trapdoor and tunnel system beneath Hoxha's house, he would have been captured. That night, everything had changed.

Adham had tacked up another photo in his hut: Captain Chayton "Jake" Mahegan.

Looking now at both photos, Adham powered up his MacBook, logged into his Facebook page, and then looked into the small camera that was streaming live.

"Greetings."

Adham was piping his feed into outer space, redirecting off several satellites before hosting on a specific bird to which all of the major cable channels had access. His beard would not come in as fully as he might want, so he had used henna to darken the hair.

"America, the attacks have begun. Women and children, especially, beware. These are *inverse* attacks and we are not sparing the most vulnerable. Actually, we are targeting *them*. Today you saw some unique explosives. If you want answers, ask your Captain Chayton Mahegan of the US Army. He knows exactly how we are doing this. And next, coming soon to a computer near you: beheadings. We have captured American spies and things will get pretty crazy from this point on, so let's chat tomorrow. Peace, out."

The camera panned past Adham sitting cross-legged on his prayer rug, beyond the AK-74 leaning against the wall, and to a kneeling individual bound at the wrists. The person was wearing a US Army combat uniform. On either side of the captive were two hooded men wielding long, curved swords.

A tan-colored sandbag covered the prisoner's head. On the front in bold black Magic Marker were the words, "*Life's a Bitch.*"

Chapter 5

Dare County, North Carolina

As Mullah Adham was making his announcement, Mahegan was halfway across Croatan Sound on his return trip. He was in a perfect rhythm, arms wind-milling through the slight chop that had followed the sunrise and the accompanying winds. With each stroke closer to Roanoke Island, and farther away from the wildlife refuge, his sense of foreboding grew.

A sharp pain rocketed through his left arm as it struck something hard just beneath the surface. He thought: *bull shark.* Frequently they came this far into the sound through Oregon Inlet to the south. Presently, it was the middle of mating season when they inhabited the brackish water the most. Mahegan had scraped with a bull shark or two in the past year and knew that they accounted for the majority of shark attacks inside the sound and along the Atlantic coast.

He snatched the knife from his leg strap and pushed away, blade open and at the ready. He was expecting the bump and bite technique the sharks employed to stun and then attack their prey.

But nothing came thrashing toward him. Then he thought: *alligator*.

He saw nothing above the water and could not see land. He placed himself in the channel, about a mile from Roanoke Island. He floated perfectly still and blew out some air, deflating his lungs so that he would submerge. Keeping his eyes open, and knife at the ready, he saw a dark mass about five feet to his front ambling slowly with the tide, which was moving to Mahegan's right. Going out.

He studied the mass for a moment. His initial impression was that it was a dead animal of some type, killed maybe by an alligator. Perhaps it *was* an alligator. He cautiously approached the object, registering what looked like floating hair on one end and different colors, like clothes swaying with the ebb and flow of the water. Coming closer, Mahegan noticed brown work boots and a frayed rope tethered around the ankles of what he knew now was a human being.

He quickly closed the distance, using the knife to cut the ropes tied around the body's ankles, then pulled the dead weight above the meniscus of the water. He put a hammerlock around the body's torso, bringing back the memory of the last time he had done this: dragging Colgate out of the vehicle a year ago.

Mahegan sucked in some air and turned to look at the face to determine if this was a rescue or a recovery mission. He had seen his share of combat brutality and its effect on the human body: blown-off heads, sucking chest wounds, and amputated limbs. But the mangled face that stared back at him was as horrific as anything he had ever seen. Half chewed, half bloated and distended, the person was unrecognizable and certainly dead.

Recovery mission. He tucked away his knife and positioned himself to sidestroke the remaining mile to his landlord's boat, or wherever he might wind up on the island. He tied the length of cut rope around the body and had just enough to tie a bowline knot around his waist, easing his tug just a bit. The tide was beginning to move and with the extra weight, he would almost certainly wind up farther south than his start point. He let the pull of the tide, which was southeasterly, help him, didn't fight it, and he surged toward Roanoke Island.

Mahegan hit the first of the marsh about a half mile south of where he had hitched the boat to the buoy. Not bad for dragging an extra two hundred or so pounds. Though now he had to wade through a hundred meters of mud and saw grass. He lifted the corpse onto his back and trudged through the muck, each step becoming easier as the ground became firmer. Only once did a moccasin coil. He simply stepped away quickly from its thick head and hurried on.

Mahegan placed the body on the sandy soil above the marsh line and took notice of his location. He wanted to remember everything for his report to the police. He turned and looked at the sound. Mahegan figured he was right that he'd found him about a mile out, though the trip back had felt longer with the body. He could see the cut in the land to his north where the boats would pull out of Millionaires' Row into Croatan Sound for their big fishing trips into the Atlantic Ocean. He figured he was about three-quarters of a mile from there, and Midgett's boat would be tied up about three hundred meters south of that. So, he had about a half mile to go. With those calculations locked in his mind, he turned to the body.

He had laid the corpse faceup and guessed that by the build and size of the body it was a male. Black hair was matted to the purplish remnants of his face. A black jacket, like a Windbreaker, covered part of his bloated neck. He saw a blue T-shirt beneath the jacket and the man was wearing denim jeans over brown work boots. The man's hands were chewed and he could see several of the bones on both hands. Where there was skin left it was bloated and dark like the face.

He rolled the man over halfway and removed the rope he'd been using to tug him. He felt both pockets for a wallet and came up empty. Returning to the front, he checked both Windbreaker pockets and both jeans front pockets. Nothing.

He unzipped the jacket and checked a small inside pocket. Nothing. He wanted to remove the man's boots, but the leg swelling would make it too difficult to replace them and he figured he had done enough investigating.

Mahegan did one more check of his location, looked at the man, his path through the marsh, and one last look at the remaining rope around the man's left leg. He knelt down again, and then moved the rope above the line of the hiking boot. He untied the left boot and pulled at the uppers. The skin bloated out and he knew he wouldn't be able to get it back the way it was.

All of his life Mahegan had been writing his name inside his shoes and boots. Living in cramped or communal quarters such as he did, he wrote his name on everything, not so that people didn't steal his stuff but so that he could kick their ass when they did.

As he checked the left boot, he saw a black letter *T*, a couple of unreadable letters, a *C* or *O*, an *H*, followed by an *S*, and a new word, *PET*. He looked harder, pulling at the leather and determined it was a *C*.

"Tchspet?" he muttered.

He retied the boot as best he could, opened the right one, and was able to fill in the blanks.

"Teachspet."

At least he had a name.

He shook that boot once and noticed it felt slightly heavier than the previous one. Both were waterlogged, so it was something else.

He placed the boot on the ground, reached in, pulled up the insole, and shook the boot. Still nothing. He angled the boot so that he could see inside and noticed a small rectangle directly beneath the heel. He lifted the rectangle with his fingernail and got it on the third try.

The sun caught the yellow glimmer of something wedged in the base of the shoe. The notion of a round peg in a square hole occurred to him as he reached in and pulled the object out.

He held in his hand a shiny gold coin. Flipping it over, he noticed it had an eagle on both sides and a small "c" beneath the talons. It looked so perfect it seemed fake. Probably was a good-luck piece of some sort.

Then Mahegan looked at the man's decaying face and thought, *This didn't bring him any luck at all.*

Chapter 6

On Roanoke Island near the Queen Anne's Revenge guesthouse, Sheriff's Deputy Roland Williams said, "What you got here is your basic A-one dead body."

Williams was dressed in his starched khaki Dare County police uniform. It was a warm September afternoon and he wore the short-sleeve summer khakis, making him look more like a park ranger than a law enforcement officer. Mahegan stared at the reflecting aviator shades that allowed a veiled glimpse at his pea-sized eyes and thin eyebrows. Heavyset, Williams tried to suck in his hanging gut as the crowd gathered, but his attempt to defy nature was unsuccessful.

Not exactly Barney Fife, but close, Mahegan thought.

"Say you found him when you were swimming in the sound?"

"That's what I said," Mahegan replied.

"About a mile out?" Suspicious this time. Mahegan noticed Williams's hand drifting ridiculously close to his pistol. Spying the bulge in his top left pocket beneath Williams's name tag, Mahegan wondered if that was his one bullet.

"That's right. Dragged him in about a half mile down the island and then carried him up here."

"You one of them Copperhead carpetbaggers?"

"Not sure what you're talking about, but it's just me," Mahegan said. He knew about the tension created when contract companies swept into small town America. Some created jobs, others didn't. He had to assume that there was some animus between the locals and Copperhead.

Mahegan said, "Well, anyway, here it is. I am happy to help if you need me."

He had laid the body at the intersection of Old Wharf Road and the trail he had followed from his landing point. He didn't want to bring the corpse all the way up to Queen Anne's Revenge, so he stopped about a hundred meters short, hid the man in some tall grass, walked up to the restaurant, called 911, and then walked back to the body and waited. Williams got there twenty minutes later with lights flashing, calling for backup, which still hadn't arrived. Leaving his flashers on, Williams guaranteed drawing a crowd, which was now about twenty strong.

Mahegan studied the group closely, not really paying attention to the babbling deputy anymore. He saw four preteen kids with fishing poles who were on their way to the sound when one of them saw the lights and then the dead body and said, "Cool."

He saw one of the four whip out a cell phone, do some texting, and within five minutes seven of their buddies showed up along with some local adults that Mahegan recognized from the restaurant and infrequent visits to town. A jacked-up truck with knobby tires pulled up behind the cop car and two twenty-something locals jumped out, whooping and saying, "What we got here, Rollie?"

Rollie. As in Roland Williams, Mahegan figured. Mahegan looked back at Williams, who hitched up his pants and said to Mahegan, "I'm talking to you, boy. You got a name?"

Then he looked back at the two guys who had jumped from the truck. Both were bare-chested and wore backward-facing ball caps. One sported a fuzzy goatee and the other had a soul patch under his lip. Goatee was barefoot. Soul Patch wore some type of sandals. Both looked to be Williams's age.

It was already well into the warm afternoon and Williams took a step toward him and began reaching his hand out to turn Mahegan in his direction.

"Don't touch me," Mahegan said. His voice was just above a whisper.

Williams hesitated just enough for Mahegan to know that he was calculating what to do.

"I'll do whatever the hell I want to do," Williams said. But he didn't touch Mahegan. "You might even have something to do with them attacks in South Carolina this morning. Now let me see your identification."

Mahegan raised his arms in a half shrug. His swim trunks hung low below his navel and a solid year of swimming and running, rehab as he called it, had further refined his powerful, cut frame.

"I told you I was swimming. I don't have ID on me," Mahegan said. "Name's Mahegan. What happened in South Carolina?"

"Don't let him give you any shit, Rollie," Goatee razzed and then whooped again, this time with a fist pump. "Damn, a dead body."

"Everyone back away," Williams said. "This is a crime scene. The nation is under attack, just like nine-eleven."

Mahegan knew it wasn't a crime scene but he supposed that the deputy had to consider that perhaps it was one. *And what had happened in South Carolina?*

"Is that a first name or a last name? Mahegan?"

"Chayton Mahegan."

"Chayton?" Soul Patch said. "Is that some kind of gay name?"

Williams looked at Goatee and Soul Patch, smiling as if Soul Patch had just landed a good punch on Mahegan.

Mahegan stared at Williams, then turned away, calling over his shoulder, "Tell your boss to call me if you need me for anything else."

"You stay put," Williams directed. "Right now you are the number-one suspect in this."

"Oh, give me a break, Rollie," Sam Midgett said. The owner of the Queen Anne's Revenge had walked the hundred meters toward the sound after listening to Mahegan call the police from the lobby of his guesthouse. He was wearing khaki shorts, white socks, brown deck shoes, a short-sleeve, button-down shirt, and a yellow Windbreaker. He had thick white hair parted on the side. "This boy's staying with me, doing some groundskeeping, and he called from my place. Why in hell would he call you if he had something to do with it?"

Then Midgett turned to Mahegan. "Fort Brackett got bombed this morning. It's on the news."

Mahegan looked at Midgett, and then noticed the black pickup truck cruise by the scene without stopping. The tinted windows prevented him from registering who was driving the vehicle. But it was the same one he had seen cruise his apartment twice.

"He's still a suspect, Sam," Williams protested.

"And with those bombings at Fort Brackett, we can't be too careful."

"Don't be an idiot," Midgett replied.

Mahegan had taken a couple of steps away from the deputy, but was still watching the pickup truck. He nodded again, as if to second Midgett's words, all the while processing that Fort Brackett had been attacked.

Mahegan noticed in his periphery that by now the crowd was probably thirty people, mostly kids. Because the street was a dead end, he knew the truck would have to turn around and give him another look. North Carolina didn't require front plates, so he was going to have to try hard to get the back plates if he could get a view past the crowd.

"You may be an accessory, Sam, if you don't watch it," Williams said, still basically standing about ten feet from the body, unsure of what to do.

"Handled many dead bodies?" Mahegan asked, again quietly, trying not to provoke.

"Mind your business, stray dog," Williams said.

Stray dog. Mahegan figured it was a reference to his unknown status in the eyes of the locals. He knew that in the Outer Banks there were locals who grew up there and scratched out a living; rich homeowners who vacationed there in their second homes; tourists who came and left within a couple of weeks; and drifters, stray dogs, who were somewhere in between all of that. He suspected that Sam Midgett knew something about him, maybe that he was former military, but no one else in this town had a clue. He had trimmed hedges, mowed the centipede grass, and planted a few shrubs in the less than two weeks he had been on Roanoke Island. That was enough to merit free room and board.

"Either charge me or I'm leaving," Mahegan said.

"You're not going anywhere," Williams protested.

Mahegan noticed the black pickup truck had turned around and was cruising slowly past them again. No plate on the front. Ford F-150. Through the front windshield he saw two men with short hair. The tinting made it impossible to determine anything else. He kept following the truck and thought one of the men locked eyes with him, though he wasn't certain. They didn't look like Coast Guard and that was his main concern, given what had happened on the Ocracoke ferry less than two weeks ago. His position in the crowd would single him out as someone of import or concern. He was juxtaposed from the deputy sheriff and triangulated with the body. Sam Midgett had come closer, but was still part of the horseshoe-shaped throng that continued to grow.

Another siren was wailing now, not because there was an emergency, but because there was a line of vehicles and gawkers coming from all corners of the island, Mahegan guessed. As the pickup continued, a maroon Buick Riviera with the flashing bubble in its windshield passed just as Mahegan would have been able to see at least part of the license plate.

No joy.

Mahegan noticed the Buick driver's head swivel toward the pickup as they passed one another. After coming to a stop behind the crowd, an older gentleman jumped out of the Buick and walked quickly to Williams.

"Talk to me," the man said.

"I've got a dead man laying right here in the grass. This man here claims to have found him in the sound when he was swimming." Williams pointed at Mahegan.

The man turned to Mahegan.

"Swimming?"

Mahegan looked at the man, who was dressed in civilian clothes consisting of dark blue work pants and a light blue, short-sleeve denim shirt. He was wearing work boots not unlike the ones on the dead man. He had white hair and a weathered face that spoke of the relentless sun and wind here in the Outer Banks. Mahegan gauged he was maybe sixty years old, but in good physical condition.

On his lapel was a badge that read: DARE COUNTY SHERIFF.

Before he could say anything, the sheriff asked, "You the one who's been out there in the channel every day?"

"That's me," Mahegan said unaware that anyone had actually noticed his early morning swims.

"Sheriff Mitch Johnson here," he said. "Garland Grimes sees you in the morning from his shrimp boat. Says you're crazier than a loon out there swimming. He wants me to arrest your ass just for that."

Mahegan didn't respond.

"What's your lot in this, Sam?" Johnson asked, looking at Midgett.

"Hundred yards from my property and the boy's been staying a week or so in the garage apartment, tending to the place."

"Staying with you?" Johnson eyed Mahegan suspiciously. "A drifter?"

"Look at that prison tat on his left arm, sheriff," Williams said. "Got a shiv cut, too." Williams and the prison lingo didn't fit. Johnson leaned toward his left arm and took in Mahegan's Ranger tab tattoo and the scar.

"Ranger?"

Mahegan nodded. "Army."

"Still in?"

"No."

Mahegan watched Johnson go through a series of mental calculations which he figured went something like: *drifter, stray dog, ex–Army Ranger, biggest guy in the crowd, dead body at his feet, Sam Midgett standing up for him, I've got a county to run and a reputation to keep up*.

"Going to have to take you in, son, if only to get your statement."

Mahegan nodded. "I understand." He turned toward the maroon Buick as Johnson opened the back door for him.

"Need the knife, son," Johnson said.

Mahegan stopped, bent over, and began pulling at the Velcro straps that secured the knife to his lower leg.

"Slowly!" Williams shouted, rearing up with his pistol.

"Oh, put that away, Rollie, for crying out loud," Johnson said.

Mahegan finished removing the knife and briefly considered flipping it at Williams, securing his gun, jumping in the sheriff's tricked-out Buick, and getting an early start on Arlington and Colgate's gravesite. Sometimes thoughts like those galloped through his mind, barely controllable. Maybe that's why he wouldn't have ever made it past the rank of captain. He was too primal. Or maybe he was still sick over Colgate's death and revenge wasn't in the anticipation at all, as Mark Twain had argued, but in the execution. Regardless, he reined in the maverick notion and handed the sheath and blade to Johnson.

"I'm getting this back," he said, locking eyes with the sheriff to remove any doubt that he was handing over a prized possession.

Stepping inside, he found the vehicle interior to be

the same as a standard black-and-white police car. No lock tabs on the two back doors, steel mesh separating front from rear, and bulletproof, opaque glass behind the headrests of the driver and passenger seats. He spotted two personal digital assistants that looked like smartphones plugged into an aux power source that was slaved to the cigarette lighter. What could have been mistaken for a citizens band radio, Mahegan knew to be a high-frequency radio, and suddenly he understood more.

As Johnson situated himself in the driver's seat after a brief conversation with Williams, Mahegan said, "You're Dare County, not just here on Roanoke, right?"

Johnson turned, his thin silver hair adding contrast to the tanned, creviced skin.

"That's right, son, but we're headquartered about a mile away, so we'll get your statement ASAP. You want a lawyer? I can call ahead and have one standing by for you."

He kept his eye on the radio. Dare County ranged about one hundred miles from north to south. The sand spits jutted into the Atlantic Ocean like the right side of a parenthesis. Further inland were Roanoke Island and the chunk of land called Dare Mainland he had swum to this morning. The sheriff would need an HF radio to talk to all of the minor municipalities from Hatteras to Duck and monitor what mostly consisted of tourist-related crimes and problems.

"Don't need a lawyer," Mahegan said.

Johnson gave Mahegan a wry smile that said, "I've heard that a million times." They arrived at a flat cinder-block building painted brown. A big sheriff's badge was painted on the side to remove any doubt that this was the headquarters. Mahegan could see a newer structure built onto the back of the older building, which he guessed was the jail, where he presumed he was headed.

Johnson processed him quickly. First, the sign-in roster. Next came the mug shot, then fingerprints, and a quick Q-tip swab inside the cheek for DNA. Johnson then moved him beyond some metal bars and sat him in what he guessed was the interrogation room. The idea of being questioned made him think about Hoxha the bomb maker, whom he had killed and not questioned. That made him think about Colgate, which reminded him that he needed to be out of here in a few hours so he could get to Arlington.

Johnson came back once and said, "Why don't you have a middle name?"

"I go by Jake, but ask my father."

"We looked. Can't find any record. Your mother's dead, but your dad, nowhere in the databases."

Mahegan shrugged.

"No other family?"

"Just me . . . that I know about."

"Town of Maxton. That makes you Lumbee Tribe, right?"

"Partly, I guess. Originally from Frisco."

"Saw that. Chayton. That an Indian name?"

"I think the politically correct phrase is Native American or American Indian, but yes."

"Why you got blond hair and blue eyes, then?"

"Dominant gene? Manifest Destiny?"

Johnson thought about it, and then smiled. "Good one. Okay, I've got to head over to Duck. Some congressman's wife beat the shit out of him at their beach house. She showed up and the mistress is there, too. Should be fun."

Shortly after Johnson departed, he heard Williams's

voice boom through the chamber that separated the new structure from the old building.

"Looks like we got us an A-one dee-lemma."

Mahegan watched as Williams turned a key in the metal door and stepped through with a large uniformed African American man by his side.

"Why you looking at him?" Williams prodded. "He's your prison bitch, dude."

Mahegan made a small turn of his lips, as if to smile, but that was about all anyone would ever get out of him. Williams placed his hands on the gray metal table where he was seated and leaned forward, putting his face inches from Mahegan's.

"Think it's funny, stray dog? You want Johnnie's nightstick up your ass?"

"You his boy?" Mahegan said to the tall black man. Johnnie had his arms crossed, which, coupled with his shaved head, made Mahegan think of him as a black Mr. Clean. The blue uniform told Mahegan he was a local cop, not a county officer, which told him that Williams had found the biggest guy possible to try to come in here and frighten him.

"Ain't nobody's boy. Don't talk to me," Johnnie said. The voice didn't match the man. He sounded more like Michael Jackson or Mike Tyson, high-pitched and effeminate. Mahegan strained to see the man's name tag, which was turned up beneath a beefy forearm.

"That's right, stray dog. Now answer me this," Williams began as he sat down. "How is it that for over two years we have no suspicious deaths in this area and you show up and suddenly we've got one dead body and one missing person?"

Mahegan thought about it a minute and then said, "I only found the one."

"But you killed two? Is that what you're saying? Did

we catch you before you were able to try and hide the other one?"

Mahegan kept his anger at bay, but he felt a storm offshore.

"Not my problem you've got one dead, one missing," Mahegan said. He looked at Johnnie, who had lowered his arms so that he could read the name tag, which spelled WALKER. Mahegan wondered then if Johnnie was his real name or a nickname someone had given him a long time ago.

"You must not be listening, punk. This is exactly your problem. You are in this prison because you are the number-one suspect for both of these murders."

"I reported it. At first you said one dead, one missing. Now you're saying two murders?"

Mahegan believed the one he had found was a murder. The rope around the ankles was the primary clue, and he had never heard about people killing themselves by tying a rope and cinderblock around their legs, which seemed to be a hell of a lot more trouble than just about any other way.

"We got us a prime A-one forensics team. Gunshot to the head for the first one. When we find the second one, we'll know. The missing person is the nephew of a prominent Roanoke Island citizen," Williams said. "And you reporting the dead body? All that does is move you to the top of the list. One of them voyagers."

Voyagers? Mahegan figured Williams meant *voyeur*. He knew that killers often had a penchant for returning to the scene of the crime; their prime motivation for murder was to watch the drama, the chase that played out all because of them. It was not unlike combat in many respects. You plan a mission, execute it, and then follow up. The Army had taught Mahegan to call it "battle damage assessment." He had to watch the aftermath to determine whether he destroyed the target or not.

Changing tack, Mahegan asked, "So you haven't found the other body?"

"Where'd you hide it, dog?"

No longer *stray*. Just *dog*. Mahegan looked down at the man's pistol, and then thought about the fact that they had not handcuffed him. He played it out in his mind. Before Williams could move, he could grab the pistol, shoot Williams, fend off Johnnie Walker, and probably escape in one of the police cruisers outside. Yes, it would be stupid, primarily because he doubted if Williams's gun was loaded, but also because he would have to fight his way out, which he could do, but not without taking some time on Walker. By then he would probably have more police coming in with weapons, which would get ugly.

He recognized it as one of his overreactive fantasies and was about to respond when he heard a sharp female voice on the other side of the passageway from where they sat. His hearing was in the top one percent of every hearing test in every decibel range. Mahegan felt fortunate, given the amount of loud machinery he had been around for the last ten years. He attributed this finely tuned sense to his Native American heritage. He listened to the high-pitched voice carry over a softer bass tone that he recognized to be Sheriff Johnson's.

"I'm telling you I saw him in the water swimming! He didn't kill anyone! Especially Miller," the female voice said. The two were walking inside the police station and the voices carried.

"We don't know that just yet, Lindy. Rollie's in there questioning him now and the Coast Guard called about

him the other day, so I've got to call them, too. We're
pretty devastated about Miller and concerned about J.J."

"Rollie's a moron and you know it. Why in the hell
would you trust him with something like this?"

On that note, Mahegan looked at Williams, turned
his lip up a fraction, and locked his eyes on Williams's
round, meaty face.

"Your wife?" Mahegan prodded.

Williams was up and moving around the table toward Mahegan. Mahegan stood in time to position himself with Williams in between him and Johnnie Walker,
figuring Walker for the better fighter. This alignment
would force them to fight him piecemeal, one at a time.

"Sit down, asshole," Williams screamed.

Mahegan was a good ten inches taller and much
broader than the heavyset deputy. He thought he saw
Walker swallow hard. Williams stopped about two feet
from him.

Walker was moving now toward the opposite corner
and Mahegan shifted to his right just enough to keep
Williams coincident with his line of sight on Walker.
They were opposite ends of an invisible line that had
Williams as its center.

"What the hell is going on in here?" Johnson said,
opening the barred door. Mahegan had rotated into the
southeast corner while Walker had mirrored him into
the northwest corner. Williams, Mahegan guessed, was
scared, so he stayed where he was.

"I'm thinking we need to lock him up, sheriff,"
Williams said.

"Well then, why didn't you cuff him? Big guy like
this and you're in here playing around like you want to
kick his ass. You're armed and you've got Walker in
here, and we all know he's nothing but a big teddy bear,
so knock this bullshit off."

Teddy Bear. Mahegan's cheek twitched, the closest he had come to smiling in a long time. His crow's-feet crinkled slightly on the left side.

"You can fight?" Johnson said. "You move around like a boxer."

"I can defend myself, if that's what you're asking. What happened to your congressman in Duck?" Mahegan said.

"I got diverted by an eyewitness out here that says she saw you swimming in the sound. Says she was kayaking out there and saw you take old man Midgett's johnboat out early, tie it off at the buoy outside Millionaires' Row, and then swim into the sound. The medical examiner has already looked at the body and given me twenty-four hours as Miller Royes's time of death. So that means you couldn't have done it today, though you could have done it a day or two ago and were looking for the body."

Johnson let it hang out there like a question.

"That make sense to you, sheriff?"

"Not really, but you're not denying it."

"I didn't do it. Why would I reveal my own crime? This falls into the no good deed goes unpunished category. I'm not from here, so you treat me like I not only have no rights but that I don't know anything about what's supposed to happen in here. You've got Barney Fife and Teddy Bear in here and you're lucky I didn't have to defend myself."

"I need a statement from you that details what you saw and what you did. Then I'm going to direct that you not leave Roanoke Island until we get a bit more fidelity on this issue. Especially since we've got another man missing. Might have something to do with those Copperhead folks."

"I can do the statement, but I'm heading to Arlington, Virginia, tonight or tomorrow."

"Not going to happen. I'll lock you up if you're telling me you're a flight risk."

Mahegan thought about it a moment. "I'm not a flight risk." Of course, he was a flight certainty, but he would come back after he had visited Colgate.

He provided his statement, which took another hour, signed it, and then was brought forward by a different deputy, who had him sign out of the log and told him, "Wait for the sheriff."

As he waited, Mahegan looked through the window and saw the black pickup truck cruise slowly past the parking lot.

Chapter 7

Mahegan studied the walls inside the police station. Little League trophies lined the bookcase in the foyer. There was a low shelf that ran along the length of the building, separating the civilians from the police. The two green ledger books Mahegan had just signed were open on the shelf.

"Have a seat," Johnson said, leading Mahegan into his office. The sheriff was holding a manila folder with Mahegan's name on it.

"You understand I have to be thorough here, correct?"

Mahegan nodded and sat in a gray padded chair.

"Ever been here before? To Roanoke Island?"

Mahegan nodded again. He remembered his father telling him about the Lost Colony that had once resided on Roanoke Island but had strangely disappeared in 1588. As part of his father's never-ending search for their roots, they had explored the entire Outer Banks one year.

"My dad brought me here once. We studied the Lost Colony, debated the two theories that either the Croatan killed the settlers or helped them."

"Where do you come down on the issue?"

"I figured the Englishmen got bored with the whole settlement thing, had been eyeing the squaws, and started nailing some Croatan ass."

"Could be," Johnson said. He kept a straight face. "Birth certificate says Frisco? But the database shows something happened in Maxton, North Carolina, too."

Mahegan hesitated. He didn't want to revisit the Maxton issue until he had enough information to do something about it. He thought of his mother in Frisco: blond hair, freckles across the bridge of her nose, and willowy, like a runway model. She was constantly teaching him about the sea and his Native American heritage. Then he thought about the move and all they had left behind in Frisco and all that he had lost.

"Yes, born on Hatteras Island. When I was a teenager, we moved to Robeson County, where there were more jobs for Native Americans. The Lumbee tribe is there."

Mahegan spoke in clipped sentences, the only way to control his ragged emotions that he associated with the contrasting memories of his peaceful childhood in Frisco and the violence he had experienced in Maxton.

"You've got a sealed juvenile file. Care to explain?"

"Nothing to explain. Sealed for a purpose, sheriff."

"News reports say your mother was killed by a group of rednecks bearing Confederate flag tattoos and shouting, 'Indian lover bitch.' That's got to give a kid some rage, right? Enough to . . . kill? And like it?"

"You seriously want to go there with me?"

Mahegan's anger began to surface. He had compartmentalized his mother's death and what he had done afterward.

"Point is, there might be precedent here for murder," Johnson said.

Lightning flashed in Mahegan's mind.

"I was fourteen. Four men raped and killed my mother. I came home while it was happening . . . and defended myself." As a nearly six-foot-tall fourteen-year-old, he had critically injured all four of his mother's assailants. The memory was like shards of glass slicing through his heart.

"Shows you spent two years in the juvenile system. Just doesn't say what for."

After two years in the juvenile homes, he had disconnected from society, lost without his parents. His mother was gone and his father disappeared, heartbroken. He didn't blame his father for vanishing because Mahegan remembered his own inner compass then spinning wildly out of control, lost without bearing.

"That file ought to show you I got my shit together, too."

"It does. Shows you joined when you were seventeen. Took some college classes, made it through basic, airborne, Ranger, and even made officer. Then Delta. But with an asterisk."

"Asterisk is none of your business, sheriff."

Johnson looked up at Mahegan through sun-baked eyelids, then back at the report.

The asterisk, Mahegan knew, was the diagnosis of impulsive, aggressive behavior.

The doctor had said, "Probably traceable to the attack on his mother." Mahegan had wanted to pummel the doctor, but hadn't, and he later proffered that as an explanation to General Savage on how he could keep it under control.

Johnson flipped the folder shut and stared at Mahegan.

"And the dishonorable discharge?"

"That's pending," Mahegan said, less confident this time.

"Like football referees watching an instant replay? Currently under review?"

"I don't watch much television, sheriff. I served honorably and there's one ass hamster who wants to use me for his political gain. Feel free to read up on that on your own time, but it's bullshit." Mahegan had appreciated Savage's terminology for General Bream.

Mahegan studied Johnson as he paused. The man wore a thoughtful expression, pensive, as if he was reflecting on his own run-ins with people trying to tear him down. As a politician, Mahegan figured, Johnson had to have experience with that.

"You're free to go," Johnson said. "I find out you've left town, I'll find you and throw your ass in jail. You're staying with Midgett, so check in with me or one of my deputies every day."

"Me not being from here and all," Mahegan said.

Johnson looked at Mahegan's Ranger tab tattoo, paused, and said, "Listen. Thanks for bringing in the body. It's not every day we get one of these. I know you served our country. I'm former Navy myself. Good luck with the discharge determination."

Mahegan nodded, and then said, "Knife?"

Johnson shook his head.

"Holding it for evidence . . . and as insurance."

Mahegan locked eyes with the man for a long moment. A thousand megawatts of current were coursing through his veins and he was pulling back on the urge to react violently. What had made him such a good soldier and leader was exactly his ability to feel the raw emotion while keeping it in check. Mostly. Except for a few instances such as Hoxha the bomb maker. What he was feeling now was somewhere halfway between normal and what he felt when he heard the bomb destroy Colgate's vehicle. He could feel the combination of the brutal deaths of his mother and his best friend weld together to form a formidable catalyst in his mind. An undercurrent of emotion, which he could not afford and now struggled with daily, was usurping his reason. So he worked hard at suppressing the anguish and all of the anger that welled forth.

Mahegan shook his head. "I'm getting my knife back," he said, and stepped past Johnson into the hot September sun.

As he began to walk the mile back to the Queen Anne's Revenge, he heard a familiar voice.

"Hey, you. Swimming guy."

He stopped and saw a blond female who was probably in her mid-twenties. She was wearing a neon pink bikini top with a half T-shirt torn so that the left shoulder was exposed. On the shirt were the letters "OBX" shorthand for "Outer Banks." Wearing Daisy Dukes and Tevas, she was leaning against a yellow Land Rover Defender, complete with brush-guard and a rack of four spotlights fixed to the black roll bar. Mahegan knew that this was not an inexpensive vehicle. She was wearing black Dolce & Gabbana sunglasses.

"Yeah, I'm talking to you," she said, pointing at him. "I saw that in there. Pretty good. Rollie's an idiot. Glad you're out."

He noticed her voice had an Elizabethan English lilt to it. He remembered the distinctive dialect of the Outer Banks from his childhood.

She walked over and held out a slender hand. "Hi. I'm Lindy Locklear and I officially busted your ass out of jail."

Mahegan nodded. "Thank you."

Her grip was strong, teeth perfect, face flawless, and her muscles cut tightly beneath bronze skin. She had parked at the far end of the lot and nodded toward her Land Rover.

"C'mon. I'll give you a lift back."

"Why would you do that?"

"Because you intrigue me?" She playfully tossed the comment out as a question.

"I could be a serial killer," Mahegan quipped.

"That would be the most interesting date I've had down here."

"Date?"

"Yeah. You're going to buy me dinner on the way back as a thank-you for vouching for you."

Mahegan contemplated his choices. Walk back barefoot along the hot pavement from the jail to the Queen Anne's Revenge or catch a lift with this attractive woman who only asked for some chow in return for breaking him out of his bind.

"I can grab a quick bite. I have someplace to be," he said thinking of Colgate.

"Well, hope it's on the island here, right?" she said, coyly.

Mahegan looked away and then back at her, thinking he would find a way to get to Virginia in the next twenty-four hours. "Okay. It'll have to be an IOU, though, unless I get my stuff first."

"That's okay," she said. "I'll buy. They rough you up?"

Mahegan looked at her. "What do you think?"

She looked at him, then said, "Didn't think so," and walked to her Land Rover. Mahegan followed.

As they pulled out, he looked back at the police station. The sheriff was standing at the window, watching them.

Chapter 8

Lindy Locklear drove the Land Rover like a pro, shifting effortlessly. The wind tossed her hair like a long yellow scarf blowing in the breeze.

"Mind if I get a shirt first?" he asked. "Maybe some shoes?"

She reached back into the flatbed where four seats faced each other in the unique British design and grabbed his mocs.

"Here. Try these on." She tossed them on his lap and looked down at his chiseled frame. "Since I'm driving and it's not cold out, I say 'no' to the shirt. Besides, you don't need one where we're going."

Mahegan thought a moment and said, "You grab these from the boat or did the sheriff give them to you?"

"I kayak every morning right off the beach by my house. I take these binos with me and watch," she said, holding a pair of Bushnell Elite 8x43 binoculars.

Mahegan looked at the binos and then at her. "Those are for hunting, not watching."

The corner of Locklear's mouth twitched before she broke into a grin and looked at him. "Maybe I'm doing both."

"So, from a half mile away you've been watching me swim the past week?"

"Yep." She smiled.

"What were you looking for before you were watching me?"

Locklear slowed the Land Rover as she wound through a series of roads that led past a high school, a botanical garden, and finally a gate, which was open. Warm air spilled over the windshield and through the open half doors. She pulled onto a gravel road that paralleled the beach. He knew they were at the north end of the island and moving west, as they had just passed a sign for the Lost Colony Theater.

The gravel road ended at a quaint tan bungalow that appeared to be half home and half office. A sign on the front of the building read: CROATAN HISTORICAL SOCIETY.

"I thought we were eating?"

She jumped out of the Rover and jogged past the bungalow onto a small beach that sat on the tip of Roanoke Island. The sun was hanging low in the western sky and in about an hour they would have an unobstructed view of the sunset in the nexus between Croatan Sound and Albemarle Sound to the north. Mahegan could hear the slight buzzing of traffic whipping across Route 64 and it reminded him that he needed to ask Sam Midgett to borrow his truck.

"I just need to pick something up," she called over her shoulder. Mahegan watched her take two steps with one leap onto the covered porch that faced north. He stepped out of the vehicle, took two strides, and stopped. He stared at a ship in the sound to the north about a half mile out. It appeared anchored, or at least stationary, and seemed to be a replica of an old sailing ship. Mahegan didn't know his boats as well as he'd like, but maybe it was a brig or a simple merchant carrier. There were black holes dotting the side of the ship like windows and it occurred to him that they might be a battery of cannons. The bow of the ship was angled to the northwest and the sails were wrapped tightly around the three massive masts.

For a better look, he reached inside the Land Rover and pulled out the powerful binoculars, held them to his face, adjusted the eyepieces to fit his vision, and zeroed in on the bow of the ship.

Painted in gold letters were two words.

Teach's Pet.

Intrigued, Mahegan slid the binoculars along the starboard side of the ship and noticed that the portholes were squares and housed either replicas or actual cannons. Interesting. He noticed ropes and lines coiled tightly around the masts. The ship was motionless, dark, uninhabited.

Hearing a noise to his rear, he turned slowly, moving to put the Rover between himself and the noise. A dense wooded area separated the bungalow and beach from the road on which they had traveled inbound. He used the binoculars to scan the forest and caught some movement. It was just a flash of light, could have been anything, but Mahegan was experienced enough to trust his instincts.

He had spent the better half of a day recovering a dead body, being questioned, and filling out a statement, and now he was trapped on the sand between an unknown entity lurking in the woods and a row of cannons on the *Teach's Pet*, which he now knew was a ship's name.

Mahegan placed the binoculars in the front passenger seat and was about to move into the first cut of the woods when Locklear came charging out of the bungalow, Tevas slapping against the wooden porch and blond hair trailing behind her like a vortex.

"Why didn't you come in?" she asked. Mahegan noticed she had placed a gold necklace around her neck, which suspended a large gold *C* on the torn T-shirt above her moderate breasts. The way she came bounding off the porch demonstrated an athleticism that smacked of lacrosse or maybe field hockey, though she was tall enough to have played basketball.

"Wasn't invited," he said, keeping his eyes on the forest. He noticed a mixture of tall oak, birch, and maple spotted with a lower canopy of dogwood and magnolia. The density of the forest, so close to the beach, surprised him.

"What?" she asked, following his gaze to the woods.

Mahegan gave her a glance and then looked back in the woods, but he couldn't recapture the white flash.

"See Virginia?" Locklear asked.

"Virginia's north of here. Can't see it from this far," Mahegan said.

She smiled and said, "Virginia Dare. Her spirit roams the island."

"First English child born in America, right?"

She punched him on the arm. "Not bad."

"Part of the Lost Colony, right?"

"That's right," she said. "Born on August 18, 1587. The county's named after her." Locklear was moving into the driver's seat by now and Mahegan kept his eyes on the trees. He didn't completely dismiss the story. He was a spiritual man in many ways, often wondering about a higher being and his place in the world. His father had said, "The Spirit lives" as if it were the answer to almost anything. He did feel connected to the earth and something beyond, but he had difficulty discerning the tangible, that which he could sense in a physical way, from the intangible, which wholly required faith. He had so palpably tasted death and witnessed the basest behavior in mankind that he did believe the only thing that could balance such depravity was an all-powerful goodness, perhaps God. His logic went like this: If there was evil in this world, and there most certainly was, then an equally good and powerful force was out there to balance things. *The Spirit lives.*

So did he believe that Virginia Dare's spirit was floating around the forest? Maybe. But the more likely explanation was that the sheriff had someone tailing him.

He eased into the passenger seat as Locklear tossed him an extra-large T-shirt reading IF IT'S TOURIST SEASON, WHY CAN'T I SHOOT THEM?

He held it up and said, "I'm not wearing some guy's shirt."

"This is my sleeping shirt."

He pulled on the T-shirt and it smelled of fabric softener and recent laundering.

"So did she live?"

"Who?"

"Virginia Dare. Did she survive the colony?"

"I wish we knew, Jake." She looked at him as if she had known him all of her life and put a hand on his shoulder where his scar was hidden beneath the shirt. "I've been working with the Lost Colony Research Center and they've got clues that lead to Dare Mainland, near the bombing ranges. Can you believe it? The military put in bombing ranges where the Croatan used to live and now there's evidence that the Lost Colony had actually fled there."

"What evidence?"

"The contractors found Moline crosses on some coffins over there when they were digging for bombs."

"So it was an English or French colony."

"Right. But there's no record of the French ever colonizing here."

"Was there an infant female in the coffins?"

Locklear looked at him. "No. But they found parts of a necklace made of whalebone with her name carved into it."

"Virginia? Or Virginia Dare?"

"Virginia. And then an 'r' and an 'e.' There are those that think it was like a souvenir or tribute to the new land, but it would fit the neck of a ten-year-old girl."

Mahegan nodded, wondering why she seemed so emotionally attached to the story. He decided not to pursue the matter. "People were smaller then."

"Maybe. There's the research that shows Eleanor Dare married Chief Manteo. That could have something to do with it also."

Locklear started the Defender again and slammed it into gear. As they were pulling out of the winding asphalt road that led past the botanical gardens and onto Route 64, Mahegan noticed the black pickup truck parked about a half mile away to the west, directly before where the bridge lifted over Croatan Sound.

Teach's Pet, black pickup, and Virginia Dare, he thought as she pulled into a west side restaurant called "Blackbeard's." They sat at a rear deck table that gave them a fifty-yard-line view of the orange sun diving into the far bank of Croatan Sound not far from where he had swum earlier this morning. The deck had about twenty tables scattered about with a few umbrellas for shade. Waiters and waitresses in black T-shirts with skulls and crossbones silk-screened onto them scurried around carrying giant trays of seafood and alcohol.

"So you swim ten miles a day?"

Mahegan shrugged. "Never measured it."

"I have. It's five miles each way."

He smiled. "You probably just made it harder now that I have to think about it."

"Doubt it. You have a good stroke."

"So are you stalking me?"

"Something like that, but probably not like you're thinking."

He turned away from staring at the sun and looked into her blue eyes, then at her necklace.

She sighed. "It will take me back to our previous conversation. You sure?"

"It didn't bother me before," he said. "Lindy starts with an 'l.' What's up with the 'c' on your necklace?

"Croatan. My mitochondrial DNA shows I'm linked to Virginia Dare. Eleanor Dare is an ancestor. I believe the Dares moved with the Croatan to protect baby Virginia from everything that plagued Raleigh's Lost Colony: disease, famine . . . unsympathetic Indians. So in a sense the Croatan protected me."

She let the comment hang out there. He had noticed her high-fashion sunglasses, the $60,000 British Land Rover, the perfect teeth, and her accented Elizabethan English. Being a direct descendent of Virginia Dare was probably as close to royalty as someone could get in North Carolina. So, she had some funding, but what was she doing?

"I thought the Croatan slaughtered the English," he said.

"White man's illogical deduction. John White comes back after two years and can't find anyone, so he and his men assume the worst. Meanwhile, a few generations went by and the Croatan all looked like North Europeans, blond hair, blue eyes . . . like you. But now they're saying there are no Croatan left in the world. Extinct."

"I think I'm Lumbee," he said before he could stop himself.

She cocked her head. "Really?"

"Perhaps." Changing the topic and getting to a point he wanted to discuss, he asked, "What do you know about the *Teach's Pet*?"

"The ship? Lots. Why?"

"Just saw it out there off your beach," he said.

"It's really just a prop for the *Lost Colony* production, which is an outdoor drama put on every year from May until September. In fact, the cast party is tomorrow night. But it is parked out there in a strange spot."

"How so?"

She shifted uncomfortably in her seat as a waiter brought two waters and menus. He was about twenty years old with an earring in both ears and colorful tattoo sleeves that stopped abruptly at his wrists.

Once the waiter left, she said, "Treasure hunters are looking for pirate treasure all around it."

"Pirate treasure?"

"Teach? Edward Teach? Blackbeard?" she said, waving her hand and looking around the restaurant. "I guess growing up around here we all know Blackbeard's real name was Edward Teach. Personally, I'd go by Blackbeard also if that was my real name."

Mahegan vaguely recalled something about Edward Teach being Blackbeard the pirate and now put the two names together. *Teach's Pet* was obviously a play on the common phrase "teacher's pet."

"This far inland?"

"Why do you think all this Blackbeard stuff is around here? Heck, where you're staying, the Queen Anne's Revenge, was the name of Blackbeard's ship once he stole it from the French in the Caribbean."

Mahegan nodded. "Got it," he said. "But how do you know where I'm staying?"

Locklear paused and smiled without looking at him. "I've got connections."

Mahegan watched her, something flashing in his mind. It was a comment she had made earlier, but the thought disappeared when she continued speaking.

"Anyway, legend has it that Blackbeard ferried his treasure north into Croatan and Albemarle sounds and up the Blackwater River. Then apparently he hid it in various locations in North Carolina and Virginia. You know Buffalo City, North Carolina, at all?"

Mahegan shrugged.

"Back in the 1850s a Doctor Thomas Johnson bought an ironclad ship called the *Curlew* he used in the sound because of its shallow draft. He would ferry his family and friends back and forth to Nags Head on the beach. Even back then it was a resort spot. He did timber and cotton, stuff like that."

Mahegan shrugged again as if to say, "So?"

"During the early stages of the Civil War, the rebels took control of the ship when the War Between the States broke out and began using it initially as a troop transport to move men up and down the Outer Banks. Then they tricked it out with some guns and made it a fighting ship, like the *Monitor* and the *Merrimack*. It was shot and burned very close to where the *Teach's Pet* sits right now."

"What's the connection?"

"Legend has it that Warren did more than take his family on vacation. We're told that he raided the SS *James Adger*, stole two million in gold, and was moving it around the sounds on the *Curlew* kind of like an armored car."

"How do you know this?"

Mahegan noticed her affect change from playful to determined as the conversation continued.

"I think I should stop there," she said.

"Okay . . ." Mahegan remembered the gold coin in the key pouch of his board shorts. He got the sense that she was working some angle on the gold and clearly some had been found. He had hauled someone named Miller Royes in from the sound and Royes had a gold coin hidden in his boot.

He turned to look over the deck railing at the glassy smooth sound. The sun was slicing into the haze just above the horizon, which came together with the east bank of mainland North Carolina and the nexus between the two sounds. An orange stripe painted its way along the mirror of water like the wake he had created this morning. He pieced together the information from the day.

"But you need me for something," he said, turning toward her.

She nodded.

"Something to do with this treasure stuff."

Not a question.

She nodded again. "Strong *and* smart," she said.

"You go out in your kayak on the west side of the island away from where you live. You paddle into the sound every day and see me swimming, so you're wondering if I've got something to do with searching for this treasure or if I'm a Copperhead carpetbagger. At first I'm an idle curiosity, but then you determine that I might actually have value to whatever end it is you have in mind. You figure I'm not with Copperhead and maybe decide to approach me later, but then I found the dead body and the sheriff is threatening to arrest me, forcing you to act. You need someone who's not a local and whom you can trust. The first part you've got figured out and you're working on the second part."

A frown grew on her face. "Am I that easy to figure out?"

"But what I can't figure out is why Sheriff Johnson apologized to you about Miller Royes and whoever J.J. is," Mahegan said.

Locklear looked away over the deck of the restaurant and into the tranquil sound. He thought he saw tears well in her eyes, but she quickly regained her composure.

"Ah. Miller was a friend. And J.J. . . ." she said. Her voice saddened and she couldn't finish.

"And J.J.?" he asked. But the waiter interrupted by asking for their order. He ordered a Mahi fillet and she ordered a vegetarian dish. As the waiter was turning away, Mahegan noticed a movement to his three o'clock. He looked in each direction using all of his senses, including imagining his magnetic field scanning like radar. Mahegan believed every animal had a spirit and an energy field, which was part of the reason he preferred being alone. Get mixed up with the wrong energy overlapping his all the time, he figured, and he might lose his tenuous bearing on magnetic north.

He turned slowly and saw a large man with a close haircut sitting at a table at the far end of the deck. The man looked vaguely familiar if for no other reason than he had seen that look, build, and haircut a million times in the military.

Then he thought about the black truck and excused himself.

"Restroom," he said to Locklear, standing to leave.

As he walked toward the restaurant's rear door, he caught in his periphery the large man nodding to someone he could not see. Careful not to turn his head, Mahegan saw that there was a window looking onto the back deck. As he entered through the back door, he felt the intent stare of another man whom he could make out in the corner of the restaurant. This man was big and muscular with a tight military haircut also.

He walked to the front of the restaurant into the main lobby where the bathrooms were located and with purpose continued to the parking lot where he saw the black truck parked in the far corner. He walked to Locklear's Defender and grabbed the binoculars from under the seat.

Mahegan bent down and acted as though he was working on the Defender's right rear tire. He held the powerful binoculars to his face and focused on the license plate.

US Government. He memorized the plate number and scanned the sticker on the left top portion of the plate. Virginia.

Pentagon?

He used the binos to scan through the driver's side window but the tint was too dark. He moved slightly and adjusted his angle to see through the rear window. Though the window was clear, he could not make out anything but the presence of a green three-ring binder. He recognized it as a dispatch log the military used for keeping track of who signed out what vehicle when and how far they drove. On the log were the words: Fort Belvoir. Then, CIDIG. CID, Mahegan knew, stood for the Army's Criminal Investigation Division. IG was the acronym for the Army's Inspector General, every soldier's enemy. The IG was exactly like any police force's internal audit function, only exponentially more powerful and far reaching.

Recalling Savage's warning about General Bream,

the Army Inspector General, he put the binos under the seat of the Defender, brushed off his hands, and walked up the steps.

These were Bream's goons?

He turned right and positioned himself at the end of the long covered porch. There were four rocking chairs on either side of the main entrance, cigarette butts littering the sun-bleached deck. The porch encircled the entire building, so he moved just off the periphery as the two men came charging out of the restaurant, believing he had probably escaped from the tight net that they had cast about him.

He walked back into the restaurant and sat across from Locklear.

"Everything . . . okay?" She arched a barely visible blond eyebrow.

The waiter had brought two house salads and a greasy basket of hush puppies.

"Two guys are going to come barging back in here in a second and I want you to level with me. Do you know them?"

"I can already tell you. I've never seen them. I noticed the one sitting at your four o'clock and the one who followed him out of the restaurant when you'd been gone more than a minute."

Mahegan stared at her a moment, half smiled, and nodded.

"Good. I like that."

On cue, the dark-haired guy came walking in too fast directly toward their table. He had a slight bulge under his Windbreaker and, up close, Mahegan saw the man had a broad build, much like a football lineman, but on the softer side, perhaps a guard not a tackle. He was probably good in his day, but Mahegan noticed in his walk that his legs weren't powerful enough for his frame so he pushed out with every step instead of fully forward. He had to turn sideways to weave through the smattering of tables, which didn't help as he was wide in both directions.

He stopped directly in front of their table and before he could say anything Locklear looked up at him and said, "You know, I think we will have another appetizer. Some of that calamari looks good. And we'll have a bottle of Sonoma Cutrer Chardonnay also." Then she looked at Mahegan and smiled, reaching her hand out to his on the table. "Don't you agree, dear?"

Mahegan nodded, looking at Locklear, but kept his antennae up. "Sounds good to me." He returned his gaze to the interloper, taking in his Doc Marten boots, pressed no-iron slacks, big rodeo belt buckle, and the cheap blue Windbreaker. He memorized his pock-marked face and high-and-tight haircut and pegged him for military police.

"Captain Chayton Mahegan?" the man asked.

"That's me." Mahegan stood slowly until he was fully upright and nearly chest to chest with the man. He was proud of his name and proud of his service and he would never deny either, no matter who this stranger was or what he might want. "But it's Mr. Mahegan now."

"I'm Chief Warrant Officer Paul Paslowski with Army Special Activities Division in the Army Inspector General's office. Lieutenant General Stanley Bream directed me to either apprehend you or ask you to come to the Pentagon for questioning in regard to the alleged murder of Commander Hoxha in Nuristan Province, Afghanistan, a year ago."

"Murder?" Locklear spat.

Paslowski shifted on his feet and actually backed away from him a bit. Mahegan tensed, ready to fight.

"Murder. That's the allegation and it's really all I can say."

"What kind of jurisdiction do you think you have down here?" Mahegan asked.

Paslowski slid the Windbreaker back a tad so that Mahegan could see the butt of his Beretta pistol.

In his periphery, Mahegan noticed Locklear fidget with her purse. While he didn't know her very well, he wouldn't be surprised if she had some kind of small firearm tucked away in there. The lady had an engine, but he wasn't sure she had a governor on her carburetor. She seemed to be full throttle with a methodical bent, like a fighter pilot. Reckless but in control.

"Afraid that's not going to get you a whole lot down in this region, chief. I put in my paperwork less than a year ago, and I'm on a date with this beautiful woman."

"Well, captain, we can try it either way. You can sign this document stating that you will appear at the Pentagon to answer questions, or we can use this document," Paslowski said. He had removed two folded pieces of paper from his jacket pocket. Now he held one in each hand like a shopper comparing two different products. Mahegan didn't care what either piece of paper said.

"Not signing anything and really don't care about your paperwork. Now if you're done, I'm going to eat my chow."

Mahegan turned his shoulder slightly, but he knew what was coming. He saw Paslowski's baseball mitt–sized paw moving at a rate of speed indicating that he was totally unprepared for what Mahegan was about to do. The hand got within a centimeter of his "Shoot the Tourists" T-shirt when Mahegan's right hand grabbed Paslowski's wrist and used the man's momentum to pull him forward while Mahegan slid under the big, fleshy arm that was softer than he had anticipated. His left forearm pressed Paslowski's head into the deck railing, giving the investigator a direct view of the flooring of the restaurant. Meanwhile, he ratcheted the man's right arm up so far he thought he heard a slight pop from the shoulder.

"Six o'clock," he said to Locklear, who was already standing and pointing a baby Glock at the light-haired version of Paslowski who had come running from his station near the door. Not suspecting Locklear, Paslowski's partner had missed her leveling her pistol before he could retrieve his weapon.

"Don't even think about it," she said to him.

"You are messing up big-time," Paslowski grunted. "This will have bearing on your discharge determination, too, asshole."

Mahegan said, "Maybe, but you've got a whole restaurant full of folks here who saw everything. And because I'm such an honorable guy who deserves an honorable discharge, I'm going to do two things. I'm going to take your weapon and your friend is going to hand his weapon to my friend, because you know what? She's crazier than I am."

Mahegan added some torque to Paslowski's arm as he reached around with his left arm, removed the pistol, released the magazine, caught it with the heel of his hand, and slid the pistol on the table to Locklear. He thumbed the rounds out of the magazine and they plunked into the still water just over the deck's edge. Without being told, Locklear held the pistol over the sound and jacked the slide, but no round expelled.

"I'm insulted," Mahegan said. "Not even worthy of you chambering a round."

"Next time," Paslowski grunted.

"Maybe," Mahegan said.

Locklear had retrieved the second man's pistol, jacked

his rounds into the sound, and checked the chamber, again empty, about the time Rollie Williams came busting through the door.

"What we got here is an A-one situation," he said, standing in the middle of the now empty deck, several of the frightened diners peering around either side of the restaurant.

"Oh, Rollie, put a sock in it, will you?" Locklear said, moving toward the deputy while she kept her pistol trained on the light-haired special agent.

"Lindy, damnit. You've got no right to be talking to me like that here, especially in front of this murder suspect."

"He's no more a murder suspect than I am. Now what you need to do is take these two big badasses and lock them up because I think they may have more to do with Miller Royes's murder and J.J. being missing than anyone else here. Here's two pistols. Start running ballistics on them. Make yourself useful."

Mahegan was still pinning Paslowski to the deck railing and he felt a lot of the fight go out of the man. He knew he had probably separated the man's shoulder and eased up a bit, turning Paslowski toward Williams.

"Here you go, deputy. You can have him."

"It ain't him I want, you moron," Williams said.

Williams glared at Locklear as he grabbed Paslowski by the shoulder to steady him. Mahegan could see the agony painted on Paslowski's face, which looked like a theater tragedy mask.

Mahegan wiped his hands on the swim trunks he'd been wearing since this crazy day had started and he thought for a minute about the red wolves and how centered he had felt with them. For a moment, he wondered how Locklear and Williams were connected. Then he thought about Colgate. He needed to get his ass in gear if he was going to make it to Arlington tonight. Then he had an idea.

"These goons want to take me to the Pentagon, Williams. You going to let them?"

Mahegan could see Williams thinking. He also saw Locklear snap her head toward him.

"Why would you go?"

Mahegan shrugged and said, "I changed my mind. Maybe it will be my chance to show I'm an honorable guy."

She was still aiming her baby Glock at Paslowski's partner. Then she seemed to remember and dropped her arm.

"All this bullshit for nothing?" she asked.

"Maybe not," he said. Turning to Williams, he noticed Sheriff Johnson pounding his way through the restaurant and onto the back deck.

"Damnit, the two of you again?" the sheriff said. Then he saw Locklear and stopped. "Lindy, what did I tell you about carrying a pistol around here?"

"All these damn treasure hunters, contractors, tourists, and such, you know I'm not going to stop, Uncle Mitch."

Uncle Mitch. Interesting. He could see the connection. Both Locklear and Johnson were athletes. Johnson was a big man, like a linebacker, and still looked fit and cut in the same way Locklear appeared sinewy and strong.

"Just because I deputized you, Lindy, doesn't mean you get to wave that damn pistol around," Johnson barked.

Deputy? Certainly didn't look the part, Mahegan thought. Victoria's Secret model, Billabong surf-wear babe, and actress would all fit. But deputy? No.

Johnson turned to to Mahegan. "What's this about the Pentagon wanting you?"

"Ask them," Mahegan said.

"That's right," Paslowski said. "The Army Inspector General, a three star, wants to question Captain Mahegan about an enemy prisoner of war who died while in his custody. Maybe murder. Given today's incident at Fort Brackett, the situation is more serious than ever. His discharge determination is hanging in the balance, too."

Mahegan had gone from complete anonymity for the last 364 days to wanted man at both the state and federal levels. Not good. He watched Johnson swivel his head from Paslowski to him and back to Paslowski.

"Murder?"

"That's right. That's what we call it even in combat when a combatant is unlawfully killed."

Mahegan watched Johnson weigh his options. He'd got what he considered to be the Feds down here to pick up someone whom he probably initially thought was telling the truth and an innocent do-gooder. Now, the new information colored his lens of perception. He didn't want to give up his prime suspect, but he didn't want trouble with the Feds.

"How serious is this? Is he being charged?" Johnson asked.

Mahegan watched Paslowski, who was holding his right arm up in a position as if it were in a sling. Paslowski looked at Mahegan and then at Johnson.

"Murder is the allegation. The Inspector General has extralegal powers. For you and your courts here, Mahegan is innocent until proven guilty. That's a pretty high bar. For us, it's the preponderance of the evidence. That can mean a lot of things."

"And what does it mean regarding Mahegan?" Johnson asked.

"It means the evidence is looking pretty good for conviction. Otherwise, we wouldn't be down here. General Bream ruled him a dishonorable discharge, but his daddy, General Savage, a two star, mind you, filed an appeal. So General Bream, B Three as we call him, is reconsidering based upon S Two's recommendation."

Mahegan rolled his eyes. The staff jockeys had an annoying habit of combining the first letter of a general's last name with the number of stars he bore. Just more unnecessary Pentagon jargon.

"Are you going to lock him up, or will you send him back to answer my questions when you're done with him?"

They talked as if Mahegan were invisible. Two men were hashing out his fate in front of the waiters and patrons who had come around the corner of the restaurant when Sheriff Johnson had arrived. Mahegan looked at Locklear, who was just staring at him. Just after they exchanged glances, he had a thought. Maybe she'd sent it to him somehow, he didn't know.

"Gentlemen, if you send me up to DC under the supervision of Sheriff's Deputy Locklear, you can kill two birds with one stone." Bad analogy under the circumstances, he thought, but he kept going. "She can drive me up there, wait for me while I'm questioned, and then drive me back here. I'll be in her custody until such time as the Inspector General takes custody of me and releases me back to her, should they decide to do so."

"You're crazy," Rollie Williams spat.

Mahegan could tell that Johnson, though, was considering it. He looked at Locklear.

"I'm good with it," she said. "As long as it doesn't take too long." She looked at Paslowski.

"Should be a day of questioning. If we decide that the evidence is against him, all bets are off."

"Sheriff, you can't be seriously considering this, can you?" asked Williams.

"Stay out of it, Rollie. I trust Lindy and if we've got to keep an eye on him, she's about as good as we've got."

Locklear was better than Rollie, and Mahegan figured it wasn't even her full-time gig.

"Fine," she said. "Where do you want me and when?"

"Ten hundred hours tomorrow morning in Crystal City," Paslowski said, handing her a document. "The address is on there."

Locklear took the sheet of paper, nodded, and said, "Roger."

"And Mahegan?" Paslowski said.

Mahegan pulled his eyes from the paper he was straining to read in Locklear's hand, and stared at the man's beefy face, pockmarked with acne scars. Paslowski hefted his separated shoulder as much as he could, wincing.

"Once this heals, I'm going to show up sometime where you least expect it. Hell, it might be your prison cell in Leavenworth, who knows?"

"And you want me to get the other one? Give you a matching set?"

"Watch it, shit for brains. I have input into this case," Paslowski said.

"Why don't we just give you assholes pistols and you can duel? Put us all out of our misery," Locklear said. "Barring that, Mr. Mahegan, you are in my custody." She came around the table, wedged herself between Johnson and Paslowski, and grabbed Mahegan's thick triceps, guiding him past the throng. She stopped and turned toward Paslowski.

"Does he need a lawyer for your line of questioning?"

Paslowski gave her a wide grin that showed bad, crooked teeth. "That's the beauty of the Inspector General. He can't even have one."

Mahegan trained his eyes on Paslowski and could see the man was serious. He hadn't known this, hadn't known much at all about the bureaucracy in the Pentagon or the uniform code of military justice. All he'd known was what was right and what was wrong and he'd lived by that code. Well, it looked like he was going to learn, and the notion began developing in the back of his mind that there were many different ways a massive organization could squeeze even the guys who wanted nothing more than to do their jobs and serve honorably.

"Well, that seems like a load of bullshit," Locklear said.

"Lindy?" asked Johnson.

"Yes, Uncle Mitch?" Mahegan watched Locklear keep her hard gaze fixed on Paslowski as if she was calculating how deep the Inspector General could drill into someone's life without the civil protections of the American justice system.

"Never mind. Doesn't matter what the hell I say."

"About right," she muttered as she guided Mahegan past Paslowski to her Defender in the parking lot.

Mahegan allowed Locklear to escort him to the passenger seat and theatrically placed her hand on top of his head as she guided him beneath the roll bar into the passenger seat.

"Thanks. That was a close one," Mahegan said.

"Watch it, you're in my custody now." Locklear grinned.

She jumped in the driver's seat, cranked the engine, and waved good-bye to the newly assembled throng on the front porch of Blackbeard's.

Chapter 9

Twenty-two miles across Croatan Sound and up the Long Shoal River the CEO and president of Copperhead, Inc., Samuel Nix, cradled his Fabbri 12-gauge over/under shotgun in the crook of his elbow as he lifted a wad of Red Man chewing tobacco into his mouth. He stood on the edge of Alligator River National Wildlife Refuge, contemplating what to do next.

"This shit better not get out of hand," he muttered to himself.

Though he hadn't really planned on killing anything today, he kept the weapon on hand in case one of those menacing red wolves decided to come after him. He'd shot a few already and had them stuffed for his Copperhead, Inc. company headquarters near Edenton, North Carolina. He considered them excellent trophies.

That afternoon he had driven up Route 264 on the east side of Dare Mainland and looked through his binoculars across the Croatan Sound at the gathering that was forming near the Queen Anne's Revenge restaurant. Mildly curious after receiving a text from someone in the crowd, Nix knew he would be able to regain control if the situation unraveled, so he wasn't particularly worried. He had studied the commotion for a few minutes, turned his Ford King Ranch truck around and found the cove he had told his partner to locate using the new GPS they had installed in Vader.

What bothered him right now was that Vader was late, which was not good. Much of their post-Afghan and Iraq war revenue plan depended on the reliability of the submersible fighting machine. He walked back to the cove, which was completely concealed from any road or waterway, save a small channel. Nix stepped over clumps of tall grass, picking his way down to the glassy pool of water that was about ten feet deep.

His trained eye noticed a line tracing along the water as if in pursuit, maybe a largemouth bass in high gear ready to attack a lounging bullfrog. The water was clean but not especially clear. The ecosystem here mixed rich soil, freshwater, salt water, and abundant plant life to create a food chain that ranged from plankton to bull shark.

But most important, Albemarle and Croatan sounds were the perfect testing bed for Vader, Copperhead's prototype bid for the Navy and Coast Guard request for proposals on shallow-water armed submersibles.

Nix watched as the submersible crested the meniscus of the water, barely discernable. He let a crooked grin set on his face as he pushed the stopwatch function on his Tag Heuer Gran Carrera black titanium watch. Vader had made the fifty-nine nautical miles from Edenton to where he was standing in one hour, fifty-eight minutes, and thirty seconds. Better than any prototype out there and averaging thirty miles an hour through the shallow waters of Albemarle and Croatan sounds.

A former senior staff officer at Norfolk Naval Station, Nix believed that Vader could already win the Navy's contract to supply a formidable array of shallow-water capabilities to combat forces. They were like fighter jets under the ocean. The Coast Guard would also want it for fighting the diesel submarines used by drug runners from South America. At the moment, though, he was holding on to the trade secrets his team had developed. They had created a radar-avoiding skin they called MeshLink that combined the buoyancy of fiberglass with the protection of armor via multiple overlapping thin tiles, like fish scales. And he wanted to know he had every possible profit anticipated and accounted for before he submitted the prototype on the final bid to the Navy.

Nix was fifty-six years old with the small, tight build of a cage fighter. His black and gray hair was trimmed neatly around his ears, just long enough for the wind to toss and make him appear disheveled, a look he preferred. His eyes were dark, almost black, with no delineation between iris and pupil. As a submariner during his Navy career, his lack of height had served him well. At five and a half feet tall, Nix never had to duck as he transitioned between compartments. He always fit just fine in his bunk, and he moved efficiently around the submarine's tight confines.

He had been near bankruptcy when he retired from the Navy fourteen years ago, just before 9/11. He founded Copperhead as a limited liability corporation, mainly as a way to funnel money away from his ex-wife, who was constantly suing him for child support and medical bills. He had lost contact with both of his daughters, who had opted to take on their mother's last name, Wisenewski.

Nix had given his relationship with his wife and daughters the college try, but at the end of the day marriage wasn't for him. Truly, the military really hadn't been his thing either. He just wanted to cruise through life, hammer some chicks as often as possible, and make more money than everyone he knew. Toys were important to him and so his collection of fishing boats, Jet Skis, and airplanes were his metrics of success.

His fortunes had risen and fallen and they were on the uptrend again in the give-and-take of a business. If he was able to convert on just one or two of the product lines over the next week, though, it was game over, and that was what he was counting on. He had finally figured out that it was all about product lines and market diversification. In the beginning, he had said to his small crew, "Let's keep the main thing the main thing."

Then, after the embarrassment he and his Copperhead employees had caused by allegedly abusing detainees in Iraq and Afghanistan, his company was radioactive. Nix's singular focus on the lucrative private military contractor business had almost led them to insolvency. The US State and Defense departments banned them like lepers to a remote island. Court challenges led to one meager contract, the bomb disposal grunt work here on Dare County Mainland at the Dare County Bombing and Electronic Warfare Range.

But the bomb-clearing contract had led to other unexpected opportunities and suddenly he was all about market diversification.

As Vader One surfaced, only the glass bubble of the cockpit was evident to the naked eye. The MeshLink was loaded with 2400 pixels of color and constantly imaged its environment, like a chameleon, changing hues to blend.

Nix watched the wing tips break the surface of the water and he was staring at the almost perfect image of a fighter jet, but one built for moving undetected through shallow water. It had two small torpedo tubes on either side of its "wings" that looked more like small cannons. Nix's design created a vacuum fed conveyor belt into each wing that allowed the guns to rapidly fire miniaturized torpedoes with significant warhead explosive capability, either by line of sight or with predetermined GPS coordinates.

The hatch popped and his partner, Vinny Falco, stepped out, slid down the MeshLink surface, and splashed into the chest-deep water. He took a few steps and lashed a snap link through a countersunk eyelet and then fed some rope through his hand, securing Vader as if it were his steed. Falco pulled down on his wetsuit zipper to let some air in and emerged from the water looking like the Creature from the Black Lagoon.

"Boss," Falco said, his gold earring reflecting the sun.

"Vinny. You're late."

"I know. Sorry, boss."

"Though it appears the GPS works well," Nix said.

"Almost plowed into a damn shrimp net. You're right, the radar did well, though. Caught it just in time."

Nix had designed Vader with futuristic global positioning systems, forward-looking infrared radar, and thermal capabilities all downloaded into a single integrated platform with a heads-up display that gave the pilot just-in-time information to make crucial decisions about steerage or combat.

"That's good. Good." Nix looked into Croatan Sound and changed the subject, letting some of his anger show. "Some drifter found the body."

"Really?"

"You sterilized it, right?"

"Yes, completely."

"Next time, we use Vader to haul any bodies out to sea. Got it?"

"It'll be the first time we punch her through Oregon Inlet, but aye. Thought the old concrete block at the bottom of the sound was good enough. Hell, drop 'em at sea and they can still wash in. We caught a bad break, that's all. There was the other matter with his boat I had to deal with, too. A lot going on."

"Cut the lungs out next time. They'll stay down." Nix paused, holding back. He and Falco had served in Desert Storm together and had been on a variety of low-level, noncombat missions when they got bored with the military scene and retired. Nix had retired as a Navy captain, which accorded him a decent pension, except that his ex-wife got half of it. Falco had retired as a Navy chief petty officer, which also accorded him a decent pension, except he spent every minute off in Nags Head chasing women or in Atlantic City gambling. He was awash in debt and had needed the business as much as Nix had.

"I've got a phone conference today with Fort Brackett, so we'll see. They called after this morning's incident. It seems as though they need some security. Seems our willingness to do the bomb cleanup has got us some traction with DoD again."

Falco frowned.

"Saw the news right before I got in Vader. Lots of casualties?"

"Check. They're saying it was a lone jihadist targeting a major military facility. Front gate security cameras picked up a guy running into the crowd. This could be an opportunity for us."

Falco stood in knee-deep water holding the submersible that wafted back and forth with the chop kicked up by the breeze. About one hundred meters to their rear through the thick forest was Route 264, though it saw only the occasional car this time of day.

"We've got a lot of projects going, boss. I know we got our ass handed to us, but we can't spread ourselves too thin. Where will we get the personnel if we get the security contract? Can't be the same as who we've got clearing bombs, that's for sure."

Nix was losing his patience.

"Vinny, need I remind you that you were part of the Afghanistan debacle? We need the work, and if we need people, we'll find people, just like we found people to clear those bombs." He hooked a thumb over his shoulder in the direction of the bombing range a few miles to the north.

Nix studied Falco closely, keeping in check his pent-up anger over what Falco had done in Afghanistan.

"Understand. I'm just saying, boss. We got tons of shit going on. Almost like we're throwing spaghetti at the wall. See what sticks."

Nix nodded. "What's sticking is this dull-ass bomb disposal. But it's steady work and, as you said, cheap labor. We have a good chance at the Vader thing. I think we can sell that puppy to the Navy once we get our use out of it. Two prototypes. So do whatever keeps the cheap labor coming. We're going to need it."

Falco smiled. "Okay. Got it, boss."

"Plus, now we've got the biggest military base in the country maybe asking us to provide security. I'd say things are looking up, wouldn't you, Vinny?"

Nix watched Falco break eye contact, something not quite right.

"You know it, boss. Plus we've got the Rainbow."

Nix paused and then nodded. "We don't talk about Rainbow until it's a sure thing."

Falco started to speak, but Nix chopped a hand through the air and shut him down before pointing a finger at him.

"And Vinny? I don't know how that asshole floated to the surface, but don't let it happen again."

"Understand."

"And the other? The 'missing person?'" Nix used his fingers to make quotation marks.

"We're handling it."

"Okay. Dismissed."

The Navy captain had spoken to the chief petty officer; the businessman had not spoken to his partner. Nix knew Falco didn't like it, but tough shit. He also knew Falco was not being completely honest with him about what had transpired with the dead man named Miller Royes the drifter had found.

Nix watched Falco pull up his wetsuit zipper, unlash the line, step onto the stirrup just below the cockpit, and swing into the seat. Falco closed and sealed the hatch and then looked over his shoulder at the cargo bay. In Nix's view it had been crucial to keep the cargo hold as small as possible so that the submersible could carry more ammunition. In addition to the two turbo-propulsion engines, he had designed Vader with a flotation system so that it could elevate completely out of the water with a twenty-four-inch freeboard for activities such as transferring passengers or cargo.

As he watched Falco back out of the cove, he thought about all of his product lines: the bombing range clearance project, Vader, potential security work, and, of course, Rainbow.

Rainbow was the game-changer. It was his ticket to financial independence.

Chapter 10

The sun had set, it was eight p.m., and Mahegan watched Locklear navigate the narrow roads out of Manteo, up through Nags Head and Kitty Hawk, into Chesapeake, Virginia, and then onto Interstate 664 through Suffolk, over and under the Monitor-Merrimac Bridge Tunnel, and past the Hampton Coliseum on I-64 toward Richmond.

He watched her hold the steering wheel with her knees and text for about five minutes. When she seemed to have finished her business, she looked at him and said, "What?"

"You might want to watch the road."

"Making you nervous?"

Changing the topic, he said, "Johnson's your uncle?"

"That's right."

She was wearing the same outfit she had on when he had first met her. They had left Blackbeard's Restaurant, made a quick stop by her beach bungalow on the north end, and then departed for Arlington, Virginia. He was still wearing her IF IT'S TOURIST SEASON, WHY CAN'T I SHOOT THEM? T-shirt. The September evening had grown cool and Locklear had opted for the soft top. The air whipped through the gaps in the canvas and Mahegan closed his eyes, letting the wind buffet him.

"You're a deputy?" he asked.

"Sort of. During the tourist months, the sheriff needs all the help he can get. I'm really an engineer. Marine biology engineer to be specific."

Mahegan let that sink in for a moment. He ran the last twenty-four hours through his mind and something caught in one of the gears. He kept working through it and thought that Locklear may be able to help jar it loose.

"You kayak in the sound. You carry a Glock. You're deputized. You know all about the *Teach's Pet*, and you know all about the Croatan tribe."

"That's right, though the Croatan thing is sort of a hobby. As a direct descendent of Virginia Dare, I'm curious. The Croatan protected Dare and we know she survived, but can it be true that there are no Croatan bloodlines left in the world? I don't think so. An entire people extinct? Can't be."

They passed a sign for Fort Eustis, which Mahegan knew was a transportation command headquarters along the James River.

"You mentioned something about the private military contractors and no jobs for the locals. Can you tell me more about that?"

Mahegan felt he was close to what was hanging in his mind. When he added up the events of the day, her comment about the contractors was the only thing that did not make sense to him.

"Over in Alligator Wildlife Refuge the Navy and Air Force have a bombing range. After all the protests and threatening to vote out our congressman, they finally closed the place down two years ago. Can you believe it? Jets bombing in the middle of a wildlife refuge for black bears and red wolves. Unbelievable."

"The contractors?"

Locklear pulled onto I-295, bypassing Richmond as she moved north toward Washington, DC.

"Right. Copperhead, Incorporated won the contract to clear the 46,000 acres of all the ordnance. As you may know, for every ten bombs dropped, two don't detonate."

"At least that, but forget what I know. Why would you know that in your world?"

Locklear turned and smiled at him, the dimly lit dashboard casting a faint orange glow across her face.

"I'm a researcher."

Mahegan nodded, as if that explained everything.

"So, the contractors come into Manteo and hang around?"

"Only a few of them do. Mostly ex-military. Copperhead is that company that was protecting all the State Department and nongovernmental organizations in Iraq and Afghanistan and lost their contract after Abu Ghraib and the Bagram scandals. A prick named Sam Nix is their CEO and founder."

Mahegan knew from his time in Afghanistan that Copperhead had mostly rogue operators who would ride hanging out of windows, firing at anything that moved, aggressively pushing citizens and other vehicles off the road all in the name of getting their principal safely from point A to point B. Most of them lied about being former Delta Force or Navy SEALs. He didn't know of Nix, which told him something right there. Nix wasn't part of Mahegan's community of shadow warriors. Mahegan had known the Copperhead thugs left in their wake a scorched path of destruction that the maneuver commanders would have to then reconcile with the indigenous people, often costing military lives to increased numbers of roadside bombs and ambushes from angry citizens. Their interrogators would push the limits of the law and decency, believing that slapping around a few prisoners would yield the gold nugget of information such as Adham's exact location in the form of a ten-digit grid coordinate. It was not only shortsighted but plain stupid. Mostly, Mahegan knew these rookies just liked getting off on the power, having complete control over another human being.

"You know these guys?" Locklear asked.

"I know of them. Loose cannons, mostly."

"What nobody can figure out is that they really haven't hired any locals. During off-season our unemployment goes through the roof and everyone was hopeful. First, to get the bombing range cleaned up so that the wildlife preserve could actually preserve some wildlife. Imagine *that*. Second, the contract is for several years and folks were hoping for some good-paying jobs. Times are tough."

"But no jobs?"

Locklear nodded and Mahegan could tell she wanted to say something more, but she didn't. They drove on in the darkness, merging with the constant I-95 traffic heading toward the nation's capital like bees to pollen.

"Is Lindy short for something?"

"Why do you ask?" Locklear stiffened.

"Normal question, isn't it?"

"Is Jake short for something?"

"In fact it's a nickname. Chayton is my first name. Couldn't say it as a kid. Kept coming out Jake, so Jake it is."

"Cute."

After another five minutes of driving, Locklear relented even though Mahegan hadn't pressed her.

"Elizabeth."

"Pardon?"

"Lindy is short, sort of, for Elizabeth."

Something clicked in Mahegan's mind at the name, but he lost the thought as they pulled into the parking garage for the Hilton in Crystal City. It was one o'clock in the morning and Locklear changed the subject. "You're in my custody, you understand?" she asked. "I take my duties for Dare County seriously. Don't make an asshole out of me. And then there's this."

She showed him her iPhone. Mullah Adham's statement from this morning's attacks was on the screen.

"Captain Chayton Mahegan knows how we are doing this, so if you want answers, it is best to ask him."

"I want answers," Locklear said.

Mahegan processed the information. Williams had mentioned the attacks and he had heard intermittent references to the casualty count. But why would Mullah Adham implicate him? How would he even know who he was? But he immediately knew he had underestimated the enemy. Of course, Adham knew who he was. Mahegan had been assigned the task of capturing The American Taliban.

"I don't have any . . . right now," Mahegan said.

Locklear seemed to understand. "Fair enough, but I thought you should know."

"Thanks."

"This whole Pentagon thing may be more about this," she said, pointing at the phone, "than something that happened a year ago."

"A year ago, today. It's all the same. We are fighting a war and nobody really cares. The generals in the Pentagon go home every night and the soldiers in the field get shot at every night. Then they use the 8,000-mile screwdriver to tighten your ass up and decree whether you did right or wrong. Happens every day."

Locklear looked out of the window of the Defender into the dark parking lot. Mahegan saw her eyes narrow, as if in deep thought. He noticed, not for the first time, the beauty of her profile. Subtly strong chin, high cheekbones, thick blond hair, and light freckles across a nose that could be every plastic surgeon's inspiration.

"You're talking about the dishonorable discharge." Not a question.

"Partly. There is a great divide, Lindy, between the wheels that spin in the Pentagon," he said, pointing in the direction of the five-sided building, "and the machine that goes to war."

"But for you, a dishonorable discharge would be wrong. Unfair."

"I don't get into fair or unfair. It is up to a three-star general to decide. My record was spotless until I killed Hoxha. He was handcuffed. My intentions were irrelevant. I should have been more careful."

"Careful? You were in combat. He could have escaped and killed more of our soldiers!"

Mahegan was surprised. He had not mentioned any of the details to Locklear. Recalling that General Savage had said the news had covered the incident, he gauged Locklear differently. She had researched him. When and why, he wondered?

"This much is true," Mahegan said. "It's late. Let's move."

She parked the car and checked them into separate but adjoining rooms. Mahegan took a twenty-minute shower to wash off the day. While the memories of what happened that night to Colgate would never leave him, he thought he had left the legal ramifications behind. His command had conducted an investigation and

had cleared him of any wrongdoing. Savage had recommended him for an honorable discharge and Mahegan had quietly received a chest full of medals when
he'd departed the Army. He didn't care about the medals,
but the discharge characterization was important to
him. He had served honorably and deserved that per-
manent moniker on his record. General Bream pursuing a change in Savage's recommendation to perhaps
characterize the discharge as dishonorable gave even
his last hold on honor a bitter aftertaste.

And now this? Adham mentioning his name in connection with Fort Brackett?

Turning off the shower, he heard a light rap on his
door. He wrapped a towel around his waist and peered
through the peephole. He saw Locklear's face distorted
by the bubble as if she was looking at him.

He opened the door and she stepped in, nervous and
carrying a hanging bag she pushed into his hands.

"I had a friend go by Big and Tall as we were driving
and get you clothes for tomorrow. I don't know what
the Army requires you to wear to something like this,
but I guessed at your sizes; forty-six-long jacket and
thirty-two waist by thirty-six pants. Size twelve shoes,
which I knew from inspecting the mocs. Close?"

"Close enough. Thank you. A friend?"

"That's right. When I was driving with my knees
and texting? Anyway, she had to buy off the rack because anything else would need to be tailored."

She held out a navy blue suit, white shirt, red-and-
black rep tie, black dress shoes, and a bag of white
T-shirts.

"What do I owe you?"

"We'll settle up later," she said.

Mahegan retrieved the items and hung them in the
closet, setting the shoes and the shirts on the top shelf.

Then he turned toward Locklear, realizing for the first time that he was naked under the towel. He caught her staring and she flushed.

"Sorry," he said. "Just got out of the shower."

"Obviously. I wasn't checking you out. . . . Well maybe just a bit." Locklear smiled.

"I'm sure you got a boyfriend and all that comes with it."

"No boyfriend," she said. Locklear moved to the bed and sat on one corner. "No nothing. You got tourists who come and go and all they want to do is get laid or cheat on their significant others. You got a few contractors who come over to the island and the Outer Banks to get drunk and then get laid. You got rich guy millionaires who keep their boats on the sound, who just want to get laid in their fancy boats."

"I spent a little over a week on Roanoke Island and I didn't pick up on all that sex," Mahegan quipped.

"Try being a hot blond chick," she said.

Mahegan sat on the opposing bed, still dressed in his towel. He wasn't quite sure if he should excuse himself, but he did not want to put on the same clothes he had been wearing all day. He was fighting his male instincts. Here she was still in her beachwear, tanned shoulder exposed through the ripped OBX T-shirt, long legs crossed and honed and flexed and smooth.

"No thanks," he said. "I'll leave that task up to you."

She flipped her green eyes up at him and smiled.

"I should leave," she said, but didn't move.

"Yes, you should." Mahegan didn't move either.

"Or . . . we could hang out a bit."

"I would feel awkward with you not in a towel, though." Mahegan smiled for the first time since he could remember.

Locklear lowered her face and apologized, "I'm

sorry. You're half naked and we don't even know each other."

"I'm okay with this, Lindy, but I need to understand something," Mahegan said, feeling himself stir under the towel.

"Yes?"

Mahegan scanned her again with his eyes and said, "You're gorgeous. Sexy. Smart. Usually women like you are taken twice over."

"I have trust issues. Besides, you're not so bad yourself and you're alone."

"That's different."

"Really? How so?"

Mahegan thought for a moment. He had no vehicle, no home, minimal possessions, and about $90,000 in combat pay left in the bank. He didn't consider that he had much that would attract a woman nor was he in pursuit of affection. Besides, his mind was its own torture chamber. One day he would be mentally flogging himself for not saving Colgate and his other men, and the next he would be figuratively waterboarding his brain for killing Hoxha. He had tortured himself enough for not saving his mother, which had given him good practice for the additional guilt he now carried. The doctors had diagnosed him with significant post-traumatic stress when he'd processed out of the Army. Regardless, before he could be good for anyone, more than just sexually anyway, he would need to make himself whole again, at least mostly. Before he could do that, he needed to come to terms with Colgate and Hoxha.

"Can you trust me?" he asked.

"Can I?"

"I'm going to do something and I'm not sure how you're going to react."

"Okay," she said. He could see she was nervous but excited. Her breasts seemed to harden through the T-shirt and her cheeks got flushed. "I'm sure I'll be fine."

He stood, leaned over, and kissed her on the lips. She responded by reaching up to him and placing her hands on his shoulders. Her tongue darted into his mouth and before he let himself get carried away, he said, "Sorry, can you excuse me for a moment?"

She tugged on him as he pulled away, clearly not wanting to let him out of her grasp, which seemed almost desperate. Her response made his next step more difficult.

"Make yourself comfortable," he said.

He stepped into the bathroom, quickly put on the same clothes he had been wearing all day, stepped into his mocs, flushed the toilet, and let himself out of the bathroom.

Then he darted out of the hotel room. He jogged quickly to the stairwell, jumped in, and circled fourteen flights to the ground floor. He dashed into the lobby, out the front door, and began jogging toward the nearest metro stop. Mahegan saw that it was closed and kept running.

He jogged beneath I-395, passed the Air Force Memorial that looked like three giant spikes curling into the air and then found an asphalt path. Hooking onto the jogging trail, he ran parallel to Highway 110. To his left were the white headstones, standing erect like soldiers in formation. He was separated from the expansive Arlington cemetery grounds by a small three-foot-high stone wall.

He moved toward the southeast portion of the cemetery and jumped the wall when he was near Section 60 where the Iraq and Afghanistan War veterans were buried. He was certain that the cemetery was under constant surveillance, but if he moved swiftly, though, he could do what he needed to do. He did the math in his head. Colgate was killed a year ago. Since then there had been about 150 servicemen and women killed in those wars. Mahegan figured about two thirds would be buried in Section 60, which would mean 100, while another third were probably buried near their hometowns. As he studied the rows of headstones, there seemed to be about 100 across, so he went to the second row back from the first incomplete row.

Seventeen headstones toward the middle he found:

Wesley K. Colgate

As he knelt, his mind spun. Kneeling before Colgate's headstone, the memory came rushing back at him like an arrow shot into his chest.

They were jumping with Army Rangers on static lines at 500 feet above the Iranian countryside and he was poised against the inside door of the Talon, the new J-Model plane with four feathered propellers and turbine engines. His stick buddy, the jumper next to him, was Sergeant Colgate standing directly in front of him as they held their yellow static lines above their arms. Mahegan was the primary jumpmaster, so he was looking at Colgate, his best friend, who was the number-one jumper on the left door of the MC-130 Combat Talon. Twenty-nine camouflaged Rangers were standing behind Colgate, also holding their static lines above their left arms.

Mahegan gave Colgate a half smile as if to say, here we go again, bro, and barked his commands alerting the jumpers to stand up, hook up, check equipment, and sound off for equipment check. He got the, "All okay, jumpmaster!" from Colgate, who pointed at him with an outstretched hand, his smirk showing white teeth offsetting his black face.

Mahegan looked away from Colgate as the Air Force loadmaster opened the door to the Talon with a loud whooshing sound now that the 140-knot slipstream was rushing into the airplane. Mahegan turned to a Ranger paratrooper who was strapped into a counter-sunk D-ring on the floor of the aircraft wearing a monkey harness and parachute. He shouted, "Safety! Control my static line!" The safety grabbed the yellow nylon cord running from Mahegan's parachute to the snap link hooked onto the outboard anchor line cable consisting of one half-inch twisted steel that could hold thirty-two jumpers. Mahegan kicked at the two down-locks that held the jump platform in place. He put a heel on each edge of the outer platform and used his large hands to grip the rails inside the aircraft as he leaned into the 140-knot slipstream that was trying to suck him out of the aircraft. As he held on to the frame of the aircraft, Mahegan was now an inverted cee bow-ing into the powerful current of air riding along the slick exterior of the aircraft. His face whipped into de-formed shapes as the wind pushed against his exposed skin. His rucksack full of ammunition, water, and med-ical supplies was rigged in front of his legs and was the biggest threat to his stability. Mahegan was powerful and his arms were near hydraulic, locked on to the frame of the aircraft.

He looked to the rear. The other aircraft was blacked out and there was no moon so he barely saw the sil-houette of the second Talon. It was slightly higher than them, which was good. He looked to the front and saw a group of lights about two miles to the aircraft's ten o'clock, near the Iraq border, Mahegan figured. He calculated that they were on course. They should be. The MC-130 pilots were the best in the business.

The Delta credo was to blend in with whomever they were fighting. If they were working with a bunch of Afghans, then they wore local garb. If they were working with Rangers, they wore Army combat uniforms and Ranger scrolls on their sleeves, as Mahegan, Colgate, Patch, and the rest of his team were wearing tonight.

Mahegan pulled himself back into the aircraft and turned to his assistant jumpmaster, a Ranger who gave him a nod, indicating he agreed they were on track. Mahegan tightened his grip again as he leaned back into the night. Looking forward he saw the grouping of lights now off to their nine o'clock, which was the one-minute signal. He pulled himself back in and held up his right index finger. He heard the entire airplane of sixty-four Rangers and Delta operators echo, "One minute!"

He leaned back outside of the aircraft and spied the faint reflection of a mountain lake. The thirty-second mark.

Pulling back in, he held up his thumb and forefinger, as if to indicate a small amount. Thirty seconds.

He heard the paratroopers echo, "Thirty seconds!"

And that's when it all went to shit.

Mahegan leaned out for his final door check to make sure the second aircraft was higher than theirs so when the green light came on the Talon wouldn't chop up their parachutes with those new propellers. As he was about to spin back in and give the thumbs-up to his assistant jumpmaster and say, "Stand by!" he saw a rocket glowing and smoking its way from the ground toward the trail aircraft. They were close to the drop zone, which was a suspected manufacturing site of copper plates, electrical components for bombs, and possibly a nuclear facility as well. Their mission was to jump 130 Rangers and Delta operators onto the facility and go through it with a fine-tooth comb . . . and M240B machine guns.

But now Mahegan must act on instinct. He whirled inside the aircraft when he saw the chaff of his plane's aircraft survivability equipment escaping into the air, smoking hot white flakes of metal corkscrewing behind the aircraft, to trick the missile's heat-seeking guidance system. They couldn't jump into that.

Mahegan grabbed the loadmaster and screamed, "Tell them to turn that shit off! We're jumping now!" He watched the loadmaster bark into the microphone on his crewman's helmet and a moment later the chaff stopped.

Mahegan stepped into the door, turned to his stick of jumpers, and yelled, "Follow me!" He was out of the back end of the MC-130 and bunched into a tight ball holding on to his reserve parachute that was snapped onto his parachute harness across his abdomen, one hand covering the ripcord grip so that it wouldn't get pulled free by the slipstream. He was buffeted about by the airfoil from the Talon and by the time his parachute fully inflated, he felt like his testicles were cinched up into his throat. Mahegan knew the pilot was going over the 140-knot drop speed to evade the missiles just by the ferocity of his opening shock. He saw good silk above and as he spun, he saw Colgate coming down about fifty meters away. Bullets laced with burning green tracers were whipping through the sky like a fireworks display. Mahegan registered that for every tracer he saw there were four other machine gun rounds. The Talons were still powering through the drop zone at 500 feet above the mountains of northern Iran along the Iraqi border.

The ground grabbed Mahegan and he rolled, hating the T-10 parachute because it was just a round piece of nylon that he couldn't steer. On the ground, completing the paratrooper's first task, to land safely, he pulled his rucksack in, having decided not to lower it, given all of the machine gun fire. More protection. Quickly, his next task was to put his weapon into operation and Mahegan pulled his M-4 from the inside of his parachute harness waistband. He chambered a round, snapped his night-vision goggles on his helmet, and saw a group of enemy coming directly at him. His parachute risers were still attached to the canopy release assemblies. With the wind blowing away from him, he popped both of the release assemblies and his parachute sailed directly toward the shouting men with their AK-47s. He used the obscuration to roll just a few meters to his right. In a prone position, with his rucksack between his legs, he popped the lowering line and used his feet to push it back, all the while putting his infrared-aiming laser beam on the first combatant to emerge from the parachute. He fired five times, hitting every man coming toward him, but then there were more than he could count. They were like apparitions backlit by some kind of light, nothing but shadows coming at him, and he knew he was about to be surrounded. This was the paratrooper's most vulnerable moment, the first couple of minutes on the ground before he could link up with a single buddy.

Suddenly, he heard another weapon firing from behind him. "Mahegan, I'm here, man."

It was Colgate, who came rushing into the craziness with orange and green tracers whipping around like angry hornets.

"Thanks, Half-mil," Mahegan said using the nickname that only Colgate let him say. Colgate landed

about five meters from him behind a rock. Their combined firepower bought them a couple of minutes, but Mahegan noticed three men flanking them from Colgate's direction. Suddenly, they were on Colgate and Mahegan couldn't get a clean shot. He was up with his knife and his pistol, moving into the fray. He shot one with the pistol and cut another, leaving Colgate with one, whom Colgate handled with a butt-stroke of his M-4. Mahegan put the knife in the man's throat and they'd bought some more time.

"Man, don't ever lose that knife," Colgate said about the time they noticed more enemy troops gathering on the crest of the ridge. Patch had jumped in with an M240B machine gun and suddenly it was singing as it pumped fifteen rounds every second into the gaggle of Iranians reacting to their vertical envelopment.

Mahegan and Colgate threw their rucks on their backs and ran toward Patch about seventy-five meters away. Now there were three of them. Soon Pucino and a couple of Rangers linked up by calling out the password, "Buckeyes," a name picked because the regimental commander was an Ohio State grad.

Mahegan noticed that they had gathered about fifteen men now, everyone coming toward the safety of Patch's machine gun.

Mahegan said, "Okay, men, follow me."

Patch stopped shooting to bound forward with them when another machine gun picked up the pace from about a quarter mile away. The plan was coming together. Mahegan took his group up to a fence. They cut the wire, moved into the first building by kicking the door in, shot two armed guards, and checked fire on two scientists wearing white smocks.

"Flex-cuff them," Mahegan said and he was moving

to the next building, which was a warehouse where they found thousands of copper discs that had been machine struck and milled by makeshift presses, like a coin press. Their products, though, were six-inch-diameter metal Frisbees that when shot from a PVC pipe turned into a molten fist that cut through tank armor. They'd hit the mother lode. Mahegan thought about all of the men and women who were missing limbs or were dead as a result of these munitions. He felt his emotions begin to gallop away from him like a herd of mustangs, but he kept them in check. He and Colgate moved into another room and, as he scanned with his flashlight secured on the rail of his M4 carbine, he said, "Look at this shit."

Colgate looked and they were staring at floor-to-ceiling boxes of MVX-90 multi-wave receiver transmitters made in the USA by MVX Entertainment, Inc. in Raleigh-Durham, North Carolina's Research Triangle. It said so directly on the boxes. Mahegan knew this technology because Delta got them fresh off the assembly line in their beta prototype state for enhanced frequency hopping to avoid enemy communications intercept.

"Grab one," Mahegan ordered. Colgate cut open a cardboard box that had a dozen MVX multi-wave receivers in smaller containers about the size of an Amazon book-shipping box.

"Got it," Colgate said. "Unbelievable. The acquisition guys told us the only people who had these were those who made them and tested them, and us."

"They lied," Mahegan said. He signaled to Colgate before tossing a thermite grenade in the room, shouting, "Clear!" The explosion rang loudly in the warehouse, echoing throughout the valley.

It was fifteen minutes before the helicopters would land at the soccer field about a quarter mile away. They had been on the objective an hour and Mahegan decided it was time to leave.

The Ranger demolitions team rigged the warehouse for destruction, though Mahegan knew that without enough firepower, all the explosion would do was kick out hundreds of those copper plates that could be milled again and later used to hurt more Americans. He grabbed the Air Force tactical controller by the body armor the way a football coach grabbed the quarterback by the face mask and said, "Either get me one of those bigass daisy cutter bombs or a bunch of Tomahawks from the squids. The moment we leave here, I want this place to melt."

The controller smiled and said, "How about both, sir?"

"Whatever, but do it." Within minutes, he got the thumbs-up from the Rangers that the demo was rigged and he checked one just to be sure. He saw a block of C-4, a well-seated blasting cap, and detonation cord, and nodded.

He rallied his men and they moved out to the soccer field as the helicopters came blowing in. There was some residual enemy fire, but nothing significant. He called into the regimental commander that he had everyone and everything he was supposed to have and they lifted off, spitting dirt and rocks in all directions heading back toward a secure compound in Iraq, which this time, ironically, meant safety. Sitting on the edge of the Black Hawk helicopter, his legs dangling in the cool night air as the pilots sped toward the nearest US Army base, Mahegan saw the warehouse erupt in a *ball of smoke and he felt the shock wave from the explosions. A few seconds later, a daisy cutter bomb, a fuel-air explosive and the closest thing to a nuke without being a nuke, incinerated the place, melting all those copper discs.*

Mahegan had the two scientists on his helicopter and he could see Patch, Pucino, and Colgate. They all locked eyes and he nodded as if to say, "We've done good, men." It was all a soldier ever needed, to know that he'd done his job well.

Suddenly his body ached with loss and mourning. Classic post-traumatic stress reaction, the doctors had told him. Like a magician's trick, not there one moment, and then appearing somewhere unexpected the next.

Together they had destroyed the primary copper disc–manufacturing warehouse of the Shia, who were supplied and funded by the Iranians. After their raid, the lethal, explosively formed penetrator attacks against the Coalition had dropped dramatically, and it was near miraculous that no Americans were killed and only a few wounded. Mahegan was most proud of the copper disc raid in Iran. Remembering the moment he'd been surrounded, Mahegan knew the mission would not have been casualty free and he would not be alive had Colgate not been there. Because an MVX-90 had ultimately led to Colgate's death, the irony made for a bitter memory.

It was four a.m. and the September morning in Arlington National Cemetery was heavy with dew, waves of moisture beginning to come down almost like a light rain. Mahegan reached out and touched the headstone, reading the words again.

WESLEY K. COLGATE
STAFF SERGEANT, US ARMY

~

Iraq, Afghanistan
1987–2014

Silver Star, Purple Heart,
Combat Infantryman's Badge

~

A Loving Son and a Good Friend

"Roger that," Mahegan whispered. He looked beyond Colgate's grave, saw thousands of others just like
it, and knew that his friend was in good company.
Trace Adkins's song "Arlington" played through his
mind as he bowed his head and closed his eyes.

The Spirit lives. He hoped so anyway.

He ran his hand along the smooth, white granite stone,
and felt a bump. He tugged at a small tube, not much
bigger than a one-hundred-pound-test fishing line.

Suspicious now, he followed the tube with his hand
all the way to the back of the headstone, where he found
a small battery pack.

Before he could look more, he heard car doors slam
about a hundred meters away and he could almost see
Colgate smiling at him, saying, "Better get your ass out
of here, man."

He was up and moving among the fallen. Soon he
was back over the fence as shouts echoed behind him
with flashlights crisscrossing his path.

He was back to the hotel by five a.m. He let himself
into his room and found Locklear inside the door,
pointing a pistol at his face, her eyes cold and unfor-
giving.

Chapter 11

Millions of megabytes away from where Mahegan stared into the black hole of Locklear's pistol barrel, Mullah Adham proudly watched the video of the Fort Brackett slaughter. It had gone viral all across the Internet, so much so that it became impossible for the American government to shut down or eliminate. He had been careful not to post it to his Facebook page . . . yet.

Seated before him were two new jihadists. Two new ghosts. They watched him eagerly as he stood and walked toward them inside his small cave. A generator somewhere in the distance was pushing enough electricity to keep the lights glowing brightly.

He squatted before the two men who had been delivered to him over a week ago. One was an eighteen-year-old Pakistani boy named Hamasa. He was thin with black hair, a wiry beard, and deep-set, hollow eyes. Hamasa knew that one day soon he would be a suicide bomber and perhaps, Adham thought, his mortality was registering with him.

"Don't be afraid," he whispered, running his hand across the boy's face.

"I am strong, Mullah," Hamasa said.

"How, then, were you captured?"

Hamasa looked away.

"They came for me in the night. We were sleeping in the *qalat* with the animals. Our guards had gone to sleep also. They killed the others and took me."

Very good, Adham thought. The Copperhead Capture Team was performing well. He had presented his idea to the Quetta Shura two years ago. The hard-core fighters had been tiring of fighting only in Afghanistan and wanted to help al-Qaeda carry the fight back to America. Adham had drawn in the sand a map of Afghanistan, the Atlantic Ocean, and the United States. Fight here, he'd said to the Quetta Shura, pointing at the US, not here, as he pointed at Afghanistan.

One of the Shura members stood and walked to the sand map and used Adham's stick as he said, "If we fight here, then they will fight even harder here." He pointed at the first location and then Afghanistan and Pakistan. Then the man pointed at America and said, "And who will we get to fight here?"

"Ghosts," Adham had said, smiling. He had heard reports from detainees released from Bagram Detention Facility that one in ten prisoners had never been officially logged into the Department of Defense system. Private military contractors were in charge of most field detention sites where the Americans first brought the prisoners into detention. Adham knew the well-publicized rule was that within four days of capture the US Army infantry units had to notify headquarters that they had captured an enemy prisoner of war and to make a decision on whether they were going to move a prisoner to Bagram. But often with the pace of operations, detainees languished in a void. And some became ghosts, with no official record, yet stashed

away in containers around Afghanistan and Iraq. With
tens of thousands of soldiers and contractors on the
battlefield, there was potential for abuse of the system.

Adham saw it as an opportunity. Legitimize the ghost
operation through the most vulnerable contractor on
the battlefield. At the moment, that had been Copperhead, Inc. He motivated the tanking contractor by offering an endless pipeline of free labor, ghost prisoners,
who could travel back on their private charters from
Kandahar to a remote runway in North Carolina.

Hamasa was part of that plan. So was Uday, the
Iraqi. Sometimes US military forces captured their
prisoners and left them in the care of Copperhead, too
busy to follow up on the prisoners' status. Other times,
rogue Copperhead Capture Teams would target specific individuals to keep the pipeline of labor flowing.
After their detention by US military forces or Copperhead Capture Teams, Copperhead evacuated the ghosts
to Adham's location for training. They had performed
well. Top of their class—of ghosts.

Adham nodded, and then looked at the Iraqi, a twenty-
two-year-old combat veteran who had served in the
Shi'a militias that were funded by the Iranians. Joining
al-Qaeda, he had traveled to Pakistan, trained young
recruits, and then led them into battle near Kandahar
where he, too, had been captured.

"And you, Uday, how were you captured?"

The Iraqi had the hardened eyes of a criminal, of a
man who had seen too much death for one lifetime.
Uday was a large man. How *had* his Capture Team wran-
gled this man to the ground?

"They were civilians," Uday said. "Electric guns."

Adham nodded. The Capture Teams carried lethal
weapons and stun guns. They killed the bystanders and
stunned the prey to preserve for shipment overseas.

"Do you know what comes next?"

Both men looked at him expectantly.

"You will complete your training and then you will conduct jihad in America."

"But, Mullah?" Uday asked. "Where are we? I was blindfolded for days and knew that I was on every form of transportation. Airplane, truck, and ship. Many ships."

"At this moment, you are nowhere. You are ghosts. For years in both Iraq and Afghanistan the Americans have taken our brothers as prisoners, documenting most and officially imprisoning them in their jails in Abu Ghraib, Bagram, and Guantanamo. But they keep a few of our brothers in torture chambers without ever documenting them. The Americans call them *ghosts*. I have saved you from torture so that you can conduct jihad."

"*Inshallah.*" *God willing*, the men said in unison. They were thankful and knelt before The American Taliban's feet.

"We will step outside and you will see your new environment."

Adham led the men from his cave where they climbed a long staircase and stepped outside into the bright sunlight. Instantly, they heard the Islamic call to prayer, the *Adhan*, beckoning them.

The two men turned to Adham and asked, "Which way is Mecca?"

Adham paused, then pointed and said, "South. That way."

Immediately, the men dropped to their knees and began their supplications. Adham followed suit, lest they think he was a fraud. He put his forehead in the dirt, keeping his eyes on his new ghosts until they were done.

Standing, Adham walked his men around the small complex, which consisted of small homes, a mosque, and a few stores. A few people milled about, but the town was essentially vacant.

"Where in Iraq are we, Mullah?" Uday asked.

"We are at a training base far away from anywhere you have ever been, Uday. I know you are from Basra and that you are a Shi'a. You fought the Americans mostly in East Baghdad and specialized in making explosively formed penetrators. You have never ventured to this town, called Srab Qyrh."

"Srab Qyrh?" Uday asked.

"Yes. I know what you are thinking. Literally translated, it means Mirage Village. It is a ghost village for ghost prisoners, and we built it for you and others like you who want to train to attack Americans. Everyone believes I am in Afghanistan or Pakistan or even Iran. But no one knows where I am or that you exist, and we will use that advantage to destroy America on its own soil. Now that the Americans have all but left Iraq and Afghanistan, we have more freedom and can hide in plain sight. And once you graduate, you will move onward, your final voyage."

Hamasa and Uday watched a group of men doing push-ups on an athletic field. They were led by a man with lighter hair and a thick beard wearing camouflage fatigues. He was calling out to them in Arabic, though Adham knew that the men were a mixture of Iraqis, Pakistanis, and Afghans.

They were the perfect jihadists.

And he had created the perfect way for them to conduct jihad.

"Follow me," Adham said.

They walked down a stairwell into the basement of one of the concrete buildings. As he descended, Adham looked up at his satellite dish, hidden below an awning.

It was facing southwest and angled high into the sky. As he ducked through the low door, the shift from extreme sunlight to utter darkness momentarily blinded him. He felt the presence of his two new ghosts behind him. Opening a secondary door, the smell hit him first. His prisoner of war was not going to last much longer. He would kill him tomorrow on television.

"This is the enemy," he said pointing at the huddled figure in the corner. The man still had the sandbag on his head. Adham had punched some airholes in the burlap so the person could breathe. The Army combat uniform was soiled with urine, feces, and vomit.

"The two of you will behead him tomorrow on television," Adham said.

Hamasa and Uday nodded.

Uday said with some conviction, *"Inshallah."*

Adham returned his trainees to their quarters and then entered his hideout, where he powered up his computer. He typed a new status update on his Facebook page announcing another attack.

"If you thought Brackett was bad, just wait until the next attack. It doesn't get any better than this. Well, actually it does. But more to follow on that. Just FYI, beheading tomorrow. Last thing, friends, watch out for former army Captain Chayton Mahegan. You will soon be calling him 'Traitor' Mahegan. He is wanted for murder in North Carolina and by the Inspector General of the US Army."

Then Adham went to his Twitter account and typed: "CPT Mahegan is traitor. In NC hiding. Mobilize America and stop him before he does more damage. Ft. Brackett his idea . . ."

Next he sent a Twitter direct message to Chikatilo from a dummy Twitter account.

@TuffChik, get ready to shop at Walmart!

Satisfied, Adham stepped outside again, turning his face toward the sun. Reflecting on his ascension to power, Adham thought again about Camus, which made him think about the duality of life. Which made him think about his father. Who was never there.

His mother, however, was ever-present, nurturing, and loving. Perhaps she believed she had offset the absence of his father, who for a brief period of time was so close, yet unreachable.

Then the FBI raided their home, stole his gaming code, and ruined his chance at legitimately making a name for himself as he'd planned. It didn't matter. Now, he had developed a bigger, better way. And it would make things tough on good old dad.

Payback was a bitch, indeed.

Elizabeth Carlsen, the researcher from the library, had briefly offset the pain. She, too, had nurtured and perhaps loved him. Elizabeth had also urged him to pursue his passion in web design, which had really been no passion at all. His prime motivator was expanding his universe through the web, not being a functionary. *Monument Hunter* had brought together thousands of online gamers. Elizabeth had unknowingly motivated him into hacking into the domains of the most powerful. Seeing the level of corruption everywhere had further tainted his innocence, dropping him into despair. Knowing too much too soon in life had catapulted him into depression. His happiness had turned to sadness, just as Camus had philosophized.

He emerged from his teen years shattered by the government corruption that had stolen his creativity and a father who had stolen his childhood by never acknowledging he existed. In a sense, he was a ghost as well.

And so he decided: if you can't beat 'em, join 'em. Or even better, beat them at their own game. Mullah Adham was partly still the young Adam Wilhoyt, longing for the love of his parents. Unfortunately, he didn't have many good memories and had reconstructed the steel frame of his character as best he could with the help of the madrassa leaders of the Taliban and al-Qaeda. Knowing that he wasn't buying anyone's bullshit, Adham became a mercenary for power. At times he hesitated. Others, he was sure of his path. Today he was certain.

As he saw it, he wasn't like those garden-variety kids at Columbine, or the Sandy Hook slayer, or even Julian Assange from WikiLeaks. He was better. He rode the competing forces of good and evil to the top like a lava vent erupting. Forged by love and the absence of love, by loyalty and betrayal, and by guidance and misdirection, Mullah Adham reasoned that it was not his fault at all. He had simply stepped onto the world stage a product of modern society: crazy, competent, and ready for power.

And he had amassed an army of anonymous loyalists, his ghosts, who were prepared for the next step: terror in the suburbs of America.

Chapter 12

Mahegan stood in front of the desk of Lieutenant General Stanley Bream, the Inspector General of the United States Army. He knew very little about either the man or the position other than what he had heard in the news and could see scattered about the walls and desks.

There were several photos of Bream dressed in Army uniforms posing with a variety of presidents, other generals, and entertainers. He saw dozens of plaques and awards scattered about the personal display. It wasn't something Mahegan would have done, not that he could if he'd wanted to, as his own awards were classified.

On the bookshelf there was a round bomb insignia of an ordnance officer and a variety of maintenance and ammunition references throughout the office. So, Bream was at one point in his career either in charge of Army maintenance or ammunition, or both, for the units in which he served. There were some naval photos of old ships in stormy seas and a large glass case directly behind his desk with a set of matched dueling pistols facing each other in a velvet box. His eyes found a series of plaques from different postings around the country.

Bream apparently had served in the Mojave Desert at the National Training Center and also at Fort Hood, Texas. Curiously, Mahegan saw a photo and certificate from the Director of the FBI thanking him for his liaison tour with the Bureau. There was a plaque titled, "The Rock," which indicated a tour of duty at Rock Island Arsenal in Illinois. From the looks of it, Mahegan thought, Bream had mostly been in charge of units that fixed tanks or delivered ammunition, but had at some point migrated to investigations and inspections. Mahegan could see the reflection of Bream's computer screen in the shiny glass.

On the wall was a framed *Washington Post* article titled "The Army's Chief of Integrity." He saw a picture of General Bream and scanned the first few lines about Bream's stellar career and how he may be "the military's shining star of integrity and veracity." Bream was the man who had felled corporate giant Copperhead, Incorporated, and disclosed their evil deeds in Afghanistan and Iraq. The article catalogued prisoner abuse, theft, obstruction of justice, and an assortment of other crimes that Bream had relentlessly pursued with his extralegal powers. Accordingly, the year-old article relayed, Bream was next in line to be Chief of Staff of the Army, the equivalent of the CEO.

What was missing, Mahegan thought, were family pictures. There was one photo of Bream with an attractive woman who was probably in her fifties. His wife. No kids. Not that unusual, as most senior officers relished their contact, however fleeting, with dignitaries until they imagined themselves to be one. But Mahegan still found it odd that he would have only one picture of his family among dozens of celebrities.

Moving to the bookshelf, he noticed more pictures of General Bream with politicians, usually in Washington, DC, with the Capitol or White House in the background. He read the titles of books: *The Pentagon's New Map, The Clash of Civilizations, Ship of Gold in the Deep Blue Sea, The Looming Tower*—

A voice interrupted his perusal.

"Captain Mahegan." Mahegan turned and saw a tall man wearing an Army combat uniform coming out of a door, probably a private bathroom, at his left. Mahegan's first thought was that the uniform's digitized tan-and-olive pattern looked strange on him. He looked more like a congressman or CEO than a military guy. He had gelled black hair that was too long for Army standards, but neatly parted from left to right. He looked toned, muscular, and an inch or two shorter than himself, but nearly the same weight. He flashed white teeth that looked like a row of Chiclets. He had brown eyes and a smooth face. His grip was strong as he grasped Mahegan's own hand.

"General," Mahegan said. He stood there in his navy blue suit with white shirt and red tie, all of it feeling unnatural and uncomfortable. He figured it beat wearing an "If It's Tourist Season: Why Can't I Shoot Them?" T-shirt over dirty swim trunks. He had hidden the gold coin beneath the passenger seat of the Defender just before Paslowski had picked him up from a grumpy Lindy Locklear standing guard at the Hilton.

Locklear had barely spoken to him since she'd had her pistol in his face and didn't seem to care about the explanation he'd actually wanted to offer. Her jokes and flirting were gone and she'd become the distant, resigned jailer doing her job.

Paslowski had driven him the short way to the Pentagon, where they walked through several vault doors on an inner ring of the building to enter the IG's office. He had been waiting twenty minutes in the general's office, standing in front of the big wooden desk with no paper or appearance of functionality other than a laptop computer with a red Ethernet cable and a white Ethernet cable serving both his secure and nonsecure internet and e-mail networks.

"Chief tells me you're wanted for murder in North Carolina."

"That's not true," Mahegan replied.

"That's not true, *sir*. Right?"

"Right."

"Right, sir? Right, captain?" Bream corrected him again.

Mahegan saw where the general was headed and decided to avoid the "Who's on first" conversation. Arrogant prick. "Yes, sir."

"So, Chief's not telling the truth?"

The general was standing in front of him now, about three feet away. They were nearly eye-to-eye, but Mahegan knew that Bream gained an inch or two with the Army boots. Bream leaned against the outer edge of the polished mahogany desk. There was a phone on the credenza next to the dueling pistols behind the desk and beneath a rare window in the inner rings of the Pentagon.

"Just saying he's wrong, is all. Sir."

"You're just being investigated, then. Right?"

Mahegan suddenly got the distinct impression that the general was playing him the way an interrogator might begin to work a prisoner of war. His first clue was the general's version of the "stress position" by making him wait for twenty minutes standing in his office as opposed to sitting on the sofa directly outside the door. Second, he began with the classic, "When did you stop beating your wife?" question. He could answer at his own peril.

"I was swimming and found a dead body. I did the right thing and turned it in," Mahegan said.

"Like finding a lost watch. You just turned it in?"

"Something like that."

"You keep dropping 'sirs' around me, soldier, and we're going to be having an entirely different conversation."

"Sir, I'm not in the Army anymore. What do you want? How did you even find me?" Though Mahegan thought he knew the answer to the last question, he remained concerned about the ultimate purpose for his visit to the Inspector General of the Army.

Bream crossed his arms and rested them on his chest. He dropped his head and stared at his boots, as if he was thinking.

"As you know, your sugar daddy, Bob Savage, has formally challenged my dishonorable discharge ruling. I'm willing to listen to a West Point classmate, but I've taken some heat in the media over that ruling, too. So, what I want with you is to go back to exactly one year ago and have you tell me about how you killed the detainee, Commander Hoxha, you had in your possession. With my investigation into Copperhead, we've learned some things and received some statements that compete with your and your team's version of events."

Exactly as Mahegan had expected, Bream did not address the question about how the Inspector General goons found him. As Bream had referenced, Savage and Bream had been West Point classmates. How Bream had been promoted past colonel, much less beyond Savage's rank, was a mystery to Mahegan. Mahegan had heard that Bream had taken a few jabs from conservative talk show hosts about his challenge of Mahegan's honorable discharge.

"Sir, we all provided statements on what you're asking me. General Savage reported it up the chain of command, and we were all cleared after an independent investigation. And what does Copperhead have to do with this?"

"That's not telling me anything I don't know, Mahegan. Copperhead was the crew that got called in to clean up your mess. While you were down in the valley airlifting Colgate's remains back to Bagram, the Copperhead forensics team went in there. It was their last mission. They were in the second vehicle."

Mahegan remembered wondering why the contractors were milling around the intact Humvee.

"I've got nothing to add, sir. And this is the first I'm hearing that Copperhead had stayed behind. I thought the entire scene was evacuated."

Bream seemed to consider this. The man probably thought Mahegan was being insubordinate.

"You lawyering up? That it?"

"I was told you don't allow lawyers," Mahegan replied, edging toward confrontation.

Bream looked away, a creepy smile crossing his face.

"They're allowed to be present. They just can't say anything."

"Sounds like the Taliban. Judge and jury," Mahegan said, and then after a noticeable pause, "sir."

"How many detainees have you taken off the battlefield?"

"None lately, sir."

"Captain, are you the least bit concerned with your discharge rating? Do I need to read you your rights and sit your ass down in the interrogation room?"

"General, am I being charged with something here? I served my country. I've got my papers. The way I see it, my odds are slim with you because you've already made up your mind. This is just bureaucratic bullshit. Combat is tough. I've lost friends. And *I've* spent a lot more time getting shot at than second-guessing soldiers' instincts while in combat from behind a mahogany desk in Washington," Mahegan said.

Then he added, "Sir." He looked at Bream's right-shoulder sleeve, which was noticeably bare of the US Army "combat patch." In today's environment, Mahegan could not understand how anyone other than a new enlistee could have escaped combat duty. Mahegan had had eight combat tours in the last thirteen years. A quarter of his entire life had been dedicated to fighting his nation's enemies and while the general in front of him may have had a distinguished thirty-plus-year career, Mahegan was incredulous at the idea that the man could have avoided combat duty during his entire tenure.

Bream's eye twitched in irritation, but he took in Mahegan's challenge without comment before continuing. "Captain, I make the final call on your discharge. Honorable or dishonorable. You are not helping your case." Bream paused and smiled. "As I said, we have some new evidence."

Mahegan wanted to say, "Bring it on," but knew better than to further antagonize someone who appeared to be an impossibly powerful individual with unlimited ability to do harm. Like Hoover when he ran the FBI, Mahegan thought. But, the general was dangling something in front of him. A deal, perhaps?

"What do you know about The American Taliban and his Nuristan hideout you raided that night?" the general asked.

Mahegan stared at him. He knew a little more than what everyone else knew from the television accounts that had been playing endlessly since yesterday morn-

ing's attack at Fort Brackett. He and his men had hunted
Adham with every resource allowable, and some that
were not. How did this desk jockey know about Adham's Nuristan sanctuary, and why was he asking? That
information was specially compartmented at the highest classification levels.

"Other than the news the last twenty-four hours, I'm
not sure what you're talking about, sir."

Bream moved from the desk and stood so close to
him that Mahegan could count the crow's-feet on the
corners of Bream's eyes. Three on the left and two on
the right. There was a small injection mark at Bream's
hairline. Judging by the smooth forehead, Mahegan
figured the general had regular Botox injections. Ap-
pearances were important here in the Pentagon, Mahegan surmised.

"Why would Mullah Adham mention you in connection with the Brackett attack?"

"Sir, I have no idea. Maybe because my team was
assigned with putting pressure on him and we killed
one of his most wanted men?"

"Maybe," Bream said. "But it looks bad for you . . .
and for us. Brings this whole thing with Hoxha back
into play."

Mahegan thought he understood now. Once Adham
had mentioned Mahegan's name, the Inspector General's initial investigation would be suspect. And the
first rule of bureaucrats, which Bream decidedly was,
was to cover one's ass.

Bream changed his tone.

"I see you looking at my right sleeve, Mahegan. You
don't know me and you don't know where I've been. I
see the wheels spinning through your mind, sizing me
up, figuring you can take me. Maybe you can. It would

be a tough fight for a wounded man. And of course you know it wouldn't do you any good."

Mahegan almost smiled.

"I played tight end for West Point in 1979, the last class with balls. You know what that means?"

Mahegan shrugged. "You've got a pair?"

Bream squinted and shook his head.

"Last all-male class at the Academy. I keep in shape and I've served my country. There's no need to square off with the man who is likely to be the next Chief of Staff of the Army. You should think about that."

"Not squaring off, sir. You're a general. I'm not. It's that simple. Chief of Staff or not."

Mahegan knew one of two things was happening. Either the general was trying to provoke him into violence so he'd have Mahegan on a detainable charge, or he was probing him for unreported details on Adham. It was a classic lose-lose situation. He either reacts to the provocation or reveals details that are still classified beyond the general's security clearance.

"Back to Adham. We've got intel you may have captured him," Bream said.

The comment caught Mahegan off guard. To his knowledge, Adham was still on the run.

"Sir, are you asking me to discuss specially compartmented information with you? And how could he be in detention if he's all over the Internet?"

"Listen, Mahegan. Clearly Adham has something working here in the United States. When you raided and then killed that bomb maker, there was intel that Adham was close by. Then he fell off the radar. And now he's got hostages. We've all seen the footage. And out of over one million service members, he mentions your name? What kind of coincidence is that?"

Mahegan stared at Bream, debating what to say.

"I thought you said Copperhead went into Hoxha's compound after the medevac. Standard docex."

Docex was short for "document exploitation." Even that name was a misnomer because the team, usually contractors, retrieved information off computers, hard drives, cell phones, and other forms of media.

"Why didn't they go in with you on the mission?"

"Sir, my mission was kill and or capture. You should ask General Savage. What I will say is that we had eight seats on the Little Birds. I needed all the firepower I could get. Some of my team went through the shack and collected some intelligence. Scraps of paper. Hoxha's diary, bullshit like that. The biggest find was the MVX-90s."

"I didn't know about the MVX-90s. That's interesting, to say the least."

"It was all in the report."

Bream turned and walked to his window, which opened to a gravel maintenance area and gave him a view of another ring of the Pentagon.

"You ever ghost a detainee, Mahegan?"

Mahegan knew the term "ghost" was both noun and verb. A ghost detainee was an individual seized from the battlefield and never entered into the official prisoner of war tracking system. Ghosting allowed the interrogators to avoid Geneva Convention standards for questioning or to extend the official holding period if the capturing unit was unsure of the value of the detainee. Bream was asking him if he had ever taken a prisoner of war and held him without officially documenting his capture or entering him into the Department of Defense database. But while he had taken his share of detainees, he always rapidly turned them over to the Joint Special Operations Command detention center and from there he was unaware of the process.

He truthfully answered, "No, sir. I have never ghosted a detainee."

"Why do I not believe you, Mahegan?" Bream continued to stare through the window at the opposite ring.

He wanted to say, *Maybe some insecurity manifesting itself, sir?* Instead, he followed with, "Sir, I'm an operator. I seized my share of prisoners and turned them over to the proper authorities." After a pause, he added, "And I've killed my share of enemies on the battlefield as well."

Bream smiled and turned toward Mahegan.

"You view me as an enemy?"

"That would be unwise of me, wouldn't it, sir?"

Changing tack again, Bream said, "The forensics from yesterday's attack at Ft. Brackett show DNA from a Middle Eastern male. Probably the same one pictured on the video. The fingerprint database in West Virginia gave us a dossier that indicates he once fought in Nuristan Province for the Taliban, was captured, fingerprinted, and then taken to Bagram, where he was released after a year. Then nothing until this. The question is: How did he get into the country?"

"Sir, if I might say, this seems different from why you had me come here. What specifically are you asking? Detainees are released all the time. Sometimes they're recaptured on the battlefield."

"You said you're an operator, Mahegan. You and your men went into Nuristan. Did you pull anyone off the battlefield without telling us? You killed that one prisoner of war. Did you haul any others back and torture them to seek your vengeance for Colgate and your other team members? Maybe fly one back on those secret JSOC airplanes? Maybe he escaped?"

"Sir, I think you've insulted me enough for one day. I served. I defended. I upheld the Constitution. I did it all honorably. I made one big mistake in killing Hoxha. But to answer your questions, no, I didn't do any of what you suggest."

This seemed to satisfy Bream. He nodded and said, "Okay." Then added, "But something else is not adding up."

"I've already said too much."

"No, you've answered the Inspector General's questions."

"Can you answer one of mine, sir?"

Bream studied him a moment and smiled. "Maybe."

"What's an ordnance officer serving as the Inspector General doing asking sensitive intelligence questions about combat operations and an enemy operative?" Mahegan could guess. Bream was vying for the top position in the Army. He was competing against hardened combat veterans who had led troops in Iraq and Afghanistan. If Bream could bring Adham to his knees through his special police squads, then that might give him an advantage. It was all about positioning to these generals.

"Fair enough," Bream responded. "As I said, someone thought there was a nexus between you, Hoxha, and Adham. *My information* tells me you were near Adham when you captured Hoxha. I'm told it's even possible that Adham is the one who remotely detonated the bomb, not Hoxha. And, of course, we've already mentioned Adham's statement on Facebook today."

Mahegan's mind reeled. Savage had told him that he, Mahegan, had sent the deadly transmission that had killed Colgate. Was it possible that Adham had killed Colgate and the others?

"How does any of that involve you?"

"We were asked to reinvestigate your killing of Hoxha the bomb maker."

Mahegan paused. Passive voice. *We were asked.* Who asked? Instead of pursuing that axis, he said flatly, "But I was cleared."

"No such thing as double jeopardy here with this office. We can keep coming back to the well, son. Especially since Savage asked for your discharge to be honorable. That's still under review, as we have discussed."

Bream smiled and patted Mahegan's left arm, then rested his hand on the deltoid, pushing just enough to make Mahegan feel his scar burning just beneath the warm palm.

"I'm going to turn you back over to Chief Paslowski. I wanted to talk to you man-to-man before I made a final ruling on your discharge and proceeded with this investigation. The Army gives me wide latitude in determining what should be checked out and what should not be. I haven't made up my mind yet, and will likely base my decisions on your level of cooperation."

Mahegan listened to the man, who now sounded more like a lawyer than a general. This time he wanted to say, *Sounds like a fishing expedition*, but chose discretion over further verbally sparring with the general. He didn't like being at the center of this controversy. There were his teammates, who all had submitted statements, and Hoxha, who was dead. He wasn't sure if any enemy had remained alive on the objective that night, but he was pretty certain his team had killed all of the guards. They were combatants and that was combat.

"Where are you getting your intel, sir?" The only thing Mahegan could think of was that it was the

Docex guys that coughed up some information. If it was the Copperhead team, he knew a few things that could be screwing up the facts. First, they were not accustomed to being in the field on objectives. They did most of their interrogation at Bagram's prison. Second, they had little to no experience on black operations. Last, they were in a pile of trouble with the Department of Defense and, like tortured prisoners, might have said anything to stay "alive."

Bream smiled, knowing he had Mahegan's attention.

"I'm not at liberty to discuss that, Mahegan. It is a most unusual source, though."

"How unusual?"

Bream stood and walked over to a map of the world, which hung in a teak frame on his wall. He looked at it, his eyes scanning the oblong cut-out portions that appeared as if a child had taken scissors to a round globe and cut it to lay flat. He seemed to contemplate something, running a finger along his lips.

"Extremely unusual."

At that moment, Chief Paslowski came in the door, big and bulky, his right arm set in a sling, his left arm straight down by his side as if he was hiding something.

"Chief, I'm done with him," Bream said.

"Roger, sir." Paslowski moved toward Mahegan in the large office. Mahegan was calculating what he could do when Paslowski came up fast with a leather sap and brought it down on Mahegan's injured left deltoid with force.

"Make another move, asshole, and I will have to defend the general again," Paslowski said. Mahegan didn't go down—he just rubbed his arm as if simply bitten, though it was a solid blow. He looked at Paslowski's right arm in a sling from where Mahegan had separated it and figured Paslowski had been practicing the left-handed strike. He also figured that Paslowski had looked in Mahegan's military medical records that showed he had been wounded from flying shrapnel, resulting in the severed rotator cuff and torn deltoid that had left his scar.

The pain was sharp, as if the blow had unhinged something important that had mostly healed. He turned to look for Bream, but the general had disappeared.

"Chief, if the only way you can get to me is by having your daddy in here set me up, then you might as well eat the barrel of your pistol because you're a bigger pussy than I figured you for."

He looked at Paslowski, whose eyelids were half closed, as if he was drugged. He was breathing heavily and it occurred to Mahegan that he might have to fight his way out of there, potentially even hurt Paslowski more than he had the day before.

"I'm sure the general's office is wired for sound and video and I'm also sure he knows exactly what is happening here," Mahegan said. "So, if you're really into this, let's have at it, wild man." Mahegan prepared for a fight. He studied Paslowski's face, which was covered with a developing film of sweat.

Paslowski backed down, saying, "Get out of here before I have you arrested."

Mahegan cocked his head and stared at Paslowski. "Only shot you can take is a cheap shot? That right, chief?" After holding everything back with Bream, Mahegan could feel the emotions galloping, tugging hard at his control the same way they had after the bomb hit Colgate's vehicle.

"You'd better take the only opportunity I'm giving you, captain."

"I turned in my papers, asshole. I'm Mr. Mahegan to

you. Or else I could have your ass arrested for striking a superior officer."

Paslowski's mouth twitched into his version of a smile, appearing more like a lecherous grin.

"That's the beauty of the IG, Mahegan. Right now you're a mister. Tomorrow we could bring you back to active duty to stand trial. Make you a captain. Just like that. And all we'd need is a preponderance of evidence. Maybe you swung at the general first. Think about it, asshole." He shook the sap, which he was still holding in his left hand.

Mahegan took a step toward Paslowski, who flinched. He brushed past the heft of his body and exited the large office. He walked past a series of dark wood desks lining the outer sanctum of the IG's office, nodding at the young officers in charge of managing the general's schedule, keeping his paperwork, and tending to his needs.

He walked through the Pentagon to the parking lot. Were it not for his immaculate recall of paths taken, he might have been lost in the place for days. He walked past the security guards, then around the 9/11 Memorial, across busy Route 110, and stepped over the small stone wall into Arlington National Cemetery. He found Colgate's headstone, pulled up the camera device on the back, and separated it from the wooden stake to which it was taped. It was a fiber-optic camera.

General Bream, or someone, had cast a wide net searching for him.

Chapter 13

"Just drive," Mahegan said to Locklear when she picked him up at the cemetery.

"Don't be an asshole." Locklear shifted the Defender and pulled onto I-395 for the long trip back to the Outer Banks of North Carolina.

At least she was talking to him again. After about two hours of driving, just south of Richmond, Virginia, Mahegan broke the silence by looking at Locklear and saying, "Don't call me an asshole."

Locklear seemed to take this in for a moment and nodded. "Quit being one and you've got a deal."

A long moment passed. Finally, Locklear asked, "Those guys got anything on you?"

Locklear had obviously gone shopping. She had changed into a silk navy business suit with white blouse and three-inch heels. She had pulled her hair into a ponytail and had applied light makeup. Tiny gold hoops hanging from her earlobes matched her modest gold necklace with the Croatan *C* hanging just above her cleavage. Mahegan thought the professional Locklear was perhaps even more seductive than the laid-back Locklear, though it was a close call.

"Nobody's got anything on me," Mahegan said. "But everyone thinks they do. What does your uncle have to say about that?"

Locklear turned her head toward Mahegan and said, "Well, they say it's looking good."

"I don't think that means for me, right?"

"Probably not."

"Then why tell me? I could jump and run the next time you slow down."

"Then I'd have to cap your ass," she said, patting the pistol in her purse next to her. "Besides, I think you're curious about Miller Royes and J.J."

Mahegan didn't respond. She was right about his curiosity. He still hadn't asked again about the missing person, J.J., and figured the less they told him about that one the less they thought it was connected to him.

Locklear's affect turn serious when she asked, "What makes Colgate different from the other men you lost?"

The question caught Mahegan unprepared.

"Who said he was different?"

"I know where you went last night. I got a call from the Inspector General's office asking why I had lost control of you."

"Sorry."

"I said I had authorized you to visit your friend's grave. Not to save your ass, mind you, but to save mine." She stopped, and then softened her tone. "It is kind of messed up that they were watching you like that."

"Thanks."

Mahegan wrestled with his unfamiliar emotions, having stuffed them neatly in a tightly sealed compartment in his mind for the last year.

"Colgate was a top-notch soldier, just like they all

were, but there was just something else about him. He was just this big, happy guy, always smiling. I cared about all of my men, but something clicked with Colgate. He saved my ass. I saved his. We all get close to somebody. Sometimes we choose them. Sometimes they choose us."

"You chose Colgate?"

"I can't say it was that simple. We were Ranger buddies and that's enough to make you either hate someone or be forever grateful for the friendship. But it was more than that. I never had any siblings and he was, well, like my brother I guess."

Mahegan turned and looked out of the window, recalling Colgate's toothy grin and affable demeanor.

"Sounds nice. Most people don't get that, ever," Locklear said, her voice a bare whisper above the sound of the wind.

Mahegan wondered if it was better to have "that" and lose it or to never experience it in the first place. Was the high of the friendship worth the low of the loss? That thought made him think of the horrible way in which he had lost his mother when he was fourteen.

He decided to change the topic.

"So, what's with the businesswoman outfit?"

Locklear turned and looked at him. "I'm an actress. Well, sort of."

"What? Like in movies and stuff?"

"No. At least, not yet. You know I told you that the *Lost Colony* is an outdoor drama. It runs from Memorial Day weekend to Labor Day weekend. We reenact what might have occurred. I used to stay in the dorm with all the other actresses and actors. It was fun. Great summer gig."

Mahegan nodded. "You play Eleanor Dare, I take it?"

She paused. "That's right. Today I went to the Kennedy Center to discuss next season's performance while you were doing your macho stuff at the Pentagon. Hence, the professional attire." She waved her hand across her business suit.

"In this performance you reenact the colonists and the Croatan living forever in bliss?" But Mahegan was thinking something else. The name. Elizabeth. Eleanor Dare. Elizabeth Locklear. What else? What was still catching in his mind?

"Something like that." Locklear paused and then said, "Don't you get it? The fact that my mitochondrial DNA shows me connected to Virginia Dare means that some of the colonists survived. How could they have survived if the Croatan had not protected them? And if Dare survived, then the Croatan did, too."

"Everybody's linked to somebody," Mahegan said, still chasing his intuition.

"Sheriff ran your DNA, you know."

Mahegan looked at her. They had crossed into North Carolina and were cutting through Currituck County. The afternoon was warm and as they drove away from the sun toward the Carolina shore, the resolution of the landscape was in high definition. There was no haze and the rural countryside stood out boldly with the stark colors of red barns, green fields, and black asphalt roads.

"There are a lot of theories that say the Croatan migrated south and west and integrated with the Lumbee. You've got the blond hair and blue eyes of a Croatan. Maybe you're Croatan, not Lumbee? Maybe the last Croatan?"

Mahegan half smiled and looked at her. "So, we are going to blend effortlessly into the night, you and me?"

"After last night? Keep dreaming." But she laughed.

Mahegan had never had much of a problem finding suitable women to date, though he had spent multiple tours in combat away from said suitable women. As he processed the last forty-eight hours, his instincts were telling him two things. First, she was certainly a beautiful woman and he was interested. Second, this might be too easy. Normally the first instinct would trump the second without hesitation. But being at the center of two murder investigations, Mahegan found himself wondering why she had blown off her anger so quickly, why she was being so . . . accommodating.

As they crossed the bridge onto Roanoke Island, she turned past the Lost Colony Theater and onto the beach with her bungalow.

She shut off the ignition of the Defender and looked at him.

"Want to go grab some 'chow,' as you say it?"

"You cook?"

"I didn't say that. But I can feed you," she said. "Sheriff says they don't need you until tomorrow. Says you might want a lawyer."

"Okay. Let's eat."

He stepped out of the car and slid his hand under the floor mat where he had placed the gold coin.

"Looking for this?" Locklear asked, holding up the double eagle.

Mahegan nodded. "Not anymore."

"Found it on Royes's dead body, right?"

She took off her high heels and walked toward the cottage. Mahegan grabbed a shopping bag with his swim trunks and the "If It's Tourist Season" T-shirt. He followed but remained fixated on the gold coin in Locklear's hand. His only clues in this entire affair were the gold coin and the boots that bore the name of the ship. He stole a quick glance at the *Teach's Pet* sitting idly in Croatan Sound.

"Right. What do you know about the coin?"

"It's a perfect double eagle made in Charlotte, North Carolina. Was being hauled by the SS *James Adger*, which shipwrecked about four miles off Oregon Inlet."

"Washed up?"

"Gold doesn't 'wash up.' It's too heavy. In water, it drops straight to the bottom. With thieves, it gets hidden."

"The dead guy, Royes, was a gold thief?"

"I don't think so. I knew him. I think he found it and was protecting it. He probably wasn't sure what to do with it."

"Gold's hard to turn down. Money is money."

Locklear shook her head.

"Not with some people. Anyway, we've got a pizza on the way from Angelo's."

Mahegan nodded, sat on the porch swing, and stared at the *Teach's Pet*.

"Why is that out there again?"

"It stays there. Like I said, for the reenactments. The county also has a communications relay on there."

Mahegan thought for a moment about why a faux pirate ship would have a communications role and then he remembered the sheriff's car and the broad area he had to monitor.

"What about these gold diggers you were talking about?"

Locklear smiled. "Treasure hunters? They sniff around there, near the *Curlew*, which is still down there. They haven't found anything. As an environmentalist, my main concern is to make sure they don't damage the environment, especially the Alligator River area."

"Where I've been swimming?"

"Which is why I've been kayaking and watching you."

She sat next to him on the wooden bench swing that hung from the covered porch ceiling and faced the beach and sound. The water's edge was about fifty meters away.

"You ever go out there?" he asked.

"No. Why?"

"If you're the environmental police, then I would think you would've scoped the ship out."

"Not much going on. Occasionally, a barge of some type stops, probably for upkeep of the communications equipment out there, but mostly there's some locals that dress up as pirates and schoolkids go there for field trips."

"Playacting? Blackbeard?"

"Aargh." She smiled.

"A lot of history," Mahegan reflected.

"Hang on."

A Jeep pulled up and a young man in a T-shirt and swim trunks jumped out. "Hey, Linds," he said, approaching her and handing her a pizza box.

Mahegan watched her pay the delivery boy and then disappear inside the bungalow.

She reappeared a few minutes later wearing a halter and sarong with the Teva sandals she had been wearing on the trip to the Pentagon. On her first trip out to the porch, she brought the pizza box. On the second, she had a wine bottle cradled in her arm and was holding two wineglasses between her fingers. In her other hand, she had a printout of an online news article, which she held out to him.

"See this?" she asked.

Mahegan grabbed a slice of pizza and read.

SUSPECTS AND SECURITY
AFTER THE FORT BRACKETT ATTACK

FORT BRACKETT, SOUTH CAROLINA: At 6:12 a.m. yesterday morning several bombs detonated at Fort Brackett's main entrance, killing at least 28 people, including seven children. Police say that eyewitnesses described a large blast from the north side of the gate. Then, 20 minutes later, a secondary device ignited from within the crowd, possibly initiated by a suicide bomber.

The American Taliban has taken credit for orchestrating the attack and has already posted video images of the attack on the Internet via YouTube and Facebook. The American Taliban is a U.S. citizen named Adam Wilhoyt, who goes by the moniker Mullah Adham. Wilhoyt has stated that his army of jihadists will continue to target women and children throughout America and that "this is only the beginning." He also claims to have prisoners of war and will begin beheading them soon.

Curiously, he also implicated former Army Captain Chayton "Jake" Mahegan in the attacks. Department of Defense officials say they have talked to Mahegan and he denies any involvement. The Army Inspector General is currently reviewing Mahegan's discharge in the wake of his killing an enemy prisoner of war last year. The Federal Bureau of Investigation and Department of Homeland Security are working with the Department of Defense on the investigation.

"I have personally spoken with former Captain Mahegan about this situation and will continue to monitor all leads," said Army Inspector General Stanley Bream, called the Army's "Chief of Integrity" by some and believed by senior defense officials to be in the running for the next Chief of Staff of the Army. While officials tentatively corroborate Mahegan's alibi, the former Army captain remains a person of interest in the investigation.

Police Captain Jeremy Sidenstricker said, "We're working with the Internet company to remove the video and we think we'll have it down soon. We feel that there may be evidence contained in the video and having it out there is insensitive to the families of those killed and injured."

Ironically, due to the high operational deployment tempo of military police forces in recent years, Fort Brackett had in the last two months published a request for bids from private security companies to begin force protection of the Fort Brackett base. Negotiations faltered when Copperhead, Incorporated, rumored to have the lead in negotiations, was blacklisted from doing business with the State Department after a year of litigation resulting from accusations of excessive use of force in Afghanistan and Iraq. While Fort Brackett falls under the purview of the Department of Defense, Copperhead, Inc. has become a pariah in the private military consulting world not unlike Blackwater, Inc.

When pressed on the matter, the base military commander said, "We are right now focused on taking care of the wounded. I mean we are still pulling bodies out of the wreckage. Our first course of action is to check all of our procedures at the gates and outside the gates. Of course, as this was very clearly an attack, we intend to respond with the proper security measures."

The American Taliban has already had over 20,000 Facebook comments with over 1,000 "likes" on the video, possibly indicating international terrorist support for Adham.

This is a developing story. Stay tuned for updates.

Mahegan rubbed his chin.

"Damn. Bream works fast. Covering his ass, big-time."

"Why would this Mullah mention you?"

"Maybe it's because I chased his ass hard. Killed lots of his people. Or maybe he wants heat on me because I understand classic Taliban tactics. Hit the gate hard, let an even larger group gather, and have a secondary device ready to go. Probably a suicide bomber. Just outside the gate, they let their guard down and didn't secure the scene. They should have pushed security out and not let anyone into the chaos once the first one went off. Slow is smooth, smooth is fast."

"'Slow is smooth; smooth is fast'?" Locklear had a quizzical expression on her face.

"Roger. Be deliberate and efficient and you will be quicker than just reacting. Let logic drive your actions, not emotion. Racing to respond, they tripped up their procedures and ended up causing more harm than good. They blew it."

"A tad harsh, don't you think?"

"Not harsh enough. Lax security got a lot of people killed. Period."

"What do you know about this American Taliban guy?"

Mahegan paused. There was enough in open source information that he could give her a brief sketch.

"He went to high school in Davenport, Iowa. His mom was an executive assistant at an Army base out there. No father in his life. Pegged as a 'Columbine kind of kid' by his principal. Developed a massive online video game where the goal was to destroy famous American landmarks. When he was sixteen, FBI came into his house and seized computers, phones, everything. He got a plea deal. Curiously, the FBI agent

retired and made a marginally different game with different landmarks using the Adam Wilhoyt code. That's
his real name. Adam Wilhoyt. The kid says, 'Screw it,'
and moves to Pakistan, joins a madrassa, calls himself
'Mullah Adham,' the name of the bad guy in his video
game, and the rest is history."

Mahegan felt a buzz as he provided an unclassified
version of Adham's dossier. There was something bothering him about the Army base where The American
Taliban's mother worked. He couldn't remember the
name of the installation, but recalled it was not anywhere he would ever have been. It wasn't a base for operators. Just the opposite. It was for logisticians, people
who handled ammunition and maintenance.

Tucking the thought away, he paused, realizing what
had been sticking in his mind before. He added, "And
he was supposedly in love with a young woman named
Elizabeth Carlsen."

He studied her intently, looking for any micro-
expression: a twitch of the cheek, a slight aversion of
the eyes, or a nervous hand movement.

He saw nothing. Then he looked at the *C* necklace
wondering if it really stood for Croatan.

"Seems you know a lot about this man."

"I hunted him for a year."

"Grudge to bear?"

Mahegan wasn't sure if she was talking about him
or Adham.

"Maybe," Mahegan replied. "I lost good men trying
to capture him."

During the long stretches of silence on the trip back,
he continued to wonder why Adham would mention his
name. Unable to discern a reason good enough to settle
on, he changed the subject.

"Can you tell me anything else about Copperhead across the sound?" Mahegan asked.

"Hmm. Just that they are clearing the bombing range that was just shut down. Every once in a while you'll hear an explosion over there."

"I heard one yesterday morning. What do they do with the bombs they've cleared out?"

"Beats me. I've seen some barges leaving out early in the morning, though, when I'm kayaking. There's an old ghost town on the other side of the peninsula there called Buffalo City. It's an old timber town from the mid-1800s and runs adjacent to the Alligator River Wildlife Refuge. They raked the area clean and moved out. Copperhead's also done some construction over there and I think the Army uses it now. Perfect symbiosis don't you think? A bombing range next to a nature refuge?"

"Well, I'm glad they're clearing it now," Mahegan said. "Nobody needs to be bothering the wolves who are doing nothing but minding their own business over there."

"Really?" Locklear was looking at him as if impressed.

"What?"

"I know you're Native American and all, but I wouldn't have pegged you for a defender of the natural habitats of animals."

"Nature's all we've got." Mahegan shrugged and turned to watch the sun dip into Croatan Sound. It was a perfect orange circle slicing into the calm waters, masked faintly by a few wispy clouds and the low horizon of the wildlife refuge about seven miles across from the northern tip of Roanoke Island. He studied the land as if there were answers to be found, like a Bev Doolittle painting where the images revealed hidden messages. He visualized hundreds of workers sawing down trees and mules dragging the lumber to a rail line, where the train would carry the wood to a sawmill or pulp factory to make lumber or paper. There would have been barracks for the lumberjacks, who cut the trees until the peninsula had been deforested. What Mahegan had seen from the shore after his swim was a marshy, nearly uninhabitable piece of terrain that was practically impossible to get to without swimming or boating five miles. If the place had been abandoned for nearly one hundred years, he wondered what, other than the standard duties of bomb clearing, might be happening over there.

He tucked away that thought and ran through the last two days in his mind. He wasn't much on coincidences and while he might believe it was just happenstance that his left arm had slammed into a dead body in the middle of the sound, he could not accept that Paslowski, Bream, and Locklear were chance encounters. He stared at the glass of wine with its condensation beading on the stemware. He couldn't tell a Chardonnay from a Chartreuse. When he drank, which wasn't often, he preferred regular beer such as Budweiser or good whiskey, such as Maker's Mark. He let the wine continue to sweat.

"Question," Locklear said.

"Okay."

"You seem like a guy who lives off the grid. How did they find you?"

He had asked himself that same question: How had Paslowski found him? He had been aimlessly drifting up the Atlantic coast like a fugitive. He had only taken jobs that either paid in cash or trade, such as his residing in the Queen Anne's Revenge for some yard work. There was little chance of blowing his cover there.

When asked for his name, he would offer only "Jake." But it hadn't taken him long to figure it out.

"There was a kid on a ferry from Ocracoke to Hatteras a couple of weeks ago. I was taking the ferry up from working a job in Carteret County and happened to see him just as a car rolled forward to crush him between two cars. Some moron had left the car in neutral instead of park, and I had to bust his BMW grille to create a gap to release the kid. The owner had been halfway across the lot when it happened, and he came back pissed. So he snapped a picture of me, then e-mailed it to the cops."

"A visual 911? Interesting. Why didn't they snatch you right there?"

Mahegan studied Locklear for a moment, listening to the lap of the sound against the sand and nearby bulkhead.

"I slipped off the back end and swam a mile up Pamlico Sound before they got there. Walked back into town as the Coast Guard and cops were heading out."

The cops must have matched the BMW prick's photo with a photo of him on the black and gray list distributed by Homeland Security upon his return from combat. Bream had probably put him on that list as part of his dragnet to find him. The cameraphone image had to be a pretty good one and it wouldn't have taken long for someone to identify him.

Savage had warned him. Every port of entry—air, sea, and land—would have him on the "gray" list, possibly detain, saying something like, "He's probably killed at least one prisoner, former Delta Force, dishonorable discharge, loner, no family, post-traumatic stress, high security threat."

In the Outer Banks, the Coast Guard reigned supreme

and would be diligently monitoring the black and gray lists for must-detain and possibly-detain personnel.

"Earth to Mahegan," Locklear said.

Mahegan reeled himself in from the memory. It had only been a matter of time before he popped up on the radar, and he had done well to stay undetected this long.

"I'm here," he said.

"So you're quick on your feet. I like it. You're not drinking your wine, by the way."

"Sorry. Got any beer? Goes better with pizza."

She cocked her head and said, "Yeah, sure."

He watched her bounce into the cottage, the screen door smacking against the frame of the house as soon as she cleared the doorway. He picked up another slice of pizza and turned his gaze toward the *Teach's Pet*, calculating the swim. It was a little more than a quarter mile, no more than a half. Easy. The hard part would be disengaging from Locklear again.

She reappeared holding a Coors Light. If he was going swimming, he didn't want alcohol in his system, and Coors was the closest thing to water he had ever drunk, so he took it.

"Thanks," he said.

"Sure. So what were you just thinking about?"

"You," he said.

"Really? Me?" She smiled and tucked her feet up under her legs, which moved her torso closer to him. They were a few inches apart on the swing.

"I can figure out most things," Mahegan said. "But so far you're a challenge."

"Believe me, I don't try to be, but I've been told that before. My energy has me all over the place."

"Hey, I didn't say it was a bad thing."

Locklear nudged a bit closer, running her hand along the back of the swing. Mahegan felt her arm resting along his broad shoulders. He could smell the light scent of her skin. Her breath was sweet with the taste of wine, her second glass.

"Actress?" he asked.

"Hmm-hmm." She nodded.

"Cop?"

"Rog," she said.

"Marine biologist?"

"Yep."

"What else?"

She turned her gaze from her wineglass to the water, facing *Teach's Pet* and lost in her thoughts. Her eyes sparkled in the faint light from the cottage window behind him. She was close enough where he could move maybe four inches and kiss her, which seemed like a pretty good option right now.

"Lots of things," she said. The eyes flashed at him, followed by a smile, more subtle this time. "Historian. Cultural genius." After a pause, she slid her lips toward his, whispering, "Good kisser."

He received her kiss, letting her melt into him. Soon she was straddling him, her knees on either side of his legs, her mouth working his lips while she moved her hips slowly against him. He set his beer bottle on the wood deck, wrapped both of his arms around her waist, stood, and carried her into the house. She crossed her feet behind his back and her arms around his neck as he maneuvered through the house, kicked over a couple of things that didn't break, found the bedroom, and gently set her down on the bed.

"You sure?" he asked, staring into her eyes.

"I'm sure," she whispered, but it was a low moan as

she pulled at his shirt. Soon they were naked and Mahegan couldn't remember the last time he'd been with a woman, but for this moment he forgot about the two murder investigations, the bombing at Fort Brackett, the fiber-optic camera on Colgate's headstone, and the gold coin—everything. He even allowed himself to briefly tuck Colgate to the side, still present somewhere, but not dominant.

For a brief flash he permitted himself the pleasure of a beautiful, uninhibited woman, which he'd known before it started was a bad move.

Chapter 14

Mahegan took a deep breath. Locklear's head was on his chest and her leg was kicked across his pelvis. He held his arm around her back as he turned his head toward the clock.

After an hour of fierce sex they were spent, and his mind began to crowd again. Three macro themes appeared that he could not erase. First, was the name of the ship inside the dead man's boots connected to the gold coin? Second, why would Inspector General Bream call him to the Pentagon, and how was any of this connected, if at all, to Adham? And last, why was Adham implicating him in the Brackett attacks?

He turned her away from him, gently moving her farther onto the bed, leaving his suit clothes crumpled on the floor. He picked up her sarong, which had a small cutout pocket. It was heavy with the weight of the gold coin. He retrieved the coin, stared at it, and decided to keep it. He didn't want her having evidence he had hidden from authorities.

He walked naked into the living room and found the shopping bag in which he had placed his swim trunks, mocs, and her T-shirt. Slipping on the trunks and the mocs, he rummaged for a scrap of paper and pen, and left her a quick note that said, "You're an amazing woman. Gone for a swim. Didn't want to wake you." He quietly let himself out of the bungalow and stepped onto the beach. He tucked the gold coin in the small pocket insert inside his swim trunks.

Turning toward the bungalow and the woods behind it, Mahegan saw Locklear's Defender to his left and, beyond that, her kayak. He presumed she had tipped it over to prevent rain from gathering inside. Thinking it might be more efficient than swimming, he moved to the kayak and quietly knelt into the sand. When he lifted the fiberglass hull, its weight surprised him. He had expected something lighter. He heard something slide toward the bow, like metal. Concerned about making too much noise, he quietly returned the kayak to its original position. As he knelt, he rested his hands on the kayak's hull, which was facing upward. He was thinking, pressing his knee into the sand to stand, when he felt something hard crunch into his kneecap.

It was small and round.

He removed his knee and sifted away the sand with his fingers until he found a circular object. He held it up to the moonlight, and could make out the faint outline of two eagles on either side of a gold coin.

Immediately, he checked his pocket, certain that it had somehow come out as he inspected the kayak.

The original was still in his swim trunks.

Mahegan secured the second gold coin in his swim trunks, vowing to return it to Locklear after he had a chance to think about what it meant.

Standing, Mahegan walked to the edge of the nearly still water of Croatan Sound and stared at the dim lights on the *Teach's Pet*. Like most evenings, tonight the water was warmer than the autumn air, somewhere in the mid-seventies, Mahegan estimated.

It was dark, maybe three a.m. He liked this time of darkness. As a kid it was when he would sneak out of the trailer in Frisco when he couldn't sleep, find a sandy hilltop, and take comfort in the steady rhythm of the ocean and the marsh with all of its inhabitants. He would envision himself blending with them. He would also think about his parents. His father wasn't a bad man. Not at all. Mahegan loved him as well as he could love anyone. He had loved hearing his father's stories and now, admired even more his father's drive to uncover his lineage, an interest and awareness he had passed on to Mahegan. His father's name was Makwa, Algonquin for Bear. Like his son Chayton, the senior Mahegan was a huge man and thus found it easy to find work on the fishing boats or in construction. And like Mahegan was doing now, his father had drifted, though always dragging Jake and his mother along until that day in Maxton that everything had changed for fourteen-year-old Jake Mahegan.

But thinking about his father made him think about his mother, and if he thought about her loss for any period of time, he lost control. So his anger remained safely contained like a pit viper in a terrarium, snapping at the glass, but unable to do harm unless unleashed.

Now, he noticed the faint outline of the schooner's rigging cut against the dotted lights of Kill Devil Hills across the sound and to the northeast. Closing his eyes, Mahegan visualized what he was about to do. Swim to the ship, climb either a ladder on the side or shinny up the rope or chain that held the anchor, investigate what might have happened to Miller Royes, and swim back.

Mahegan was not an overly sympathetic man, at least not outside his immediate circle, which without family or love was reserved for his brothers in combat; so he had no interest in avenging whatever happened to Royes. But he *was* uniquely concerned about his own freedom, and being even a "person of interest" in Royes's death vested him in determining what had actually happened to the man.

With the early morning sounds of the tidewater filling his senses, he opened his eyes, walked into the dark water, and stopped. Thinking of the second gold coin, he turned and looked back at the kayak leaning against the house and wondered if it would float with a dead body in tow. Specifically, could Locklear have dumped Royes's body so that it would drift into him?

He looked at the house where he presumed Locklear was sleeping, and then continued walking until the water was deep enough for him to slide quietly into a silent overhand Australian crawl. He let the taste of the brackish water fill his mouth as he pushed off the loam and attempted to gain his rhythm of rotating his head every other stroke in opposite directions. After the sex, the swim actually felt good. He was leaving and moving away from the beautiful woman who had bound him.

He set himself on a directly perpendicular azimuth to the ship. It was canted with its bow pointing to the northwest and Mahegan was coming at it from due south. If he didn't waver on his approach, he would hit the port side of the stern. He wanted to minimize lateral movement because he knew that the human eye could more easily detect anomalies moving across its

field of vision than directly at it. The first settlers learned
quickly from the Native Americans to approach their
prey, and their enemies, from a perpendicular path.

The first thing he noticed, though, as he tried to ease
into his rhythm, was that the sucker punch from Paslowski had inflamed the injury. Though a year into the
healing, there was plenty of scar tissue and he could
feel the arcing pain with every left shoulder windmill.
Anger flashed in his mind as he pulled through the
darkness. He scolded himself for not being quicker
than Paslowski and for not crushing him afterward.

Thankfully, the swim passed quickly and turned out
to be about a half mile. Compared to the lengths he had
been swimming, this pace and effort was welcome,
though he was concerned about the shoulder. As soon
as he knew he was close, he slowed, treaded water for a
few seconds and visually scanned the ship. He was
about twenty meters away, his head in the water like an
alligator's, eyes and nose barely cresting the surface.
He tasted the musty water as his arms slowly pushed
back and forth to avoid causing ripples.

He saw lacquered eight-inch-wide tongue-in-groove
wood panels that created the massive hull of the ship.
His eyes flicked left, then right. It spanned about one
hundred feet, thirty-three yards, a third of a football
field, not counting the end zone. A decent-sized rig for
its day, but not especially large by today's standards.
Still, it was an impressive replica.

The ambient light from Kill Devil Hills and the
sliver of moon allowed him to see the gold painted letters, "*Teach's Pet.*" The letters were large and cursive,
and the *s* looked more like an *f* as if it was written in
Elizabethan English three hundred years ago. But that
was wrong, thought Mahegan—the long *s* was used at
the beginning of a word in Old English, but never at the

end—and the error gave him some information about the owner of the ship. It was a minor point to debate while treading in Croatan Sound, but he knew the smallest cues could be indicators of something more important, so he tucked away the thought as he began to scan the cannon battery. The portholes were square and black and he could not tell what may or may not be hidden in the wells of each window. But Mahegan figured not much. If Locklear had been correct and the ship had been out there for years, the crew would be rotating all of the time, bored stiff, and most certainly asleep at this point in the morning.

Perfect timing, he thought.

But Mahegan also knew that the apparent dormant state of the ship from the outside might indicate something else altogether, such as a decent technological barrier or scanner.

He watched the ship from the water for about five minutes and saw no noticeable activity, so he dove silently underwater and pulled hard until he was about fifteen feet deep. His left shoulder bit at him, but he continued downward at a forty-five-degree angle. He figured the keel on the ship was at about seven feet and wanted to give the vessel's bottom as wide a berth as possible in the shallow sound. Its beam appeared to be no less than thirty feet. Thirty yards long and ten yards wide, he figured. Seemed like good math, though he was no kind of mariner and his only affinity for the water was that over the past year it had rehabilitated his shoulder.

When he felt he was deep enough, he blew out a small amount of air to deflate his lungs and went deeper. What little light there was in the sky could not penetrate the dark water, and the world was entirely black at this depth. Keeping himself level, he kicked

and pulled, trying to replicate a pace count in his head.
On land, Mahegan knew that if his left foot hit the
ground fifty-two times, he had just traveled one hundred meters. In the water, he had developed a decent
gauge of his overhand stroke, that for every left arm
pull, he had gone five meters, or fifteen feet.

He slowed at the last second as the ambient light reflected back at him and he knew he was beyond the
ship. He nosed just above the meniscus of the water,
quietly sucking air in through his mouth and expelling
it through his nose. He rotated so that he was facing
south and silently used his hand to clear the water from
his brow so that he could assess what he was viewing.

The first thing Mahegan saw was a two-meter wall
ten feet in front of him. He treaded backwards to gain a
better angle on the structure. What he was looking at
was too big to be a dinghy and too awkward looking to
be the *Teach's Pet*. Pushing back, he saw that he was
looking at a barge of some type that was secured to the
starboard side of the ship. He heard voices and the dull
whine of machinery.

"Okay, let's lift it," a voice said.

"Aye, got it. Heavy bitch."

The sound of hydraulics pumping coughed briefly
and Mahegan looked to his right, to the west, and saw
the outline of forklift arms raised high against the
backdrop of the towering masts of the *Teach's Pet*.

On the forklift was a container that appeared to be
ten feet by ten feet square.

"Hope he doesn't drop it," the first voice said.

"Famous last words," the second voice added.

Mahegan searched for the two men he could hear
and thought he saw one head in the center of the workboat on the northern rail, which would explain why he
could hear them so well. He also got a better view of

the vessel and flashed back to Ranger school when he was doing the mock assault on Florida's barrier islands. They had used military landing craft, nearly the same as the Army and Marines used in World War II and Korea. This one was newer, of course, but essentially the same. There was a forklift at the aft end near the enclosed pilot's bridge, which was elevated above the gunwale. Now, he could see one man leaning out away from him and shouting in a loud whisper to the other man on the deck. He treaded the water with his arms doing silent back-and-forth motions and a slight kick from his legs every few seconds.

"Okay, just got word. She's three minutes out. This needs to be quicker than a Dale Earnhardt, Jr. pit stop, understand?"

"We're getting pretty good at this, mate. Don't sweat it."

"Well, one more of these and we're done with it."

Mahegan wasn't sure what exactly was three minutes out, but he figured it involved some kind of transshipment of whatever was on the forklift and that he would be directly in the channel of whatever might be heading toward the ship. He drew in a deep breath, slid vertically under the water, dropped about ten feet, then frog-pulled toward the vessel. He had calculated the landing craft to be only about fifteen meters long and as he disappeared under the water, he noticed spud wells, like on a barge, for driving long poles into the floor of the sound and holding steady against the current. It was a landing craft that someone had converted to a workboat.

This time he anticipated the flat bottom and surfaced slowly until his hand was touching the boat's barnacled underbelly. He walked his hands toward what he knew to be east, and away from the forklift, until he found the slight upward curvature of the bow. He slowly pushed his nose and mouth out of the water, pulled in some air, and remained motionless.

After a minute, he treaded toward the port side of the boat, remaining concealed under the low hang of the bow. He could hear the voices again, though more muffled this time for two reasons. First, he had the thick hull of the boat between him and the voices and second, they were drowned out by the approaching low idling thrum of powerful engines. He repositioned now between the new boat and the landing craft. He could tell the approaching boat was a deep-sea fishing rig. Having worked on one for a couple of weeks out of Wilmington, as the fishing vessel slowed near the landing craft, he recognized it as an Albermarle 410, which was a state-of-the-art offshore deep sea fishing boat with two powerful Caterpillar 710 horsepower C-12 engines.

He watched as one person on the sleek white fishing rig tossed two marine fenders over the gunwale and the person in the elevated bridge expertly worked the throttle back and forth until the rubber bumpers were crushed between the fiberglass of the just arrived boat and the steel of the barge.

"Let's do it, jerkoffs," a new voice said. "Two minutes."

"Hoorah," one of the two original voices said.

Mahegan heard the whine of the forklift and knew that the container was being loaded onto the deck of the fishing boat. A minute passed, and then another, and the forklift stopped. As he was noticing that the waterline on the fishing rig had risen considerably, he heard the voices again.

"Where is the other box?" the voice from the fishing boat said.

"What box?"

"The MVX-90s, dickhead."

"We packed them in with the rest of the stuff. On the top."

Silence ensued, except for the ricochet of waves lapping between the three vessels in tight quarters. Mahegan imagined that the fishing boat pilot was gauging whether he could trust what the two on the barge were telling him.

From the bridge, the pilot said in a low whisper, "Let's go."

"Jackasses."

Mahegan's mind reeled. He had destroyed a warehouse full of the lethal MVX-90s along the Iraqi border in Iran; an MVX-90 had killed Colgate and his team; and now some Americans in North Carolina were shuttling them from ship to ship in the Croatan Sound? He had to wonder if the MVX-90 was somehow involved in the Fort Brackett attack yesterday.

He heard the original boat guy say, "Tomorrow night, same time. And I want to see the rest of the '90s. Got it?"

"Hoorah."

Hoorah was a distinctly US Marine term as opposed to "Hooah," the Army version. Mahegan didn't like either because both could be used to mean, "Roger that," or, "Go fuck yourself."

It was another clue, and he hadn't even boarded the *Teach's Pet*. A Marine, a landing craft converted to a workboat, MVX-90s, and something very heavy in a box on a state-of-the-art offshore fishing boat.

He watched as one of the two men on the fishing vessel stepped back onto the boat, placed a hand on the lines securing the fenders, and as the pilot worked the two inboard Caterpillar engines, which were deathly quiet, yanked the fenders onto the deck, undid the half-hitches, and then set about lashing the ten-foot-by-ten-foot container to the sides.

He overheard pieces of a conversation between the men on the fishing boat, but the only word he thought he could make out was "Galaxy," which made no sense at all.

The whole thing took no more than three minutes. Dale Earnhardt, Jr. would be pissed, Mahegan thought. But not bad, otherwise. The boat had come in from the northwest, as if from the north point of Dare Mainland and Alligator River National Forest, or from the west side of Roanoke Island.

As the boat pulled away to the southeast toward Oregon Inlet, Mahegan saw someone already sliding a tarp over the wooden box. A Zodiac Bombard dinghy was evident as well, secured tightly to the aft end of the boat on the swim platform. Mahegan, his hand keeping him steady next to the barge, watched the boat slip past him ten feet away.

Close enough for him to see the name of the departing fishing vessel, perhaps headed out to sea.

Lucky Lindy.

Chapter 15

About twenty miles away on a straight-line azimuth of two hundred degrees from where Mahegan treaded water in Croatan Sound, Samuel Nix sat inside his command bunker in what was formerly known as the Dare County Bombing Range. Today the front gate off Route 264 near the Dare and Hyde County borders bore the distinctive Copperhead, Inc. insignia, which was a gaping snake's mouth with the word "COPPER-HEAD" written in taupe across the white background of the mouth, the fangs hanging menacingly over the letters and supplying the spine to the second "P" and the "H."

Nix recalled how he had lifted himself out of bankruptcy by convincing the Department of Defense that he had the best Navy bomb technician in Vinny Falco. Mine clearing and bomb removal were the least attractive contracts a company could go after, but after losing everything he'd had to start somewhere. The work was unglamorous, labor was difficult to find, workers got maimed, and lawsuits were aplenty. In Afghanistan, Copperhead had won a small contract to clear the Russian mines around Bagram Air Base, the main headquarters of the US forces there. The perception of Copperhead's competence in the mine-clearing effort at Bagram, coupled with a lawsuit appealing their black-listing by the Army, led the Defense Department to award the Dare County contract to North Carolina-based Copperhead, Inc.

On average, when performing similar mine removal tasks in Afghanistan, Nix had lost a worker a week to a mine. It didn't matter, he reasoned, because they were locals and it was a combat zone, meaning there would be no lawsuits he'd have to deal with. But here in the United States, where people sued over hot coffee, the Defense Department was having a difficult time finding an affordable contractor. He had outsmarted that problem and knew he could still make millions while nobody could underbid him.

For Copperhead, the contract to clear all of the ordnance from Dare County Bombing and Electronic Warfare Ranges was a gold mine. Nix had badgered every contact he had on Capitol Hill to win the ten-million-dollar annual deal. It had one base year plus five option years, of which they were in the first option presently. Now in their second year, they had already grossed twenty million dollars with the base plus one option year paid in full. As Nix had done his research, the real cost in the ordnance business was labor. It was simply hard to find people who wanted to wander around in the equivalent of a minefield. There were unexploded GBU-28s, bunker busters, sticking up like lawn darts in the sandy soil. They were finding five-hundred-pound MK-89s in every quadrant, even near the tower. Worse still, the Air Force had let pilots drop the infamous BLU-97 cluster bombs that scatter out the back of a canister while on descent from the delivering aircraft like seed tossed in the air. Despite the shortcuts he'd had to take to deal with the labor costs and laws, Nix believed he was earning every penny.

The biggest find, though, had been the GBU-43/B Massive Ordnance Air Explosive, otherwise known as the "Mother of All Bombs." One of his three-man clearance teams had been trudging through knee-deep swampland wearing hip waders and waving mine detectors as if they were divining rods when they'd come face-to-face with the exposed body of a thirty-foot-long by four-foot-wide cylindrical body of the largest nonnuclear bomb in the world. The bomb was hanging from parachute suspension lines that were connected to a nylon G-type parachute, which had become stuck in the tall pines and had never detonated. It had hung less than a meter from the swampy carpet.

In addition to being Copperhead's vice president, Vinny Falco was, first and foremost, a chief explosive ordnance technician in the Navy, which had given Copperhead, Inc. the competitive advantage in winning the contract. Upon finding the MOAB, they had waited a week before contacting the Navy and Falco had spent a full two days alone with the beast, toying with it before he determined that it was inert, full of concrete, though not without value.

Nix knew that in August, 2007, the US Air Force had "misplaced" several nukes from Minot Air Force Base. Then in 2013, the DoD had fired the general in charge of all nuclear and near-nuclear weapons, which spawned a nationwide inventory. Of the fifteen MOABs in existence, one had been stored at Dare County Bombing Range. When the Air Force came calling for the live MOAB, Nix gave them the inert round, practically undamaged from its descent.

A fully functional MOAB, commonly called a Daisy Cutter, remained in storage on the compound. *His* compound, as he was beginning to see it.

Nix stood and walked to the window of the command center. The windows were twenty-four-inch ballistic material designed to withstand shrapnel from the dumb bombs that were sometimes let loose by a hungover Navy F-14 or FA-18 pilot after a night of chasing women at Oceana Naval Air Station's Officers Club in Virginia Beach. There were a few chip marks to show for it in the glass of the octagonal-shaped tower that was akin to an airport control tower.

He had divided the entire bombing range into zones. He had 46,000 acres to clear and six years to do it, unless he wanted to squeeze another contract out of the Department of Defense. He had agreed to do 8,000 acres a year of surface clearing, which, technically defined, meant that Copperhead, Inc. was to till to a depth of three feet where possible and that there was a ninety-five-percent "guarantee" that there was no unexploded ordnance in the cleared area. To clear deeper would require different technology and more time, and of course another huge contract, which was all part of the plan.

Already they had cleared a good portion of the western edge of the peninsula near Buffalo City, the Army's Military Operations in Urban Terrain (MOUT) training facility. MOUT was the technical term for a small city in which the soldiers could train in urban combat, arguably the toughest type of fighting. Delta Force, Rangers, SEALs, and the 82nd Airborne Division had used the facility for live-fire exercises to prepare for combat in Iraq and Afghanistan. Because the MOUT facility was in the bomb release impact area, they were able to call in live artillery and air-dropped ordnance. The village was about the size of a small town with all the trappings of a spaghetti Western movie frontage: restaurants, stores, and homes fronting paved streets. Of course, once the trainees moved through the door, there were friend or foe target mock-ups they would shoot, or not, and nothing but plywood walls filled with sand to prevent ricochets and pass-through rounds.

The troops had added piled-up junked autos and tires. They also installed speakers that could blast riot control directives, homeland security warnings, or Islamic jihad music to add to the realism. But with the wars on the wane, and pressure from Congress to close the range, the Department of Defense Inspector General had shut down operations for the time being.

Standing in the control tower in the center of the bombing range and using his night-vision device, Nix looked south toward Route 264 and the inlet off Croatan Sound fed by Long Shoal River. As he scanned, he saw the series of moats that were ever increasing concentric squares emanating outward from his position. The moats were actually ten-meter-wide ditches filled with water moccasins, snapping turtles, alligators, and, of course, copperhead snakes. Each ditch ran parallel to a gravel road that the military had constructed to either provide access to the control tower and associated command buildings or to head into the impact area.

The entire peninsula was called Dare County Mainland and was a chunk of land that looked on the map a lot like the state of Michigan.

Nix heard his partner, Vinny Falco, ascend the steps and walk through the door.

"Thought you were with *Lucky Lindy*?"

"Saving myself for tomorrow night, boss. Wind is picking up and the chop is kind of sucky out there right now."

"Former Navy bomb tech scared of a rough ride?"

Falco lifted his coffee cup. "Nah. It's four in the morning and the sun's coming up in a couple of hours. We've got workers getting ready to plow the fields. I feel like a plantation owner. Life is good."

"So who's got the run on the *Lindy* this morning?"

"Lamont and Tyler. They're good. I'm told they hit the *Pet* and were away from there in under three minutes."

"That's too long. Needs to look seamless. Someone from the shore on Roanoke or Kill Devil Hills needs to look, turn away, and then look back, and that bitch needs to be gone."

"There was a minor debate about the MVX-90s," Falco said. "Morons had packed them in with the other stuff, so we didn't get those."

"Is the LCM coming back for the last run?"

"Yeah. We'll do one more load and then I'll personally dive down there and ensure we got everything."

Nix nodded. He didn't like using the *Teach's Pet* wide open in the middle of Croatan Sound, but there was a certain simplicity to Falco's recommendation to use an old ship that just sat there as a pivot point for their operation. He needed to send certain things out to sea and the landing craft couldn't weather the rough seas, nor did it have the range to go where Nix needed it to go. All of the cargo was heavy and use of the landing craft in Stumpy Point Bay was guaranteed in his contract with the Department of Defense. Neither could they bring the *Lucky Lindy* into the Long Shoal River for trans-load operations. It was too big and would be noticed by the fishermen.

Plus, Copperhead, Inc. owned the landing craft, or LCM, and Nix wanted to ensure that he owned what he was transporting on the barge, because it was not a done deal, by any stretch.

"Okay, have you worked the Wikipedia site?"

Falco smiled, nodding. "I've got a dummy page up and ready to go. I'll load it tomorrow, when things get serious."

Nix looked at Falco, noticing his soul patch, earring, and skull-and-crossbones tattoo. "You look like Blackbeard."

Falco laughed. "Blackbeard was British. I'm Italian and I get more pussy."

"That you do. Okay, so let's·get these guys rolling into Zone Foxtrot. Need to get the buffer zone clear," Nix said.

Falco walked to a map that hung in the sparsely appointed room and pointed at a section.

"Foxtrot it is," he said.

They had divided the map into relatively equal-size chunks labeling the southern tier of zones using the military phonetic alphabet Alpha through Echo, the middle tier Foxtrot through Juliet, and the northern tier Kilo through Oscar. Clearing Alpha through Echo had been relatively easy, but it had taken eighteen months because it was mostly swampland, all salt marshes and some woodland cut by narrow, straight creeks in similar byzantine fashion to a Louisiana bayou. They had found the MOAB in Zone Charlie.

They had used thermal imaging with a slow-flying airplane tracking back and forth at night looking for heated anomalies. Part of the contract included their purchase of a King Air twin propeller aircraft tricked out with state-of-the-art forward-looking infrared and thermal recording devices. They had included the cost of the airplane and the Thermal Imaging Systems, Inc. Nightfire Ball into the contract, which pumped it up another two million dollars. For annual maintenance for all six years of the contract, he charged the government an estimated $100,000 per year. Nix knew he wouldn't need that much, as they got the Nightfire for a steal by agreeing to prototype the new Generation II High Definition camera with megapixel thermal and low-light cameras in exchange for feedback on functionality. Thermal Imaging Systems, Inc. was in competition with FLIR, who made the SAFIRE ball. In essence, Nix would give them all of the imaging data for the first two years of the contract and Thermal Imaging Systems, Inc. provided them a rebate of $500,000 for the first two years.

Copperhead, Inc. was then allowed to charge the government for the equipment, get its rebate without having to pass it back through to Uncle Sam, and keep the equipment. Not a bad deal.

"You hearing anything about Royes?" Nix asked.

"They're looking at that guy. A drifter named Mahegan. Says he was swimming in the middle of Croatan Sound and bumped into the body."

Nix laughed. "That sounds so crazy I bet it's true," he said.

"But it also sounds crazy enough to be bullshit," Falco countered.

Nix pursed his lips, took a sip of coffee, and said, "You still talking to the right folks over there?"

"Nothing's changed, boss."

"What do you know about Mahegan?"

"Ex-Army. Ranger. Dishonorable discharge."

Nix considered this for a moment. "Get me some intel on him. Call your friends in the Pentagon. I'll talk to the sheriff."

"You looking at making this stick to him?"

Nix smiled. "Actually, yes."

"Well, you should know he had a knife on him."

"Even better. Sheriff Johnson have it?"

"That's what I'm told. Coast Guard was looking for him, too. Something about an incident on the Ocracoke Ferry."

"See if you can't lock that down for us."

"Aye, boss."

Falco scampered down the stairwell and disappeared into the headquarters hut behind the control tower.

Nix thought about what Falco had mentioned. Again, it was all about product lines. Definitely in today's economy any business needed to diversify. Copperhead, Inc. had had a setback, but now they had some momentum. They were growing despite the headwinds. The more product lines, the better.

He picked up his binoculars and watched as one of his men followed the mine-clearing crew into the swamps. The crew consisted of dark men with black hair and tattered clothes. If one of them died today, no one would mourn his loss. That mourning had already taken place.

The crew was chained together at the waist as they high stepped through forbidding terrain wearing snake boots and hip waders, each carrying a World War II mine detector.

Escape was not an option. They would work until their bodies fell apart or he no longer needed them.

But if one of them got loose, the whole scam would unravel.

Chapter 16

Floating beneath the landing craft in Croatan Sound, Mahegan had a decision to make, which was to either explore the *Teach's Pet* or jump on the landing craft before it pushed off. He watched the two men operating the boat begin to untie from the *Pet*.

His calculation was that if the landing craft was lashed to the *Pet*, then the *Pet* was some kind of staging base for whatever was happening. What he knew was that some MVX-90s had just been loaded onto an offshore fishing boat in the middle of the night. Chances were that it was an illegal transshipment and those devices were going to wind up in the wrong hands. Had they come from the workboat or from the *Pet*?

Mahegan knew that MVX-90s were small, lightweight devices, each the weight of a home Internet router. A bargelike vessel would not be required to ship even a thousand of them. Whatever the landing craft had transferred to the *Lucky Lindy* was heavy and had required a forklift. The MVX-90s seemed like an afterthought, as if they had been added to whatever the main thing was.

The workboat was probably empty, but the two men

on it might hold some useful information. Where had they come from and what were they carrying? Would they even know? They had spoken about the box as if it might be fragile. Confronting them would certainly lead to the possibility that his identity would be revealed, as if he wasn't in deep enough with the authorities in Dare County.

The active lead, the actionable intelligence, was on the workboat, he decided. He climbed the six-foot free-board by using the spud pole sleeve, which was jacked up and hidden inside the metal cylinder in telescope fashion.

Pulling up out of the water and then pushing with his arms, he slipped over the gunwale and took a knee behind a generator that was secured with chains to four-inch metal eyelets. The forklift was near the bow, to his left. Other than the two pieces of equipment, the landing craft was an open, flat deck without cover or concealment. He huddled there until he felt the craft move and turn away from the *Pet*.

He knew he was in a precarious position. The two men were either in the pilot's cabin or on the deck, and the moment he moved away from the generator they would see him unless they were distracted. Also, he had no idea where they were going or how long they would be gone. He instinctively reached down for his knife and cursed himself when he realized it was still at the police station.

There was enough starlight for him to see both men in the pilot's cabin. A dim light shone from the instruments into their faces. He felt the boat backing up instead of moving forward and put together three separate thoughts. First, the light in the cabin would hamper their night vision. Second, since they were backing up, they would be looking over the aft portion of the ship, away from him. And third, the cabin was elevated above the deck of the landing craft and its base would in fact be the most covered and concealed position on the vessel. Dead space, in military parlance. To a soldier like Mahegan, dead space was that piece of ground where he could hide protected, if not undetected, out of the line of sight of the opposing forces. Here specifically, the two men would not have the angle to see him if he pressed himself against the base.

He slid around the rusted generator. Masking his movement was the loud roar of the two diesel engines that were kicking up silt and churning the shallow sound. He forced himself to be deliberate, remembering what he used to tell his teammates when they were about to enter a building and clear it of the enemy: *Slow is smooth, smooth is fast.*

Keeping his maxim in mind, he crossed the thirty feet, ten yards, from the generator to the base of the cabin. He moved to the starboard side where there was a bulkhead and which was opposite the door to the pilot's cabin. He would have two options if spotted.

Fight it out or slide over the side and live to fight another day.

The landing craft churned for at least two hours. Huddled against the base of the elevated captain's platform, and separated by sheet metal at the bottom and ballistic glass at the top, Mahegan felt himself stiffen against the hard metal flooring. Watching the darkness fade into a faint gray hue on the eastern horizon, he also realized that this was about the time he went swimming every morning. He wistfully thought of Lindy Locklear and how much he would prefer to be entwined with her right now as opposed to crouching low on a workboat.

With daylight creeping toward them, he felt a subtle

shift in the engines and the craft slowed, then turned sharply. He gauged their direction of travel from the *Teach's Pet* to have been south in between Roanoke Island and Dare County Mainland past the line of his morning swim off the Wanchese marsh. Now he felt as if they were hooking west and northwest.

He saw the faint outline of tree branches hanging over them like skeletal arms creating a welcoming cordon and marking the transition from the sound to an estuary of some sort. With the migration from sound to river or creek, the density of the foliage actually provided him more concealment in an added layer of darkness. Until the giant spotlight came on.

A powerful rectangular beam of light punched through the blackness and lit the front of the landing craft with its bottom arc while creating a faux daylight into the river and surrounding woodlands. Mahegan could not see much above the lip of the vessel but, based upon his experience in hunting terrorists in caves, he judged this to be an industrial-grade searchlight, perhaps 200,000-candlepower. It was like a Xenon headlamp on a new German car, only 100 times more powerful.

Its ambient glow cast downward onto him, putting his position at risk if he were to move or if one of the two men in the bridge decided to venture onto the deck. The river would narrow, Mahegan figured, and one would steer the boat and the other would move forward from the cabin to lean over the bow and ensure clear passage, perhaps with a handheld searchlight. The din of the engines slowed from its high pitch to a low thrum as the vessel began to decelerate.

Another shift in the engines caused the boat to slow again, to what Mahegan figured was about five knots, slow enough to be looking for something. It was mo-

ments like these where endless scenarios began playing through his mind like several chess pieces, moving
to checkmate and then resetting before considering another way to win and then another.

The door to the cabin opened with a creak.

"Okay, I see the tree up there. We need to shut off
the light."

"Gimme a sec to throw the line."

"Hurry up then. Copperhead Six tells us not to use
the light at all. So no more than another thirty seconds."

"Six" was usually the military suffix for the commander. Mahegan presumed Copperhead Six to be the
radio call-sign for Nix, the person Lindy had mentioned as running the Copperhead operation.

One of the men moved quickly past Mahegan, no
more than ten feet away. He walked the entire distance
to the bow and grabbed a coiled rope. The man was lit
in high definition by the searchlight, making him appear like a rock star on a stage, the beckoning forest his
fawning audience. Mahegan closed his left eye and
counted down from thirty seconds, protecting his night
vision and intending to move as soon as the light shut
down.

With fifteen seconds to go, he felt the boat shift to
the west side of the diminishing creek. One of the motors slipped into reverse as he watched the man on the
bow slide to his left, toward the port side, and focus on
the shoreline.

As soon as the light went out, Mahegan stayed low,
hooked a leg on the gunwale, and shinnied over the
boat's edge on the starboard side, grasping the top rail
as if he was prepared to do a pull-up. Opening his left
eye, he pulled himself up enough to observe, his legs
still hanging in the cool water below.

The man on the bow tied the rope to a tree as the pilot reversed and revved the engines rapidly to crab the landing craft sideways before gunning the engine and pushing the vessel up onto dry land, leaving only the engines and Mahegan hanging in the water. Not knowing the depth of the river, he lowered himself so that only his fingers were visible on the top rail of the craft. He remained suspended, pressing his head against the metal hull.

"Get the rifles and let's boogie," the pilot called out as he shut down the engine.

"'Kay. Gotta cover the boat first. Sun will be up shortly."

"Screw it. We've got one run left and we're here."

After a pause, the other voice, said, "Aye. Let's bolt then."

Mahegan heard footsteps clang off the metal deck, then the rustle of two men walking through the forest. He waited another ten minutes, concerned that there might be a setup. He wasn't sure about the pause. Maybe there were some hand and arm signals indicating that he was hanging off the back of the boat. Or maybe he was just thinking too much.

His arms tiring, he executed a pull-up until his chin was above the top rail of the gunwale. His eyes had adjusted to the darkness and his night vision was intact. He shinnied back over the rail and knelt on the deck for another few minutes, silent. He saw the forklift and the generator, and could still feel their heat.

He moved quickly into the pilot's bridge and studied the interior cabin. He saw a large steering wheel, two gearshifts, several instrument displays, and a state-of-the-art portable Loran Global Positioning System. Before powering the GPS, he searched a couple of empty boxes in the corner of the cabin, but the most helpful thing he found was a pencil. He tore off the lid to a liquor box, stepped outside, saw nothing, and then returned to the cabin.

He stood where the pilot had been standing and looked to where he had been hiding. He had chosen the perfect position. The height of the cabin made it impossible to see into the blind spot he had selected.

Mahegan powered up the GPS, which cast his face in a bright green glow. If anyone were within a quarter mile of his position, they would notice. He quickly scrolled through the functionality, discovered the waypoints, and then stopped.

With each waypoint appearing on the left side of the display, an accompanying map was displayed on the right side. Mahegan pushed the down arrow and scrolled through six different map shots with what he presumed were latitude-longitude numbers on the left. Immediately, he recognized the *Teach's Pet* position off the north edge of Roanoke Island, about fifteen miles away. There was a map of the south edge of the island near Oregon Inlet. There were two points in the Alligator River near Buffalo City, one off Milltail Creek, and one point off Mann's Harbor, which he knew was on the east side of Dare County Mainland. The navigation device announced major landmarks in bold letters in the same fashion as an automobile GPS, with big block letters highlighting significant areas and smaller words identifying less prominent ones. This maritime GPS also identified all creeks, rivers, sounds, bays, and oceans.

The last point in the GPS was located in the Long Shoal River, which he decided had to be his present position, though the river seemed wider on the map than where he believed the landing craft was.

He quickly scribbled onto the cardboard the lat-longs for each of the points, stuffed it in his waistband, and then shut down the GPS. Hearing a noise in the distance, he knelt inside the pilot's cabin until his night vision returned.

The noise seemed to grow in intensity and he suddenly realized that at least two men, if not more, were heading toward the landing craft.

He silently moved to the most advantageous position in the pilot's cabin, which wasn't saying much. He was at a forty-five-degree angle from the door, catty-corner from the instrumentation. He figured that if anyone came up the steps, they would move toward the instruments, away from him, giving Mahegan an opportunity to attack and disappear down the long end of the vessel, perhaps even over the side into the forest.

"Okay, nobody knows about this shit, you understand?"

He recognized the voice. It was the one of the men who had piloted the vessel.

"Yeah, got it."

A new voice.

"What about Lars?"

"Lars won't be bothering us. We'll take this last load and go," the pilot said.

"I'm with you. Just don't want Copperhead Six on my ass," the new voice said.

The two men boarded the landing craft and stopped.

Mahegan looked above the rim of the pilot's cabin through the ballistic glass. He saw two large men talking next to the generator where he had initially hid after he boarded.

"We're talking several million dollars, Jimmy."

Jimmy was the pilot, Mahegan deduced.

"Damn right. And we've earned it."

Another pause, and then, "Okay, I'm with you. But if that asshole Nix finds out before we can disappear, we're toast."

"That's a chance I'm willing to take," Jimmy said. "I'm tired of driving this bitch around while he gets rich. Plus, all those damn ghosts give me the creeps. I've seen what's down there. Falco thinks he's hiding all that, but I've read about Tommy Thompson and know what the hell is going on."

Mahegan's mind reeled. Bream's office. *Ship of Gold in the Deep Blue Sea* by Gary Kinder. He had seen another name on the book's jacket: Tommy Thompson, the treasure hunter. On the trip back from the Pentagon, he had borrowed Locklear's phone to Google the book because it seemed out of place. The synopsis described Thompson as a genius explorer who ultimately found the SS *Central America*, a ship that in 1857 had sunk in a hurricane off the coast of Cape Hatteras with practically the entire California gold rush onboard. Thompson had spent three years at sea searching for the *Central America* two hundred miles offshore in two miles of ocean.

Gold.

This was about gold. Mahegan fingered the gold coins in the inset pocket of his swim trunks. Miller Royes had a gold coin in his shoe. Locklear had talked about treasure hunters. She had a gold coin in her kayak.

What did MVX-90s and gold have in common?

Mahegan could not summon an immediate answer to that question, because something else had caught in the back of his mind.

Ghosts.

What were they talking about? Mahegan remembered his conversation with Locklear. Was Dare County haunted by the Lost Colony or were the crew members talking about something more tangible? General Bream had asked Mahegan if he had "ghosted" any prisoners of war. Were these men now talking about prisoners?

The two men were now moving toward the cabin, discussing the merits of mutiny within Copperhead, Inc.

"Nix is doing okay. He was rich, then broke, and now he's rich again as soon as this stuff is legit," Jimmy said.

"But how do *we* make it legit?"

"We'll figure it out. Possession is nine-tenths, finders keepers, and all that good shit," Jimmy said.

"Probably harder than all of that if Copperhead Six is going through all this bullshit."

"We'll find our own ship. . . ."

Mahegan immediately recognized the unmistakable sound of rifle fire in the forest. The sharp zipping sound, the echo through the woods, the high-pitched whine, the two men falling to the deck of the landing craft, hit.

Someone had initiated a perfect ambush or perhaps even an assassination. Regardless, Mahegan immediately began to calculate that if the assassin had seen Jimmy and his co-conspirator, then there was a good chance that he too had been spotted. At a minimum, the shooter would come to the landing craft to inspect the bodies. If he was lucky, there would be just one, but his military mind told him that there was a small chance of that.

He began to think about what was at play.

Gold. Apparently, a lot of it. Whoever was running the operation would want to keep people in the know to a bare minimum. So maybe just one shooter. If he was lucky.

He waited until he thought the sniper might be moving. Worst case, he thought, was that one was keeping watch on the ship while another was moving. Classic over-watch.

He heard the rustle of footsteps moving quickly through the forest toward the boat. Mahegan looked down at the two bodies not more than twenty feet from the entrance to the pilot's cabin. Both were dead, he was sure. Headshots. Infrared scopes, close distance, and infrared aiming lights.

Mahegan wished he had his night-vision goggles. Knowing he was at a disadvantage, he stayed in his protected corner until he heard footsteps board the landing craft. Looking above the rim again, he watched as a man pressed his hand against the neck of each corpse. He was carrying an M24 sniper rifle with mounted thermal scope and infrared aiming device.

When done, he turned toward the bow of the vessel and spoke into a handheld microphone.

"Copperhead Six, this is Copperhead Three. All secure."

"Roger, out."

Mahegan heard Copperhead Six's voice through the microphone on the shooter's radio. His first thought was, authoritative. Crisp and clear, the voice sounded like an Army commander. He was giving orders, monitoring the situation, and receiving the report he desired.

Confident. No mistakes. Good to go.

"Roger, out," Copperhead Three said.

The "Three" suffix was usually the operations officer, a worthy chess piece to remove from the board. Mahegan sprung from his hidden position and leapt onto the shooter's back, striking him directly on the carotid artery. He felt the man buckle and loosen his grip on the rifle. Mahegan held the sniper, who was a big man, as he slid down onto the deck.

For good measure, Mahegan struck him in the back of the head with his forearm, a concussive blow as opposed to anything lethal.

Searching the man, Mahegan removed his radio, his weapon, and a knife.

He pulled a small Maglite from the man's tactical vest and searched the rest of his body, finding a hand-held Garmin GPS Map and a Copperhead swipe card. The identification on the card read "Lars Olsen." He had made the classic rookie mistake, carrying identification on a combat mission. Mahegan pocketed the high-tech GPS device and ID card as he quickly searched the two dead men. One of them had been carrying a duffel bag, which he unzipped, revealing an oxygen tank for scuba diving, a regulator, mask, fins, a yellow waterproof searchlight, and a block and pulley with rope already fed through the grooves. He also found a K-Bar knife, standard Marine fare to match the "Hoorah," he had heard earlier in the evening. He secured the knife and scabbard.

If he'd had any doubt before, Mahegan was now convinced that these men had discovered gold somewhere nearby, most likely in the water, and the bodies littering the deck of the landing craft had clashed over its ownership.

In addition to three sets of PVS-16 night-vision monocles, Mahegan also found a military officer's Beretta pistol on one of the dead men. He handled it, popped the magazine, saw the hollow points packed inside, then jacked the bolt open, catching the expelled round. He replaced the shell in the chamber, slid the magazine back into the well, charged the weapon, slipped the safety to "on," and moved toward the sniper rifle.

This weapon was more interesting. But not wanting to spend any more time on the landing craft, he simply

snatched it, and removed the black backpack from Lars
Olsen, who was moaning now and trying to roll over.
Mahegan lifted the pistol and prepared to forcefully
strike Olsen near the base of his skull. But before he
completed the downward arc, he thought about Colgate and the MVX-90s and stopped.

Instead, he stuffed two of the night-vision devices,
the handheld GPS, K-Bar knife, block and tackle, lat-
long cardboard, and Beretta pistol in the backpack,
loosened the straps to full length, slung it over his shoulders, grabbed the rifle, and high-kicked over the gunwale onto a well-worn path in the dense forest. He leaned
the rifle against a thick cypress tree, its roots jutting
upward in sharp edges. He returned to the landing craft,
deadlifted Olsen, and dumped him over the rim of the
boat on the forest side. The big man landed half in the
muck and half on the roots. Mahegan heard Olsen
groan as he leaned over and lifted him into a fireman's
carry.

He secured the night-vision monocle to his head,
flipped the switch, picked up the rifle, and followed an
obvious trail, now displayed in the vivid green hues of
infrared imagery through his night-vision goggles.

Mahegan moved about a hundred meters before
stopping. Olsen was wakening, the trail was well worn,
and he wanted to get away from the certain inbound
traffic. The morning sun was now making it light enough
so that he did not need the goggle, so he removed it,
held it in his free hand, and carefully picked his way
through dense underbrush to a minor opening about
thirty meters off the trail.

He dumped Olsen onto the edge of the opening and
knelt next to the man. Shards of light were knifing
their way through the canopied forest, just enough for
him to clearly see Olsen's face.

He had a tight haircut, military style. Even in the relative darkness, Olsen's hair looked blond. The man was probably over six feet tall, almost as big as Mahegan. He was wearing black cargo pants and a long-sleeve polypro shirt.

Mahegan used the flashlight to inspect the remainder of the backpack's contents, revealing little of interest other than some rags that smelled of gun oil and a secure, handheld Motorola personal mobile radio. Mahegan had used similar devices in Afghanistan and as he looked into the bag with the pistol, knife, night-vision goggles, GPS, and radio, and the rifle lying across his lap, he couldn't help but think about the raid he'd led a year ago to capture a key bomb maker in Afghanistan. He had carried much of the same equipment into that fight. But now, why did his attempted retreat from that world refuse to take hold? He looked at the thick, partially broken canopy above him, shut his eyes, and tried to think. He heard the rhythmic sounds of millions of insects, the frequent rustle of small animals, and the occasional growl of what had to be a black bear. Now that he knew his location to be just south of where he had been swimming just a few days before, he wondered if the red wolves were nearby.

He had tossed away his career, his passion, his life, but he'd simply been throwing a boomerang, as here in his lap had returned the means of war, the tools of his trade. A warrior's arsenal.

He thought about the MVX-90s and the gold and how they could intersect, if at all. He replayed in his mind Locklear's words about the *Teach's Pet* and about Copperhead, Inc. There in the forest he pieced together what he knew, what he believed, and what he was going to do about it. What he knew: Colgate was dead. Some-one had used an MVX-90 to defeat US jamming capability. The MVX-90 was a uniquely American invention, tested at the Dare County Bombing and Electronic Warfare Range. Copperhead, Inc. had lost tens of millions of dollars' worth of contracts in Afghanistan and Iraq. They had also been sued by the foreign governments of Afghanistan, Iraq, Pakistan, Iran, Jordan, and Saudi Arabia for their harsh treatment of detainees and indiscriminate shooting of civilians. Fort Brackett had been attacked and Adham was claiming responsibility. Adham was promising more attacks and beheadings as well as implicating him, Mahegan, in the plot. And Copperhead was moving gold and MVX-90s on a deep-sea fishing boat.

What he believed: Copperhead, Inc. was a business that had either gone bankrupt or was about to file Chapter 11. They had started out selling the MVX-90s to the highest bidder and somewhere along the way found the gold after securing the bomb-clearing contract, a decidedly unsexy contract for a bunch of folks who considered themselves trained killers. Last, Mullah Adham, aka Adam Wilhoyt, wanted to duel with him, and was taunting him from afar.

What he was going to do: Find out if Copperhead, Inc. was responsible for Colgate's death and, if so, then make every last son of a bitch pay.

And then find Adham and give him what he wanted: a duel.

He looked at Olsen, who was rubbing the back of his head.

"Son of a bitch," he said.

Mahegan put his knee into Olsen's sternum, pushed the rag into his mouth, rolled him, tied his hands behind his back using the rope from the pulley, and then winched the rope around a sturdy oak tree. He looped the rope around Olsen's waist, positioning him so that he was sitting with his back against the tree. Then Mahegan used the pulley to severely tighten the rope until Olsen's eyes began to bug out.

Tight enough, he thought.

"Okay, Lars, here's the deal." Mahegan retrieved the pistol and knife from the backpack and thumbed the safety to the "off" position. He laid the pistol in his lap and stuck the knife in the ground next to him as he sat in the center of the clearing about five feet from his captive.

"I'm going to take that greasy rag out of your mouth, but I will stick this knife in your heart if you try to scream for help. We're going to use quiet voices here and I want you to nod that you understand me."

He waited and watched Olsen, whose eyes were still popping from his face like some kind of Amazonian tree frog. His cheeks were red and Mahegan knew that the oil-soaked rag probably impaired his breathing. When Olsen didn't respond, Mahegan took the knife from the ground, sharp tip up, and rested it beneath Olsen's chin, pushing slightly upward without drawing blood.

"You guys need to sharpen your knives, wild man. Now let me know if you're hearing me." Mahegan removed the knife and Olsen nodded, eyes shut, probably fearing the future more than the present.

"Okay, now before I remove the gag, I've got one of your buddies on the other side of the trail and he's already starting to talk. I'm a crazy son of a bitch and so what I've decided is I'm going to ask you both the same questions and figure out what reality is here. I'm going to know who's lying. It's a game called 'prisoner's dilemma.' I'm sure you used it on some of your detainees in the sandbox. Whoever talks the most wins. It's that simple. You're going to wonder how I know all this, but don't waste your time. You can't even figure out how I got here or why you're cinched up with this pulley. So, keep it simple and keep it real. You got it?"

Olsen nodded.

Mahegan lifted the pistol, stood, and walked toward Olsen, who tried to kick him, but missed. Mahegan sidestepped the lame effort and stopped.

"Listen, asshole. I can assume the other guy is telling the truth. The one who lived. You got his buddy pretty good in the head, but the other guy came to before you did. He's talking. He's talking about gold and MVX-90s and all kind of shit. Hell, he's even giving me grid coordinates, asking me to split it with him. He's told me about the *Lucky Lindy*, too. All that sounds pretty real to me. So what am I going to do? I've got three options. Leave you here for animals to eat. Shoot you dead, which is really a subset of the first option. Or let your ass go. Your call. Give me a sign, because I'm losing momentum here."

Deflated, Olsen nodded as if to say, "Okay."

Mahegan removed the gag, aiming the pistol directly at the man.

"This is going to be quick. In what building are the MVX-90s located?"

"Who the hell do you think you are?"

Mahegan cocked the hammer to the Beretta, a largely meaningless move, but one that got Olsen's attention.

"What building?"

Olsen's lip was trembling and Mahegan didn't know if he was going to cry, shit his pants, or both.

"Warehouse near the tower."

"Okay, your buddy on the other side of the trail gave me that plus a direction. From the tower, what cardinal direction?"

Lars paused and said, "Screw it. Only a few left anyway. Northeast."

"My man across the trail said, 'North by northeast,' but I'm going to accept your imprecision this time."

Olsen shook his head. "Screw him. I'm telling the truth, man. It's about fifty meters northeast of the tower."

"Okay, now how about the gold?"

"What gold?"

"My man across the trail tells me that you assholes found a shitpot full of gold and are using the landing craft and the *Lucky Lindy* to move it around."

Olsen stared at Mahegan, struggled against his binds, and then sighed.

"Don't know anything about that."

Mahegan said, "Fine, I'll ask him again. If he gives me the same information twice, I'm going to assume you're lying and come back here and kill you. Pretty simple."

Mahegan started to walk and Olsen said, "Okay. Okay."

"I'm still moving. What's the deal?" Mahegan stepped over a log in the direction of the trail.

"The gold is gone."

"I thought there was one more shipment?"

"How do you know—?"

Mahegan smiled.

"I'm inside your head. I'm inside Copperhead, Incorporated. So the only thing you need to understand is that if you don't tell me the truth, you die."

Olsen shrugged. "You're going to kill me anyway, so go screw yourself."

Mahegan walked back over the log, lifted the pistol, and swatted Olsen across the face using the back of his hand.

"Next time you get a bullet. I'm tired of wasting my time and your partner has far more information than you. He figures he's dying anyway. Told him you shot him so he's talking."

Olsen looked up at Mahegan. The sun was beginning to burn away the early morning fog allowing some light to seep through the high canopy.

"One more shipment. The way it works is that we pull it up from the river, take the landing craft to any number of locations, conduct a transfer, and then the *Lindy* takes it offshore. Not sure where."

"Offshore?"

"Yeah, asshole, like out to sea."

"Two more questions."

"I ever get out of this I will personally hunt you down and cut open your guts and use them for fishing bait," Olsen croaked.

"Cool. Now tell me about the ghosts."

Olsen's face went white, but remained impassive. "No ghosts around here, man. Just wolves howling all the time."

"Okay, try something easy. Is the *Lucky Lindy* named after Lindy Locklear?"

Olsen smiled.

"You tapping that shit? That's Nix's girl."

"Lindy Locklear is Nix's girlfriend?"

"Thought you were inside my head, douche bag?" Olsen mocked.

Mahegan considered the information. Why would she come on to him? It had to do with the gold. Some kind of falling-out over the gold?

Mahegan retrieved Olsen's GPS and scrolled through its stored grid coordinates. Like the Loran navigation device on the landing craft, the Garmin had a "my favorites" option. He punched the screen and saw several of the images appeared the same as the one on the Loran. A few were different. One was an anomaly: It was in the middle of the Atlantic Ocean about 150 miles due east, offshore.

The very first image was what he believed to be the landing craft docking point on Long Shoal Creek. The second was about a mile away through the forest and across Route 264 in the middle of what looked like a swamp surrounded by rectangular moats. The alternating light green and blue lines gave way to a piece of land that appeared to have a few dirt roads and some buildings scattered in a tight area.

The bold letters next to the buildings read: DARE COUNTY BOMBING AND ELECTRONIC WARFARE RANGE.

Mahegan punched the "navigate" function, watched the device triangulate the satellites and then point in the direction he needed to walk.

He repacked the rucksack, ran a strip of duct tape over Olsen's mouth, and with soldierly skill carried the sniper rifle at the ready as he followed the GPS arrow.

Chapter 17

Samuel Nix turned to Vinny Falco and said, "Something's wrong with Lars. He took care of the two defectors but he hasn't called in or returned." He paused and said again, "Something's wrong."

"I'll head down there."

"We've got visitors coming soon, too."

"Army pukes, right?"

Nix smiled. "Yes."

"Well, just keep them dancing, boss. That's your line of work. Meanwhile, I'll go find out what's happening with the boat. We've got one more shipment and then we reverse the process. Everything's ours free and clear."

"Which is why I figured those morons might try something stupid such as running off with the last load," Nix said.

Falco rubbed his goatee with an open palm and then tugged at his diamond stud earring.

"No worries, boss. I'll find Lars and dump the bodies for the gators."

Falco was a shade under six feet tall, but his muscular frame seemed to occupy more space than men much bigger. Both his edgy personality and brawn mixed to create their own magnetic field that actually pushed people away. When Falco walked into a room, people noticed his wide shoulders cutting an arc like a scythe and his penetrating gaze sizing up and assessing anyone in his field of vision as a threat or nonthreat.

"Cut the lungs out so they sink this time," Nix said. He nodded and turned to his bank of cameras that covered every point of entry into his compound. He started at the periphery and worked his way inward. On Route 264 he had cameras facing both directions, tracking the only two routes into the compound. Both gates were locked tight, though he knew that Falco would be exiting out of the south gate in a few minutes in his white Ford F-150. He checked the east gate about four miles to the north and east of the south gate and saw it was locked. One of the first tasks Nix gave the ghosts was to move large boulders and dragon's teeth, tripods of iron bars, on either side of the chain-link fencing. The first layer of early warning was video coverage coupled with Slew-to-Cue technology. If something moved, a camera would automatically adjust its direction and zoom in on the movement.

On the perimeter fencing, which Copperhead, Inc. had billed to the government as part of the contract, Nix had installed top-of-the-line magnetic, infrared, audible, and passive vibration technology. If someone tried to climb, dig, or cut through the fence, one of the systems would cue one of the hundreds of cameras, which would then zoom in and focus on the anomaly using change-detection technology. Each camera stored an image database of every square inch of its sector of fence line. Each day, the cameras stared and recorded. Simultaneously, a back-end software system overlapped the current digital video with previous pictures, building a composite picture over time, accounting for minor changes such as trash, debris, or animals making changes to the terrain, such as a gopher digging a hole. Larger manipulations, though, would be presumed to be man-made and would be flagged by the software. After eighteen months on the job, Nix had to inspect the fence a dozen times, often in challenging locations. Each time, a bear or alligator had ripped through the fencing or burrowed underneath.

Such instances tended to dull his concern toward someone coming into the compound through the marshy terrain. Still, Nix was confident that if the fence didn't keep intruders out, the camera would probably spot them and his team could react. Nix kept a three-man quick reaction force and pickup truck with a .50 caliber machine gun mounted in the bed like the Tec Vehicles the Somalis used. He had billed this security equipment to the government under his ordnance removal contract.

In essence, the government had paid for a secure compound from which Copperhead, Inc. could conduct all of its activities.

As he watched Vinny Falco's Ford F-150 wait for the remote-controlled gate to open, he heard the high-pitched single beep of a fence alert along the southeast portion of the property. It was an outer perimeter fence that they had constructed along a dike separating two swampy ditches.

Nix turned and looked at the camera as it began to turn, tilt, and zoom onto the fence.

Mahegan studied the highway and the ditch-fence-ditch setup he would have to navigate. He was on the south side of the highway with Route 264 twenty meters to his front. He was camouflaged well enough by the dense undergrowth and deadfall. About ten feet from his position he saw a water moccasin coiled on the log behind which he was hiding. Its elliptical eyes watched him, the forked tongue flicking and sensing his presence.

He turned away from the snake, feeling safe enough. The road and the canals were classic danger areas that required caution on many levels. First, a random car could turn the corner and spot him, which might not be tragic, but the likelihood that Copperhead, Inc. kept tabs on vehicular traffic near their gates was high. Going across the road put him at high risk for detection, as was attempting to breach the fence in the early morning sun.

He studied the moccasin again, which hadn't moved. Its thick black-and-brown body was coiled like a climbing rope atop the deadfall. Mahegan looked farther east and saw a steady stream of water moving toward the Long Shoal River. His eyes followed the flow upstream and he spotted a large drainage pipe.

With a nod, he bid the snake farewell, moved about ten meters into the dense foliage away from the road, and then moved laterally toward the stream. The thorny vines and poison ivy were plentiful. The swim back would wash most of it away, he figured. Thick oak and walnut trees gave way to cypress as he stepped into the rich, black soil of the stream. As he approached the culvert, he could see that the near end was open and that the far end, about twenty meters away, had some type of mesh covering. He figured there were probably sensors embedded in the culvert denial system as well.

Mahegan moved back toward his position near the moccasin, which was still coiled tightly in a new block of sunshine that was angling through the high canopy.

In his periphery he saw the southern gate to the Copperhead, Inc. compound open as a white Ford F-150 pulled through and then crossed directly onto the dirt road, which led to the landing craft's anchor point on Long Shoal Creek.

Mahegan suspected that this person was a one-man investigation team in response to radio silence from Lars Olsen. Having no idea how many men worked at Copperhead or what their true security posture might be, Mahegan was at a disadvantage. He was in recon mode as opposed to assault mode. He needed more information and while the GPS and maps were useful, what he really needed was to be inside the compound. He also knew that whoever was driving the white pickup truck was going to find some dead Copperhead, Inc. employees at the landing craft launch site and eventually Olsen as well. Mahegan would become public enemy number one in the eyes of Copperhead, Inc. He knew that the corporation hired mostly ex-military and some ex-police, all of whom had some kind of expert skill sets, whether hand-to-hand combat, marksmanship, or several combinations thereof.

He looked at the snake, completely still, nearly invisible to the naked eye, and thought the serpent had it about right.

Lie there, observe, and strike when ready.

Chapter 18

Lindy Locklear slipped into the dream again. Each time, she knew it was a mixture of her personal experience, her research, and a bit of creative license on behalf of her subconscious.

It was September, 1857, in the Atlantic Ocean off the coast of Nags Head, North Carolina. The SS James Adger, a side-wheel steamer, was pushing through heavy seas. With winds gusting over 120 mph, the captain was using the 240-horsepower Allaire Iron Works steam engine. They were burning through mounds of anthracite coal ferrying $3.5 million in gold from the Dahlonega, Georgia, and Charlotte, North Carolina, mints. They had lost their main sails and their steam engine was flooded. The ship's captain knew they had passed Hatteras light so he searched for Oregon Inlet and the Bodie Island lighthouse where there was safe harbor.

Meanwhile, Dr. Warren Johnson, owner of the Curlew ironclad steamer, received a telegraph from Charleston, South Carolina, that the Adger left port with large quantities of gold. He quickly devised his plan. He hauled kerosene-soaked logs onto the high sand dunes of Kitty Hawk, several miles north of Bodie

Island, set them on fire, shot the foreman of the Bodie Island lighthouse, and snuffed the lighthouse flame. As the floundering Adger *angled toward the ersatz lighthouse, it ran aground in the shoals where the Gulf Stream and Labrador currents met.*

Johnson's crew raided the Adger *and took some casualties, but escaped with nearly two million dollars in gold as the flat-bottom* Curlew *glided back into Oregon Inlet. Johnson murdered the remainder of his crew and hid the gold in the Long Shoal River.*

Lindy Locklear passed the Curlew *in her kayak, her stroke quiet and stealthy. She was scared that Johnson might shoot her as well, but now she knew where the gold was hidden. She paddled hand over hand, her fit triceps propelling her through the still waters until she was floating in the Long Shoal River above underwater mountains of gold gleaming up at her like shiny pyramids. Finally, her research had paid off and she had discovered the missing treasure. But the felled crewmen of the* Curlew *were staring at her, eyes open, faces pale, hair wafting in the tidal ebb. "Stay away," they seemed to be saying to her, their mouths moving. "Stay away." But two million in gold was too much to ignore.*

Locklear bolted awake, sitting upright immediately, wiping sweat from her brow. She checked the clock with the panic-stricken thought that she was late for something.

Ten o'clock a.m. Her mind reeled through the last twenty-four hours. She remembered returning from the Pentagon, drinking with Mahegan, the sensual lovemaking, and falling asleep exhausted. She recalled waking and secretly watching him stride confidently into the water as he swam toward the *Teach's Pet.* Then she had snuggled back into his warm spot in the bed.

She was surprised that she didn't care this time that

he had left. From this point forward, the situation was not in her control, and she would follow the leads wherever they appeared.

And she would reclaim the gold.

But first she needed to go check in with the sheriff, so she showered, combed her hair wet straight back over her head, and tossed on a bikini, T-shirt, shorts, and her Tevas.

"Hell with it," she muttered, realizing she was nervous. She liked the guy and wondered where he was, what he was doing, and what he might discover. While clumsy, he had turned out to be an affectionate lover, which she found appealing.

She leaned over the sink, stared in the mirror, taking in her almost platinum hair, pale green eyes, and clean, lightly freckled face. She smiled with perfect teeth grinning back at her. On the way out, she picked up her Droid cell phone, checked her voice mail, texts, and instant messages, most of them reminders about the season closing cast party tonight for the *Lost Colony* production.

She hopped in her Defender, flipped her sunglasses over her eyes, and drove the quick four miles to the sheriff's office. As she entered the building, she almost bumped into Rollie Williams, who was barreling out of the building. She spun around, grabbing his arm. "Hey there, Rollie, where are you going so fast?"

"Don't mess with me now, Lindy, I've got a mission," Williams shot over his shoulder.

She watched him leave and then went straight to Sheriff Johnson's office, where she found him standing and talking with two other men.

She leaned over Johnson's assistant's desk and asked Lorraine Wilson, "So what's shaking, wild thing?"

Lorraine was a throwback. She had lived in Dare

County all of her life and had held the sheriff's assistant position for over forty years. She dyed her hair brown, had one face-lift already, and at sixty years, Locklear thought she looked pretty damn good.

"Love the police outfit, Locklear." Lorraine smiled. The two women got along usually and mostly because Locklear deferred to the elder nearly one hundred percent of the time. In fact, most people did.

"You know better than anyone, Lorraine, if you don't use it, you lose it."

Lorraine smiled again. "You got that right, girl. What's shaking, yourself?"

"You going to the cast party tonight?" asked Lindy. Lorraine had played a variety of extras over the years in the *Lost Colony* theatrical production.

"Of course. Wouldn't miss it unless this new information on Miller Royes and J.J. causes us all to work late." Lorraine winked.

Locklear picked up on the hint and, leaning forward, said in a whisper, "So what's the deal?"

Lorraine bent toward Locklear and said, "We've got military police in the office asking questions about Miller and J.J. Word is that they were out on the *Pet* last week when they went missing." Lorraine tilted her head in the direction of Johnson's office.

Locklear chewed on a fingernail, concerned that she might need to deal with these federal investigators. *What in the hell had they found out?*

"Thanks, Lorraine, we'll see you tonight then?"

"Sure thing, honey."

Locklear took a step, then stopped and turned around, catching Sheriff Johnson's eye. She nodded and then leaned back into Lorraine. "Think I can catch a minute with the sheriff when he's done with the military guys?"

"He's always got time for you, dear. Why don't you just pull up a chair?"

The outer office was sparsely furnished with old government furniture consisting of gray cloth chairs to match Lorraine's gray desk. There were a few paintings on the wall of Chief Manteo, the Croatan tribal leader during John White's settlement in 1587. Locklear noticed there were none of Chief Wanchese, Manteo's main rival during the Lost Colony days.

After thirty minutes, the two investigators, whom Locklear immediately recognized as the two men she and Mahegan had confronted at Blackbeard's, came walking from Johnson's office. Johnson was saying in his Elizabethan English, "I thank you all for coming down. We had no idea that Royes was anything but a worker on the *Pet*. You know that ship stays out there year-round except when we haul it in and scrape all the crap off the bottom and get it ready for a new season. And we're just worried sick about my nephew, J.J. I've got everyone in the department looking for him."

The man Locklear recognized as Paslowski said, "We were going to Copperhead today but we decided we would start with that ship first based upon some information we got from headquarters."

"We can work that out. Give me a day to get it set up. Now that the theater season's over, they have a business they run out there. Kids go out on field trips from the schools. They have guys playacting as pirates. Five hundred dollars a pop and they do at least two visits a day. They've got some official Edward Teach artifacts out there on display. Plus, it has radio and antennae stuff on there and acts as a relay station so I can communicate to all my deputies across this big county, so we're going to have to be careful."

Paslowski slewed his head toward Locklear like a
T. rex looking for game and then returned his gaze to
Johnson.

"We'll be ready tomorrow morning," said Paslowski. "That's when we'd like to get out there. If you
can be ready sooner, so will we. I've got a warrant
coming from the federal judge in a few hours, but I'd
prefer to start when we'll have a full day to spend out
there."

"Deal," Johnson said. He stood there in his denim
shirt with the embroidered "Sheriff" above the left
breast pocket and his khaki pants.

"And on the other, about Mahegan. He's in deep shit
with the Inspector General. So, we'll defer to you for
now, but the evidence that he murdered a prisoner of
war is looking pretty good from our end." Paslowski
turned and looked directly at Locklear, who took that
as her cue to stand.

Paslowski's eyes did a full-body scan of her, which
caused Locklear to shiver as if to shake off the residue.

"How's the arm, slugger?" Locklear provoked him.

Paslowski's mouth turned into a wicked, lips-sealed
grin making him look like a Gila monster. "Probably
better than Mahegan's. Where is he, by the way?"

"I've got him locked up," Locklear said confidently.

Paslowski paused, started to say something, and
then the two men departed.

Once they were gone, Sheriff Johnson looked at her.
"What in the world?" he asked. "Lindy, we've talked
about this. Either you're on duty and dressed appropri-
ately or you don't come in here like that."

She grabbed his arm, pulled him into his office,
closed the door, and said, "Listen, you don't pay me
enough to work full-time. I'm trying to pull some

things together that will help the case. You're not seriously going to let them tear apart the *Pet*, are you?"

"Don't have much choice in the matter, Lindy. You heard the man. They've got a warrant from a federal judge. Royes and J.J. were doing some work for Copperhead and Royes apparently had called the feds. Something about the expense report for the bomb-clearing effort there. They're spending money on construction when all they're supposed to be doing is finding bombs. Miller didn't get real specific, but they said he was worried about something. And another thing Paslowski told me was that there is an issue with the paychecks for the people who are clearing the bombs. So, we know they're up to something, but until now there's been nothing but secrets."

"What I never got about Copperhead is that they've got this big contract to clear the bombing range and they've never hired a single local person to do it. I couldn't ever get Nix to talk about it," Lindy said, sitting in another gray chair inside Johnson's office. She pulled at her lip, thinking.

Johnson sat in his chair and leveled his eyes on Locklear.

"Lindy, I've thought about the same thing. All we ever see is that guy, Falco, who is bird-dogging chicks during tourist season—"

"Doesn't have to be tourist season. He's always bird-dogging chicks," Locklear countered.

"And sometimes Nix is over here, but you'd think there would be workers."

"You're the sheriff of Dare County. Can't you go over there and check things out?"

"Federal property. We got no say," Johnson said.

Locklear paused, then asked, "What do you think they'll find on the *Pet*?"

"You would know better than me," Johnson said. "You're always out there in that kayak."

She frowned. "Never boarded the damn thing, though."

"I'm hearing that Mahegan found a gold coin on Royes's body," Johnson said. It was more of a question directed at Lindy than a statement of fact.

Lindy held his gaze and said, "News to me."

"Well, you just spent the last twenty-four hours with him so I would assume you would have pumped him for as much information as possible."

"I did. And all I've got to show for it is I don't know where he is. Left last night. Saw him swimming out to the *Pet* and from there I don't know."

"Swimming to the *Pet*?"

"That's what I said."

"Shit. He probably boarded it and knows more than we do."

Locklear stood, leveled her eyes on Johnson, and said, "I'm counting on it."

"Think he knows what happened to J.J.?"

"That's what I'm hoping."

Chapter 19

Chikatilo had a new mission. He received his orders through innocuous text messages, tweets, or direct messages.

@TuffChik; party at Suffolk Walmart today at 1030 am ;)

Needing to keep up the momentum after the Brackett attack, Chikatilo was moving quickly in a new vehicle, a Dodge minivan, to Hampton Roads, Virginia.

He kept at the speed limit along Route 58, picked up Interstate 664 in Suffolk, Virginia, and then pulled into a Walmart parking lot across from what he knew to be a classified military training compound. A fifteen-foot-high fence with razor wire surrounded the leased facility's twenty-five acres. Chikatilo knew that the compound was hiding in plain sight among the neighborhood eateries, local stores, and the Super Walmart. Still, there was a formidable gate that required breaching if he was going to be successful.

And he also knew the front gate used Harris radios to communicate with the roaming security teams.

He had the remaining ghost from the Fort Brackett attack, a man he called Bundy, lying on the floor cargo compartment of the minivan with a retractable tarp pulled over him. He had activated the door locks using the "kid-lock" function on the driver's console. Tucked around Bundy were enough explosives to do the Suffolk job. But they parked next to a panel truck that was being driven by a ghost Chikatilo called Dahmer.

The plan was for Dahmer to fill his vehicle with barrels of ammonium nitrate to augment or accelerate the attack. They moved quickly, with Chikatilo lowering his window in tandem with Dahmer.

"Salaam Alaykum," Chikatilo said.

"Inshallah," Dahmer said in return, completing the bona fides.

Chikatilo nodded and stepped out of his vehicle, unlocked the rear compartment, and led Bundy to the driver's seat.

"You know the drill. We've rehearsed this," Chikatilo said. "Your front end is reinforced steel and will easily break the gate. Your engine is turbocharged, so approach slow, pass the van, and then about twenty meters away, floor it, break down the wooden arm, and then plow into the main lobby of the big building, keeping it floored until you explode and go to Allah."

Bundy nodded, ready for jihad.

"Once you pass him, Dahmer will be directly behind you and will bore a deeper hole into the headquarters, then detonate the fatal blow. You are the breaching force. He is the assault force. You must succeed for him to be successful. Understand?"

Again, Bundy nodded.

"It's ten-thirty a.m. Time for you to go before everyone heads to lunch."

"Inshallah," Bundy said.

Chikatilo nodded as he turned toward Dahmer, a large Pakistani man recruited by Mullah Adham.

"Peace be with you," Chikatilo said, then flipped the switch on Bundy's MVX-90. The next radio call from the Harris radio would ignite Bundy's considerable arsenal. Chikatilo was banking on the security guard calling in Bundy's breaching of the wooden arm about the time Bundy crashed through the front of the building. The MVX-90 would, as it had in Fort Brackett, send an electrical current to the explosives wrapped around Bundy and those stored in the back of the minivan. If the guard did not make the call, Bundy had a rocker switch he could simply press that would ignite the car and, subsequently, himself. Either way, he was meeting Allah this morning.

Dahmer nodded and followed the slow-moving minivan. Chikatilo walked into the Walmart, bought a novel and some toothpaste, then returned to the parking lot, found the Honda Accord with the North Carolina license plates. He reached under the front left wheel well, found the magnet with the key, and entered the car.

As he turned the ignition, he heard the first explosion and for a stricken moment believed that his accomplice had rigged his car with a bomb. Not the case. He saw a plume of smoke and fire billowing from the headquarters building across the street. About the time several onlookers in the parking lot registered that a bomb had detonated in the lightly defended military compound, a second explosion in the compound sent shock waves roiling across the parking lot. The Honda Accord rocked a bit and Chikatilo smiled. They had done their duty.

And there was much more to do.

Chikatilo pulled slowly out of the Walmart parking lot, turned onto I-664, and quickly made his way through

Portsmouth's midtown tunnel and onto I-264 into Virginia Beach, where he was to await further instructions.

After forty-five minutes of bridges and tunnels he located Seashore State Park, which fronted the Chesapeake Bay. He pulled into a sandy parking spot next to a white, rusted Sunnybrook Edgewater recreational vehicle. He used a key to open the door and turned on the generator and then the air conditioner.

Sitting in a tufted captain's chair, he switched on the satellite antenna and lifted the satellite radio's black handset to his mouth.

"This is TuffChik."

He heard slight buzzing noise, waited a few seconds, and repeated his first call. After a minute, he got a response.

"Go ahead."

"Welcome to Walmart."

"Roger, out."

Chikatilo switched off the satellite antenna and receiver and looked at the waters of Chesapeake Bay shifting with the tide.

Looking to the west, he watched an aircraft carrier slide effortlessly toward Norfolk Naval Base, the next target.

Chapter 20

Mahegan approached the stationary white Ford pickup truck with caution. On his back, he carried the small rucksack he had lifted from the landing craft. He had placed the GPS and pistol in the rucksack and moved slowly with the M24 sniper rifle at port arms.

His acute hearing told him that the truck was still idling. From fifty meters away, he could not see a driver in the truck's cab, so he immediately began scanning the surrounding area. He stopped and knelt next to the base of a large oak tree, listening. The buzz of insects ran through the forest. He could hear the lap of the water against the hull of the landing craft nearly one hundred meters away.

The driver of the truck had parked in the same clearing where the two now-dead men had parked in hopes of making off with the remainder of the gold. It was a small gravel turnaround that gave way to the trail that led to the creek. Mahegan held the rifle up to his cheek and looked through the scope, scanning. He started by checking to his rear, to ensure the driver had not circled back on him. After a few seconds of using the scope and checking closer in, something the troops called the "five and twenty-five," he determined there was no threat to his rear. He always checked the first five meters around himself and then broadened the scan to twenty-five meters. If he consistently performed this drill, as he had in combat, Mahegan knew he would pick up on most threats.

Turning back to the truck, he heard a noise not indigenous to the environment. These were careful footfalls, spaced apart evenly, as if the owner were trying, unsuccessfully, to avoid the underbrush. But they were cautious, indicating awareness of a possible threat. Most likely, Mahegan figured, the driver of the truck had seen the two dead bodies on the landing craft by now and was trying to avoid whatever had befallen them. The trucks, side by side, were in between Mahegan and the footfalls, blocking his field of vision. To his ten o'clock, he could barely see the landing craft through the thick, downward sloping terrain. The trail ran from the side of the circular gravel area away from Mahegan and toward the landing craft.

Through the scope, Mahegan could not see any obvious movement, until he saw the slightest tipping of a green-leafed dogwood above the hood of the idling truck. It might have been a squirrel, Mahegan thought, but more likely it was a man leaning against the tree to lighten his footfall and avoid making noise.

As if he were an apparition appearing out of nowhere, a man with a goatee and an earring cautiously stepped onto the gravel behind the other truck, a black Ford Ranger. The man with the goatee opened the truck, less careful now. Mahegan assumed he was checking for Olsen. After a few seconds, the man quietly closed the truck door and then angled around the back of the pickup bed toward the white truck with the Copperhead logo emblazoned on the driver's door. Skirting around the back of that truck, the man approached the driver's door, opened it, and then leaned inside, extracting a shotgun. Mahegan thought it looked like a basic Remington. Good enough to do the trick.

Apparently feeling secure now with the weapon, the man knelt in the vee developed by his open door and the frame of the truck. His back was fifty meters from Mahegan, framed by the still crosshairs of Olsen's sniper rifle. Holding a personal mobile radio to his mouth, the man with the goatee whispered loud enough for Mahegan to hear. Mahegan secretly congratulated himself for turning off the mobile radio he had secured from Olsen.

"Copperhead Six, this is Copperhead Five, over."

"This is Six, go ahead, over."

"Two dead at landing craft. Copperhead Three missing. Has he returned to HQ?"

"Negative on three. Secure the area. I will be there asap."

"Roger. Standing by. Out."

Mahegan watched the man with the goatee put the radio on the seat of the truck. Bad move, he thought. He should have kept it on him. Mahegan calculated that he had less than five minutes before Copperhead Six, presumably Sam Nix, the CEO of Copperhead, Inc. would arrive on the scene. Mahegan had one play and only one if he intended to get inside of Copperhead for a quick inspection. And he had to move quickly.

He decided that the man with the goatee had yet to do anything that might cause Mahegan to shoot him. Though he presumed that the man was plenty evil, Mahegan wanted evidence before he could pull the trigger from fifty meters and send a bullet into someone's heart.

He watched the man with the goatee carry the shotgun at the ready. He was expanding his zone of security by walking toward the wood line in Mahegan's direction. The man stepped into the wooded area less than twenty meters from his position, moving toward Olsen, who was one hundred meters away, near the mouth of the creek.

The man reappeared less than ten meters from Mahegan, circling back onto the gravel. He could make out the man's face, weathered, tanned, angular, and determined. He noticed the penetrating eyes, calculating what had happened and what might happen. The man's buzz-cut hair, goatee, diamond earring, and searching eyes made for a menacing look. Mahegan noticed beneath the polypro Under Armor T-shirt a chiseled body that bespoke a man as accustomed to the gym as Mahegan was to the water.

Not an easy takedown. He watched the man carefully. Two minutes had passed, with less than three remaining. If Mahegan did not move now, the opportunity might be lost.

As if sensing his move, the man with the goatee turned in his direction, alert, the same way a deer popped up its white tail when it sensed danger. Mahegan had not moved, so he presumed the man was cuing in on an instinct. Maybe he sensed his presence. Mahegan knew he was well camouflaged behind the tree and dense foliage, but there was the matter of his rifle and scope, barely visible.

The man with the goatee seemed to be looking at the trail directly next to the thick oak behind which Mahegan had obtained cover. Footprints, Mahegan thought. He was looking for footprints. The piercing eyes were focused at a forty-five-degree angle downward on the trail. The man disappeared behind the oak tree and was to Mahegan's immediate left. Motionless,

Mahegan listened intently, following the sound of the man's footsteps, now at his eight o'clock.

Now or never.

Mahegan sprang from his position, catching the man with the goatee fractionally off-guard. He noticed his opponent's head had been scanning to the right, away from Mahegan, when he'd decided to make his move. Mahegan dropped the sniper rifle, lunged at his prey, and grabbed at the shotgun. The man was swinging the Remington as if a covey of quail had just surprised him to his rear, lifting and aiming at the noise. Mahegan caught the weapon mid-traverse, and snatched it from the man's hands while delivering a high kick to the solar plexus. He heard an *oomph* as the man bent forward. Mahegan turned the shotgun and stroked it across his opponent's face.

He tossed the shotgun to the ground and used the rope from his rucksack to tie the man and gag him behind the oak. He bound the hands and legs, then coiled the rope around the tree, working quickly. Using the knife, he cut a portion of the man's shirt away, stuffed it into his mouth, and tied it around the back of the nearly shaved head.

Retrieving the sniper rifle, the shotgun, and his backpack, Mahegan jogged to the man's truck, checked inside, saw the keys, turned the ignition, and spun out of the circular driveway toward the road. Reaching the hardtop, he yanked a hard left and floored the gas pedal until he was around the nearest bend. He slowed and pulled onto the shoulder in time to see another truck exiting the Copperhead gate. He watched carefully as the truck stopped, the man reached up and pressed something, and then the gate opened. The truck passed through the gate and stopped, the man reached up, and the gate closed behind the truck. Mahegan had taken a left purposely to be on the far side of the driver's visual path. Most drivers glanced to their right, but looked hard to their left, where an oncoming car could do serious damage to the driver's side.

Mahegan looked up at the visor in the appropriated truck and saw the sending unit, much like a garage door opener. *Perfect*, he thought.

He gave the driver a full minute to pull onto the gravel drive and travel out of his field of view. He considered many things in the minute that passed. Copperhead had seven confirmed personnel outside the gate. He presumed the two on the *Lucky Lindy* were still out at sea. Then there were the two dead men on the landing craft. There were Lars Olsen and the man with the goatee. Now presumably Sam Nix had left the compound. Mahegan remembered that Locklear had mentioned that she had only seen a few Copperhead contractors around town. Normally, Mahegan knew that the place would be awash in transplanted personnel doing a job for a few years, like migrant workers. But Locklear had also said that Copperhead had not hired much locally. So that meant they had a small, flat organization and were performing much of the labor themselves, unless, of course, they had the equivalent of a sweatshop hidden behind the gates. Perhaps there were ghost detainees? But surely they would be, well, detained, Mahegan figured. So, the problem with flat organizations was they lacked depth. Mahegan figured there had to be a back way out of the range.

On that thought, he gunned the engine and pulled back onto the hardtop, drove the half mile to the gate, and pressed the sending unit. The gate began to creep open to his left. He studied it closely. This was more than a chain-link fence. It was a reinforced iron gate with miniature I-beams cutting across its width to prevent ramming.

Again, perfect. He looked at the receiving unit, which was situated about ten meters inside the fence line. It looked like a miniature barbecue grill. A hard outer shell iron casing protected the actual brains of the device. He saw a gap, covered by Plexiglas, which he presumed was where the signal was received. As the gate opened, he pulled the truck through and stopped. He passed the sending unit again, and the gate began to close behind him.

As he watched and heard the latch close and lock the gate, he stepped out of the vehicle and used the silenced sniper rifle to put two near point-blank shots into the Plexiglas. He reached into the truck and pressed the button on the sending unit and nothing happened. He tried again. Nothing. Good.

He reentered the truck and drove along the main road toward the tower, which Mahegan presumed was the air traffic control tower.

Seven outside, how many inside, he wondered?

He pulled to the base of the tower and visually scanned his surroundings. He figured he had ten minutes before some alarm would sound or whoever was left inside would scramble and come after him. Unsure of what exactly he was going to find, he prioritized his search by looking for the MVX-90s. Anything beyond that would be beyond his expectations. Olsen had mentioned the warehouse. He saw a row of Quonset huts to his front left, eleven o'clock. To his left rear, seven o'clock, he saw two administrative buildings. To his right front, at two o'clock, he saw the only building that could immediately qualify as a "warehouse."

He drove the quarter mile to the gray metal structure, aware that he had seen no one moving inside the garrison area. On the door of the warehouse, Mahegan saw the now familiar Copperhead emblem with a white diamond background, the gaping snake's mouth and fangs. The door was locked by a standard heavy-gauge padlock, which Mahegan quickly removed with a butt-stroke of the shotgun.

Opening the door, he stepped into a dark cavern filled with boxes, crates, forklifts, and other machinery. Mahegan jogged into the middle of the warehouse, surrounding himself with the detritus of years of random neglect and spotty efforts to organize, followed by more years of neglect. He had a brief flashback of the jump into Iran and their destruction of the warehouse filled with copper plates and boxes of MVX-90s.

He saw a stack of neatly formed boxes about two-thirds of the way into a warehouse he figured to be the length of a football field. Inside was sweltering from the lack of ventilation. Pushing toward the neatly stacked boxes, he noticed another forklift and a second door. He also saw fresh tire tracks in the dirt floor.

He pulled up short and stopped. Staring at a twenty-foot-high stack of palletized MVX-90 boxes, Mahegan saw the distinctive triangle evident even in the dim light. High windows cast an eerie pallor across the expanse of the warehouse, highlighting dust and dirt particles that floated like lazy insects.

Mahegan reached up and grabbed a box from the opposite side where it was clear the forklift had whittled the mountain down to within his reach. He pulled open the top flap and saw the smaller thin cardboard boxes that contained the actual devices. He counted ten across the top row and figured the box to be two deep, giving him twenty per container.

He heard a loud noise begin to wail above him, like

a siren. There it was, Mahegan thought. Whatever and whoever was in this compound was on alert. He grabbed two of the smaller boxes and ran toward the truck, stopped at the door, led with the shotgun and, seeing no one, moved toward the vehicle.

He stuffed the MVX-90s into the backpack and cradled the shotgun as he closed the door, started the truck, and slammed it into gear. With his foot on the brake, he searched inside his rucksack, found the GPS device, and powered it up, all the time looking in the mirror. He saw a dust trail coming from the opposite side of the control tower. Probably, Mahegan thought, the quickest alternate way in . . . and out. He fidgeted with the GPS, found the save function, and entered his location. He watched it save and then pulled it up again to make sure he had performed the task properly. He had, so he powered off the GPS and crammed it into the backpack.

With the dust trail coming closer to the tower, he released the brake and picked a gravel road that fed away from the tower to the northeast. For all he knew he was driving smack into the middle of the impact area of the bombing range where the pilots had for years dropped their bombs. Thankfully, the truck had a built-in GPS map on the dashboard, which Mahegan now used to navigate toward what looked like a viable exit on the northeast side of the fenced area maybe two miles away.

By now Mahegan was creating his own dust trail that would be easy to follow. Staying focused on the road, he noticed on his left a built-up area maybe two miles on the other side of what was clearly the impact area, like an oasis shimmering across a vast desert. Mahegan registered it to be either a range facility or an urban-training live-fire facility for the military. For years, the Navy and Air Force had dropped bombs in this one-square-mile zone that now looked like Verdun after the infamous World War I battle. There were craters, trees sawed off at the stump by shrapnel, and others burned by the explosions. He picked his path carefully, following what appeared to be recent tire tracks. What looked like a massive burn pit appeared to his eleven o'clock. Mahegan guessed it was where Copperhead detonated the unexploded ordnance they found throughout the bombing range. He was reminded of the blast he had heard on his swim.

Looking to his right, he saw winding, dense foliage that usually indicated a stream or swampy area. Looking ahead, he noticed the road was on a path to cross the stream about a half mile away. Looking back, he noticed the dust trail had stopped, perhaps because he was in the impact area, or perhaps because there was someone circling around Route 264 to cut him off.

Or perhaps there was no way out of the area.

Processing all of this information, he looked back to his left again and saw more buildings a few miles across the impact zone. He was convinced now that he was seeing a Military Operations in Urban Terrain, or MOUT, training facility. Having spent his share of time inside these makeshift cement and wood "villages," Mahegan tucked away the information and continued searching for a way out.

Abruptly the road dove into the creek and it was plain that it did not continue on the east side. An overgrown trail appeared twenty meters away across the black water of the slowly winding creek.

The recognition of a water obstacle to his front coupled with the sound of an airplane flying low behind him signaled to Mahegan that his position was soon going to be untenable. He grabbed the sniper rifle and considered exiting the vehicle as the personal mobile radio sitting on the passenger seat chirped to life.

"Give it up, Mahegan. We know who you are and you've got nowhere to go."

Had to be Copperhead Six, Samuel Nix, Mahegan figured. He listened as the airplane circled low. It was a King Air with photographic substructure, so they could track him using digital and thermal cameras with full motion video. If they had been digging out bombs, they would have that capability. He could try a lucky shot at the airplane or disappear into the dense foliage to his front.

The creek was broad and Mahegan thought it might have once been a ford site and therefore might be passable in the vehicle. If he could get to the opposite side, the GPS map told him he might be able to get some tree cover, which would at least give him the opportunity to confuse the pilots.

In the end, he decided to back the truck about fifty meters from the creek and lock the hubs by pressing a button that read "4Low" on the dashboard. He gunned the engine, feeling all four wheels engaging the dirt separately now. The power was evident and he hoped it would propel him through to the less-traveled side of this road.

As he sped toward the creek, he heard the pop of rifle fire and caught the flash of a muzzle coming from the airplane that was circling higher now. The first bullet pinged off the hood and hit something that caused smoke or steam to begin to ease from the seams of the truck. The second shot glanced sideways off the windshield, splintering the glass. A third bullet shattered the front windshield altogether.

As Mahegan hit the water, he felt the truck dip precipitously, water rushing over the hood and into the cab, but the rear tires propelled him forward until the truck leveled at about four feet deep, midway up the driver's side door. All four wheels were pulling him now as a fourth shot pinged through the roof, surely meant to kill as it punched into the passenger seat. Though progress was slower through the creek, he was still moving. The locked hubs were powering him through the creek bottom, which he figured now to be firmer than he had originally anticipated.

The front wheels banged into the far bank and for a moment Mahegan thought the worst would happen. He would stall, the sniper in the airplane would be perfectly angled for a headshot, and the secret of the MVX-90s would be forever hidden.

But the front wheels chewed at the firm surface of the far bank, gaining purchase sufficiently to allow the rear wheels to keep from spinning in the muck. Inch by inch, the tires spun but made progress until he finally shot up the bank, gaining some air and landing with a thud on the front axle, followed by the rear axle slamming into the trail. Mahegan gunned the vehicle, which was responding nicely despite the puncture in the hood. He wanted to get off Dare Bombing Range property as soon as possible, and the GPS was indicating that if he stayed on this less-used trail he would hit a convergence of several roads.

Thankfully for Mahegan, this path, while rutted and overgrown, had sufficient canopy to mask the sniper's aim. He felt two more bullets ping in the rear of the truck. Going for the gas tank, Mahegan figured. All he could do was push the button to unlock the hubs and then race the speedometer to seventy-five mph. As he calculated his position, he knew that he was safe from the ground vehicles that had been pursuing him from behind. He also knew it didn't take a strategic genius to figure he would be popping out of the trail at the only location on the east side that fed onto US 264.

The truck's GPS indicated that he was less than a half mile from the exit point when he saw a dirt road on his right angling toward an intersection. He bounced through a significant pothole that splashed water onto his face through the space where the windshield had been. To his left he saw another dirt road converging into his path. He determined he was at the limits of the bombing range when he approached a gate similar to the front gate he had breached and disabled. He pressed the remote button but got no result.

Gunning the engine and strapping himself into the seat belt, he tried the remote one more time to no avail. He was doing ninety-five mph when he dodged some poorly placed dragon's teeth and the front end of the truck broke through the heavy gate. The screeching of metal tearing from its hinges sounded like the wail of angry demons. The truck listed to the right as the hinges on that side were less forgiving than the gate latch on the left. The power of the truck, though, won over. The truck's nose remained embedded in the gate while its rear spun freely onto the road.

Mahegan quickly steered away from the spin, encouraging its momentum, and the truck performed a 360-turn, the smoking hood breaking free from the gate as it wheeled in the direction Mahegan was spinning the tires. Abruptly, he stopped, gained his orientation, and floored the truck as another shot pinged the driver's side door and blew the stuffing out of the headrest.

His warrior instinct wanted him to stop, whip out the rifle, shoot the plane from the sky, find it, and slit the throats of anyone who tried to cause him harm.

These could be the men who had supplied the MVX-90 that had killed Colgate and his extraction team.

But he compartmentalized and kept driving. The mission was more important than his personal satisfaction. He was about a quarter mile from the entry onto 264 and he had two options.

First, he could stop, move into the forest, and then approach the intersection under cover. He, of course, would have to get the money shot first on the King Air's substructure so that the pilot and engineer could not follow him through their full-motion video and thermal capability.

Or, more reasonably, he could blow through whatever might be waiting for him. At most, he figured Nix had found the goatee man and possibly Olsen, all of whom would be anxious for revenge. He thought that maybe one of the three might be in the airplane, leaving two on the ground. Heavily armed.

He looked at his weapons. Shotgun, sniper rifle, pistol.

As he rounded the curve in the dirt road, the path widened and was framed by two ditches on either side, much like he'd seen at the main entrance. He also saw a truck parked at an angle near the intersection between the dirt road and 264.

He saw a muzzle flash from near the truck and his rear windshield shattered. The warm air rushed through the truck and he brushed glass fragments from his hair. Meanwhile, the airplane was circling tighter. Nix was intent on preventing his escape. But he had escaped worse in the past. There were generally two methods of evading an enemy. The first, and preferred, was to silently move without detection until free from possible interception. The second, and least preferred, was his current method, which he called: Go Big *and* Go Home.

In the past, if Mahegan and his men were detected, they became the 800-pound gorillas on the battlefield. Either be invisible or dominate. Half-measures didn't work in combat.

Another call came in on the radio. "Mahegan, you're every bit as tenacious as your military file suggests, but we've called the local police and they will be waiting for you. So either let us talk to you and we don't press trespassing charges or, on the off chance you make it outside, you will be a wanted man."

Mahegan ignored the comment. Hell, he was already a wanted man. Less than a quarter mile to go to the blacktop. Well-aimed sniper shots from ahead and above. He looked at the GPS. The dirt road ended at a T-intersection with Route 264, beyond which the display showed an almost immediate blue body of water.

He could deal with water.

He fidgeted with the cruise control device, ramped up his speed, and pegged it at eighty mph. He stuffed the pistol into the bulging backpack, zipped it up, and wiggled an arm through the strap. He heard the snapping of more fire coming his way. Out of the corner of his eye, he saw a man on the left side of 264, which was less than fifty yards from him now, walking slowly backwards, waving his arms.

It was too late when he noticed that the man was backing a loaded wood-hauling truck into the intersection to block his egress. Mahegan turned the steering wheel slightly to the right. He gunned the accelerator as the man backing up the wood truck dove out of the way. The sniper from the right side of the dirt road fired successive shots into the cab. One of the extended pine logs clipped the side of the truck, snapping the mirror with a loud explosive pop.

Mahegan saw he was about to T-bone a small guardrail along 264 protecting drivers from absently driving into Croatan Sound. The guardrail would be no match for his barreling pickup truck. He did feel it though. The truck ramped upward and shot at a forty-five-degree angle into the air, clearing some rip rap rocks intended to prevent erosion and beef up the shoulder of the road.

Mahegan felt the weightless moment where the truck soared and then saw the front end begin to nose over toward the water. He unsnapped his seat belt and placed his back through the open front windshield as the truck plummeted into the water. The truck stalled and Mahegan surged through the open hole where the windshield had been, tumbling into the churning water with one hand looped through his backpack. He kicked hard off one of the headrests and into the depths of Croatan Sound.

He swam deeper, holding his breath and pulling himself far away from the truck, which was now capsizing. On his descent, he saw a buoy about a quarter mile away to his eleven o'clock from the nose of the truck.

Staying low, near the bottom of the sound, Mahegan pulled in that direction, wondering how long he could hold his breath.

As he swam, he saw the worming bullets from the airborne sniper bubbling their way through the water like chucked spears.

Chapter 21

Several hours later, as night fell, Mahegan sat on a bare zebra-striped mattress exactly like the cheap ones he had slept on in basic training. He was in the vacant dorm used to house the actors and actresses for the seasonal theater production, *The Lost Colony.*

Three minutes and twenty seconds had been the longest he had been able to stay beneath the water. It had been sufficient.

Mahegan had made it to the buoy and found an air gap inside the channel marker. He had stayed inside the bubble for what he calculated to be an hour and then began a series of long underwater swims, not unlike a porpoise, surfacing only for air and staying beneath the water until he reached the western shore of Roanoke Island near the bridge. From there it was a quick thirty-minute walk through the woods to Locklear's place, where he had scouted the bungalow from the forest, concealed by the foliage. He had watched Sheriff Johnson's maroon Buick come and go. After that, Paslowski's black F-150 had looped through. His blond-haired counterpart had jumped out and pounded on Locklear's door. Then an airplane had flown slow and low overhead, but presumably didn't loiter because of air-space issues.

They were looking for him. Local cops wanted him for murder. The Inspector General wanted him for questioning. And Copperhead, Inc. wanted him dead.

Figuring the procession would continue, he broke into Locklear's house, left her a note, and then proceeded through the woods another half mile to the theater. There he found a marginally hidden building to the east of the outdoor stage that he figured was the dorm. The rows of bunk beds and gang latrines proved him right.

Sitting on the bunk, he waited for her, digesting all that he had discovered, which he knew was only the beginning. But for the first time, he felt hopeful that he could uncover how the MVX-90s fell into enemy hands. What had taken a year to develop now had to be resolved quickly. Adham's attacks had claimed dozens of lives and it was clear he was using MVX-90s as trigger devices.

He heard the screen door bounce lightly against the wooden frame of the old dorm. "So you found this place, I see. Sounds like you've been busy," Locklear said.

Mahegan watched her approach through the darkness. He sat on the far bunk, nearest the latrine and the back exit. She was holding the white slip of paper in one hand and a reusable grocery bag in the other.

"Where'd you hear that?"

Next to Mahegan on the bunk was his rucksack packed with appropriated equipment: pistol, GPS, and two MVX-90s. The rest was lost in the crash and was probably at the bottom of the sound.

"Jesus," she said when she saw him up close. "You look like you've been through a meat grinder."

"You should see the other guys, as the saying goes."

He knew he looked rough. Mahegan had stared in the latrine mirror at his assorted cuts and bruises from the vines, thorns, glass, and impact of the truck crashing into Croatan Sound. His chest was covered in mud and slime from the marsh. Streaks of blood and muck angled across his face like a football player's eye-black. For a moment, he felt like a Croatan warrior, barechested, camouflaged, and defeating the scheming interlopers. Two showers later, with small white bars of soap remnants, the adrenaline wore off and the pain crept back into his left deltoid. Otherwise, he felt fortunate to be whole.

"Here," she said, holding out a T-shirt.

He looked at the silkscreen on the front: "Visit Chernobyl: It's Electrifying!" The dot beneath the exclamation point was a radioactive warning symbol.

"Thanks. Just when people were starting to take me seriously."

Locklear smiled. "Don't think you have any issues there, bud."

Mahegan put on the T-shirt. It fit snug, but was okay. "So what have you heard?"

"Word gets around. Heard Copperhead, Inc. blew up today."

"Sounds about right," Mahegan said.

Locklear put the canvas bag on a facing bunk and sat.

"You okay?" she asked.

"Better than some others."

"As I would expect you to be."

He watched her study him for a minute.

"Do I pass inspection?"

"A few dings, but it looks like you'll live. Want to tell me about it?"

"I'm thinking you know as much, or more, than I do," said Mahegan.

"Could be about right," she said. "Me being a deputy and all."

"So, let's start with you first."

Locklear paused. Mahegan wondered if she was calculating how much to tell him or trying to determine how much he knew. Probably both.

"The first thing is that there is a party about one hundred yards from here in an hour, so I can promise you that some folks will be wandering over here to hook up."

"We have time. Talk to me."

Locklear nodded. "Word is that there are four dead contractors, but nobody can find them."

Mahegan wondered about Olsen and whether he had survived. Didn't sound like it.

"Copperhead roped the place off, though, and declared the area a weapons hazardous domain, pursuant to their contract."

"You know why they did it, right?"

Locklear paused again, and then nodded.

"I suspect you saw some things," she said.

"I suspect I did."

"They're stealing gold," Locklear said.

"Stealing?"

"Yes. They found the *James Adger* gold and are doing something with it."

"I'm not sure whose gold they found, but I know for certain what they're doing with it," Mahegan said.

"What?" Locklear said, eagerly.

"First, tell me about the *Lucky Lindy*," Mahegan said.

Locklear dropped her eyes, and then set them on Mahegan.

"I dated Nix for a few months. He named his boat after me," she said.

"Big commitment for such a short amount of time."

"Guy was crazy. Possessive. Obsessive even."

"How long ago?" he asked.

"What is this, *Oprah*?"

"I'm piecing things together. Elizabeth."

She cocked her head, the smile fading.

"Problem with my name now?"

"Nix first."

"Okay. A few months ago. Probably explains why he hasn't changed the name yet."

"What's his boat doing at the *Teach's Pet* at two in the morning?"

"What?"

Mahegan gauged her reaction. She seemed genuinely surprised, though he considered that she was an actress.

"I took a little swim this morning."

"I watched you," she admitted. "But I didn't realize the *Lucky* was making pickups at the *Pet*."

"Wasn't a onetime thing," Mahegan said.

She reached into the bag and pulled out a six-pack of longneck Coronas. She twisted two off and handed one to Mahegan. He accepted. Then she reached in and retrieved his knife.

"Figured you'd need this," she said. She expertly flipped the blade with her wrist and it stuck into the wood floor like a shot arrow. She handed him the sheath.

Mahegan looked at Locklear and then at the knife. Reaching out, he plucked it from the floor, inspected it, and laid it on the bunk.

"Smells like Luminol. You guys are big-time here."

"They checked it for blood," she said. "Seems you clean up well in all regards."

"I didn't kill Royes and you know it."

Locklear averted her gaze and asked, "What's your interest in the *Pet*, the *Lucky*, all of this?"

"Aside from the fact that someone tried to kill me today?"

"Yes. Aside from that." She smiled.

"Might be personal," Mahegan said. He looked at her and then through the screen window where he could see the sun hanging in the western horizon. He found both distracting.

"Is this about your nightmares?"

Mahegan wondered if he had said anything in his sleep. Part of the reason he went for the swim this morning was to avoid a deep sleep with her. Rarely had a night passed where he did not wake up from a dream of Colgate's vehicle burning.

"You a shrink, too?"

"I heard you mention your friend, Colgate, several times in your sleep."

Mahegan nodded, saying, "Not surprised."

"I see. You're still trying to figure out if you can trust me?" Locklear prodded him.

"That, too."

"So, tell me what you know about the *Adger* gold," she said.

"Not yet," he said. "Tell me what you know about Adam Wilhoyt."

Mahegan had intentionally used The American Taliban's birth name to gauge her reaction. "Elizabeth" kept sliding through his mind and he had remembered from JSOC's extensive dossier on Mullah Adham, aka Adam Wilhoyt, that his lost love had been named Elizabeth Carlsen. Locklear had so many occupations and interests that they all seemed to collide into one synthetic persona. Who was she really? Was the *C* necklace really a gesture to the Croatan or could she be a Carlsen and the necklace was a Carlsen heirloom?

He watched a cloud pass across her eyes as they darkened and looked away at the mention of Wilhoyt's name. The first time he had mentioned the name, she'd given no tell. This time seemed different.

"I don't know much about him other than what I read in the paper. The American Taliban. Murdering civilians. That's it. Why do you ask?"

Her response was passable, but suspect, in Mahegan's view. He said nothing.

As if to change the topic, she said, "There was another attack today. Suffolk. Over fifty dead."

Mahegan remained focused, but couldn't help wincing at the mention of more innocents killed, most likely involving an MVX-90.

"Now you tell me something useful," Locklear demanded.

"Get me a small airplane and a parachute and I'll fill you in."

Locklear broke her sullen mood and smiled, then laughed. She *was* an actress, Mahegan thought.

"I can actually do that, but I need more to go on," she said.

Mahegan shook his head. They stared at each other for about ten minutes, drinking their Coronas. Mahegan thought about the hundreds of combat missions he had led. Whether in Iraq or Afghanistan or some other fourth-world country there was always that moment where he had to decide whether he had any cards to be played and, if so, when to play them. He had dealt with duplicitous Iraqi terrorists, scheming Afghan warlords, and two-timing Balkan hucksters.

And yet, he had not figured out Locklear. She played too many roles, from deputy to treasure hunter to actress. His instinct was that none of them were real. Mahegan's gut was telling him that he was on to something having to do with Colgate's death and at the moment that was all that mattered to him. But the pieces of the puzzle had begun to fall into place for him, mostly.

"I'm not one for playing a lot of games or for a lot of bullshit. I'm thinking you found Miller Royes's body somewhere and floated him into me. I mean that's an awful big chance for me to hit a dead body in wide-open water. You've been watching me and think I can help with the gold, which I can. But it begs a few questions. Did you kill Royes? I don't think so, but there's the chance that you did. Are you working with Copperhead? Again, I don't think so, but I look for the second and third layer of stuff. On the outside you're this reasonably hot chick with quirky connections to the sheriff and other locals, plus in DC and the Pentagon. I've got you figured to be a government type of some sort. Maybe Treasury because of your interest in the gold. Always connecting the dots. But there's something bigger you're connected to and I haven't quite figured that out yet. And I'm trying to determine if you know more about Adam Wilhoyt than you're letting on."

He paused. He noticed a slight tic in her cheek. Her countenance never changed, but she got a faraway look in her eyes.

"But I will figure it out," he added.

He watched Locklear take a long pull on her beer, much more than a sip. As she removed the bottle from her lips, he noticed the perfectly formed teeth and the deep, smooth tan on her face.

"Reasonably hot?"

Mahegan nodded.

"Within reason."

Locklear smiled back. "Keep thinking. You're doing

great. Want to go to the party? Then we can get your 'airplane and parachute,' big guy." She made quotation marks with her fingers, mocking him a bit. She stood and showed him her ass through a set of pink running shorts as she turned, picked up the bag, and stepped outside.

Mahegan stood and stretched. He ached. He thought about Nix and the private military contractors who would be coming after him. It was no secret in this small community that he had hooked up with Locklear. A sniper could have him in the crosshairs at this very moment. He didn't feel it, though. What he felt was that he had bored a hole the size of Montana through Copperhead's operation. The gold, the MVX-90s, the dead contractors, the *Lucky Lindy*, and the landing craft. Still, he didn't think he had it all.

In fact, he knew he didn't. He needed to make contact with General Savage, and he needed an airplane and a parachute. During his brief interlude in Locklear's bungalow, he had borrowed her computer and even left her a few clues, which he was certain she would discover.

He was 150 miles from where he needed to be. The problem was that the Atlantic Ocean was a big place.

Chapter 22

He waited at the dorm while Locklear went back to her bungalow to prep for the party. An hour later he was walking with Locklear to the amphitheater for the *Lost Colony* production cast party to close down the season.

She was dressed in a paisley sarong, a green halter, and sandals that were similar to her Tevas. She had showered and smelled like fresh citrus. He had taken his third shower of the day in the dorm, but still wore the Chernobyl T-shirt. He'd popped two Motrin that she had brought him from her medicine cabinet, but he still ached.

"Won't I be conspicuous?" he'd asked when she'd offered the ridiculous T-shirt.

"Hiding in plain sight, right? Fuck 'em if they can't take a joke. You want to trust me? This is how we do it."

"Did you kill Royes?"

She cast a sideways glance at him.

"No, but you're looking good for it." She smiled. Mahegan didn't. When they arrived, she led him past the cedar shake–tiled box office and onto the landing of the concrete mezzanine. Mahegan looked down and saw the stage some hundred yards away with rows of seats angling up toward him, spreading outward like a fan. Above the set he saw Croatan Sound and the *Teach's Pet*, innocent and idle. Beyond that he could see the dunes of Kitty Hawk and, farther over the dunes, the Atlantic Ocean.

"Stick with me," she said, clasping his hand. "There are some real freaks here."

They entered the stage from the west, which blended actual forest with the set. Mahegan picked his way along the trail as Locklear led. Standing on the edge, he saw the klieg lights blazing onto a stage filled with over one hundred actors and actresses dressed in period costumes from the sixteenth century. Noticeable were the dozens of American Indians who were dressed in their tribal garb. The men had streaked war paint across their chests and faces. For a moment, Mahegan could see the commingling of British colonists and American Indians as it might have happened five hundred years ago. And he saw himself only a few hours before, staring in the mirror of the dorm bathroom after his narrow escape from Copperhead, the cuts and bruises mimicking the actors' war paint and warrior image.

Then they stopped at a tree with "Croatoan" carved in the bark.

"The colonists left this sign," Locklear said. "Either they were attacked and slaughtered or they migrated west across the sound or south to Hatteras."

"The Moline crosses," Mahegan said, quietly.

"That and other signs speak to migration, not slaughter." She hesitated and said, "Plus, you might be Croatan. You would never do that, right? You would defend. Protect."

"You don't know me."

She smiled. "I know you better than you think. Anyway, the East Carolina University research project found a Kendall family ring in Hatteras, too. The new theory is that the settlers split up to increase chances of survival. Some went to Hatteras, some to Dare Mainland where the bombing range is, and some went to what's now a golf course across from Edenton."

Mahegan listened as he scanned the assortment of actors milling to their front.

Locklear introduced him to Adrian Dakota, the Lumbee Indian who played Wanchese, Chief Manteo's rival. Dakota looked the part. He had painted his bare, chiseled chest with white spirals and streaked his face with red and orange war paint. Dakota's shaved head glistened with sweat.

"Adrian, this is Jake Mahegan, a friend of mine."

"Mahegan?" Dakota said. "Wolf."

They shook hands and Mahegan nodded. "One interpretation. It was 'Mohegan' but got changed somewhere along the way."

"Iroquois?" the man asked.

"Probably."

"You're too fair to be Lumbee," Dakota said. Then he added with a chuckle and a sweeping hand across the set, "Perhaps Croatan?"

"Locklear seems to think so." Mahegan studied Dakota. If he closed his eyes, he might imagine the man wearing a business suit instead of five-hundred-year-old Indian warrior garb that looked like an early predecessor to the modern-day jockstrap.

"Ever see the production?" Dakota asked Mahegan.

"No."

"He just got out of the military," Locklear said.

Mahegan wondered why that would disqualify him from having ever seen *The Lost Colony.*

"I grew up in Frisco, but never made it here," Mahegan said. "But I know of it."

Two more "Indians" approached.

"Hey, Adrian, let's go give Manteo a wedgie," said the first.

Mahegan watched the two younger men, one who was not American Indian, but deeply tanned and could play the part from afar.

"Grow up, guys. We want him back next year."

"Manteo? You think he did a good job? You were so much better," Locklear said.

"That was five years ago, and he did well enough to take it over. I liked being the bad guy too much," Dakota said.

"Adrian, Jake would like to ask you a question," Locklear said.

Dakota looked at the two role players and gave them a nod. "Go mess with Manteo, but don't piss him off."

Mahegan gave Locklear a curious look.

"You wanted to ask Adrian what he does for a living, other than being a kick-ass bad guy Indian that slaughters the white man."

Dakota flinched. "That's your version."

Mahegan cut to the chase. "So, what's your second job?"

"Nicely put. I fly the advertisements up and down the beach, drop skydivers, shuttle people around the OBX. You know, 'Eat at Joe's Fish Market!' banners. That kind of thing."

"You're a pilot?" Mahegan asked.

"Yes. I fly a de Havilland Dash Six, Twin Otter."

Mahegan nodded. "I would like to talk to you about leasing your services," Mahegan said. "One way."

"I charge either by the hour or depending on where you're going, by the distance."

"I'm sure we can make an arrangement. You got a GPS on that thing?"

Dakota furrowed his brow. "Never really needed one."

"I've got one, as long as you can hold an azimuth."

After a pause, Dakota said, "This is legit, right? No drugs, man."

"Totally legit. Consider me a one-way trip. I'll need a parachute."

"But I still have to come back. What drop zone?"

"So charge me round-trip and for the parachute. I'm good with that. We'll discuss the drop zone when we are at the airplane."

"When do we leave?"

"How soon do you get done here?"

Dakota laughed. "I thought you'd never ask. I'm tired of wearing this bullshit."

"Wait a minute," Locklear said. "You're leaving now?"

"I'm thinking we don't have a lot of time here," said Mahegan.

"Give me thirty minutes and meet me at the airfield across the street," Dakota said, referring to Dare County Municipal Airport less than a mile away. "I'll park my pickup truck along the fence. Plane's just on the other side. How far are we going?"

"About four hundred miles round-trip."

Dakota whistled. "That's pushing my comfort zone. We'll need to refuel at the destination."

"No chance for that," Mahegan said. "I'll explain more at the airfield."

Locklear walked Mahegan to her Defender.

"You going to tell me what this is all about? I noticed you took a wetsuit and my smartphone charger from my place."

"Observant," he said. "I'm figuring you got me involved because you knew Copperhead was on to the gold, but you couldn't figure out what they were doing with it."

"About right."

"I don't trust you. Plain and simple. So all I'm going to tell you is that Copperhead figured out a way to make the gold theirs. You find the gold inside the state limits, the state owns it, especially if there's a historical record like the *Adger* gold, as you call it."

"That's right. Insurance companies and the state of North Carolina will tie that up in court and the discoverer will be lucky to get anything other than reimbursement for their efforts to find the gold. Peanuts," she said.

"Well, Copperhead not only found the gold, they found a way around the law."

Mahegan jumped out of her Defender, ducked into the dorm, and grabbed his rucksack, knife, and the recharged GPS, powered up by Locklear's smartphone charger. He scrolled through the saved locations, checking to make sure his destination was still there. He powered down the device, saving precious battery life. He checked his pistol and decided it was still usable. He triple-bagged the ammunition and the weapon, packed his rucksack, pulled on the dark wetsuit he'd found in Locklear's closet, and strapped his knife to his leg.

"That was an old boyfriend's. Looks better on you," she said.

"I can't be choosy here, but I need this tonight."

"Tell me this. How can they make it theirs?"

Mahegan paused. "I will trade with you. Can I trust you that much?"

"Of course," she replied, locking eyes with him. "I'm serious."

"So am I." He handed her the box with the MVX-90. "I need you to do me a favor. This is what killed my friend in Afghanistan. They make them in the Research Triangle and there's a warehouse full of them that were tested at Dare County Bombing Range. I think Copperhead found these when they won the contract for the bomb disposal and clearance project and then figured out how to cash in on them."

"By selling them to the bad guys?"

"Exactly. So, on the off chance I don't make it back, can you get this to a friend of mine at Fort Bragg? His name is Patch. We served together. He'll know what to do with it."

"Patch? Of course," she said. "But you'll make it back just fine." She looked at the phone number scribbled on the box and nodded.

"A deal's a deal. Go to the bookstore or download it on your iPad, but find a copy of *Ship of Gold in the Deep Blue Sea*. Read it and you'll figure out what I'm doing. Just remember I'll be somewhere in the Galaxy."

She looked at him curiously. "Okay," she said, drawing out the last syllable. "That narrows it down for me."

"Actually, it does. Quite a bit."

They were quickly back in the Defender and she was dropping him off at the airfield. He kissed her on the cheek as if he were just another commuter heading to work.

Which, in a way, he was.

Locklear decided to skip the rest of the party. She walked into her small living room and sat on her sofa as she tugged at her laptop. She flipped up the screen, powered on, and waited as the MacBook came to life and connected with her Wi-Fi. She went straight to Google and typed in the book Mahegan had mentioned, *Ship of Gold in the Deep Blue Sea*.

Of course any treasure hunter worth her weight in unfound gold knew about Tommy Thompson and his amazing discovery. But what did that have to do with what Samuel Nix was doing with the *Adger* gold, she wondered?

On instinct, she went to the history section for her browser and tracked the last websites her computer had visited.

As she suspected, she didn't recall the last three.

The first was the Virginia Beach Municipal Court website that showed a recent PDF download. She went to her download folder and found a document filed earlier that day by Copperhead, Inc. to establish a one-square-mile box around a latitude and longitude referenced as being 140 miles east of Cape Hatteras.

What the hell?

The second website was the Wikipedia link to the SS *Central America*, a gold-carrying partner of the *James Adger* that sank in the same hurricane back in September, 1857. Treasure hunter Tommy Thompson and his Columbus Ohio Discovery Group had located the shipwreck and retrieved nearly a billion dollars' worth of gold from the ocean floor. Beneath that link was a Google link that searched the term, "Galaxy."

The last link was an open records search of the government contract the Navy had with Copperhead, Inc. and all associated purchases, to include a C-12 airplane with sonar search capability, the landing craft, assorted buildings constructed on Dare County Bombing Range, a 180-foot side trawler called the *Ocean Ranger*, and multiple vehicles.

Locklear snapped the top of her MacBook shut and stared at the wall clock. She thought she heard the hum of the de Havilland buzzing low over her bungalow as it made its way toward a spot 140 miles offshore.

How Mahegan had figured it out, she didn't know, but she was certain now he would lead her to the gold.

Chapter 23

The assembly line was in motion.

Actually it was in continuous motion. Samuel Nix stared at the blinking dot on the map. While he was still reeling from the destruction that Mahegan had wreaked on his operation, he thought it was all still salvageable.

Nix's thermal and radar-imaging plane had found the *Adger* gold by pure chance. Six months ago, the pilot had flown a north-to-south track over the bombing range and imaged the gold sitting in twenty feet of water in a cove riddled with water moccasins and alligators. No wonder no one had found it. He sent Falco on a dive mission, and he confirmed they were indeed bricks of gold nestled deep in the silt. He and Falco had studied, schemed, and developed their plan before beginning a sophisticated series of logistics.

One hundred and forty miles offshore was a shipwreck site that explorer Tommy Thompson had called "Galaxy," in 1987, wrongly believing the location to be one of the top three most likely locations of the SS *Central America*. While the gold Nix had discovered had nothing to do with Thompson's gold find, the legal

precedent of "finders keepers" had everything to do
with Nix's strategy to keep the gold.

Nix knew that Thompson had briefly inspected the
shipwreck two miles below sea level using his underwater robot. He had found mounds of anthracite coal
used to push a side-wheel steamer, but no gold. Nor
had he been able to identify the ship. The location, in
Nix's mind, was the perfect solution to the "problem"
of their gold discovery inside US territory.

Nix, a Navy man, knew about the twelve-mile
coastal boundaries of nations and the "finders keepers"
law that Thompson's eventual discovery had begot. Before the law, over eighty insurance companies had
crawled out of the woodwork, laying claim to the one
billion dollars in gold Thompson had found. After
much legal wrangling, a judge in Virginia Beach, however, issued a verdict that Thompson and the Columbus
Discovery Group of investors that had funded Thompson's operation were entitled to keep 92.7 percent of
the gold, or roughly $927 million.

Of course, no one had seen Tommy Thompson or
the gold since then, but Nix knew all he needed to do
was use the same methodology Thompson had.

He continued to look at the map. He could see the
triangular point of Cape Hatteras where it reached outward into the Atlantic. The Labrador Current pushing
down from Nova Scotia met with the Gulf Stream flowing northward to create this series of arrowhead-
shaped sand spits.

He had a world map on his Vizio high-definition
plasma display, which he had billed to the government,
of course. On this map were a series of lighted indicators. He could scale the map in or out using a remote
control. The United States and other countries were a
tan neutral color with the oceans indicated in deep blue,

almost black. In his command post on the Dare County bombing range, Nix looked at the digital map with the green blinking light indicating a position one hundred and forty miles to the east of Cape Hatteras. That light indicated the side trawler, *Ocean Ranger*, was operational.

Another green blinking light indicated that the *Lucky Lindy* was moored next to the *Ocean Ranger*.

A third green blinking light, moving from south to north and heading directly toward the side trawler, appeared to be right on schedule. His plan was coming together. The *Lindy* should have already delivered the last pallet of gold and munitions. He had made an executive decision to leave a few gold remnants in the Long Shoal Creek. He had even rationalized that if anyone argued he had taken it, he could simply "discover" the gold and point at the remaining gold bricks as the entire find.

He pressed the remote twice and a series of blue lights appeared on his map, beginning in Karachi, Pakistan. The south-to-north green blinking light was a ship that had been at sea for two weeks, having departed Karachi and made port in Dar es Salaam, Capetown, Grenada, and Great Inagua, Bahamas, before closing in on its designated latitude and longitude. All of these stops appeared as blue lights, which indicated no problem.

All good, Nix thought. He smiled. Mahegan had disrupted their operation, but only one of the product lines. Mahegan was focused on the MVX-90s, which Nix would destroy tomorrow as they did another controlled detonation of several hundred found warheads. Mahegan didn't have the smoking gun he thought he had. Selling the MVX-90s was just a product line that had run its course, and Nix didn't need it enough to risk getting caught with the warehouse full of weapons. But the gold, that was another line that would pay off hugely. Project Rainbow. It was all about sustainable business practices and diversification.

He punched the remote again and was now watching the radar from the *Ocean Ranger*.

As the radar scanned, a small airplane appeared off the bow of the north-facing ship. It was flying slowly at 10,000 feet.

Unusual but no threat, Nix thought, and then shut down the monitor as he began to think through everything he had going on.

Vinny Falco came into the room and said, "Just got word that Mahegan hooked up with Dakota at the cast party for *The Lost Colony*."

"The pilot?"

"Yep."

"When?"

"About two hours ago."

"Long enough to fly a hundred and fifty miles," Nix said more to himself than to Falco.

Chapter 24

Mahegan checked the GPS and said to Dakota, "See anything?"

Dakota was flying by instruments, but had a PVS-14 night-vision monocle that he'd strapped onto his head. They were nearly 140 miles east of Cape Hatteras over the Atlantic Ocean.

"I'm going to tilt the nose about forty-five degrees to the horizon. We're at ten thousand feet so should be no worries. This goggle should tell me if anything with lights is on the horizon."

Mahegan felt the airplane tip noticeably forward as Dakota punched the autopilot button. The wind buffeted them a bit, but they held in a steady dive as Dakota searched the black expanse nearly two miles beneath them. The GPS put them approximately six miles to the north of the lat-long Mahegan had found on the Loran navigation device, the location that also corresponded with Wikipedia's lat-long for Tommy Thompson's original Galaxy site. To Mahegan, Dakota's night-vision goggle reminded him of so many combat missions he had led. That thought put him at ease.

Just another mission.

After about thirty seconds, Dakota said, "Not seeing anything, man."

"Let me see the fourteens," Mahegan said, referring to the night-vision goggle.

Dakota leveled the Twin Otter and reset his autopilot before reaching up and removing the head harness. Mahegan placed it on his head, refocused the lens, and said, "Okay, give me another tilt."

"We're at eight thousand feet. If whatever we're trying to find has any radar, or worse, then we could be screwed."

"Then climb and point it back down," Mahegan said with little patience. He removed the goggle from the harness and placed it to his eye like a pirate searching for land from the bridge of a ship. As he felt the nose tilt over again, he saw a small wink of light from his two o'clock.

"There," he said. "Two o'clock. That's got to be it."

"Can't see it with the naked eye, man, but if you say so. I'm about to hit my halfway point on fuel."

Mahegan stepped out of the co-pilot seat and into the cargo bay of the Twin Otter. He pulled the parachute onto his back, fastening the leg straps and then tightening them. He secured his rucksack with two snap-hooks to the D-ring that would normally hold the reserve parachute. Once again, he held the night-vision goggle to his eye, catching a bead on the winking light, and then secured the goggle in his ruck.

He looked at Dakota, who said, "Sorry about not having a reserve parachute for you. Jumping with no reserve? Huge balls, man."

Mahegan focused. "What are the winds?"

Dakota looked at the anemometer and said, "Thirty knots south by southwest up here. Probably less at sea level. I'm doing one hundred knots. So your net is about seventy."

"Thanks for the lift, chief."

Mahegan heard Dakota say, "Now get out of here—"

And then he was gone, floating through the warm night 150 miles off the tip of Cape Hatteras, arms spread, stabilizing his flight for the first few seconds, then diving and plunging through the air like a comic book hero.

Not only was this stupidly dangerous with no re-serve parachute, he had no altimeter either, which was reckless. But it was all the equipment Dakota had on hand without a two-hour diversion to his equipment shed in some other county. Mahegan kept his eye on the light and calculated that once the facility got big enough to recognize, he would deploy his parachute. Good plan, he told himself sardonically.

That moment came sooner rather than later. It had taken him less than a minute to career nearly two miles through the sky. With simple gravity pulling him down, the trip should have taken three minutes. Yet he had an-gled his body to accelerate his speed and to fly toward the light marking what he hoped was the ship he be-lieved to be over the Galaxy site, cutting by a full third his air time. He tugged at his parachute cord and felt the risers release from the pack tray. The ripstop nylon parachute caught air, slowing his descent to the point that the leg straps made it questionable whether he might ever produce children of his own.

As he grasped the toggles, he steadied his descent and began to fly toward the light. He held his path into the wind to maintain altitude. Using one hand to steer his square parachute, he used the other to retrieve the goggle and assess his positioning relative to his target.

Which was moving.

He quickly determined he had deployed his parachute at about two thousand feet above sea level, which was high. Though, better high than low. In the green-lit world of the night-vision goggle, he saw a ship moving from south to north. By Mahegan's estimation it was no more than one hundred feet long, looked cargo in nature, and was moving slowly . . . as if it was looking for something.

He switched the goggle to his other hand, steered his parachute toward the north to follow the ship, and lined up behind the stern of the vessel. He was now some one thousand feet above sea level. The equivalent of three football fields was between him and the Atlantic Ocean.

He could smell the salt water and feel the thrum of the ship churning to the north. Seconds before he was to plunge into the ice-cold water, he grimaced. He was jumping into a lat-long coordinate that was on a thief's global positioning system. The boat beneath him could be chugging steadily to Bangor, Maine, for all he knew, and the coordinates could have been a decoy or old waypoint. His calculation was that Nix and Copperhead, Inc. were spiriting the found *Adger* gold to this little-known shipwreck location where they were conducting a "reverse find."

What he had put together was the *Lucky Lindy* was moving a pallet at a time out to sea as if the boat were doing Mahi deep-sea fishing runs daily. The *Lindy*, he guessed, was offloading the gold onto the government purchased side trawler where some Copperhead, Inc. employees would then use the winch to lower it into the shipwreck on the ocean floor. They probably let it sit there for a few days to accumulate some of the local detritus in its engravings so that the experts who would surely examine the gold would declare it found in the deep blue sea as opposed to originating from the silt of the Long Shoal River.

Doing some quick calculations, Mahegan figured his best shot was to steer toward the steaming ship and perhaps find a landing spot there instead of the ocean. He toggled hard with the wind and quartered a bit to the west so that he could ride against the southwest wind into the moving ship. It was a bit like landing on an aircraft carrier, he presumed, without knowing his own speed, the speed of the ship or, with any certainty, the wind direction and speed at landing altitude.

Other than that, he had it figured out.

As he accelerated and descended simultaneously, Mahegan saw that the lights were searchlights off the nose of the ship. The lights were scanning the water for something, moving back and forth as if in an auto lot with fantastic savings to be had. With the focus of the crew to the bow, Mahegan aimed to the aft end of the ship. Knowing that there was bound to be some superstructure and that he was coming in at great speed, probably twenty knots, if not more, he needed to circle wide and land into the wind. To do so would possibly force him into the path of the searchlights or, at a minimum, into the field of vision of the forward facing crew.

He took a chance and whipped past the rear of the ship doing about thirty knots now at about two hundred feet above sea level. What he saw was not promising. The ship was a merchant cargo rig with a cabin and command center all the way in the rear. The deck was relatively clear, save a few containers. The gunwale appeared to be forty feet above sea level. Ideally, he could swing out to the bow and land on top of the containers, which were probably solid. To do so, though, would put him in the crosshairs of the searchlights and whatever else might be onboard, so he excluded it as an option.

Options: suicide run up the middle of the searchlights; land on the head of a pin atop the bridge, laden with all its antennae and satellite dishes; land in the water as close as possible to the ship and find a ladder.

He had about five seconds to make up his mind as he turned back into the wind about one hundred feet away from the ship. If the bow of the vessel was twelve o'clock, Mahegan put himself at about two o'clock, just outside the arc of the searchlights. He adjusted his flight path to become as perpendicular to the ship as possible to avoid lateral movement that was easier for those on the ship to notice. He was quartering in against the starboard side and still hadn't decided what he was going to do, though he had, by default, ruled out the suicide run up the middle.

As the ship grew in clarity, he saw a third option. Between the bridge and the gunwale was an alley of sorts. If he could slide into the gap, he might be able to find safe harbor.

The vessel was upon him quickly. He was a bit low, but caught an updraft that lifted him over the gunwale. He pulled hard on his left toggle as his body slammed into the side of the bridge. Thankfully, he had the sense to come into the wind and slow his descent to maybe ten knots. But it still hurt as he slid alongside the steel wall, rivets tearing at his wetsuit.

The air left his canopy with a suddenness that dropped him into the alley. He tumbled head over heels once and then stood up perfectly as if he were doing a gymnastics move. He unlatched both canopy release assemblies and quickly withdrew his pistol while stuffing the parachute into a crevice.

He went to one knee, slid his rucksack onto his back, and held his pistol in a military shooter's grip aimed toward the bow.

His first thought was, *A ten from the Russian judge.*

Then he heard shouting from the bridge and the bow.

He recognized the words as Arabic.

Chapter 25

Mullah Adham, aka Adam Wilhoyt, squinted into the bright light. It was time for another television appearance. He checked his watch and remembered the nine-hour difference between Iraq time and the United States' Eastern time.

He always had to factor that into his broadcasts. When would they be looking for him? When could he slip in and out of the Internet domain with the least possible chance at detection? He was already cloning his Internet Protocol address in multiple different locations around the world, some even in the United States. He had hacked into the source code of Cisco Systems, which gave him the ability to be anywhere at any time.

He was the world's most wanted terrorist now that Bin Laden was dead.

He thought about the next series of attacks. How to characterize them? He raked his fingers through his beard, contemplating. Yes, the next attacks would be on an entirely different plane with a much larger end in mind. He needed two things: First, to continue to apply pressure to allow him to stay inside the decision-making cycle of the Americans. Second, he needed more troops, which he knew were on the way. His capture teams had been active in Afghanistan, especially.

Once he got his new troops on the ground in America, the next attacks would happen with exponential frequency. He liked that word.

Exponential. Increasing rapidly.

Let the masses think about that one, he mused. Exponential frequency. Exponential terror. The media had used his phrase, *inverse attacks*, throughout their reporting. He was glad to give their lemming talking heads another word to parrot on his behalf.

He wondered about the shipment of the prisoners and whether this next crop would have the talent for precision execution that Chikatilo and his team had seemed to pull off with minimum interference.

To Mullah Adham, it was all about human capital, and he was no different than a modern-day CEO or entrepreneur who needed to find the right people to put on the bus. He chuckled at that. *I've got the right people on the van.* Crazy motherfuckers who will one minute appear to be construction workers and the next minute blow up critical targets. And we've got the Mother of All Battles, as Saddam Hussein had once called it. MOAB, baby. But this MOAB stands for something else: Massive Ordnance Air Burst!

It's all good, he thought.

He checked the flag and the AK-74 prop, adjusted his turban, squinted at the bright lights, and said into the camera, "Listen very closely, America. Brother Osama built a deep bench. Doesn't matter that he's dead. The truth is, now the bench is better than the team that was on the field. Look at Syria and ISIS. All of us are brothers in arms and we are more brutal than ever before. Some may call us the Junior Varsity. Well, okay. Put me in, coach!"

He laughed like a Halloween haunt. This was his most animated video yet. Sneering at the camera, Mullah Adham took a more somber tone.

"Three days, three million people. Three days, three critical targets. Three days, to the third degree. *Exponential*. And this is no longer the 'Mother of All Battles,' but it is a MOAB!"

He stood and walked as the camera panned and followed. Viewers could see the hostage hunched and kneeling on the floor, hands bound behind his back. The knife glinted in the camera's spotlight as Adham cut the ties binding the captive's hands. He looked in the camera and lowered his voice, taking a much more somber and serious tone.

"I would never kill a defenseless man. And just to show you we can kill a single individual or thousands of people at once, we will do this."

Uday and Hamasa stepped into the camera range wielding large curved swords. Adham handed his small knife to the captive who still was sporting the tan sandbag over his head that read, "*Life's a Bitch.*"

The captive they had held for less than a week stood and crouched into a fighting position as Adham removed the sandbag and held it in his hand. Like a referee at a boxing match, he leaned in and said, "Fight!"

Uday's large body momentarily blocked the camera. The prisoner circled toward Uday, placing his back toward the camera, and the three men began to move in a counterclockwise direction. Hamasa swung his sword low into the midsection of the prisoner, who doubled over. Uday lifted his sword high, in what Adham knew was a choreographed move, and swung ferociously downward, severing the man's head. The body fell in plain sight of the camera while the head rolled out of view.

Adham stuck his face into the lens of the camera and flashed an eerie smile. "More hostages. More mayhem. Exponential, baby!" Adham shouted into the camera.

He stepped behind the camera, which was still live, thinking about the next move against the Americans. Where were they? Would they find him?

After all, even though they were redeployed from Iraq, they were all around him.

He zoomed the camera on the back of the bloody, severed head lying next to the "*Life's a Bitch!*" sandbag that had been the hostage's shroud. The back of the sandbag was facing up. It read:

And Then You Die!

General Stanley Bream, the Inspector General of the Army, sat in the basement of the Pentagon with several other high-ranking officials to include the Chairman of the Joint Chiefs of Staff and the Secretary of Defense.

"Do we know who was just killed?" Arthur Buchanan, the Secretary of Defense, asked.

"We have no idea without getting a look at the face. The uniform had no nametape. The intelligence teams are doing visual and audio forensics as we speak," General Frank Thomas, the Chairman of Joint Chiefs of Staff, said.

"With the attacks on Fort Brackett and Suffolk, and now this, we obviously have to take this guy seriously," Buchanan said.

"Three days, three million people? That's a stretch, sir," Thomas countered.

"Well, general, a few days ago you told me our military bases were secure." Buchanan sat back after scolding the chairman and said, "Anybody have any thoughts?"

Bream piped up. "The reference to MOAB, sir, might be a clue."

"To what? The mother of all battles?" Buchanan scoffed.

"No, sir. To the largest nonnuclear bomb in existence, called a Massive Ordnance Air Burst. DoD did a recall on all of those a few years ago. We should check them to make sure we've got them all," Bream said.

The Air Force Chief of Staff, General Mike Sharpley, was quick to comment. "We've got them, sir. But we'll be glad to do as the *Army* Inspector General suggests."

Bream took this as the jab it was intended to be and played humble.

"I'm sure they're all accounted for, sir. It's just an idea since he made reference to it."

"It's a good idea. General Sharpley, have an inventory done immediately. I want to know in an hour what our status is," Buchanan directed, and then departed.

Bream walked to the window of the E-Ring conference room, poured himself a cup of coffee, and stared at the Potomac River and the night lights of Washington, DC. His mind ran through his latest victory.

It's a good idea, the Secretary of Defense had said. Then the man had acted on his recommendation. That had settled that. It was clear to him that he was the right choice to be the next Army Chief of Staff.

After about forty-five minutes of waiting, the meeting reconvened abruptly, aides madly scurrying around passing out sheets of paper labeled TOP SECRET/SPECAT. Bream stood behind his designated chair anxious to see what information the paper contained.

Buchanan reentered the conference room looking harried, obviously already having been briefed on what they were about to learn.

The Air Force Chief of Staff looked sheepish and suddenly Bream's throat clutched. He was just digging for a good idea, grasping at another rung on the ladder. He hadn't thought there was a remote possibility that he was correct that there might be a missing MOAB.

"Ladies and gentlemen, if you'll have a seat, General Sharpley will tell us about his inventory of Air Force MOABs that was just conducted," Buchanan said.

"Sir, all of the MOABs are kept in an underground bunker in Nevada. We are supposed to have forty-two and we have forty-two."

Bream heard a collective sigh around the room, but not from him. He was waiting for the other shoe to drop.

"But one of them is a concrete dummy, which means that we have a live unaccounted-for MOAB out there somewhere."

Dear God, Bream thought. That was tantamount to having a suitcase nuke on the loose in the country. And he was probably sitting at ground zero for its detonation.

"We have to alert the President immediately," Buchanan said. Then turning to the Chairman of the Joint Chiefs, he said, "Now does three million seem so unlikely?"

Bream thought about it. If Mullah Adham was going to kill three million people it had to be in a high-density area. He had several thoughts running through his mind, but would claim victory here and live to fight another day.

"All military installations are to go immediately to full alert," Buchanan ordered. "And, General Sharpley, find that MOAB."

Chapter 26

Mahegan pressed his body against the metal frame of the ship's bridge. The bow spotlights were criss-crossing the sky like an airbase under attack with anti-aircraft gunners searching for bombers. He could hear the wet smack of the ocean swells against the hull some thirty feet below his position. Sounds of men running along the ladders and deck mixed with the metallic screech of rubbing ship metal.

He recognized the shouts in Arabic as orders to grab ropes, secure fenders, and prepare to dock.

Prepare to dock?

His initial concern that his unique entry to the boat had caused alarm ebbed quickly as he watched the choreography of a ship crew move not to battle sta-tions, but to the specific points on a ship that required manning prior to docking.

He looked to his right and saw a rope as thick as his forearm coiled around a circular winch. Three huge rubber fenders linked together like sausages were stacked directly behind him and may have been what softened his landing. There was nowhere for him to move with-

out being noticed and he suspected he was seconds
away from being discovered.

Mahegan retrieved his knife at the same time he heard
a metallic door open from the cabin. The door opened
toward him, providing him both cover and concealment for the moment. A man dressed in dark clothing
with an AK-47 slung across his back leaned over to
begin unfurling the rope.

Mahegan used the butt of his K-Bar to strike the
man on the rear of his skull. His target slumped forward, unconscious. He still wasn't clear on who was
friend or foe and didn't want to start killing anyone just
yet.

He secured the man's AK-47 rifle and dragged him
toward the rubber fenders, leaving him there as he
quickly moved toward the open door. He snapped the
night-vision goggle on his head and scanned the long
axis of the boat using the door as cover. He could see
several men scurrying across what appeared to be steel
planks covering a cargo hold, the kind street crews
used to cover a work in progress.

The boat slowed as he entered the cabin and stepped
into a stairwell, or what he knew the sailors called ladders. He raced to the bottom, spiraling four times, and
then came upon a metal door that locked from the outside. He saw a bar nestled across the door resting in
u-shaped joints, one of which had a padlock securing
the bar in place.

Curious about what might lie behind the door, Mahegan used the AK-47 to butt-stroke the lock and un-
hinge the securing mechanism. He removed the lock,
tossed it aside, and then lifted the bar, which freed the
door.

He pulled open the door and was immediately knocked
back by a stench that he recognized as sweat, feces, and

urine. He turned on the Maglite beneath the barrel of the AK-47 and saw about twenty pairs of eyes staring back at him. They were silent, cowering, seemingly expectant of harsh treatment.

He stepped back into the hall and closed the door, placing the bar over the u-joints. Then he turned around and raced up the steps. He had no idea what he had just seen. Prisoners. Like on a slave ship.

Or ghosts.

As he reached the door he had first entered, he noticed it was now closed. He continued up the ladder until he reached another door, which was open. He could see inside the ship's bridge. There were four men staring ahead, watching the bow and something else. He heard voices on the radio.

"*Le Concord*, this is *Ocean Ranger*, you're fifty meters from our stern."

Then a voice from inside the cockpit said, "This is *Le Concord*, we've got you. We will come alongside and then my crew will throw the ropes and establish the bridge."

Mahegan had been on missions in his past when he had witnessed underway replenishment, a form of transferring supplies between two ships without having them collide.

"Aye, *Le Concord*. Be careful, we've got another vessel tethered to us."

He quietly retreated to the door through which he had entered, opened it, and stepped back into his original position on the deck. It seemed that the entire crew was focused on coming alongside the *Ocean Ranger*.

From his vantage along the starboard side of stern, he saw the anchored *Ocean Ranger*, highlighted by the *Le Concord* spotlights as if on a Broadway stage. It had a big boom arm hanging over it like a construction crane. A transfer of some type was going to occur. Mahegan guessed it was going to be the prisoners. Maybe they were slave labor at the gold drop site? Or maybe they were slave labor for Copperhead?

It hit him like a roundhouse sucker punch. Locklear had told him that everyone was curious as to why no locals had been hired to help with the clearing contract at Dare County Bombing Range. It was because Nix and his minions in Iraq and Afghanistan were clearing out the ghost prisons dotted throughout the countries. Mahegan himself had interrogated detainees in these facilities spread around Afghanistan, which were little more than medieval dungeons. Each cell was a solitary endeavor with a rancid mattress on a dirt floor with no place to relieve oneself.

He saw it now: twenty prisoners chained together, stomping around the Dare County Bombing Range for bombs. Nix probably felt justified using this method because the men were enemy combatants. Mahegan couldn't argue with the concept, but still it was wrong. He knew that throughout the course of combat that they had captured as many innocent men as guilty ones. Chances were that ten of the twenty men in there were guilty of nothing more than being in the wrong place at the wrong time. If even that.

Satisfied with his knowledge gained from this ship, he found the ladder that allowed him to crawl over the gunwale. He secured his equipment, checked the borrowed wetsuit for tears, and climbed down the hull of *Le Concord*. He held on to the last rung above the water until he could see the stern of the *Ocean Ranger*.

Then he slipped into the freezing cold Atlantic Ocean.

Chapter 27

Vinny Falco watched his boss, Sam Nix, pace in the control tower. The man was nervous, he surmised. Falco had no love for Nix. He was merely a means to an end, but he played along.

"Seriously, who is this guy?" Samuel Nix asked.

They were standing in the control tower of the bombing range, which afforded them multidimensional views. First, they could see the darkened landscape of the swampy impact area and the closer confines of the base area with its warehouse and residential buildings. Next, to the east they could see the winking lights of Roanoke Island and Kitty Hawk beyond that. On their displays and terminals, they could monitor intrusion points into the bombing range where they could see the marginally repaired front gate and the klieg lights that had been established around the "crime scene" near the landing craft. They could also see a single satellite video feed from the deck of the *Ocean Ranger*. Total knowledge management.

"He's a former Army badass, like I told you. Out now, and up for a dishonorable discharge from that dick Bream. Word is an MVX-90 killed one of his Delta buddies. He's pissed about it and wants revenge," Falco said.

Falco was standing behind Nix, looking over his shoulder at the *Ocean Ranger* streaming live video. They could see the small container ship *Le Concord* nudging closer, coming alongside and feeding the ropes back and forth, transferring supplies and people.

"Whose word is that?"

"Sources, boss. I have spies everywhere."

"No shit, but you work for me."

Falco hesitated, debating what to say. "Sheriff's department. Word has it that he's a drifter with a grudge."

"Why the hell would he be flying over our Galaxy site?"

"Let's hope that's all he's doing. I'm heading over to the airfield in a few minutes to see what Dakota and Mahegan come back with."

"What are you thinking? Photos?"

"Best case, photos. Worst case, the crazy son of a bitch jumped into the ocean and swam to the ship."

Nix turned and looked at Falco.

"No one's that crazy," Nix said.

"Do I need to remind you of the hole he cut through our operation today? And I don't even think he planned on that. He's a natural fighter. Like some pilots are naturals at the stick, this guy finds a small clue, some piece of intelligence, and he goes for it. That's how these guys work. I saw it in Iraq and Afghanistan. Instead of sitting back and debating some piece of information, they grab it, pursue, and stay on the offensive. That way they never give anyone a chance to catch up with them. Keeps their opponents on their heels, makes them react by using cell phones and speeding up their decision cycles."

"We need to speed our cycle up."

"That's exactly what he wants us to do," Falco said.

"I'm not going to sit by while this dick dismantles everything we have worked so hard for."

"Not saying that, boss. I've already called the crew on the *Ocean Ranger* and they're on the lookout for him. The *Lucky* also."

"Remind me to change the name of that one," Nix said, grimacing.

Falco ran a hand over his shaved scalp, then tugged at his goatee.

"She's not all bad, boss."

Nix scoffed. "First-class lying bitch. Other than that, she's good. Wildcat in the sack."

"She could be useful," Falco suggested.

"How so? She wants the gold and she's not giving up until she gets it."

Falco countered. "All that's left are the remnants in the creek. That's what, maybe three or four hundred thousand? Let her have it. It could even help us."

"Not if wonder boy figures out what we're doing."

"Let me take care of him. The guys on the *Ranger* will feed him to the sharks."

Nix studied Falco.

"He kicked your ass today, Vinny. We've got a pilot that flew over Galaxy and a loose cannon in Locklear. If she wasn't tied in with the sheriff, I'd feed her to the alligators."

"May be the best option, anyway. Listen, let me get over to the airfield and talk to Dakota."

Nix nodded. "Did you see what that crazy son of a bitch did? Adham?"

"Saw the news. Chopped that guy's head off."

"One sick dude."

They remained silent a moment and then Nix nodded.

"Go. Do what you need to do."

Falco nodded back and raced down the steps of the tower, making a quick visit to his quarters, where he grabbed a go bag of equipment. Then he jumped in a different truck than his original one and sped down the packed gravel road. He passed around the junked security gate, spotted the klieg lights where he had two men standing guard, and turned left onto Route 264. On his right side was the sound and on his left was the vast wasteland of Dare County Bombing Range. He crossed the bridge that spanned the sound and was on Roanoke Island in twenty minutes.

The airfield was on the north end of the island. Falco pulled into the small parking lot, circled once, and then sped to the water's edge and pulled his truck into a boat ramp parking lot. He grabbed a knife and pistol, shut off the lights on his truck, and jogged back along the beach to a spot where the runway opened to the water of Croatan Sound. Nothing the construction crew could do about it, he was told. Federal Aviation Administration regulations called for more runway, so they built it into the sound.

As he was scaling the minor fence, he heard the distinct sound of a Twin Otter airplane flying from east to west, which was perfect if it was Dakota. He ran alongside the runway toward the landing aircraft and watched its tires smoke once and then bounce onto the concrete. He heard the propellers go into reverse as he began to sprint. The airplane was taxiing toward the hangar on the south side of the airfield as Falco rapidly closed the hundred yards.

As the de Havilland hit the apron, Falco was up on a skid, opening the door, and shoving a pistol into Dakota's face.

"Turn around and take off now, Dakota."

Caught in the middle of manipulating his controls and steering while speaking on the radio, Dakota was momentarily confused.

Falco ripped the communications cables from the dash and repeated his demand. "Now."

"Vinny, what the hell is going on?"

"Once more, turn around and fly this bitch. Otherwise you get a bullet. *Capisce?*"

"You can look at the gas gauge yourself," Dakota said, shaking his head. "I'm near empty. Not more than ten minutes of airtime."

"That's all I'm asking. Just get this puppy in the air so we can have a nice friendly chat about the mission you just flew."

Falco watched Dakota's Adam's apple bob once. He knew he had his mark. "Let's go."

Dakota taxied the airplane to the end of the runway, idled up, and released the brakes. They sped along Runway 5, heading east and taking off against a slight crosswind. As they got through the first layer of turbulence up to about 1,000 feet, Falco said, "Now take me over Copperhead."

Dakota obliged, the gun at his head. As they were above the Copperhead facility, Falco said, "Now put it on a straight azimuth toward Galaxy and lock it in on autopilot."

"What are you talking about?"

"Don't bullshit me, Dakota. You flew Mahegan over Galaxy and he jumped, correct?"

Dakota paused and then turned away, muttering, "Shit."

"Yeah. Shit. Mahegan did you a big favor, Tonto."

"Yes. He jumped. He had a GPS device that showed us where to go."

"You locked in on that heading?"

Dakota fidgeted with a button on the cockpit controls and said, "Yes." Then added, "You don't have to worry. I won't say anything. I don't even know why he went out there."

"No. You won't say anything, Dakota."

Falco retrieved his knife and slid it across Dakota's throat, making sure to get the far side carotid artery. The blood pumped against the window as Dakota's head slumped down against his chest.

Falco wiped the blade against the pilot's shirt, sheathed the knife, repacked his small go bag, and then donned the parachute he had stuffed in his go bag.

Cinching the parachute straps beneath his buttocks, he looked up as the engines began to sputter. They were crossing the spit of land that created Nags Head beach. Making sure he had everything he came with, he opened the cargo door, leapt into the wind, and immediately pulled the ripcord grip.

He had full canopy within seconds of exiting the aircraft and steered his parachute toward the northern tip of Roanoke Island.

He made it about fifty meters from the northern tip, and then silently landed in the shallow water. He skillfully gathered his parachute as he sidestroked to the beach. Falco took a few minutes to kneel and listen, then determined that he had not been seen, and packed his parachute into his kit bag.

As he walked into the forest, he had the thought that Dakota was actually a decent guy, but not worth risking his cut of an estimated twenty million dollars.

With one problem down and two more to go, he emerged from the trees near the Lost Colony Theater and crept toward Locklear's bungalow.

Chapter 28

Locklear held a bottle of Corona in one hand and her Glock 26 "Baby Glock" pistol in the other. She rocked slowly on her front porch swing, which overlooked Croatan Sound.

She had known when Dakota and Mahegan had departed and heard the plane as it made its return approach thirty minutes ago. She had driven her Defender to the airfield in anticipation of either seeing Mahegan or learning Mahegan's fate from Dakota.

Instead, what she had seen was a man sprinting toward the airplane from the north side of the airfield, as if he had come in from the sound. Locklear had watched as the man had entered the airplane, which had taken off again shortly thereafter. She saw it gain altitude, circle over Copperhead, and then head out to sea.

It took her three boat ramps before she found the parked truck with the Copperhead logo on the passenger door.

"Falco," she had said to herself. She knew Vinny Falco was Nix's cleaner and she presumed that they were now in cleanup mode. Mahegan's actions had accelerated their time line. Copperhead would no longer be able to remain under the radar.

Which was fine with her. She had severed her ties there in enough time to ensure nothing should circle back on her. Nonetheless, she was concerned that Falco might consider her a liability. In fact, she was certain of it when she heard the aircraft sputter and, as she held the night-vision goggles to her eyes, saw the single parachutist exit and pop canopy.

She rocked gently, sipping her beer, as Falco landed in the water. She watched him enter the woods and knew he would be coming from the south side in a few minutes.

Locklear debated taking the kayak out in the water and ambushing Falco or just avoiding him altogether. She knew that the operation was at a critical juncture. Mahegan may never return and the gold may be lost forever. She had certainly put several eggs into that one basket, as she had tried with Nix before. A combination of inexperience and naiveté had scuttled those plans. Had she risked too much with Mahegan?

She stood and walked off the porch when she heard the slightest snap of a branch behind her home. Leaning her back against one of her kayaks tilted against the exterior wall of the house, she remained quiet. Pistol at her side, Locklear saw a darkened figure move slowly into the sand and stop on the other side of the kayak. She watched as Falco pressed his face against the window of her living room. She had intentionally left the television on, images dancing against the wall as the program ran its course.

Locklear could see only his face through a small seam created by the angle of the kayak against the vertical wall. It was enough for her to tell that he was amped, like a drug addict on amphetamines. His eyes were wide and darting, focused intently inside the house, the lights burning up his night vision. She noticed his hand clutching and unclutching a knife handle.

He had probably killed Dakota, who had been a friend. While that upset her, it was more important to play this strategically, not tactically or passionately. Her goal was not revenge, nor was her motive entirely based on accumulating the gold.

As she raised the pistol toward Falco's face, she said, "Move and you're a dead man."

But he did move. In fact, he jumped back, shocked by her voice. She figured it was a natural response by someone who thought they were entirely alone and had the complete upper hand. His reversal of fortune was swift and complete.

He lunged at her with the knife, but Locklear was quicker and easily sidestepped the awkward thrust. Realizing his night vision had been damaged by staring through the window, she capitalized on her advantage by first planting a forceful straight kick into his sternum.

Falco doubled over, almost stabbing himself in the gut with his knife. Swiftly, she struck his head with her heel via a full roundhouse move. He staggered, dropping his rucksack and grabbing at his midsection. After a knee to his nose, she had disabled Falco.

Locklear knelt next to the suffering man.

"What, Vinny, you think you're going to come onto my turf now and kill me?"

She held the pistol to his face, which had blood sluicing from his nose. Holding him by the back of his collar, she rested the muzzle at the base of his skull.

"Give me one good reason not to blow your brains out, dump you in my kayak, paddle into the middle of the sound, and leave you for the sharks?"

Falco coughed, spit some blood into the sand, and smiled.

"You mean like you did to Royes?"

"Let's just say you're going to wind up just like him," Lindy said.

Chapter 29

Mahegan held on to a metal rung of the *Ocean Ranger*. The wetsuit had helped protect him from hypothermia and had held his injured left shoulder in place. The small rucksack of weapons and GPS devices created some drag, but nothing he could not handle. Thankfully, the AK-47 was one of the most durable weapons in the world and water had little effect on its operating capabilities.

He bobbed halfway in the water and halfway out. He had swum to the east side of the boat, as *Le Concord* had been approaching on the west side. The bow of the *Ranger* was facing to the north, putting him near the starboard rear of the ship, which in his estimation was bigger than the approaching vessel. Toward the bow, he saw another boat moored to the *Ranger* and recognized it as the *Lucky Lindy*.

He felt that combat edge surface, the thrill that always came when a mission begins to sync like well-played chess pieces on a board. He ran through his mind the variables at play.

The *Lucky Lindy* was bringing the gold here 140 miles offshore so that they could lower it onto the bottom of the ocean, however deep, creating the illusion that it was found in deep international waters. Such a move would take advantage of the "finders keepers" precedent set by Tommy Thompson's find in 1987. Mahegan's immediate thought was that it was a brilliant, if not devious, scheme. No one had really explored the Galaxy site that Thompson had uncovered, because once they found the actual SS *Central America*, miles away, no one returned to this radar anomaly.

Nix had done his homework.

But what else was going on? Why all the elaborate machinations between the landing craft, the *Lucky Lindy*, *Le Concord*, and the *Ocean Ranger*?

Well, Mahegan, thought, Nix was delivering the MVX-90s out here. Mahegan had clearly seen them loaded early in the morning onto the *Lucky Lindy*. His guess was that the MVX-90s were barter for the slaves he just saw on *Le Concord*. Arms dealers from somewhere in the Middle East received shipments of the most technologically advanced bomb triggers in the world. In exchange, prisoners were delivered to clear the bombing range and serve as slave labor on the gold ship. Nix and company pocketed the salaries intended for the workers.

Some of those prisoners, he was sure, would be on the *Lucky Lindy*, headed back to Copperhead. Others would probably remain on this ship to work the reverse gold find. He also figured that there was a fifty-fifty chance that the FAA or, worse, the pirate from Copperhead had questioned Dakota by now.

With that in mind, Mahegan calculated his play. He would go straight for the *Lucky Lindy*. He knew the intricacies of the fishing vessel well enough that he might be able to stow away on the trip back to the coast, as painful as that would be.

The other options were worse. Fight it out on the *Ranger*. And then what? Go back to the *Le Concord* and head to the Middle East?

If they were expecting him, they would assuredly be looking for him on the two larger vessels, thinking he was there to disrupt the gold shipment.

But he had that combat edge. He felt he was still a fraction ahead of the enemy. And another thought was nagging at him. How could he let a shipment of MVX-90s head to the Middle East to kill more American soldiers? It was his moral obligation to stop this cargo.

On that thought, he eased up the ladder on the side of the *Ocean Ranger*, did a silent combat roll over the gunwale, and lay in the prone position as he sighted down the aim posts of the AK-47.

He saw movement and shadows beneath a set of bright lights on the port side of the ship, amidships, near the center. There was a winch operation under way. He saw a crate silhouetted against the lights. It was a standard wooden shipping crate, very similar to the one he had seen the forklift load onto the *Lucky Lindy*. He moved quickly while others were focused on the task of lowering the cargo into *Le Concord*.

He found a ladder that dove directly into the hold of the ship. Flipping on the Maglite, he saw several small wooden containers, similar to the one being transferred by the hoist, marked with "Explosives" warnings.

Explosives?

Mahegan asked himself the question, *What does Copperhead do with the bombs they find?* He recalled the massive explosion he'd heard yesterday when swimming Croatan Sound. He remembered the giant mushroom cloud. His assumption was that they blew everything in place.

Bad assumption.

He used his knife to quickly pry the lid off one of the crates and found several artillery shells loosely stacked in haphazard fashion with, curiously enough, Styrofoam peanuts providing minor cushion. These were old shells, Mahegan determined. They were rusted and dirty, some with mud caked on them, but still fully operational.

A noise at the top of the ladder from which he had entered caused him to stop his inspection and resume a defensive posture. He shut off his light, eased the lid back on the container, and knelt behind it for cover. Scanning, Mahegan noticed there were at least twenty rows of containers that were five deep. One hundred boxes of explosives going to the highest bidder for use against American forces, he thought, shaking his head.

Was Nix running multiple scams at once? The gold, the MVX-90s, the prisoners, and the explosives?

Someone at the top of the ladder stopped with half of his torso above the deck and half below.

"We'll retract the deck and get to the rest of the cargo," the man shouted above the din of ship noises.

Mahegan heard a pinging noise above him, metal on metal. Then suddenly the entire deck above him began to open like the Dallas Cowboys stadium, retracting from the middle in two directions. He used the noise to move deeper into the rows of crates. He stopped toward the end and began prying tops off with his knife, quickly inspecting for a specific item.

While the grating metal was coming to a final screeching halt, he saw what he needed. He grabbed two of them and wedged them in his rucksack as best he could. They were heavy, but he could still maneuver.

Mahegan looked up and saw the night sky above him. From his angle he could see the long arm of the crane beginning to slide over the open cargo bay and begin its reach for the crates.

He exited the cargo bay through a steel door that would lead him somewhere aft, he believed. The door opened outward, toward him and to the left. He stepped inside and closed the door. Mahegan was in complete darkness, but sensed he was in a similar personnel hold he had seen on *Le Concord*. This was a dank, musty room that smelled of urine and feces, at best. He switched on his Maglite and saw scattered blankets, but no people. A quick scan of the room showed no other exit. He was at the complete aft of the ship.

He heard a noise outside of the door through which he had just entered and moved to the near corner, which would provide him a split-second advantage over someone coming in from the natural angle of the outward-opening door.

Mahegan heard a radio squelch break and then, "Hey, boss, we're only going to need about five of these dirtbags. We can send the rest onward."

The door opened and a man stood outside the opening, switched on a flashlight, and sprayed the room with two quick sweeps. The light settled on the blankets.

"Smells like a shithouse on a tuna boat," the man said into his radio.

Mahegan wondered what kind of radio it might be and thought it could be useful.

"Quit bitching and lock 'em up," came another voice over the radio.

"Aye, captain. They're coming across now."

With enough evidence available to make a decision that he was dealing with rogue Americans conspiring with international arms dealers and slave traders, Mahegan waited until the man turned the flashlight off. He sensed the man turning away and moving to the door.

Mahegan sprang from the corner and threw his considerable weight and force into the door as he wrapped his arm around the man's throat and clamped his forearm across the man's windpipe. He reached up with his right hand, grabbed the far side of the man's head, and snapped his neck with one swift move.

He dragged the man into the dark room, switched on his Maglite, and inspected the body. He found a Harris radio, which he took.

He also found two weapons, a K-Bar knife and a Glock pistol.

As he picked up the radio, he heard it come to life.

"Oh, hey, any sign of our expected visitor?"

"Not yet. I don't think some stupid Army guy could find us out here in the middle of nowhere."

Chapter 30

Lieutenant General Stanley Bream had returned from his heady meeting with the Secretary of Defense and now paced across his office in long, hurried strides. This news was not good. He could go from hero to zero in an instant. That's how the beltway politics worked.

Sweat beaded on his brow and he wondered how in the world he had lost Mahegan. Mahegan was key to finding Adham, and Adham was, well, key to everything. Ten paces in one direction past the mammoth desk, about face, and ten in the opposite direction. Finally, he stopped, faced his perfectly neat desk, and placed both hands on the polished mahogany.

"You're telling me he just disappeared?" Bream screamed into the Bluetooth headset sticking in his ear like a Tootsie Roll alongside his smooth jawline. Spittle sprayed the desk.

Paslowski, still on Roanoke Island, said, "We had him scoped at a party, but we got there too late. After he tore up Copperhead, we've been a step behind him ever since."

"Maintaining control of Mahegan was your only mission in life, Paslowski," Bream spat.

"I know, sir. We'll find him. In the meantime, we've got word that a small airplane crashed just offshore in the Atlantic Ocean."

"Who gives a shit? Was Mahegan on that airplane? That's the only way I would care."

"Sir, we don't know. I'm heading over to Copperhead when the sun comes up. They've declared a top-secret restricted zone around the ambush location in the Long Shoal River. No one can get in there except for us and of course Locklear. Maybe some locals."

"Go get Locklear and talk to her. She ought to know something. This thing is coming apart faster than a Kmart sweater in a washing machine."

"First light, we'll swing by there and then over to the ambush location. I'm thinking we need to call in DHS here."

Paslowski was referring to the Department of Homeland Security. That a former soldier had breached ongoing military contracting ammunition cleanup efforts was of concern. Coupled with the fact that someone had attacked two military installations with explosives in the last forty-eight hours, they could argue it was a national security issue of the highest proportions.

"We will not get DHS involved. I don't want any of the three-letter dicks, you understand. No CIA. No FBI. No DHS. Nobody! Understand?"

Paslowski paused before speaking.

"Boss, we need some help down here."

"Listen, Mahegan is our responsibility. I asked all those agencies to back off while we played him out. When he popped up on the Ocracoke Ferry, it was perfect. You tracked him to Midgett's place and that was good. I think I can keep these other agencies at bay for about two days, max. These frigging attacks on Brackett and Suffolk are out of nowhere and ruining our play. But we have a chance. I want to nail this guy ourselves."

"Roger, boss."

"And this whack job Adham is cutting off heads overseas. I mean, this country is going to go bat shit in less than twenty-four hours. Now find Mahegan, get Copperhead under control, and make this thing go away. People are starting to wonder if these bombings are connected to Copperhead. We don't need or want any more attention on our operation! Clear?"

"Clear."

General Bream punched off the phone and paced some more, muttering to himself like Dustin Hoffman in the movie *Rain Man*.

"Sonofabitch, sonofabitch, sonofabitch," he said loudly.

In his office at four a.m., he felt the uneasy surge of fear circling him like a python. A lifetime of grabbing the next rung on the ladder, of carefully sidestepping dangerous duty, of planting his foot firmly on the backs of others, was in jeopardy. He had gambled, he knew. But the potential payoff was huge. Chief of Staff of the Army . . . and more.

Having never served in combat, Bream was unfamiliar with the swirling variables beyond his control. He was accustomed to having his rank and from that rank, power. Never one to associate much with the enlisted soldiers, he knew that aloof, iron-fisted rule was what had worked for him in the past.

Now, he was alone, having made some very risky decisions. And here was Mahegan, a damn Indian, blowing up everything. It was supposed to be the other way around.

But it wasn't all lost. There was still a play to be had.

That asshole General Savage had baited him almost a year ago with an e-mail on secret Internet about how Mahegan suspected where the MVX-90s were coming from. If it hadn't been for that message, Bream wouldn't have thought twice about Mahegan.

Bream's heart rate was arrhythmic, slamming in his chest at over one hundred beats per minute. His breathing was labored and he knew his blood pressure was through the roof. Looking for his Metoprolol, he fumbled with the desk drawer, found the orange bottle, and popped two fifty-milligram tablets, chewing them before he swallowed.

"Son of a bitch, son of a bitch, son of a bitch."

He ran through what was on the line.

He had served thirty-three years in the Army. He could retire with a fat pension tomorrow if he wished. The wife was threatening to leave him because he worked all the time and she knew she could get fifty percent of his retirement pay. The kid? Well, the kid was *the* problem. Plus, he was underwater on the fat mortgage on his townhouse in Old Town, Alexandria, Virginia. In 2007, it had seemed like a steal at $900,000. Today, he would be lucky to get $600,000 for it. He couldn't rent it and had it listed for sale at $850,000 as it sat vacant across the Potomac from his government-issued mansion at Fort McNair.

But really, what was he most concerned about? His freedom. Because what he had done could cost him the most precious thing of all.

Like most potentially bad decisions, this one had seemed like such a no-brainer at the time.

Find Chayton Mahegan, reopen the Hoxha case, and get him in the crosshairs of the mighty Inspector General. Confirm the dishonorable discharge, for sure. That kind of pressure almost always made people do stupid things like contacting witnesses, covering their tracks, and generally "obstructing justice."

There was no doubt that Mahegan was on the run and that he had made mistakes. Hell, there was enough to arrest him right now if they could just find him. But his arrest was never what had interested Bream. He had wanted Mahegan in the gray area. Was he guilty of murder? Who knew? Was he capable of treason? Possibly. Was he involved with espionage? Perhaps. Was he linked to The American Taliban? That was certainly desirable from many angles. The benefit of threatening dishonorable discharge on Mahegan was that there was a carrot to manipulate Mahegan and Savage.

But it was the MVX-90s that scared Bream. He couldn't have Mahegan out there with the real story about the lethal bomb triggers.

Bream's area of expertise was inventing uncertainty. His standard for "a preponderance of the evidence" was much lower than "beyond a reasonable doubt."

He could manufacture evidence, as he had done in Mahegan's case. Hell, Bream knew the letters from Mahegan's case were all too similar to be factual. He believed with all of his being that Mahegan's Delta Force buddies had conspired to write those practically duplicated letters defending their battle buddy. It was the perfect case for him to exploit and the perfect soldier for him to hound.

Or so he had thought.

What to do?

He sat in his leather chair and leaned back, staring at the ceiling. His height and weight caused the air to blow out of the cushioned seat with a hydraulic sound.

The blood pressure pills had helped. His heart wasn't

pounding through his chest anymore. This thing was still manageable, he thought, but far beyond his comfort zone.

"How do I get control?" he asked himself out loud.

He had a thought. Maybe he was wrong.

Maybe it *was* time to bring in the three-letter agencies.

"Son of a bitch," he said. "Paslowski's smarter than he damn sure looks."

It was approaching five a.m. If he put out a BOLO for Chayton Mahegan, then he could leverage the entire law enforcement network against him. His worry had clouded his mind, but now he was focused.

He flipped on his secret computer, shook the mouse a couple of times, clicked on Microsoft Word, and began typing.

Be on the Lookout (BOLO) for former Army Captain Chayton "Jake" Mahegan. Consider him armed and dangerous. Dishonorably discharged from the Army, Mahegan is under investigation for murdering an Afghan civilian (possibly a combatant) in detained status. He was last seen on the northern tip of Roanoke Island near the Lost Colony Theatre. He is a person of interest in one murder on Roanoke Island, North Carolina, and another missing person case in the same location. It has been confirmed that Mahegan broke into the bomb disposal warehouse of Copperhead, Incorporated on Dare County Bombing Range yesterday, where three dead contractors were located. This known activity indicates a possible connection in the domestic terror attacks at Fort Brackett and Suffolk Military Compound. Department of

Defense has lead for questioning and investigation, but seeks all interagency support
in locating and detaining Mahegan. There are
initial indications that he may have been in
communications with and received payment
from The American Taliban, Adam Wilhoyt.

He typed his name and rank, always include the
rank, and title before he cut and pasted the text into a
standard format that he then placed on his secret
e-mail, called SIPR.

He pulled up his secret e-mail, pasted the text into
the BOLO format, and then clicked on the BOLO ad-
dressee list, which included the heads of all of the
three-letter agencies, as well as the service departments,
and a host of other important national security agencies. To get the big funding in today's environment,
most agencies had added either "national security" or
"counterterrorism" to their title or mission statement.
Bream figured it was sort of like BP changing their
logo after the oil well blew open in the Gulf. Didn't
mean much, but it looked good.

When he hit send, the BOLO message would, over
the next several minutes and hours, spread across the
country and around the world to agencies such as In-
terpol in Europe. This was a wide net he was casting
and the biggest gamble he had taken so far.

The task now was to plant that link between Mahegan and Adham. Bream believed he could find something plausible enough to say it was a "preponderance
of the evidence." Maybe he could secretly pad Mahegan's bank account from a Middle Eastern routing.
That was easy enough. Or, a document mentioning
Mahegan as an ally could be "found" in one of Adham's
hideouts.

They were both good options, Bream thought. If he could snare Mahegan and Adham, his career would be unstoppable.

On that thought, he made one more call. It was time for some hands-on leadership.

Chapter 31

Mahegan dialed down the volume on the Harris radio and placed it in his rucksack. He figured he had about five minutes before the world would rain down on him.

He took a moment, though, to process what he needed to do. As he climbed the ladder out of the cargo hold on Nix's *Ocean Ranger*, he stopped and scanned the deck. All hands were tending to the simultaneous transfer of prisoners from *Le Concord* to the *Ocean Ranger* and of crates in the opposite direction.

He slipped over the gunwale on the opposite side of the ship. Clearly, the crew had been alerted that a crazy man was heading their way, but they had not taken the threat seriously. Good for him.

He was down the hull ladder and in the water, passing silently around the aft end, feeling the weight of his rucksack and the chill of the ocean water seeping inside his wetsuit. He smelled the diesel fumes from the generators powering the cranes and lights and could taste the oil in the water as he swam from the *Ocean Ranger* back to *Le Concord*.

As he approached the port side of the vessel named after the French slave ship that Blackbeard had eventually captured and renamed the *Queen Anne's Revenge*, Mahegan had to admire the irony. He was staying at a boardinghouse by the name of Blackbeard's boat and now he was bent on destroying the frigate's namesake.

Slowly, quietly stroking through the ocean swells that tossed at about five feet, Mahegan studied the massive hulls of the two ships. Briefly, they overwhelmed the vastness of the Atlantic Ocean.

He was pleased that so far their security had been lax. While he did not expect that condition to last much longer, he was exploiting the intelligence he had. His training in the Army, especially with the paratroopers and Delta forces, had convinced him that acting immediately on the best intelligence available was the preferred route. Some people liked to study an issue. Mahegan preferred to seize the initiative.

He found a series of rungs on the port side of *Le Concord*, which he immediately began climbing. Based on his brief visit less than an hour ago, he knew where he needed to go.

He was looking for the engine room. Over the gunwale again, he paused and noticed the entire crew transporting prisoners and receiving crates of bombs. Again, no security. All eyes were focused on the klieg lights, ropes, pulleys, and cranes. It was an industrial operation moving in two directions on the high seas. The only thing that might catch this brief transfer was a satellite, but Mahegan knew that almost all defense satellites were focused on the regional hotspots of Iraq, Afghanistan, North Korea, China, and the Horn of Africa.

Chayton Mahegan, he thought. He remembered his father's words: The Falcon-Wolf sees and he attacks. In battle, there were moments when Mahegan would feel a primal connection to his Indian ancestry. His instincts were so finely tuned that he believed he was reaching back in time and drawing upon the strength of the warrior brethren he had learned about as a child.

This was one such moment. Knowing he was the lone defender of what was right, Mahegan knew he had no choice but to act. He could not fathom the numbers of men and women who would perish in explosions ignited by the MVX-90s and discarded Dare County Bombing Range ordnance. And while there were more MVX-90s in the warehouse and more bombs to be unearthed, he had the opportunity to disrupt a major shipment right now. Perhaps even shut down the pipeline.

He moved swiftly down the unguarded stairwell and passed the prisoner room, which was empty. Their transfer was under way.

He went down two more flights of stairs and found the engine room. He opened a steel door and stepped into a dimly lit cavern of unfamiliar machinery. Though he had spent some time working the fishing rigs in Wilmington, he'd been a grunt, not a boat driver. This was different. Pipes were routed along the walls of the room and connected to large vats, like the ones he had seen in brewpubs. The vats all had pipes connected to a main shaft that led toward the aft end of the ship. Even inside the bowels of this craft he knew his direction was facing south.

He switched on the recently captured Harris radio to listen to any communications traffic and heard the low static buzz of an active channel. After about a minute, he heard, "Listening silence acknowledged, out."

Interesting, he thought. He turned off the radio and thought for a moment. In response to his capture of the radio, whoever was controlling this operation had

banned anyone from speaking on the devices. Such discipline spoke to the professionalism of the leadership,
if not the crew. Listening silence meant that only the
individual in charge would be initiating radio calls and
those personnel not in command would only respond if
spoken to.

His plan could still work. He looked back at the gas
turbines. The diesel fuel would be burning here, making the combustion necessary to turn the screw, which
would turn the propeller. Diesel fuel, Mahegan knew,
was less combustible than straight-up gasoline, but
more explosive than jet fuel. He would need to ignite
the claymore mine he had retrieved from the crate
using one of the blasting caps he'd found in the same
box.

All he needed was some wire. He found a series of
cables and wires running along the near wall to his
right. Using his knife, he pared back the rubber insulation, revealing a series of copper wires. He touched his
knife blade to the wires, which could have been dangerous, but he got no spark. He went to work stripping
the insulation the same way someone exposes wire when
installing a stereo speaker system. He retrieved about
eight feet of wire, removed one strand, wrapped the
rest around the blasting cap, inserted the blasting cap
in the claymore mine receptor, and wedged the claymore next to one of the diesel pumps.

Next, he traced the wire back behind a steel wall, resigned to the fact that it would do little good if the
radio call came in too soon. Mahegan then led the remaining thin copper wire to a communications portal
he had seen on his initial sweep of the room. There was
a platform with three displays and a PVC pipe full of
wires coming from above. In Mahegan's estimation,
this was a radio communications mechanism for the

engine room personnel in case of emergency or during routine operations. Whatever its purpose, Mahegan knew it would transmit the radio signal from above decks to the engine room.

Opening his rucksack, he removed the remaining MVX-90 he had lifted from the Copperhead warehouse. He then retrieved his flashlight, unscrewed the facing, pulled the guts, and connected it to the power source of the MVX-90. He saw a light flicker on the MVX-90 and knew he was in business. He armed the receiver-transmitter function to transmit on reception, which meant the next time someone with a Harris radio operating within the prescribed frequency range, 30–108 MHz, made a radio call, the MVX-90 would send an electrical impulse through the wires and into the blasting cap.

Mahegan's goal was for the blasting cap to ignite the claymore mine and the 700 shotgun pellets would blast at 4,000 feet per second with enough white-hot kinetic energy to burn diesel and, with any fortune, ignite a series of chain reactions in Mahegan's favor.

All, presumably, after Mahegan departed the ship.

With all of the operations ongoing, Mahegan knew he was taking a huge risk once he connected the MVX-90 to the wires. Just about any radio call could ignite the explosives he had just rigged. But he believed this was largely a manual operation between the ships, and he knew most seagoing ships used different high-frequency bands than ground operators. Would that hold true for the internal and external communications on these ships?

He was about to find out.

Mahegan gathered his equipment, arranged it in his rucksack, slid his rucksack over his shoulders, spotted his position in relation to the still-closed door, and attached the wires to the MVX-90 terminal posts. He knew he had a good connection, and placed the MVX-90 on a ledge.

Then he ran like hell for the door.

As he approached, he heard a metallic latch click on the outside of the hatch.

When he pulled on the lever to open the door, it didn't budge.

Chapter 32

Mahegan looked over his shoulder at the wires connected to the MVX-90. The same device that had probably killed Colgate might now kill him.

Another tug on the door and he heard the latch activate. The door was opening without his effort. Mahegan stepped quickly to the port side of the hatch, again opposite the line of sight of anyone entering the door.

A short man stepped through, ducking his head even though he didn't need to. Mahegan waited a long second before moving. He was assessing three things. First, was the man armed? He didn't appear to be. Second, was he moving with any purpose to his step? Third, was there anyone following or was he alone? The last thing Mahegan wanted to do was to attack this man only to have to turn around and fight several others. He decided that the man was alone.

The man was wearing a rust-colored sweatshirt and dark cargo pants. His hair was black and matted. He seemed broad and stocky. Mahegan assessed the man was probably the engine room captain. This was his domain.

Which is why Mahegan was not surprised when the

man immediately stopped and stared at the MVX-90 sitting in plain sight on the ledge.

Mahegan watched the man reach into his pocket and retrieve a small personal mobile radio, like a walkie-talkie. Mahegan knew that most of these smaller devices operated in the 380–399 MHz range, which would not be a threat.

But he was going to disable the man anyway, so why take the chance?

He stepped forward silently, grabbed the man's arm with a swift wrestling move, secured the radio, and drove a forearm into the man's neck. He watched as the man gasped for air, grabbing at his neck as if he was choking on a piece of meat. Mahegan slid quietly behind him after pocketing the radio and snapped the man's neck. He dragged him behind a panel on the far side of the engine room.

He moved to the MVX-90 that he had rigged and quickly placed it in a less conspicuous location, securing it again to make certain the tenuous wire connections did not falter with natural ship movements. Now, moving faster than before, he leapt through the hatch, pulled it shut, and sealed the door with the locking arm. As part of the anti-flood system, all of the below-deck hatches could be sealed from the exterior.

He was up the ladder and out the port side, stopping once only to wait for a busy deckhand to pass by him as he hid in the shadows. He found the ladder and was over the gunwale again. Back in the water, he now began to swim to the one location he had not been.

Staying away from the active end of the two ships, Mahegan once again retraced his route across the stern of both vessels. Usually not one to double back on any route over land, the only harm in doing so in the sea was that he was moving parallel, not perpendicular, to any sentry's line of sight. But the swim would be too far for him to go out any reasonable distance that would make a difference and then come back perpendicularly. So, he chanced it.

He was silent as he kicked and swam a smooth side-stroke. As he rounded the stern of the *Ocean Ranger*, Mahegan noticed that his only ride home, the *Lucky Lindy*, was still available.

He snuggled closely to the ship's hull, feeling dwarfed again by its sheer presence next to him. Keeping his eye on the only way back to the coast 150 miles to the west, he heard shouts above him.

These were American voices.

"Simons is dead! The bastard has been here!"

So, he had killed Simons. The son of a bitch shouldn't have been smuggling weapons to the enemy in violation of several treason and espionage laws. Simons, as far as Mahegan was concerned, deserved to die.

"Get the *Concord* out of here now. We're done with the transfer. Also, someone tell the *Lindy* to get moving. Now!"

The second voice was an authoritative one. Decisive and commanding.

Despite their alarm, Mahegan felt relatively comfortable in the water. First, his big concern—whether the *Lucky Lindy* would still be available as transport once he was done rigging *Le Concord*—was not an issue. He had an out and was only about fifty meters away from his ride.

Second, he was in the ocean with an entire ship between him and *Le Concord*. Both the ship and the water would absorb any blast, provided his makeshift bomb worked. On the other hand, the ship that might act as his buffer had its own load of diesel and explosives.

Last, he was certain that a radio call would be made in the very near term as they arranged security on the ship. The ship-to-ship communications would not necessarily be in the prescribed bandwidth, but certainly the personal mobile radios would be.

He found the bow of the *Lucky Lindy*, approached it from a perpendicular axis, and nestled on its port side. The fishing boat was facing south, the opposite direction of its two neighbors. As he approached, Mahegan saw rubber fenders over the side and ropes tied with half hitches to iron rungs and eyelets on the side of the *Ocean Ranger*.

The sounds of pulleys being disconnected, engines revving, and weapons charging filled the air. It was a race to determine if he could get onboard the *Lucky Lindy* before its crew did, if they hadn't already. Mahegan was certain that some of the prisoners were going all the way to Dare County Mainland as new slave labor to clear bombs.

He came around the aft end of the *Lucky Lindy*, mounted the swim platform, and noticed that the dinghy, a Zodiac Bombard boat with a Tohatsu fifteen-horsepower outboard engine, was still there. He saw three gas tanks propped in the rear of what he now recognized as a Bombard Max version of the Zodiac. Mahegan figured the top speed of a new Tohatsu would be about thirty knots, or five hours of boating from this point, requiring seven and a half gallons of gas. The red plastic gas cans looked as though they would hold three gallons apiece. Nine gallons. Enough, if they were full.

He had three plays. Take the entire *Lucky Lindy*. He knew the vessel, but doubted he had time to untie the lines. Or, he could cut the rope on the small Bombard in front of him and steal away into the night. Though if he did that, the *Lucky Lindy* and crew could run him down.

He could stow away and cut the Bombard free after traveling closer to shore, giving them little time to catch him before he was safely in the woods. He suspected the third option was best, and confirmed his decision when the boat began rocking. The crew and its prisoners were coming aboard.

Chapter 33

Mahegan slid beneath the tarp covering the Bombard Max. The crew had secured the inflatable boat to cleats on the *Lucky Lindy* using a line on its aft and bow running in either direction. The tarp was angled like a lean-to from the gunwale of the boat to the swim platform five feet below.

Normally a tricked-out fishing rig, this vessel, Mahegan had seen, had a .50 caliber machine gun mounted in the deck. As he settled beneath the angled space created by the tarp, he counted the number of times he felt the boat shudder with someone jumping from the ladder on the side of the *Ocean Ranger* onto the *Lucky Lindy*. The seam was too tight between the tarp and the boat for him to see, so he had to rely on other senses.

He could hear the soft bark of commands, spoken in English. "Move. Now. Let's go. In the hold. Down below." The rattling of chains competed with the words and he missed some of them. But he felt the thud of every footfall. He resolved that the lighter vibrations were prisoners being lowered to the craft because they were shackled. The heavier vibrations were armed men jumping from the ladder with nothing to steady their descent.

If his calculations were correct, Mahegan counted four crew and ten prisoners. The crew would no doubt be the two who had originally navigated from the *Teach's Pet* to the *Ocean Ranger*. They probably had two men doing a shift change from the *Ocean Ranger* coming back to Copperhead and wanted the extra two for security.

He angled his rifle up toward the tarp as he sensed someone near him, leaning over the aft end of the boat.

"Ghosts are down below. Check the entire boat before we take off. Make sure there are no stowaways. Stay off comms."

"Aye."

These were the same voices he'd heard at the *Teach's Pet* when the transfer had taken place.

"Check the Zodiac, also."

Mahegan knew he had one play left, and it seemed like a long shot.

So far he had kept the radio on silent and was surprised that no one had communicated on the personal mobile radios since he had rigged the MVX-90. He felt the tie to the tarp being loosed in preparation for being thrown back and, ultimately, revealing his position.

So far, the men onboard the *Ocean Ranger* had not used their personal mobile radios. Either that or he had not properly rigged his improvised explosive device. He had confidence in his abilities and leaned toward believing he had done it right.

The phrase, "Stay off comms" also indicated that the crew was continuing to exercise good radio discipline.

Using his right hand to hold the rifle level near the

spot where the tarp was moving, he used his left hand to find the personal mobile radio. With his thumb and forefinger he turned the button from off to on. Next, he located the transmit button and pressed and held it in position. He was transmitting.

Meanwhile, the tarp was nearly off. One tie was loose and the next tie was about to be completely removed. He saw the tarp go from taut to slack. A hand reached underneath and began to lift the tarp. Mahegan saw the man's head begin to lower.

Even on the far side of the blast with the *Ocean Ranger* blocking the energy, he felt the blast shock wave surround him. The intensity of the heat also reached him as the cool ocean air suddenly had a searing touch, as if all of the oxygen had been sucked out of a small room.

The tarp went completely slack. Mahegan heard the man say, "What the hell was that?!"

"Let's go!" he heard the other man say. "Move, now!"

Mahegan reached up and held one end of the tarp so that it would not blow away and reveal his hiding position. He sensed that the man was no longer at the aft end.

"Man the fifty cal," said the authoritative voice.

"Aye," replied the one who had begun removing the ties. He pictured the man stopping what he was doing and moving to the large fifty-caliber machine gun mounted in the middle of the deck.

Mahegan felt the engines rumble. The gears shifted. Suddenly, they were near full throttle. The boat pulled away through the ocean at about the time he heard a large secondary explosion, followed by a series of smaller ones.

"Holy shit. That's the *Ranger*," the fifty-cal man's voice said, more to himself than anyone else.

As the *Lucky Lindy* sped away from the fireballs, Mahegan couldn't help but assess his handiwork. He moved to the starboard side of the swim platform, water spraying him in the face, and nudged between the Bombard and the boat. He saw the tarp line fluttering in the slipstream of the boat and pulled it in. He tied it to a D-ring on the rear of the boat.

As he finished, a third large explosion engulfed the entire scene. Both ships were aflame. It appeared to him that *Le Concord* was sinking.

Good, he thought.

Now if I can just make it back to Copperhead.

Chapter 34

Mullah Adham was sleeping on his threadbare mattress with a thin sheet to keep himself warm in the fall night air.

He opened his eyes and stared into the darkness. The gore of the beheading made his mind reel back in time to over a year ago. He had been staying in a small madrassa south of Chitral in the Northwest Frontier Province.

He slept lightly, but peacefully. The Imam and the villagers welcomed his full conversion to Islam. They appreciated even more his use of technology to spread the message and his constant antagonism of the Americans.

Awaking, he knew it was time. Adham lifted his AK-47 from the prayer mat next to him. Pulling on a tactical vest, he led his four-man team from their Spartan residence to complete their graduation exercise.

They were outside and moving swiftly past a Pakistani checkpoint guarding the primary trail into the mountains that separate the Northwest Frontier Province, Pakistan, from Nuristan, Afghanistan. Adham knew that the Pashtun tribal affiliations migrated from east to west. He was in primarily friendly territory despite the fact that the British-drawn border, the Durand Line, ran north to south.

After an hour, his team was safely inside Afghanistan, having reached Commander Hoxha's compound north of the Kunar River. Not far from this location was a small American outpost manned by an American rifle platoon and a partner unit from the Afghan Army. Altogether, they held a total of about forty soldiers.

Adham longed for the bona fides that would come with combat. He was tired of taunting and mocking the Americans from his virtual nest in Pakistan. As they arrived at Hoxha's compound, Adham directed his men to help the guards outside while he spoke with his friend inside.

"Welcome, Mullah," Hoxha said. "You have traveled a long way. I have food and drink."

"You are kind, commander. First, I would like to see the intelligence on the American base. I understand you have scouted this position at length."

They sat at a table as Hoxha extracted a hand-drawn map from a stack of papers. The interior of the adobe house was modest: mud walls, sticks for firewood, a smoldering fire, and the occasional piece of handmade furniture. Two large rugs covered the floors of the rooms at ground level. It smelled of wood smoke and goat meat.

Hoxha saw Adham eyeing the rug beneath their feet.

"Beautiful, yes?"

"Yes, of course, commander."

"In more ways than one."

Adham processed the coy remark and immediately knew there was an escape tunnel beneath. He saw the commander's AK-74 leaning against the far wall by the rear door. The life of a warrior, Adham thought. He felt *a surge of pride for what he had been doing, helping these frontier men carve out a living amid international turmoil.*

"Now, as I understand your mission—"

They both heard something fall outside. Other sounds penetrated the night, hissing noises, like bullets flying.

Adham watched Hoxha, a hardened combat veteran, peel back the carpet, hand him a remote control and a cell phone, and point at the trapdoor, saying, "Down here, mullah. If I call you, press the remote."

Adham did as instructed and as he lowered into darkness beneath the house, he saw Hoxha snatch his cell phone and AK-74 as he yanked a tactical vest over his head.

Moving along the tunnel, Adham figured the farther he could get from the entrance, the better. He could hear muted sounds of combat, shouting and rifle shots mostly. He made a turn in the tunnel and braced against the dirt wall.

Then, inexplicably, he heard the trapdoor open. He was about fifty meters from the opening when he heard an American voice shout, "Tunnel!"

He saw flashlights crisscrossing, moving toward him. He gripped the cell phone and remote tightly, his AK-47 hanging across his chest. Despite all his daydreams and anger, he was suddenly unsure if he could kill a human being up close.

The soldiers were so close he could hear the commands through their radios. He heard, "Out of the house! Down!"

That was when his phone lit up with a call. He fumbled with the cell phone and the remote, but managed to press the button as instructed.

One of the soldiers said, "Fuck." Adham heard something ripped open and then a metallic click, but

*more like a fork hitting crystal. The ping resonated in
his ears until the entire tunnel exploded.*

His next memory was awaking in a metal container.

*After what he guessed was a few hours, he saw day-
light seeping through the cracks in the container's skin
and heard voices outside. A door opened and two men
entered and then closed the door behind them. They were
carrying rucksacks, which he assumed were filled with
torture equipment such as pliers, scalpels, and the like.*

*He was wrong. The first man wore a goatee and an
earring. The man smiled at him as he pulled out a device that looked like a FedEx box scanner.*

*"Need a fingerprint," the man said. His partner
looked Afghan, perhaps from somewhere north where
the Russians were. Maybe he was an interpreter, Adham
figured. They were wearing black jumpsuits with the
image of a fanged serpent on their shoulders.*

*Adham played like he didn't understand English,
and the man with the earring and goatee placed his
hand on the machine, pressing down on the forefinger
to punch a button, which made a small light come on,
blinking as if on a small fax machine.*

"Sit down," the goatee man said.

*Adham wondered if his fingerprints were anywhere
in the American database. He assumed that the FBI
still had his information.*

*A few minutes later, he watched the goatee man hud-
dle in the corner of the container with the other man.
They were discussing something with a fair amount of
animation. Adham interpreted this to mean that he was
in the database and that they had identified him. He
was certain that his capture would make headlines.
After ten minutes the argument was apparently settled.
Goatee man punched some buttons and then turned to
the door, which he opened.*

Outside, two soldiers were waiting.

"What do we have—" one of them began to ask.

The goatee man turned his head and looked at Adham and then at the soldier, muttering, "Don't use my name, asshole."

"Sorry, sir."

"We got nothing. You guys got too much going on here to deal with this dirtbag, so we're going to take him back to main HQ. Plus, he came from that madrassa across the border and we think we can get some intel."

"Roger that. Don't need him here, that's for sure."

Adham recognized the lieutenant's bar on the soldier's patrol cap.

They closed the door on him, yet he still heard the radio call.

"Bring in the Copperhead helicopter. We've got cargo of one."

Adham wiped the sweat from his brow. The memory of being so close to capture by Captain Mahegan during his last raid was both nerve-wracking and thrilling, but he had survived.

Mahegan would not.

Chapter 35

"I didn't kill Royes and you know it," Locklear said.

She had handcuffed Falco to her porch column. Barring his ability to rip the column from the frame, he was secure. He was seated, looking toward the sound with his hands behind his back. Locklear sat on the swing and kicked it lazily back and forth.

"What I know is I'm damned uncomfortable, Lindy. Now let me up."

Locklear laughed. "You probably just killed Dakota and you were coming after me. Why in the hell would I let you go?"

"You got nothing on me," Falco said.

"You're probably right about that," she said. "But in this game the rules really don't apply, do they? You want me to hold you to the standards of evidence while you go about your business stealing gold that belongs to the state or the country?"

"What are you, some kind of patriot now?"

"What I am is irrelevant, other than the fact, of course, that I am better than you."

"You boning that guy? Mahegan? He's probably dead by now anyway."

"My money's on Mahegan, Vinny. But let me get this straight. You guys have MVX-90s, which the enemy seems to have in abundance now. You're selling those to the bad guys. I know that much."

"You don't know shit. You're wrong."

"Don't think so. Plus, you're taking the *Adger* gold out to sea and dropping it on Tommy Thompson's Galaxy site, pretending like it was there all along. Funny, I pulled up the Wikipedia page and it shows a new update. That gold was believed to have been on the ship that went down on the Galaxy site. And when I Google that now, I get a few random hits that the SS *Belevedere*, which is the shipwreck there, did indeed contain gold. Of course, we all know it was nothing but a mail carrier."

"Must be true then," Falco said weakly.

"You're making it true, that's for sure. So, the *Lucky Lindy*, hate the name by the way, goes out with the gold, you lower it, keep it there for a few days, then you lift it back up and say, 'Eureka!'" She paused, and then said, "Did I get that right?"

Falco shook his head and smiled. She saw beads of sweat running down his shaved head. He pulled at his handcuffs, scraping them against the wood. She saw him staring out at the *Teach's Pet*. Looking from him to the *Pet*, and then back to Falco, her mind began to process the possibilities.

"Let me go, bitch. I've got shit to do."

"I'm sure you do. I'm just trying to figure out what to do with you. Kill you or turn you over to the authorities."

Locklear heard the slight whisper of an air gun and felt the sting of an insect bite in her arm. She looked down and saw that she had a dart sticking out of her arm. She reached down and retrieved it quickly, standing to move.

The drug was moving quickly through her system as she felt dizzy and began to lose control of her muscle movements. Locklear stumbled off the porch, holding her pistol, firing it wildly at Falco at the same time arms wrapped around her.

"Now, now, Lindy, no need to go and get all trigger happy on us."

"Go to hell, Sam Nix," she managed to say.

At the same time, Falco was saying, "Take these cuffs off me, Nix. That bitch grazed me."

"Looks like she did more than that, Vinny," Nix said. "I've got to come over here and clean up your mess. Thought you were taking care of everything?"

Nix laid the now unconscious Locklear on the sand.

"I got Dakota out of the picture and I'm sure Mahegan has been caught by now," said Vinny. "Locklear's the last one and we're home free."

"Perhaps," Nix said. He stared at the *Teach's Pet* for a long moment. "What do you know about that ship?"

"Unlock my damn cuffs and I'm happy to talk about whatever you damn well please."

Nix ignored his remark. "I know we use it on occasion for transshipments, but as I was looking through Royes's stuff, I found a spectrum analysis report. Seems there's quite a bit of activity coming from that ship. Internet, cellular, radio transmissions and the like. So, again, Vinny, what do you know about all of that?"

Nix nudged his pistol underneath the chin of his partner. "Have you done something that I don't know about?" he asked.

"C'mon, boss. It's me. Vinny Falco. We were in Afghanistan together. Iraq. Every other shithole as we tried to build our business. What would I do with that stupid relic?"

Nix leaned forward and whispered in his ear.

"You better not be lying to me, cocksucker. There's millions riding on this and I have to completely trust you."

"We laid all that cable out there so that we could communicate with the team. I've never even been be-lowdecks on that thing. Chikatilo is the only one who goes out there."

"Speaking of which, where the hell has he been?"

"Not sure. Said he had some business to take care of and then he'd be back. Been a few days."

Nix pulled the handcuff key from Locklear's pocket, feeling a little more of her bare leg with his free hand than was necessary.

"She's looking good, boss," Falco said.

"That she is," Nix said, licking his lips. He unlocked the cuffs on Falco and said, "Drag her ass into the truck. She could be useful."

Falco waved his hand at Nix's pistol. "Let me just finish her off right here. End this bullshit."

"Too risky. You ever get caught, you'll be in prison for life if they don't give you the needle."

"We can blame it on Mahegan. I'm sure his DNA is all over this joint." He waved his hand around the cabin and front porch.

"Negative. We need Mahegan. On the off chance he's alive, we need bait. Which means we need Lock-lear."

"Well, using your logic, she's bait for a whole bunch of three-letter agencies."

"Not if they don't know where she is. Mahegan will know. And he'll want to do it alone. That's his mode."

They carried Locklear to Nix's truck. Falco had his hands under her armpits, his fingers rubbing her breasts. Nix had her ankles, legs spread sufficiently to give him a decent view inside her running shorts. They slid her into the back of the pickup Nix had parked a hundred yards away.

Driving back to Copperhead, Inc. on Dare County Mainland, Falco asked, "Do we have any reports from Galaxy?"

"Haven't been able to reach them. They're busy."

Chapter 36

Mahegan had secured the lines that held the Bombard in place to prevent the boat from being blown to sea just as the *Lucky Lindy's* two inboard 220-horsepower motors gunned to full throttle.

He held the pistol up toward the gunwale and remained low against the aft of the ship, crouching beneath the tarp covering the Bombard. As they raced away from the rocketing explosions, the chain of events happened better than he could have hoped.

Le Concord had lost the back third of its ship and was sinking rapidly. Its bow was angled upward at forty-five degrees, looking like a piece of modern art. The turbulent waters around the ships boiled with gasses being released and fires burning from lit detritus.

The scene was diminishing rapidly for Mahegan as the *Lucky Lindy* sped mercilessly away from the inferno. He noticed that there were further secondary explosions that had spread to the *Ocean Ranger*, which now had spotlights trained on the waters, presumably looking for survivors or perhaps even Mahegan himself.

A bit late, Mahegan thought.

It was only a matter of time until the *Ocean Ranger* also caught fire with diesel fuel blowing like a cut artery onto the water and the partner ship. Like a lighter held up to an open aerosol can, *Le Concord* was spewing diesel and flames in a brilliant arc skyward that was landing all over the faux gold mining operation. Busy deckhands were using large hoses to spray the burning fuel, which in many cases only served to spread the diesel.

By now, the thrum of the engines and the giant rooster tail spitting out the back of the *Lucky Lindy* were all Mahegan could hear of the activities onboard. As he watched the burning ships from a distance, to Mahegan's eyes the flames bundled together into a diminishing speck. He wondered why the crew of this survivable ship had not circled back to save the others. Perhaps they had their marching orders. He didn't know. In reality, what could they have done? Their load was maxed out with the ghosts and the basic rule in combat was to cut your losses.

He began to calculate his next series of moves. He felt good. He was back in the hunt. He had just destroyed a significant load of MVX-90s and saved an incalculable number of American and coalition soldiers' lives. That was some small redemption for Colgate and all of his warrior brethren. But he couldn't rest. The warehouse wasn't empty and there was more at play, he was certain.

Copperhead, Inc. had proven that they were working several azimuths, most illicit, aimed toward a larger goal. At the end of the day, Mahegan figured, it all boiled down to money. Paramount was the gold. Then came the trades of MVX-90s and bombs for free, slave labor.

Now, he looked at the problem as if he had to crack a safe. With this find, he had turned the tumblers sufficiently to have one turn left to go. But it was a difficult challenge. He believed that whatever the main operation was, aside from the gold, had to do with the prisoners held on this ship and those that were at the moment perishing on the *Ocean Ranger*.

Mahegan figured that an operation the size that Copperhead was running on Dare County Bombing Range would require maybe twenty-five to fifty employees. Yet, Locklear had told him that there was not a single Roanoke Island citizen that anyone knew of that had been hired. Could this have been what Royes had discovered? Some kind of personnel irregularity through pay records? He was more certain than ever that these captives in the bottom of *Le Concord* and now in the hold of the *Lucky Lindy* were the slave labor for the demining operation.

He could see how it might work. Import a bunch of ghost prisoners, illicitly taken off the battlefield, and use them as worker bees. Hiding a detainee was exceptionally easy. A small squad captures someone and they turn him over to the contract interrogators that the Army hired for every forward operating base in Afghanistan and Iraq. Copperhead, Inc. had the contract for several years, had done reasonably well, and then a scandal broke about how they were abusing some prisoners. An investigation revealed that they had interrogated and moved some detainees around two years ago, but the detainees had escaped. That escape had led to another investigation, which ultimately led to the cancellation of the contract for all of Iraq and Afghanistan.

Here he was on this fishing craft with about ten such "ghosts" imprisoned below and headed toward what he believed to be a future of trudging through the muck of

Dare County Bombing Range, stepping on a few mines, maybe losing a limb or two, and perhaps even being left out there to die. Again, he didn't have any affinity for these people, at least not the guilty ones, but when he compared them to the team at Copperhead, Inc., he wondered who the real enemy was.

His solemn duty was to defend against all enemies, foreign and domestic.

And more than anything, he had to see what the final destination for these men was. To be sure, he would never make it if he just stayed on the swim platform and docked with the group. What would he say when they saw him? "Hey, thanks for the lift?"

On the other hand, conducting a one-man takedown of the craft could be problematic. Aside from the detainees, there were at least four Copperhead crewmen. Such uncertainties were difficult to adequately predict. And while he was more spontaneous than most, he believed that he'd had his one big lucky break tonight with the utter destruction of the ships.

He calculated that they had traveled nearly an hour, the boat droning endlessly against the chop of the Atlantic Ocean and the black firmament above. As the crew powered the boat, Mahegan figured they were doing about sixty knots. Knowing they needed to go about 140 miles, that was three hours. Now, they were about two hours out. He thought that ninety minutes from now might make the perfect time to enact his plan.

Keeping quiet, he moved slowly and double-checked the three fuel tanks, hefting them and discerning they were either full or close to full. No problems. The problem would be keeping them in the boat. He saw two bungee cords securing the gas cans, but felt he needed more. He removed one of the lines securing the boat to the D-ring, freed it completely, and then looped it through the handles of the three gas cans while also tying bowline knots onto D-rings inside the Bombard rubber boat.

Now he checked the engine. The Tahatsu fifteen-hp outboard motor was not ideal but he knew he could get thirty knots out of it. He had the range, but not the time. The *Lucky Lindy* would be moving twice as fast as him. He knew if he didn't return to shore first, then Copperhead, Inc., and perhaps others, would be lying in wait for him.

He loosened the two ties on the tarp that were on the aft end of the swim platform. Next he tied slipknots that he could pull, allowing the Bombard to slide into the water. Securing his stolen radio inside his backpack and ensuring its watertight seal, he then used a climber's snap-link to hook the backpack into the bottom of the Bombard.

He began nudging the Bombard to the back of the Lindy's teak-stained swim platform. The boat was heavy with the gas and the engine. Nothing he couldn't manage, but it was not a simple task of flipping the boat over the side and diving in. He took the long bowline and began maneuvering the nose of the Bombard toward the aft of the *Lucky Lindy* swim platform. He wanted the motor to go in the water first to keep the weight in the back and prevent it from nosing over. He checked the latches on the motor, ensuring they were tightened against the aft of the Bombard. The last thing he wanted was to lose the engine one hundred miles away from the coast.

He felt the unmistakable shift of the fishing boat's engines until they came to an idling rest in the middle of the Atlantic Ocean. The sudden shift in momentum rolled him toward the aft end of the *Lucky Lindy*.

"Okay, go get him," the voice said.

"Aye."

Mahegan held tight, aiming his pistol toward the tarp again. He heard the vibrations of feet on the deck, but they seemed to be heading away from him.

Muffled shouts were coming from belowdecks. Mahegan felt the boat tossing with the endless swells that slapped the side of boat from the northwest. The wet smack against the hull set an ominous tone.

"Inshallah!"

"Shut up, raghead. You're the lucky lottery winner. We'll be done with you quick, unlike your comrades down there."

"C'mon, dickhead, just do your thing. Nix is gonna be pissed we cut the manpower."

"He's extra, so just let me do my thing, as you call it."

"Well, hurry up. We've got all kinds of distress signals out there and the Coast Guard is going to full alert. We're going to look pretty strange coming back into the port when we should be going out on another early morning fishing run."

"Inshallah!"

"Shut up, you piece of shit. What I'm about to do to you is more than you deserve."

"Please. Please. No kill. Interpreter for American forces. I love Americans."

"Yeah, yeah. Famous last words."

Mahegan lay still, listening to the interchange. Before he could do anything, he heard a yelp that he recognized. One of the Copperhead men on the deck had just stuck one of the prisoners with a knife and it sounded like he was working the knife inside the victim.

"Pluh—pluh," was the only noise the prisoner could make.

Mahegan knew what was next. The splash came shortly after, followed by the boat driver saying, "C'mon, no blood on the ship, man."

"Say it's marlin blood. Raise the flag upside down."

Fishermen flew flags for big game fish off the trolling rigs or masts of their vessels when coming into port. If the flag was upside down, it meant catch and release. If right side up, it meant the fish was onboard.

"All right. Raise the flag, but we're hauling ass."

Mahegan felt the boat engines gun and the rearward tilt of the boat pulled the Bombard a bit farther off the swim platform.

He checked his equipment one last time and began feeding the Bombard into the jet spray of the rooster tail behind the ship.

He secured the two lines on the tarp, reestablishing the forty-five-degree angle of the tarp from the top of the gunwale down to the base of the freeboard. In effect, if no one checked, he would be just fine. They had been moving for about ten minutes since they had killed the prisoner and he felt the moment was close at hand.

"Hey, asshole, what are you doing?"

It was the same voice of the man who had gutted the prisoner and dumped him overboard for the sharks. And it was talking to him. The man had loosened one end of the tarp and had lowered himself half over the gunwale in pursuit, chest first.

Mahegan didn't waste much time. He used his knife to cut the bowline, sending the Bombard careening into the black water. In a seamless move, he half turned his upper body and flipped the knife into the chest of his challenger, who had drawn his pistol.

The man flipped over the gunwale, grasping at the knife and letting loose a couple of errant shots. Mahegan was certain these were reflexive shots, his fingers clutching at the pain of the knife in his chest, but they would alert the crew. His attacker actually flipped over the gunwale onto the base of the swim platform. Mahegan clasped his knife, secured it in his scabbard, hugged the man, and slid effortlessly into the Atlantic Ocean. He held the man for a few seconds as they rocked through the turbulence created by the twin screws propelling the boat.

Still, the abrupt change in plans had separated him from the Bombard by at least one hundred yards, which Mahegan knew could be a lifetime in the powerful currents off Cape Hatteras. He released the bleeding man into the cold Atlantic, certain the blood gushing from his chest would draw sharks within thirty minutes, if not sooner.

He watched the corpse bob in the water and twist so that he was floating facedown. Mahegan swiveled his head and kicked away from the dead man. He saw the diminishing plume of the rooster tail heading into the darkness. In the opposite direction, he detected the faintest sliver of gray breaking over the horizon. The Bombard would be headed in that direction. He spied the rapidly evaporating wake of the *Lucky Lindy*, and it was enough to get him started in the right direction. A line of bubbles marked the centerline where the two Mercury engines had propelled the boat westward toward shore.

Without the weight or drag of his backpack, Mahegan glided about twenty meters, stopped, scanned the horizon, and repeated the process. The swells were at least five feet and he had to elevate himself by timing his kick into a rising swell. A cool wind pushed the swells higher

and he knew the weather could change quickly, especially at sea. His wetsuit was a four-millimeter; not the
worst, but not ideal by any standard for the deep Atlantic.

He bobbed in the vastness of the Atlantic Ocean, the
sound of the *Lucky Lindy* no longer detectable even to
his excellent hearing. Swells shoved him as he rose and
sank with the constant sloshing.

He swam about one hundred meters to the east,
where he predicted the Bombard had splashed into the
water. Searching for ten minutes and seeing nothing,
he let his body feel the general flow of the current.
South.

He began chopping through the increasing seas in
the direction the raft would be floating . . . if it hadn't
sunk.

Another ten minutes, twenty altogether and he saw
nothing but black water against a black horizon.

Even with the wetsuit, Mahegan knew he wouldn't
last long in the freezing Atlantic Ocean.

Bobbing hopelessly in the sea, those mustangs that
wanted to escape from Mahegan's mind and gallop
were pushing at the corral. But he could least afford at
this very moment, with hope fading, to do anything but
concentrate on the task at hand.

To find the Bombard, which was nowhere in sight.

Chapter 37

@TuffChik, come to Mama!

Standing near the pier on Milltail Creek in Dare County Mainland, Chikatilo looked at his Droid phone and deciphered the innocuous tweet to determine that Mullah Adham had ordered the MOAB into action. The Massive Ordnance Air Blast. The Mother of All Bombs.

It would take two days to reach its destination, so Chikatilo figured Adham wanted to get it moving now, for the big finale. Fine with him.

Chikatilo had driven from Virginia Beach to the Copperhead compound two hours ago when he'd learned Mahegan had attacked the operation.

He turned to Lars Olsen, who had survived Mahegan, and said, "You ready?"

They were standing at the pier in Milltail Creek. Below them were Vader One, Vader Two, and Vader Three. Vader Three was a large submersible that had been built with extra payload capacity to carry personnel or ordnance. It looked like a small submarine, motionless at the end of the pier. Copperhead had acquired it from the Drug Enforcement Agency at the low, government-subsidized price of $200,000. The DEA had seized it in a drug raid. Falco had added it to the second option year of the bomb-clearing contract once they had developed their entire plan for gaining back their market share.

When under way, the submersible could make thirty knots and was small enough to evade most radar. If Vader One and Vader Two were "Smart Technology," which they were, then Vader Three was basic blunt force, dumb technology powered by a three-hundred-horsepower diesel motor.

Falco and Olsen had cut the submersible, inserted the MOAB, and then arc welded the two parts back together. Limited test runs had proven it reliable. It sat at the end of the pier, facing west, the way out of Milltail Creek and into the Alligator River. The creek was broad and deep, running dark with the rich elements of the refuge.

The two modern Vader prototypes were on either side of the pier.

"I get two ghosts, right?" Olsen asked.

"Aye. Two ghosts. You take Vader Three up the intracoastal, into the Chesapeake, and up the Potomac. You can jump off somewhere near Mount Vernon. Best to be as far away from this thing as you can. It has old chemicals in the warhead and we're not quite sure what they will do. It's fully rigged and will steer itself. Just program it. You're just there to babysit the ghosts, so that they ride it all the way into Buzzard Point and Fort McNair at about six a.m."

"What's the blast radius of the MOAB?"

"Bitch will kill everything within two miles. You fry all those generals in the big houses and that should do the trick. They will definitely be asking for security contracts."

Olsen nodded. "Any way we can have Mahegan up there so I can fry his ass?"

"Word I'm hearing is that Mahegan is dead and gone."

"If that's true, would be none too soon." Olsen nodded toward the shore. "There's O'Leary."

A large, bearded man dressed in camouflage fatigues was escorting two ghost prisoners, his hands pushing them forward. The ghosts emerged from a manhole cover near the pier and walked through the forest toward the men, their faces sunken and hands secured with cuffs. They were dark, of Arabic descent, and dressed in brown jumpsuits.

"Okay, men, time to do the jihad thing," Chikatilo said.

They lowered the two ghosts into the semi-submersible. Olsen looked at his two partners and said, "I know Falco's got our back on this, but I still get a bit uneasy, you know? We're attacking our own military."

He shivered, perhaps shaking off the thought of how far he had drifted from his enlisted days in the Navy.

"Those generals and admirals bankrupted our company, Lars. Bow up, big guy," Chikatilo said. "Plus, not my military. Not my country, remember?"

Olsen nodded. O'Leary and Chikatilo did the warrior's clasp of hand to forearm with Olsen and each gave him a half-shoulder bump.

"Last mission for you. We've got some loose ends to clean up here and then we conduct linkup and Rainbow is a reality."

Olsen lowered himself into Vader Three. Chikatilo put a foot onto the top of the submarine hatch, and then silently slid a Master lock through a hasp, sealing Olsen's fate along with that of the ghosts. O'Leary pretended not to notice Chikatilo's betrayal of Olsen.

"Teach him to let an Indian kick his ass," Chikatilo said.

The submarine was soon under way on its programmed 276-mile circuitous route through the intracoastal waterway to Washington, DC.

Chapter 38

Hopeless.

The word had never entered Mahegan's vocabulary. He steeled himself against the despair that the situation warranted. There had to be a way.

Thirty minutes had passed and he knew that with each second the odds of him finding the Bombard diminished. He continued swimming south, feeling a slight push of cold water: the Labrador Current.

Then he felt it.

There was a subtle push against his momentum coupled with noticeably warmer water. And he actually felt himself crab a bit to the east, perpendicular to his line of travel.

He paused and floated, feeling the unmistakable current pulling him eastward, away from the coast. Salt water slapped him in the face as he rapidly crossed his arms to tread water. He looked left, to the east, and thought, *Gulf Stream*.

Could he be at that point where the Labrador Current and Gulf Stream joined? If so, what would that mean for the Bombard? It might be farther east than he had anticipated.

He turned east and swam, cutting through growing swells.

Then he saw it.

On the horizon, he spotted an unnatural outline bobbing at the crest of a swell about fifty yards south of his path. It was backlit by the dawn easing over the horizon. The current had been moving north to south and taking the lightweight craft with it. But here it had turned east, as the vector of the Gulf Stream pushed against the Labrador Current.

Mahegan chased it down after five minutes of struggling through the chop. The Bombard had capsized so Mahegan climbed on the underside, which was facing skyward, and grabbed a rope running along the top rib of the raft. Standing, he did a backward flop into the ocean while holding the line, which pulled the boat right side up.

Altogether, he had spent less than an hour from the time he cut the raft loose until he was sitting inside the Bombard. Not bad, he thought, but not good enough.

Mahegan took stock of his position. The first rule of a paratrooper was to tie everything down. His backpack was still on the boat, flipped upside down but still present for duty. The three gas cans had remained secured by the same line he had tied through eyelets atop the gunwale of the Bombard. He unscrewed their tops, checked the reservoirs, and retightened them. They were all full. The real question was whether the engine had sustained any damage in the drop from the *Lucky Lindy*.

Mahegan opened his backpack and removed his pistol from the airtight bag. He released the magazine, checked its contents, and secured it back in the magazine well. Though the AK-47 was forever lost, he was grateful for the pistol. The Bombard rocked constantly in the tossing ocean as Mahegan waited for all of the fuel lines to readjust to being upright. The wait was agonizing as he visualized the *Lucky Lindy* reversing course to look for their missing comrade.

His patience having run its course, he opened the fuel line from one of the red gas tanks, gave it a few seconds to feed into the engine, and then pulled the choke on the Tahatsu. After two cranks, the motor spit white smoke and rewarded Mahegan with a steady purr.

He looked over his shoulder at the breaking dawn and turned the nose of the Bombard into the western darkness. He opened the throttle to full and began to power through the growing swells.

He estimated in his mind that he had been on the *Lucky Lindy* for ninety minutes after the explosion. Estimating that the Copperhead crew was cruising at fifty mph, he figured he had no way to catch them. He would make landfall in two more hours if he reached a top end speed of thirty mph. So he would have to improvise.

Locking the wide-open throttle, he opened his backpack and retrieved the radio he had acquired from *Le Concord*. He turned up the volume, hoping to hear some traffic. After five minutes of static buzz and relentless bouncing in the Bombard, he began switching channels, listening for a few seconds, and then switching again. It reminded him of trying to find a decent radio station when driving through the country. Instead of fading music, all he heard was a whining squelch until he caught a faint whisper on one of the higher spectrum channels.

". . . BOLO . . . hegan . . . Coast Guard . . . he . . . say again . . . terrorist"

The words faded quickly and he held the radio high

in the air to see if he could get better reception. Mahegan knew what the term "BOLO" meant—be on the lookout—but he couldn't put together the rest. He pulled the radio down when a series of swells rocked the boat until he needed to hang on to the ribs of the Bombard with two hands.

After twenty more minutes of trying to find another station, he returned to the frequency where he had heard the fragment of information. If that frequency was the common bandwidth for the Coast Guard, then anything he heard might be helpful.

But he thought he had heard enough. Be on the lookout for Mahegan. This, coming through government channels, was a problem. Coast Guard, FBI, CIA, and DHS would all be descending on him. He had gotten inside the wheelhouse of somebody much bigger than a small-time military contractor. He knew firms like Blackwater or Xe, Triple Canopy, and others were powerful and had big-time connections, but Copperhead had gone south in a big way. They were lepers among the defense industrial complex and no public official or military officer in their right mind should want to have anything to do with Copperhead, Inc.

As he steered the Bombard into the gray morning, the sunrise was outracing his ability to get into Croatan Sound under the cover of darkness. He knew of the treacherous opening through Oregon Inlet. Buzzing along the tops of the swells, he finally saw a speck of light that he figured to be Bodie Island lighthouse, which would guide him into Oregon Inlet.

With a faint shimmer of hope buzzing through his body, Mahegan saw the orange tracers arcing through the gray dawn before he heard them hiss past him. Immediately, he altered course, knowing he would be a tough target to hit from a floating platform.

From the south he saw the boat bearing down on him. It seemed bigger than the *Lucky Lindy*, but he had only seen the craft in the dark, and light could play tricks on visual perception. Still, this looked more like a ship than a fishing boat.

"Shut down your engines!" The voice was broadcast through a speaker system. "This is the United States Coast Guard. Stop your vessel so that we may safely come alongside."

With no chance of outrunning the ship and no chance of swimming to shore, Mahegan slowed the Bombard. He retrieved the pistol from his backpack seconds before the searchlight found him. He calculated that this boat must have come from port in Atlantic Beach Coast Guard Station, which was well south of Oregon Inlet. He silently cursed the *Lucky Lindy* crew for having stopped to kill one of the prisoners. That loss of time, and the subsequent search for the Bombard, had given this ship enough of a lead to cut him off at Oregon Inlet.

"Disable any weapons that you have and keep your hands where we can see them!"

He kept the pistol in the hip pouch on his wetsuit. The Coast Guard personnel would see the weapon. Just in case they weren't actual Coast Guardsmen, though, he would have a fighting chance with the pistol nearby.

The ship looked to be about one hundred feet long, maybe more. Its superstructure was just about as high as its length. A radar dish was spinning atop a steel frame, and a .50 caliber machine gun was mounted with a night optic on top.

When Mahegan shut off the engine, he heard a slight buzzing noise above him in the sky and realized that the Coast Guard had used an unmanned aerial system to locate him. It was a smart move. They probably had only a few patrol boats, yet had reacted fast. He had been thinking tactically about getting to Copperhead as quickly as possible and had momentarily lost sight of the big strategic picture.

He had been a wanted man ever since he'd left Afghanistan. He knew that General Savage could only do so much to protect him and it appeared that coverage had ended. He ran several courses of action through his mind, but none of them seemed to be good. He had no idea what they wanted him for. He quickly surmised that whoever was moving and counting on the gold and ghosts had just received a stark wake-up call.

And whoever that person was could put in motion the United States Coast Guard. Suddenly, Copperhead, Inc. appeared more of a pawn in this operation than he had originally suspected.

As the ship pulled alongside, the searchlight shone on him as if he were the lead singer at a rock concert. He could read the letters on the side of the vessel: *Aquidneck* with the numbers *1309*.

The searchlight and the .50 caliber machine gun sealed his fate. He thought he remembered that this boat had secured the Navy fleet in the Persian Gulf at the beginning of Iraq II. If so, he knew there was a hardened crew of sailors on board that were professionals.

Underscoring this thought, up above the gunwale he could see a row of sailors with M16s trained on him. He understood the play now. He was an alleged terrorist in charge of both the Brackett and Suffolk bombings as well as the sinking of an American vessel at sea. That, coupled with the murder of one or two individuals near Roanoke Island and his history of killing a prisoner of war, spelled certain doom for Mahegan.

At least, that was how he knew authorities were spinning the story, getting their charges amped up to lock him down. Capture him.

"Keep your hands where we can see them!"

Two frogmen leapt over the side of the patrol boat and were instantly at the side of the Bombard. They popped up, looking like ninjas in their dive suits. The Bombard rocked softly in the swells as they guided the inflatable boat to the port side of the *Aquidneck*. They had ropes, which each of them looped through eyelets atop the rib of the Bombard.

A deckhand flipped a ladder over the side and one of the frogmen said, "Remove all weapons from your person and slowly climb the ladder."

Secure with the knowledge that he was among professional servicemen, he said, "I have a pistol in my wetsuit. I can see each of you has a weapon aimed at me along with about ten of your guys up on the deck. I'm not stupid. I'm going to remove the pistol and lay it in the boat."

"Do that." The voice was authoritative.

Mahegan removed the pistol and laid it on the floor of the Bombard. He reached out and secured the ladder and then began climbing. Once he was coming over the gunwale, he had about four men on top of him, cuffing him and dragging him into custody.

They sat him in a room for about an hour before a man opened the door. As he looked up, General Stanley Bream ducked beneath the lintel, stepped into the room, which was nothing more than a very small office, and closed the door behind him.

Then locked it.

Chapter 39

"**O**kay, asshole, this room is sealed tighter than a ram's ass," Bream said. "You're looking good for a whole bunch of shit and before I turn you over to the hounds, I need some answers. We've got one John Doe of Arabic descent at Fort Brackett and two in Suffolk. Who are these people and where did they come from?"

Mahegan eyed the general. It had been two days since he had stood toe-to-toe with the man in his office. No longer carrying the confident look of arrogance, the general appeared wild-eyed and just short of frightened. Mahegan had seen the look many times in combat, especially on fresh, young troops. The lack of any combat experience would account for Bream's absence of confidence here. Mahegan knew false bravado when he saw it, and this was certainly a display. Still, the general had used the old high school debate trick of attacking with a question.

Mahegan ignored the question and asked, "How can I help you?" Pausing a moment, he then added, "Sir."

Exhaustion began to claw at the back of his mind like a dredge raking his brain. The adrenaline dump had carried him through the night, but now he was feeling the cumulative impact of two days with little rest or food.

"You can help me by answering my questions or telling me what the hell happened out at sea. I'm good with either for starters."

Mahegan paused. He played out several scenarios in his mind and landed on the most probable.

"You involved in all that gold moving around out there?" Another pause. "Sir."

Bream studied him a second before replying.

"You don't have any idea what you're saying, soldier. Just tell me what happened. You're wanted by about five different agencies right now and I can help if you cooperate."

"Are you offering me a deal, general?"

Bream opened the zipper on his Army combat uniform and yanked down his T-shirt, showing his bare chest.

"Not wearing a wire, soldier. This is between us. But, yes, if you tell me what happened at sea, I will do my best to see you get treated fairly."

Mahegan's lip turned up a fraction, his best imitation of a smile.

"I have to assume, then, that if I don't cooperate, you'll do your best to see that I am treated unfairly."

"Your words, not mine."

"Well, here's what happened. I jumped from an airplane onto a ship named *Le Concord*. It was filled with Arabic terrorists. It came alongside another ship called the *Ocean Ranger*. The *Ocean Ranger* appeared to have a lot of gold and ammunition on it. I'm talking bricks of gold, like you might see at Fort Knox. And I'm talking bombs, like you might find at an old bomb-

ing range. And I'm also talking about MVX-90 deto-
nators, like you might find at an electronic warfare
testing range."

"Gold?"

"Yes, gold."

Mahegan paused. He noticed Bream leaning forward, his jet-black hair disheveled. The man licked his
lips and Mahegan thought he saw some sweat start to
bead its way through the perfect stalks of hair. The general nodded at him as if to say, "Go on."

"And so the terrorists boarded the *Ocean Ranger*
and attacked the crew. It was like something out of a
pirate movie. They then transferred all of the gold and
all of the bombs and all of the MVX-90s onto *Le Concord*. Then the terrorists blew up the *Ocean Ranger*
and it appeared to be sinking as I left."

Mahegan spoke calmly, as if he had witnessed a
simple shoplifting crime.

"Wait a minute. You're telling me the *Ocean Ranger*
sank and that this *Concord* ship escaped? With this
supposed gold you keep talking about?"

"It was dark, but that's how it appeared to me," Mahegan said.

He figured this was his only move. If Bream was
dirty and working the gold, Mahegan knew he would
pursue any chance to recover it. The Army had taught
him that the best deception schemes gave his opponent
a dose of what he wanted to believe. In this case,
Mahegan felt as though the only reason that the Army
version of internal audit might be on the scene was because of a deep, personal interest. There was no way
that a three-star general would be on a Coast Guard patrol boat in the Atlantic Ocean interrogating a suspect
unless the circumstances were extreme. Extreme to the
point of personal involvement. Mahegan also noticed

the way Bream focused on the gold, not the ammunition or the MVX-90s.

Bream studied him for a long moment, seeming to regain some of his composure. He ran a hand across his face as if to wipe away what Mahegan figured was bad news to him. When Bream looked up at Mahegan, he looked even more tired and worn than before.

"Frankly, I don't believe you. How did you see all of this?"

"What's hard to believe is that you don't have Paslowski out here doing your bidding and keeping someone between you and your problem."

Mahegan watched Bream stare him down with his best general's glare.

"Agent Paslowski is trying to find your girlfriend, Lindy Locklear. It seems she's disappeared."

Mahegan rifled through their last moments, digesting the news. She had dropped him off at the airfield to link up with Dakota. She was going to head back to the bungalow and wait. The only thing he could think is that Copperhead had come after her. Nix or Falco. Or both.

"Where's Paslowski looking?"

"That's part of a federal investigation. An agent goes missing, they pull out all the stops."

"An agent?"

"Little slow on the uptake, aren't we, Mahegan? You sure you're not in over your head? She's with Treasury. The Terrorism and Financial Intelligence Department, known as TFID. She's been tracking all this gold you've moved out to sea. She works in their terrorist finance cell."

Mahegan processed what Bream was saying. His assessment had been pretty close.

"Gold that you think I've moved out to sea?"

"You're good for the whole thing, man. I mean this just keeps getting better and better. You raced through Copperhead yesterday and stole those MVX-90s and apparently some gold. You've traded or more likely sold that to terrorists. It will take me ten minutes to add something to your bank account or toss a duffel bag of counterfeit money in your room at the Queen Anne's Revenge. And now we've got you as the last one to see a federal agent before she disappeared."

"So what do you want from me? Just book me or whatever you guys call it."

"In due time. Tell me what you saw. All we got was the distress signal that you attacked the *Ocean Ranger*. There are probably ten recorded radio calls by different ships trying to assess your location because they saw you as a threat. But we know nothing about another ship, this terrorist ship you claim exists."

"Okay. I spent most of my time in the water. You see I'm wearing a wetsuit. I found the lat-long on a GPS, that's global positioning system, and bummed a flight over the location. Then I jumped, landed on the terrorist ship that now has your gold and bombs on it and is steaming back toward the Middle East."

Bream leaned back and smiled at Mahegan. It seemed like a forced grin, almost a grimace.

"I've got nothing to do with this, soldier. I'm investigating on behalf of the Army before I turn you over to the wolves. Because assuredly, once the FBI gets its hands on you, we will never have another crack at you. All this time I was actually going to give you a break on the murder in Afghanistan. I understood that you probably snapped in combat. It happens. Maybe even upgrade your discharge."

Mahegan ignored the general's obvious attempt at provoking him.

"Right. Then why are *you* out here interrogating me, general? It makes no sense, unless . . ."

"Unless what, Mahegan? This is about national security, son. It doesn't get any more serious than this. We took an oath to the Constitution of the United States to protect and defend against all enemies, foreign and domestic. Looks like we've got both here."

"You're damned right it is. I love these lofty terms you bureaucrats use. You know what national security means to me? It means preventing my buddy from being killed while I'm doing your bidding. It's a pretty simple concept."

Another smile creased Bream's face.

"Well, you failed there, didn't you, soldier?"

The corral in Mahegan's mind went wide open and thoughts and emotions raced forward like wild, unbroken mustangs. He was actually glad he was handcuffed. Otherwise, he knew he might harm the general, maybe kill him.

Therein, he knew, lay his problem. He had an "on" switch and an "off" switch, but little in between. In the end, he refused to lose his temper in front of this pompous bureaucrat. Bream had advanced through the military, in Mahegan's view, because the organization promoted mediocrity while weeding out the highly competent and the highly incompetent, advancing those of marginal competence and risk-taking ability.

"What's the matter, Mahegan? You were all full of cock and bull before. Thinking about Colgate?"

"Yes, sir. Thinking about Colgate and how one of your MVX-90s killed him."

"I'm done with you, asshole. Here's what's going to happen. I'm going to get on my airplane and fly back to DC. I'll be in the office by eight a.m. This is a black operation and no one will ever know I was here. Meanwhile, you'll be escorted to federal custody and charged with the bombings of Fort Brackett and Suffolk Compound as well as the destruction of an American vessel. You admitted to being on the terrorist ship *Le Concord* and I will make sure the FBI knows this. Meanwhile, you'll be charged with two, possibly three, murders in North Carolina. The federal part will take a few years, during which you will be in Fort Leavenworth prison. Once convicted of treason and murder, the state courts can have their bite at you if they wish. You'll get the needle for certain, but I'm sure the families of those you killed will want their vengeance. That's how this is going to play out."

Mahegan felt that Bream was describing an "either-or" scenario to him, so he said, "Or?"

"Or, nothing. There's no way for you to recover the gold or the munitions that you sold to the terrorists."

"So there's no way to make this right in your world? Not even if Adham is involved?"

Bream paused. Mahegan knew that for Bream to survive in the "meritocracy" as long as he had, Bream must have understood nuance and subtlety. He needed to have someone between him and the problem.

"Adham? Go on."

"If I jumped into this thing once, I can get there again."

"And do what? Take over the ship and turn it around? Then waltz into a port and say, here's your terrorist?"

"No. Look. I'm a liability to you right now. I know. I know. You don't have to say anything." Mahegan held his cuffed hands up in mock surrender, as if warding off an attacker. "So the way I see it, you can gamble on the chance that I don't talk or that no one believes me that you flew all the way out here to interrogate me.

There's a fifty-fifty chance, though, that something I say will get traction. Then, at the very least, your gig is up, possibly forever. You overplayed your hand here trying to reel me in. Put out that BOLO when I fell off the grid. I can see how that might happen. It was a bold move, for sure."

Mahegan then shifted gears, turning his disgust into false platitudes. He figured Bream had been hearing it all of his life from his subordinates, from whom he required such nonsense. Figuring that Bream didn't have the spine to kill him, or have him killed, Mahegan played his only angle: Bream's ambition and inflated ego.

"So, I see it this way. You have absolutely pulled off an incredible feat here. The only problem is that you've got nothing to show for it except a loser former captain put away in prison for something he didn't do. Is that the legacy you want? I don't think so. I saw probably ten million in gold. That will buy a lot of retirement, general. And I know where that boat is going." Mahegan kept talking, not wanting to give Bream a chance to think just yet.

"So what have you got to lose? You said yourself this is a black op. You can dump me overboard when we're near the beach and I can swim in. You guys found an abandoned Bombard, but it wasn't me. I'm still on the loose. Meanwhile, I'm on the way to find your stash. The only thing I need is a way to get in touch with you once I get the ship under control."

Bream turned and looked at the locked door, then leveled his eyes on Mahegan.

"Where is it going?"

"Now why would I give up my only hole card? You know how this works, general. You've been slaving

A. J. Tata

away in the Army for thirty-plus years. The give-and-take of the bureaucracy, sir. This is just another angle you've got to work."

"I don't know what you're talking about. We found you, we can find this boat. You're so full of shit, Mahegan, your eyes are turning brown. You want to reach me? Call the Inspector General hotline."

Bream paused as if to reflect. "You know, I graduated from the Academy in 1979. As I said the other day, we were the last class with balls. All male. They brought the bitches in for class of 1980. We all had LCWB inscribed on the inside of our rings. And I'll admit it takes balls to do what you've done, Mahegan. But treason? I cannot respect that. Find me Adham, maybe."

Bream stood and walked out of the room.

A strange mix of exhaustion and adrenaline overcame Mahegan. Squaring off with an Army three-star was no small feat, yet at least he had fit another piece of the puzzle together. Bream had the inside dirt on every officer in the army. He was the J. Edgar Hoover of the military, trading secrets and trading information. Bream could place a dragnet on him one hundred miles long up and down the North Carolina coast involving all the big-name agencies. And he could walk out knowing he was spotless. Mahegan knew that one of two things was going to happen.

Every authority known to man was going to press charges against him for their piece of the action and he was going to be in the system for a long time. Or, something else would happen.

Mahegan was banking on something else.

Chapter 40

About an hour later, something else happened.

He could tell the patrol boat had been maneuvered into port by the forward-reverse machinations of the engine he heard and felt from the deck below. The motor turned off, and soon he began to wonder if he was alone. He heard no voices and, barring guards on the dock, felt no vibrations of boots moving along the deck.

He opened the desk drawer that had been facing Bream and found a heavy gauge paper clip sitting in the pen tray. He bent it and went to work on his cuffs. A minute later, he was free.

The door was locked, though he heard footsteps and muffled conversation on the other side directly before it opened.

"Well, there you are, son."

Mahegan turned to find Dare County Sheriff Mitch Johnson standing in the dark doorway.

"Sheriff, what the hell is going on?"

"That's what I'm here to ask you. Seems like we need to talk."

"Get me off this boat and let's go somewhere."

"I had to fight to get a few hours of custody of you so I can get what I need for the murder investigations. For once, locals trumped the FBI. Plus, the Coast Guard made the colossal screwup of docking here in Wanchese, which is Dare County property, not a Coast Guard base."

"Okay."

"Of course, it helps when my brother is the captain of the ship. And he docked here, not in Atlantic Beach where a few dozen federal agents are waiting for you."

Johnson led him to the top deck. Before they departed, Johnson nodded at a tall figure standing in the captain's bridge. The angle of the stairwell gave them a view into the back of the command center. "Thanks, Lonnie."

"Don't know what you're talking about, bro."

Johnson turned back to Mahegan. "In case someone notices us walking off this boat, I need to you do the perp walk off this here cutter."

Mahegan held out his hands as Johnson used his own cuffs. After thirty minutes they had departed the dock at Wanchese and arrived at the sheriff's house. Mahegan checked the clock on the sheriff's dashboard and saw that it was seven a.m. He looked out of the window and saw that Johnson lived on Croatan Sound at the end of Rogers Road. His home was a yellow Cape Cod with weathered rust-colored shake roof shingles. The shutters were black and appeared freshly painted. The driveway led to a garage in the back of the house, which also put them thirty yards from the sound. The nearest home was a hundred yards up Rogers Road on the opposite side of the road. Wetlands separated this spit of land from the rest of the homes.

It was private.

"Follow me," Johnson said, opening the door.

Mahegan followed him into the backyard and onto the deck. They entered through a French door. Inside, the home was well appointed with all the right touches, but something seemed off. Perhaps it was too sterile. Mahegan determined that it was missing the warm feel of a woman.

"Nice place, sheriff."

"Been in the family for years. Just me in here now."

Mahegan nodded. "Anything we can do about the cuffs?"

Johnson stared at him.

"I'm taking a big risk bringing you here, son. But you're my only shot. So, don't jack me over here, okay?"

"Depends on what you want me to do. If it's legal, I'm good."

"Well, we might have a problem there. I want my niece back. Those scumbags have kidnapped her. Probably killed my nephew, J.J., too. Along with Miller Royes. Legal? Who gives a shit about legal when they've got your family?"

It was back to the killings. Interesting.

"So now it's one killing, one possible killing, and a missing person?"

"Yes. While you've been playing cowboy, we've been investigating. I've got something to show you."

Mahegan nodded. His instincts from the beginning were that Johnson was a trustworthy man. He had nothing more than a few brief interactions on which to base this judgment, but sometimes those gut reactions were the most accurate, like the first answer on a multiple-choice test.

"Okay. Let me rephrase what I said. As long as it's just, I'm good."

"That's more like it."

The sheriff removed the handcuffs and nodded to a breakfast nook with a table and chairs. He was standing in an open kitchen of walnut cabinets and dark marble tile for countertops. A modern stainless refrigerator anchored one end of the kitchen while the nook with white shuttered window dressings anchored the other. There was a pass through the mudroom into the breezeway that led to the first of two garages. Mahegan could see the freestanding barnlike structure in the back near the sound.

"I'm making coffee and Rosa should be here any minute to make us breakfast. I imagine you're hungry."

"Starving."

"Okay. Do you want clothes and a shower first?"

"Deal."

He showed Mahegan to a shower and guest room upstairs. Mahegan showered for twenty minutes and stepped into the guest room, where Johnson had laid out some clothes on the bed. He had told him that his nephew in Virginia Beach was about the same size as Mahegan, extra-large. The jeans were an inch big around the waist, but otherwise the length was fine. The shirt was a black Under Armour spandex T-shirt. The work boots were tight, so he left them for when he would need them.

When he came around the corner, he smelled breakfast and saw an elderly Hispanic woman working in the kitchen. He saw two plates stacked with eggs and bacon and pancakes on the table. Johnson sat at the table waiting for him.

"This how you treat all your prisoners?" he asked Johnson.

"Only the ones who can help me."

Mahegan sat down and began to eat.

"Are we off the grid here?" Mahegan asked through a mouthful of eggs.

"If you mean, undercover or black ops as you guys call it, yes. If you mean can anyone find us here, well, yes, they can, but I've got a car at the end of the road and a boat out in the sound. We should be okay. Not airtight, but okay."

"So let's talk," Mahegan said.

They finished their meal, Mahegan devouring an extra helping of pancakes.

"Let's go to the garage," Johnson said.

They exited through the mudroom, into the breezeway, and then before entering the front garage, followed a flagstone path to the barn, which was a small replica of the house with fewer angles. It appeared more Dutch Colonial than Cape Cod. Probably a different builder, Mahegan thought.

Inside, Mahegan saw a 1965 light blue Mustang that appeared in near mint condition.

"Had that when I was a kid," Johnson said. "Nobody knew it would become a big collector's item."

"Looks like you've maintained it well."

"Love you Army guys. 'Maintained it.' Yeah, I've taken care of it."

They walked past the Mustang into a separate room. It was dark with no windows, and built with solid concrete that Mahegan figured were at least two blocks thick. They passed through a steel door like those on industrial freezers. Johnson locked that door and there appeared to be no other way out.

"We got shit for forensics and evidence techs and all of that. Oh, we have enough to make us look good and to get by on your basic stuff, but nothing to deal with the magnitude of what's going on right now."

Mahegan looked around. He felt like he was standing in the inside of an air-conditioned sea-land container. Maps hung on the long axis of the "room." At the far end were a plasma television and an army cot. At the near end were a workbench, industrial sink, and drafting table.

"So you created your own forensics lab?"

Johnson nodded.

"What I've got is two friends killed, a nephew missing, and a niece missing."

"Two killed?"

"Dakota washed up on the shore this morning. His plane crashed about a half mile out over the ocean. High tide carried him in with his throat slit. My information tells me that you jumped from his plane into the middle of the ocean last night looking for that gold. Then his plane landed briefly at the airport and took off again quickly. Then crashed into the ocean."

"Dakota was alive when I jumped. How else did he get back here?"

"I know that and you know that, but you were the last person to see him alive . . . other than whoever killed him."

Mahegan thought for a moment and changed tracks.

"Has Lindy lived here all her life?"

Johnson turned toward Mahegan and said, "Why do you ask?"

"Just curious."

After a moment, Johnson said, "She lived in Chicago with my sister for two years when she was in high school. There was a bad crowd here and my brother had to get her away. What's this about?"

"Is your sister's married name Carlsen?"

"No. Caveza. She married an Italian guy."

"Sorry. Just running down a lead. So she's really an agent with the Treasury Department?"

"Where'd you hear that?" Johnson seemed surprised. He laid his brown eyes on Mahegan, who returned the gaze. Mahegan took in Johnson's white hair, deep tan, and stoic countenance and nodded. He would trust the man.

"From General Bream, the Army Inspector General who flew out onto the patrol boat as I was being escorted back in."

"That guy? What did he want?"

"Well, it seems that you want me for murder, the Army wants me for espionage, and a bunch of other three-letter agencies want me for sinking ships and that sort of thing."

Johnson laughed.

"You're in deep shit, son. Bream's been down here a couple of times. Chasing beaver up and down the OBX. Usually rents some senator's house in Duck."

Mahegan registered this for a moment and felt a buzz, like he used to when a mission was beginning to fall into place.

"Well, the fact is, he blew her cover, if it's true."

"It's true. Lindy's the smartest thing I've ever seen. Grew up here surfing and reading all about the history of the Outer Banks. The two years she was in Chicago she got into acting and writing. She even wrote some children's books that got some good reviews. She came back and went to East Carolina, that's ECU, here on an academic scholarship, but I practically raised her and knew she wanted into law enforcement. We used to shoot right out in the backyard here. I'd put a target on the last pole at the end of the pier and it got to where she was putting a dime-sized hole at twenty-five meters through a bull's-eye. Best athlete I've ever seen. Run, jump, swim, swing a bat, you name it. Bitch of it was that when she was at ECU, she learned she's good with numbers and took a bunch of economics courses. After 9/11, when the wars were swinging into full gear, the Department of Treasury recruited Lindy to work in their intelligence and domestic terrorism. I'm the only one who knows this down here. Everyone else thinks she can't find a job. She acts in *The Lost Colony*, I have indeed deputized her, and she does that historical society thing with the Croatan. All of that is legit stuff she wants to do. But it's all cover. Given all of Copperhead's problems in Afghanistan and Iraq, Treasury wanted someone to keep an eye on them. Who better than a local girl who could blend in? Lindy thought it was babysitting duty, but she's a patriot and figured she's young so it was her way of working from the mailroom up, so to speak."

Mahegan reflected on this information for a moment, visualizing her smile, quick wit, and intelligence. He could see everything Johnson had just said. He felt electricity surge through his veins.

Mahegan sat in a chair and looked at the wall of maps. Johnson had giant maps of Roanoke Island, Dare County Mainland, and the Outer Banks all the way up to Virginia Beach on the wall. The sheriff apparently had placed tape indicators where certain events must have occurred. There was a blue sticker marking the location of where Mahegan had said he found Royes's body as well as two other blue stickers, one in Croatan Sound and one atop the theater.

"But instead of babysitting, she uncovers what she believes is a career-making kind of deal? Copperhead, the gold, and the murders?"

"That's right. And she was in over her head," Johnson said. "That's why I let her take you to DC. Liked what I saw in you from the beginning. Hauling Royes's body in from the sound. That was a class act."

"What are those for?" Mahegan asked, pointing at the blue stickers.

"You found Miller here," Johnson said, pointing at the blue sticker in the middle of the sound near a buoy. And this is the *Pet*," he added, pointing to another sticker before moving onto the next. "And here is the last known location of my nephew, Jack Johnson, known as J.J. He was leaving the theater the same morning you found Royes."

"Is this Lindy's brother?" Mahegan asked, his attention caught by a framed photo on Johnson's desk.

"No," Johnson said, shaking his head. "I have two brothers in addition to the sister in Chicago. J.J.'s father, Lonnie, who you met earlier on the Coast Guard cutter, and Lindy's father, Bob, who left after marrying a woman from Hatteras. She's a local and her family is part of the Indian heritage here. The Locklears go back a long way. Lindy officially changed to her mother's maiden name once Bob disappeared. So, you also might say we have a lot of baggage."

"No. Just a lot of life, sheriff. You're good people."

Johnson regarded Mahegan a second, and then said, "So let's look at this thing. In one day we have Royes killed and J.J. missing. Royes was working for a company called MagicAir that created the Merlin system. Copperhead has one of their airplanes with substructure that can see thermal images and such."

"The night optics Merlin? They tried to follow me yesterday when I blew through Copperhead."

"Heard about that. Ballsy move. But, yeah, the Merlin is an airplane with an optics ball underneath it that can see a pimple on a gnat's ass from outer space, or some shit like that."

"Not that good, but close enough."

"Anyway, Miller was an odd duck. He was a consultant. Did audits. Reviewed video. Did limited tech support. Jobs are hard to come by here in Dare County when it's not tourist season, so it's not unusual for people to have two or three income streams. So MagicAir hired him off the books, and I think unknown to Copperhead, to review these tapes I'm about to show you. He called me and told me he needed to discuss what was going on out at Copperhead."

He moved his gaze from Mahegan back to the map. "J.J.'s boat was found down here," Johnson said. He pointed at a small chain of islands in Croatan Sound near the mouth of Oregon Inlet. "Washed up and got covered up by some tree branches. No blood. Almost like someone drove it there."

"This has to be about the gold. Merlin shoots a thermal and an infrared beam down to see into water and even subsurface so they can find the bombs. That's how they found that gold from the *Adger.*"

Johnson paused, rubbing his chin and looking at the map, confused.

"Could be. I've got the plane's flight route sketched out here." He took the back end of a number-two pencil and waved it in north-to-south motions over the map of Dare County Mainland. The tracks were identified by straight ruler markings atop the acetate that covered the map.

"These videos were from months ago and done over four days. The green arrows here along the eastern boundary show the first day and correspond to a set of tapes. The red arrows show the second day. The blue

arrows the third. And then the black arrows the fourth
day. Each has a set of video that goes with it. There's
daylight, nighttime, infrared, and thermal. There are
four sets of everything. Royes had built this software
that overlaid each day's flight patterns over the previous days' patterns, in order to show anomalies on the
ground."

"Roger. For example, the video picks up a three-foot-
long metal object. If it looks the same on all four days
with each type of camera, it's probably a bomb," Mahegan said. It was a statement, not a question. Mahegan had seen versions of this kind of software in the
Middle East. The Army called it "Change Detection."
Some Pentagon geniuses believed that if you flew a
plane over the same road a number of times and detected the changes, the soldiers would be able to find
the bombs. It might have worked one out of fifty times,
which he guessed was a Humvee full of soldiers' lives
saved, which was good. But he also wondered about all
the money, energy, and time invested in doing all of
that when maybe the same resources could have been
put into better offensive and intelligence capabilities.
That might have worked better in Mahegan's view. But
that was always his approach. Know more than your
adversary and strike before they do.

"Right. Exactly," Johnson said.

"Do you have them here?"

Johnson coughed. "I have two of the four sets."

"Which ones?"

"The sets that go over the easternmost and the west-
ernmost, but not the middle two."

Mahegan stood next to Johnson, looked at the map,
and thought it through. The Merlin would have covered
the stretch of land from Route 264 to the Long Shoal
River and on the opposite side of the peninsula from

East Lake to Buffalo City. The gold would have appeared in the middle of the map. Those tapes were missing. Copperhead killed Royes and perhaps J.J. because they had found the gold.

"Have you watched them?"

"Yeah, but they ain't *Gone With the Wind* or anything. Boring as hell. Just a bunch of trees, mud, water, and dirt. You'll see the occasional animal. Bear, deer, maybe a gator or two."

Mahegan thought of the red wolves. He had missed them the last couple of days.

"Where do you think your nephew is? Do you really believe he was kidnapped?"

"I think he's gone. You were just lucky to find Royes. I think they were talking about something to do with Copperhead and that got them both killed."

"What makes you say that?"

"Listen."

Johnson walked over and clicked a button on his computer.

"I've got a voice mail download goes straight to this computer. This is a message from J.J. to me."

The computer speaker started out nearly inaudible, but Johnson turned up the volume.

". . . something pretty bad. I'm up here at the theater talking to Miller and we both think there's something there that you gotta investigate. We're both kind of scared." The line went dead.

"That's it. I called him back, but he never answered. Then we get word that he's missing."

"Could he be on vacation? Anything like that?"

"He's a good kid, not a deadender, but not setting the world on fire. Like most kids in their twenties he's a whiz with computers. He's the one who worked out the guidance system for the *Pet*. Midway through the show the ship sails behind the theater appearing to take John Smith back to England. It's all wireless. He does it right from his computer."

Something clicked in the back of Mahegan's mind, like the slow roll of a penny dropping into a cone and spiraling toward the bottom.

"Anyway, my brother, the Coast Guard captain, is worried sick. J.J. would never do anything like this."

"Let me ask you this," Mahegan said. "When I found Royes, I looked at his boots. They said *Teach's Pet* on the inside of them. I originally thought he was a deckhand. You're telling me he worked for a different military contractor that interpreted change detection software. Why did he have those boots on?"

"Oh, them? Like most folks who have been around here for a while, Miller worked on *The Lost Colony* production. Those boots are just part of the costumes. Miller got the occasional cameo as a deckhand, so you're right about that part. But it was just for shits and grins. Miller was handy and did the mechanical stuff—the *Pet* breaks down quite a bit—while J.J. worked the Internet, or whatever it was he did to make it go."

"Say again? Royes *and* J.J. worked on the *Pet*?"

"Well, not 'on it' as in being real deckhands or anything. But, yeah, as I said, Miller did the mechanical stuff and J.J. did the electrical stuff. Pro bono. J.J. can drop the anchor, lift the anchor, start the motor and all that from his computer. Out, in. Left, right. He had to boost the Internet capacity out there so that he could control the ship remotely. I think it's even a wireless hotspot boaters use sometimes."

"So who does stay on it officially? Work it? All that goes with running a ship?"

"Nobody. It's all electronic. That's J.J.'s job. It's got state-of-the-art communications gear. Hell, Lindy gets her Wi-Fi from there. We use it as a repeater for our radios because it covers the north end of Dare Mainland and all the way up to Duck and Corolla pretty good."

"Do you find it a coincidence that the two people who made the *Pet* work are either dead or missing?"

"I don't believe in those kinds of coincidences, son."

"Me neither," Mahegan said.

"So, what do you think?"

"I think we need to get inside Copperhead and find out what they've really got going on in there," Mahegan said. "Check their books. They have an airplane. A landing craft. A fishing rig. Trucks. What else are we missing? These guys have been shifty. And you know what?"

"What?"

"You're not going to like this, but how about you check out J.J.'s background, too."

Johnson stared at him. "Huh?"

"Look at his bank accounts, credit cards, all that stuff. If he's kidnapped or dead, there's got to be a reason. Might be something there."

Before Johnson could respond, they both turned and looked at the muted forty-four inch, high-definition plasma television playing in the background. The news channel suddenly began showing the man the journalists had dubbed "The American Taliban."

"Turn that up," Mahegan said.

". . . and today, Mullah Adham, as he calls himself, has declared that he has another American hostage after a gruesome display in which two fellow terrorists beheaded the first yesterday. He has made no demand for the hostage, but does say that more bombings and killings like those associated with the Fort Brackett and Suffolk compound can be expected."

The stock video footage of Adham showed him sitting cross-legged, mouthing something indecipherable and sitting next to an AK-74. The anchor continued speaking.

"The young American Taliban Internet phenom, Adham, has sent all news stations the following message. 'This hostage will live for twenty-four hours and then will be beheaded. As I did before, I will post the video on Facebook and YouTube and other locations. It will go viral before you can even think about taking it down.' We checked with our American forces in Afghanistan and the few remaining in Iraq and we are getting no word of any hostages taken, though we are cautioned that the head count is still pending from all of the nongovernmental and private organizations. News Channel 4 will continue to bring you the latest on The American Taliban as well as updates on the bombings."

"Why didn't you kill that bastard when you were over there, Mahegan?"

Mahegan looked at Johnson, wondering the same thing.

"No excuses. But I'm not done yet."

The anchor was now interviewing a retired military general talking head. "Bob," he said, "our most current information indicates that Adam Wilhoyt is the son of Barbara Wilhoyt of Davenport, Iowa. We have it from an exclusive confidential source that the mother of The American Taliban worked at the US Army's Rock Island Arsenal as the executive assistant to a senior officer."

Mahegan stared at the television screen, all of the puzzle pieces beginning to take shape and fit together.

Rock Island Arsenal was in Illinois. Just across the river from Davenport, Iowa.

Where General Stanley Bream had served twice, once as a captain twenty-seven years ago and most recently as a two-star general.

Interesting, to say the least.

Was Mullah Adham the son of General Stanley Bream?

Chapter 41

Johnson opened a small door off the bunker, as he called the secure room he had built. In the alcove were a cot, toilet, and shower, not unlike a prison cell.

"I'm going to see if I can't buy us some time with the Feds. You need some rest. So knock out a few while I go into town."

Mahegan looked at the cell and then at Johnson and smiled.

"I'll have to lock you in the bunker," Johnson said, "but I'll let you have access to whatever you want down here."

"Guess this is better than dealing with Johnnie Walker and his nightstick."

Johnson chuckled. "Hell, Walker's a pussycat. Played linebacker for ECU, but the coach couldn't ever get him to hit hard enough. Anyway, the deal is that I got you off the boat and now you're going to help me. We've got a few witness statements and all, but I think the secret is in those tapes. That's what J.J. and Miller were worried about."

"I think J.J. and Miller saw the gold and then got

sucked into trying to alert somebody to it. Or wanted in on it themselves."

"No, they're not like that. Neither of them."

"I saw those big, giant bricks of gold, sheriff. That would be hard for any person to turn down."

"But *you* did. That's my point. Each of them is just as good a man as you are. Or were anyway. That's why you're standing here in my bunker and not in some Coast Guard prison down in Atlantic Beach."

Mahegan ceded the sheriff's point with a nod.

"See you in a few hours," Johnson said, motioning toward the cell. "I've got some explaining to do and some ass to kick."

Mahegan went inside and heard the door lock from the outside. The front door closed as Johnson departed. He didn't like being caged like this, but it was better than most of his current options, and he appreciated talking to someone who was not an asshole.

He was tired, but his mind was reeling with the possibilities based upon the information he had just learned. Sitting at the computer, he opened the file labeled "Green Run Daylight," which he presumed was the eastern run. He watched about five minutes of the daylight flight before putting it on fast-forward. He recognized the video as shot by the same kind of technology they used in Afghanistan and Iraq. The camera had all of the latest lenses with significant intensifying power. Occasionally, the image would zoom in on a spot that might look like a bomb. He worked his way through the first tape in under an hour, seeing nothing of interest except a double pass toward the shore of the Long Shoal Creek. He recognized the terrain as that where he had tied up Lars. He saw the intricate network of roads and ditches that closed in on the bombing range like a series of concentric moats.

FOREIGN AND DOMESTIC   367

He clicked to "Black Run Daylight" and watched similar footage, but over entirely different terrain. There were two flights over water to the west of the bombing range and then the standard flights north-to-south and south-to-north as the MagicAir Merlin canvassed the terrain. He stopped the video about halfway through its run when he saw two buildings at the northern apex of a flight. He zoomed in as best as the software would let him, but the images lost resolution.

Standing, Mahegan looked at the map and figured that the airplane was probably turning just south of Buffalo City. He remembered Locklear mentioning something about Buffalo City and some construction in that area. And he remembered seeing some buildings on his escape run out of Copperhead.

Back at the computer, Mahegan ran the rest of the way through the tape without stopping. He selected "Black Run Night" and saw the thermal replay of what he had just watched. He admired the crew's attention to detail by staying on essentially the same headings back and forth and considered that they may be veterans of change detection runs in Iraq and Afghanistan. He knew that this technology would be able to find significant anomalies up to five feet underground.

At the apex of the run that put the airplane just south of Buffalo City, Mahegan noticed something that a layperson might not see. With thermal night-vision imagery, the individual operating the equipment could select either white-hot or black-hot, meaning heat would show as either white or black. Mahegan didn't have a preference; he just needed to know what the setting was. In small letters at the bottom of the screen, he could see "white-hot" as the setting.

The buildings appeared a lighter shade, holding the heat from the day, as did the concrete streets. The ground had cooled, though, and Mahegan could see the black surrounding the two buildings and the street that fronted them.

There was a faint gray line that appeared four to five feet wide running perpendicular to and beneath the road, as if it were a shallow buried sewer system.

Or an underground network.

Mahegan had seen this anomaly in combat zones and had studied similar tapes in preparation for combat missions. He forwarded the video footage slowly, frame by frame, and watched as the gray line had white spots flash on the screen inside what Mahegan saw now as an underground network.

Rewinding the video, he replayed the flight path at normal speed and watched as it banked over the two buildings. The gray line was barely discernable as were the two white flashes that appeared on the screen, then disappeared less than a second later. Most other people watching this boring film would glaze right over that and keep droning, looking for bombs.

Mahegan watched the rest of the thermal video and then closed out the window. The sheriff was right. He was tired.

He lay on the cot in the cell and thought about what he had just seen. He opened his eyes briefly, stared at the ceiling, and everything fell into place.

But sleep captured him first.

Chapter 42

Mahegan wasn't sure how long he had slept but his internal clock told him it had been about four hours. It was four hours too much and four hours too little. He needed to be out of here, to act now, but he also needed the rest. Two solid days of high-adrenaline combat and he was smoked. The breakfast had been good and the sleep better. He opened a small refrigerator in the sheriff's homemade cell/makeshift tech lab and pulled out a bottle of mineral water, drank it, and then pounded another.

With no windows, it was difficult to get his bearings. It was near one p.m. and if he was right about what he saw in the video, he had to act tonight. He checked the computer clock and it was set for midnight 1997. It didn't seem that Johnson used this computer much, though it was powerful enough to run the MagicAir videos.

He turned on the television and flipped through news channels. They were all replaying the video of The American Taliban announcing his second American hostage. The crawl at the bottom of the television on Fox News showed that the time was 1:17 P.M. Eastern time. He also saw the words, "Update" flashing across the bottom of the screen. Turning the volume up, he listened:

"And we are still monitoring the status of Mullah Adham's second hostage. He has threatened to behead the hostage tonight. He has given no specific time, but we will be watching both Twitter and Facebook for updates."

With grim inflection, the anchor reviewed the events of the past few days. He talked about the dozens of deaths at Fort Brackett, South Carolina, and in Suffolk, Virginia, and the promise of millions more. Then the television showed an image of him, Jake Mahegan, wanted for acting in concert with The American Taliban. It made for good news copy and fit into the overall picture that the Secretary of Homeland Defense had painted about returning veterans being a threat to national security. And certainly highlighted the threat Bream had made to him.

For Mahegan, everything was beginning to fit into place. Copperhead was merely a pawn in a much bigger scheme. Even the gold was a diversionary errand. While he felt good about destroying *Le Concord* and, he presumed, the *Ocean Ranger*, he had always had this nagging feeling that there was something much larger at play.

Now he knew.

He needed to begin collecting the means of combat, and he needed out of this cell. But instead of burning energy trying to figure a way out, he inspected every crevice of the cell Johnson had constructed. Certainly this was not a new structure. The room had too much wear and tear, as if the sheriff had been using it for a year or two.

First, he stared at the map of Dare County Mainland, committing to memory the area around Buffalo City, the abandoned lumber village. Once the land had been deforested, the place had become a vacant wasteland like a ghost town after the gold rush. Johnson had blowups of the bombing range and the electronic warfare range, but little in the way of detail on Buffalo City. Until he found the set of blueprints on Johnson's wall, he had wondered if he'd have to go in blind.

As he studied the roll of papers, Mahegan flashed back to his streak through Copperhead's operation. Off in the distance he recalled seeing a village of sorts. He had calculated it to be a live fire range for training in urban areas. Now as he studied the blueprints, it became clear that was exactly what it was intended to be. Underground tunnels. Speakers for blasting music and messages, shops, homes, and the rubble of combat, all done in a fashion to make the training as realistic as possible. Mahegan noticed the range was set at the northwest corner of the impact area so that the surface danger zone, or SDZ, for live-fire training would be oriented into the middle of the impact area.

During his year in Afghanistan and his year off, the military must have constructed this range to give soldiers and Marines more practice at fighting in urban terrain. Mahegan knew the technical acronym was MOUT, Military Operations in Urban Terrain. In short, he was staring at the blueprints of a MOUT facility.

But he believed it to be much more. The map and the blueprint confirmed what he saw on the night run of the black sector using thermal capabilities.

Tunnels.

And people.

There might have been a training exercise ongoing to account for them, but he doubted it. Copperhead would have scheduled the flights so that there was no chance of live ammunition being fired into the million-dollar airplane and optics ball overhead, not to mention the pilots. The plane had flown directly through the surface danger zone, as depicted on the blueprints, of the MOUT facility. This evidence led Mahegan to think about the slaves he saw strapped into *Le Concord* and transported ultimately to the *Lucky Lindy*.

Was he about to face an army of ghost prisoners?

Mahegan began to do his battlefield geometry to measure the arena in which he would do combat, again. He wasn't certain he could do this by himself, but he had little notion of whom he might be able to trust.

At the sound of a key entering the lock to the metal door, Mahegan moved swiftly to the reverse side of the door. He had noticed the one security flaw in the cell. The door opened inward, not outward, which gave him several options he might not otherwise have.

Prepared to launch, he watched as Johnson stepped through the doorway, pistol in hand and prepared for Mahegan's positioning.

"I expected nothing less," Johnson said. He was holding the pistol in his right hand and the door handle in his left while bracing his shoulder against the actual door, prepared for Mahegan's countertactics.

"I wasn't sure it was going to be you," Mahegan said.

Johnson walked into the container and shut the door. He was holding a duffel bag, which he placed on a worktable.

"Your gear's in there. I couldn't get you much more without raising suspicions. The FBI is looking for you. They think you've escaped. I've not told anyone I have you other than my brother, who is getting his ass handed to him right now by the Coast Guard. J.J.'s his son, though, and I'm hoping you'll get him back . . . alive. Same with Lindy. Alive."

"Is it your impression that I am working for you now?"

"No. I'm smarter than that. It's my impression that you are going to go into Copperhead and do what none of us can do."

Mahegan nodded. He liked Johnson's direct way. The man's face, though, carried an anxious façade. The furrowed brow, downturned lips, and lack of eye contact suggested that Johnson had a lot at stake here.

"Any leads on Lindy or J.J.?"

"Some. On Lindy, there are plenty of footprints in the sand around her bungalow for Treasury to examine. This thing is going to have more three-letter acronyms than a first grader's iPad pretty soon. Her pistol is missing."

Johnson paused.

"And, a fair amount of blood on the porch. Splatter and stream. As if she had been struck and cut."

"No chance it was just a bloody nose?"

"Looked more complicated than that."

"And J.J.?"

Johnson pulled out some documents.

"Bank records. Lots of deposits from Copperhead, Inc. As far as I knew, he didn't do any work for them."

The deposits were all between $9,000 and just under $10,000. For the past two years, Johnson's nephew had made nearly $200,000 in contract payments from Copperhead, Inc.

"Any idea what he did?"

Johnson shook his head. "The only thing he could do is Internet stuff. Websites. Routers. All that invisible stuff no one understands."

Another piece of the puzzle fit into place in Mahegan's mind.

"Then there's this," Johnson said, handing over a piece of paper.

"John Does for Forts Brackett and Suffolk," Mahegan said, more to himself than to Johnson.

"That's right. They identified all the bodies except one at Brackett and two at Suffolk. The John Does' DNA indicate Middle Eastern or Southwest Asian descent."

Mahegan nodded. Bream had said the same thing.

"Ghosts," said Mahegan.

For a moment a thought slid across his mind like a dark cloud. Were Sheriff Johnson and General Bream working together? There had to be some history there. He didn't completely dismiss the thought, but also knew he had to commit one hundred percent to this mission or not do it at all.

He stepped over to the duffel bag and opened it. Inventorying the equipment, he counted a small global positioning system, a Beretta 9mm service pistol, an M4 rifle with rail mounting system, two boxes of 9mm ammunition, what he presumed was a cut-out burn cell phone that was actually a smartphone complete with Google Maps, and some water bottles and Clif Bars.

Mahegan looked up. "Seriously?"

"Hey. It's better than what you had."

"My knife?"

Johnson smiled as he reached into his cargo pocket on his paratrooper pants and withdrew the sheathed blade. "Of course," he said. "My brother's guys figured you'd want this back."

"They were right." The Coast Guard had completely disarmed him, including his knife, which Locklear had returned to him before his jump into the Atlantic Ocean.

Strapping the knife to his leg, Mahegan said, "Thanks for the gear. It will have to do."

"And there's this. Not sure if you need it, but I found it at Lindy's house."

It was an MVX-90 box with Patch's phone number scribbled in his own handwriting. Mahegan nodded and stuffed it into his rucksack.

"I can give you a lift to Dare Mainland, but I don't want to get too close to the gold site down south. I can either take you by boat or car. Your call."

"We'll be less obvious in a car, even though I'd like to come in from the water. So, let's do the car from the north. Slow down and I'll just roll out."

Mahegan wasn't going to reveal his plan to Johnson even though he believed he could trust the man. He really needed to come in from the west, but his study of the map showed no way to do that without alerting whatever was in the guard towers, whether it was cameras or people. Plus, almost assuredly the sentries would be searching the flat water for any sign of intrusion, confident that the thick junglelike forest and its predators would deter any infiltrators.

He placed the M4 in the small duffel with back straps, opened the door, and said, "Let's go then."

Chapter 43

Johnson backed the car into the garage and Mahegan lay down in the backseat with his duffel. He had wanted to ask the sheriff if he could work the pistol and rifle a few times off the pier, as Lindy had done as a kid. He wanted to at least zero the weapons. But in the end, he didn't want to risk detection generated by random gunshots in the early afternoon.

Staring at the Buick's cloth ceiling, Mahegan recalled Johnson's intelligence trove. The tapes, the information on the John Does, and J.J.'s bank deposits all combined to put a fine polish on Mahegan's conclusion.

About the time the sheriff's vehicle stopped, the radio announced, "BOLO, BOLO, BOLO. White male, six foot, five inches, blond hair, blue eyes, Chayton Mahegan, last seen on US Coast Guard vessel near Oregon Inlet, North Carolina. Consider him armed and dangerous and possibly connected to rash of bombings involving Mullah Adham, The American Taliban. Contact FBI immediately upon sighting."

While driving, Johnson leaned over the backseat as best he could with the mesh partition blocking him.

"You're going to have all kind of people looking for your ass," he said. "I'll do my best to send them in the wrong direction."

Mahegan said, "Yeah, but I'm only six-four. They've got me an inch taller. They'll never find me."

"Sense of humor. I like it. Especially at a time like this. I'm figuring you've got less than twenty-four hours. I'm dropping you on the north side of the bombing range, which is about six miles to the south through the forest. You know the rest of the map and have the GPS."

Mahegan visualized his location as he lay there on the backseat wondering about his next steps. It was all about battlefield geometry and intelligence.

"Why the smartphone?"

Johnson looked at the duffel bag.

"I loaded one phone number in there. Use it if you need help."

"I'm thinking it's got a GPS tracker on it and you'll be watching me from your man cave back there."

Johnson nodded.

"Maybe that, too." Then added, "I've got skin in the game here, son."

"I understand."

"I'm rolling into this rest stop. If you get out low and slide into the brush, you should be okay. The rest is up to you."

Mahegan's governing thought from this point forward would be *Slow is smooth; smooth is fast*. To be thoughtful and deliberate created momentum and speed, avoiding unnecessary, time-delaying mistakes.

He was out of the door and made two smooth rolls into the wood line. He moved another twenty feet into the brush and waited. The Buick's motor faded in the distance as he calibrated his senses. His eyes adjusted to the layered canopy of the forest, ears to the conversation between animal calls and road noises. Soon, he would be deep into the Alligator National Wildlife Refuge, where the only sounds he would be able to hear would be the low growl of bears and the slaps of alligators' tails hitting the water

Kneeling in his protected spot surrounded by thick underbrush and low, full trees, he removed the smartphone from his rucksack. He sent one text message to the number preloaded into the phone, and then pressed on the Google News App. The top story remained that Mullah Adham had detained another US prisoner of war and intended to execute the hostage tonight at midnight. He pressed his thumb on the news story and a video started playing. Thankfully, the volume was muted and so he only saw the images across the small four-inch screen. This report had more detail than what he had seen in the sheriff's homemade cell by showing the actual video of the hostage, who appeared petite, dressed in an Army combat uniform, and had the requisite *"Life's a Bitch"* sandbag covering the head. Mahegan noticed that it was the probably the same sandbag used on the previous victim as there were dark stains around the edges where it was tied to the prisoner's neck. This person seemed slight and could perhaps be a female soldier, Mahegan considered. There would be considerably more impact on the American will if Adham were to chop off the head of an American woman on television. The ultimate terror. While the nation was proud of its female troops and their performance in combat, it was still difficult to stomach America's young women coming home in body bags.

He pressed the off button, having seen enough. Removing the back shield from the device and then the battery and the SIM card, he sealed all three components into a waterproof plastic bag and repacked his rucksack. He removed the battery from the GPS as well, holstered the Beretta, checked his knife, and took a minute to register his location.

He calculated that he was about ten miles north and two miles east of Buffalo City. He knew there were multiple obstacles in between his current location and his ultimate goal.

As he made his first step toward Buffalo City, he stopped. His mind replayed the video he had just watched. He had seen the sandbag and the Army combat uniform. The boots and the hands secured behind the back. He had also seen where the too-large uniform created a vee near the neck of the hostage. The sandbag did not cover all the way down the neck and the uniform did not cover all the way up, leaving a small triangle of skin just beneath the Adam's apple.

And where he thought he saw a necklace blinking in the dull light of the video.

What he convinced himself of propelled him more quickly into the dense forest, home to venomous snakes, alligators, bears, and men seeking to kill him.

Chapter 44

As a chief petty officer in the US Navy, Vinny Falco felt he had suffered at the hands of US Naval officers for decades. The way Falco saw it, the Navy had the most entrenched caste system that bifurcated the officers and the enlisted. The Army and Marine Corps, densely populated with ground combat forces that required constant commingling of leaders and led, routinely had closer ties between the officers and enlisted. Then again, Falco thought, the Air Force perhaps had the best relationships between the two strata because everyone was on a first-name basis.

The fact that retired Navy Captain Nix had saved him from the likes of Lindy Locklear had not set well with the former chief petty officer. Falco had taken risks beyond anything that Nix was willing to do. He had stuck his neck on the line in killing Dakota. He had uncovered the curiosities of Royes and J.J. Royes had resisted and J.J. had done okay until, well, until he had quit doing okay.

Falco stood directly above Lindy Locklear. With her blond hair spilling over her forehead, her hands tied behind her back, and a gag tightly secured in her mouth, to Falco she looked like the star of a bondage video. Her eyes wide with fear, she shook her head at him. He smiled.

With his gaze fixed on her slender legs and the curve of her buttocks peeking from beneath her running shorts, his hands drifted to his zipper.

He was standing in a dark cellar beneath the warehouse where Copperhead, Inc. had been storing the MVX-90s. There was the cellar, which Nix knew about, and then there was this place, of which Nix was unaware. Locklear was on the floor, her back against a concrete wall. On the opposite side of the dungeon were a laptop computer and HD monitor on a small card table. The monitor was tracking twenty-seven sensors and nineteen cameras that Falco had placed throughout the bombing range and beyond. Each was displayed in a rotating square on the monitor so that Falco could stop the changing images and focus on a particular area. As a security alert occurred, a graphic image would display on a map to give Falco the specific location and direction of movement of any intruders. With many animals moving about the refuge to the north, Falco had decreased the sensitivity of the remote sensors.

He had charged all of the equipment to the government describing their necessity in keeping innocent civilians away from the bomb clearing efforts. When, in fact, the sensors, cameras, and other technology were protecting something far more valuable than innocent human life.

This was their core business he was protecting.

Just as computer antivirus and Internet assurance companies paid hackers to create new threats every day, Falco and his longtime running mate, Chikatilo, had come up with a similar scheme. While Nix was doing all of his bullshit officer stuff, developing his product lines as he reminded them every damn day, Falco and Chikatilo were planning to increase the need for private military contractors everywhere: overseas, on the home front, and on the high seas.

Falco took his hands from his zipper and looked at his watch as the door opened to the tomblike dungeon.

"My brother," Chikatilo said, smiling.

"My man. Right on time," Falco replied. The two friends gave each other a half man-hug.

"Olsen's in the submarine, headed to DC."

"Sweet. Plan is back on track."

Falco watched his Afghan friend's eyes drift away. "What indeed do we have here?" Chikatilo remarked as he spied the bound and gagged Locklear.

"I believe it's called USDA prime beef, my brother."

Chikatilo walked over and pawed Locklear's legs and breasts. "I'm looking for the stamp. Has no one inspected this yet?"

"Well, the golden boy is about to do a video with her."

Just as Chikatilo ran his thumb across Locklear's cheek, the computer security system made a soft beeping noise. Then it did it again.

On the monitor the map displayed a flashing red dot near Boat Bay, a formidable body of water that protected the northern edge of the new Military Operations in Urban Terrain training facility they had built in the last two years.

The rotating camera display remained steady on camera twelve with a zoom into the region for sensor fourteen.

"What you got?" Chikatilo asked.

"Not sure." Falco walked over to the monitor and played with the zoom function. The camera zeroed in on an area that was thick with underbrush, marsh, and trees.

"Whatever the hell it is, it ain't going far. Probably a deer or bear. Anything smaller wouldn't trip it," Falco surmised. He spoke with the air of someone who had seen several false alarms over the past year that the system had been in full operation.

"Or someone looking for us. One last operation to go, Vinnie. I don't want no bullshit now."

"Nobody's coming for us, Chik. You load up with the new crew tonight and do your thing at the Norfolk Navy Base tomorrow morning. Then Lars hits DC with the MOAB."

"Long-ass drive. I'm smoked."

"One last op. Like you said."

"I saw them new ones. They look weak."

"This new team is just insurance in case something happens. There's also a good crew that's ready for you."

"Something happen? Thought you said they've been rehearsing?"

"Don't worry, brother."

Chikatilo looked at the monitor, which showed nothing, then at Locklear. "Shit," he said. "Lost my woodie thinking about all this. I need to get rolling if we're going to hit tomorrow morning."

"I was heading over there anyway," said Falco. "Got a little show for Miss Locklear here tonight. Once we get there, maybe you'll get that little thing working again."

Falco lifted Locklear by the arm. She stumbled into Chikatilo, who aggressively rubbed his body against hers. The two men escorted her through a sliding concrete door, like a pharaoh's tomb, which closed behind them.

Taking the familiar path, Falco began walking along a series of hundred-meter straightaways met by extreme right angles. He heard the occasional sound of water hissing above them. The tunnel through which they were traveling met the highest standards for underground passageways. Bicolor, flexible, polyvinyl chloride sheet membrane lined the entire system from start to finish. With the many trenches that had been plowed by the loggers as the lumber companies deforested the region and floated the trees to Buffalo City, Falco had only needed to drop pipes into the trench.

Thanks to Uncle Sam, the tunnel was dry, pristine, and easily passable.

After thirty minutes, they surfaced inside the urban village and looked into a small room with a prayer mat and an Iraqi flag on the wall.

They escorted Lindy Locklear into the room, dressed her in an ill-fitting, stained Army combat uniform, and slipped a tan sandbag on her head.

Life's a bitch!

Chapter 45

Mahegan studied the radar sensor from a concealed location. He also had noticed the camera about seventy meters away to his southwest and had backed off slightly to find some dead space.

His route had taken him through dense brush, but he'd had to avoid some open areas such as trails and clearings. As he approached what he considered to be the outer security ring of Copperhead's defenses, he methodically checked every tree, every opening, and every piece of fallen timber. Now he lay prone in some low ground that was nothing more than a fifty-meter-wide concave bowl with some dogwood trees and a couple of pines. The berm seemed almost manmade, but a long time ago, like earthworks of an old redoubt at Yorktown.

Or like the remains of an old Indian village.

The nuances were subtle, but suddenly he saw them. Two lowered portions of the berm that led into and out of the bowl were juxtaposed to one another. Time had beat down the sharper edges of what could have been an entire colony. Aware of all of the radar activity, he felt himself burrow into the earth a bit deeper, actually scraping away a foot or two of loose dirt and sand. His hand came across something hard as he absently burrowed into the dirt.

He stared at a square rock that was about the size of a die. There were no pips he could see, just a small cube that seemed manmade, a cube among the randomness of the refuge. He thought of Locklear and brushed the dirt away with an archaeologist's care. Noticing a small etching on its face, he pocketed the rock and then registered his location in his mind and refocused on the task at hand.

The sensor was desert tan, which made it stand out amid the greens and browns of the Carolina forest. It stood about three feet high and was mounted on tripod legs. The radar was the size of a laptop screen and spun every five seconds before coming to rest again. Recognizing the radar to be an SR Hawk, he knew it could detect him several hundred meters away, but it was useless if he got within about twenty meters. Right now he was about that far.

He noticed the slight movement of the camera and figured that the radar and camera were using the same type of protective measures the Army had used to secure their bases in Afghanistan and Iraq. Motion detectors and persistent stare cameras were the coin of the realm in fighting the roadside bomb terrorists. Now the same technology was turned against him.

If he destroyed the radar, he would raise suspicion in the operations center. If he didn't, of course, he ran the risk of detection. The only advantage he held at the moment was the concept of surprise. While they may fear him coming, they did not yet know he was on his way.

Mahegan had made good time, so he chose the opportunity to rest, drink water, and think.

The key to radar avoidance, of course, was to not cross its path. Mahegan didn't have that luxury. He knew that stealth technology involved special paints and materials, which he did not have. But he did have an MVX-90 stashed in his rucksack.

Stealth technology also involved absorbing and deflecting radar emissions to trick the radar into thinking the object was somewhere else or nonexistent.

But that was complicated by the fact that he anticipated running into several more radars and cameras. He could also cut the camera cable or stay inside the angle of view of the camera.

Mahegan determined that the best strategy would be to get inside the perimeter of the radars and cameras and leapfrog from camera base to camera base. The cameras were positioned on telescoping Erector set–like frames that each sat atop something like a boat trailer. As Mahegan conducted further reconnaissance, he was able to spot two more cameras and sensors in each direction, a picket line of technological sentries. What he didn't see was any kind of road or major path where maintenance crews might routinely ride out and check on the equipment.

He crawled low to the opposite side of the Indian grounds and looked west using the pair of binoculars that Johnson had provided. First, he studied the line of cameras and radars. So far, he believed he was undetected. But to penetrate the defenses, he would need to foil at least one of the radars.

As he studied each camera, he noticed what he could only call manhole covers protruding slightly from the ground, no different than he would see on the street. Dirt and natural debris obscured the covers, but they were there. Mahegan figured that these carried the electrical wiring for the cameras. He registered the location of the covers in relation to the Erector-set trailers upon which the cameras were perched. Obviously, the cameras, radars, and manhole covers were all connected, part of a system.

His eyes followed a canal for about three hundred meters west until it made a sharp left turn near where a large creek meandered and protected the north boundary of the urban training facility. Elevating just a bit, he focused the binoculars to study the broad body of water and the glistening fence approximately a quarter mile beyond it.

So far, the few rattlesnakes and cottonmouths he had seen had been passive. He had also spotted two red wolves, though he doubted anyone else would have seen them. They were motionless, staring at him, perhaps even urging him forward—he didn't know.

Mahegan's eyes found the narrow portion of the stream, which appeared easily fordable. He also knew that this was a readily identifiable choke point, one that would be layered in sensors, cameras, and perhaps even improvised explosive devices.

He was, after all, walking straight into a bombing range.

The sun was hanging low in the western sky as Mahegan prepared to forge ahead and barrel through the defenses. He wondered where exactly Lindy Locklear might be and how much time she had left, if any. Once they knew that she was a federal agent, they would kill her, he was certain.

And while that would be bad, it would pale in comparison to what he believed was going on and about to occur. Adham had significantly raised the stakes in his last few videos.

He burrowed into the protective mound of his redoubt as he reached into his rucksack and removed the plastic Baggies with the smartphone components. He replaced the SIM card and the battery and then slid the backing into place. Pressing the power button, Mahegan waited a minute until the phone had completed booting up. If the sheriff was tracking him, he would now have his position. He saw the GPS flashing at the top of the menu bar. Thinking of the rock in his pocket, he pressed "Mark Location."

Then he noticed that he had a text from the number Johnson had programmed into the phone.

Out of Time, it said.

Tell me something I don't know, Mahegan thought to himself.

Mahegan replied, reiterating the detailed instructions he had given in the first text. Then he disassembled the phone, stuffed it in the bag, and repacked his rucksack. There were three means of attacking this objective, he figured: over land or water, from the air, or from below.

Mahegan had looked at the MagicAir Merlin ground-penetrating radar tracks that covered this portion of the bombing range. The radar had clearly shown tunnels. The manhole covers, Mahegan figured, were probably entrances to the tunnels.

It was a risk, but dusk was enveloping the forest, and he decided it was time to move from the Indian ruins. The broad shadows from the tall pines and oaks provided a false sense of security, and the thermal cameras would have an easier time of finding him in the dark than during the day.

His reconnaissance had highlighted that he would also have to navigate his way through a minefield of cluster bombs that were sticking in the ground like lawn darts. One misstep and he could detonate a single bomb that would then sympathetically detonate dozens of others. Obviously, the pilot had been a tad off on this bombing run whenever it had occurred, as Mahegan knew the actual range was another mile south. He was fifty meters from the base of the camera. To his right was a sensor, active and scanning. He had to have alerted the Copperhead command center at some point, but he knew they were busy.

And short on personnel.

As he watched the radar spin, he made sure he was concealed from the camera and removed the MVX-90 from his rucksack. Mahegan understood counter-jamming techniques and the ground surveillance radar that used Ku Band in the 16GHz range. If he could feed back to the radar the same power it was pushing, the radar would detect no change and therefore report no activity. Locking the MVX-90 battery into the casing, he began to turn the frequency dial, but could see on the digital display that the MVX-90 had already found the radar and that it was recording it at 16.4 GHz. Mahegan looked at the power display, which presently read zero. Here, he dialed in the amount of power he wanted pushed back at the radar and set the frequency at the same GHz. Like two mirrors aimed at each other, the MVX-90 would create an endless feedback loop.

He flipped the power switch and a green light registered, indicating it was pushing against the found device, the ground surveillance radar. Mahegan waited a few minutes and there was no movement of the radar and no movement of the camera. Good enough for him.

Mahegan then navigated the cluster bomb field carefully while staying in the zone of the duped radar. He moved quickly to the base of the camera trailer and its telescoping stand that looked like a poor man's Eiffel Tower. He calculated that whoever installed this system had made a tactical error. The manhole cover was inside the detent range of the camera, meaning the camera could not see if someone was trying to break into the tunnel. Dead space, like on the landing craft and in the Indian hollow.

Exercising due caution, he crawled low to the manhole cover and paused. It was about three feet wide and made of cast iron. Probably weighed about a hundred pounds. He saw the pick hole and noticed that it was not worn, meaning that if anyone used this cover, it was from the inside.

It was a risk, but he used his knife to pry open the lid, which gave slightly without snapping the blade. He slid a hand underneath and pushed up on the cover.

Still not certain what he might expect, he found himself face-to-face with the elliptical eyes of a rattlesnake. The tail was rattling like an African shekere. What he figured to be an Eastern Diamondback was coiled and prepared to strike. With his left hand holding the cover at a forty-five-degree angle, he flashed his right hand across his face as the snake struck, its fangs clicking off the metal of the knife blade.

Mahegan flipped his wrist as the snake bit into the knife, pulling the serpent forward from its perch on a small shelf. The snake fell into the pit. Mahegan heard its body make a scratching thud after about a second or two, which put the tunnel, if it was a tunnel, at fifteen or so feet below.

He used a stick to prop the cover up, allowing him to pull the Maglite from his bag. Using the light, he saw the small shelf the snake had been resting on. How it had arrived at that location, he didn't know. Perhaps someone had left the lid open and then backed down the steps he now saw. After a thorough study, he repacked his bag, slipped it over his shoulder, and descended into the darkness. He used one hand to support the massive weight of the cover and another to push the tree branch out of the way. The cover slammed shut as he climbed to the bottom.

He heard the snake rattle, but it had moved from beneath him. Using the Maglite, he scanned the bottom and was pleased to see a snake-free cement floor.

He jumped to the cement and looked in each direction

Mahegan. Alone.

Moving to the sound of the guns.

Chapter 46

Mullah Adham looked down at the hostage sitting cross-legged on the dusty, cement floor. The tan sandbag read, *"Life's a Bitch!"* on the front, but he could also read, *"And Then You Die!"* on the back because the captive's head was slung forward, as if sleeping. This was not the television room. It was more like a locker room, and he was giving a halftime speech to his team. The hostage was the chalkboard, which he would break.

But first, he paced slowly in front of his troops, recalling himself cowering in the tunnel of Hoxha's compound, his subsequent "capture" by Vinny Falco and the Copperhead Document Exploitation Team, and the deal he had made.

He was the first shipment for Copperhead, Inc. In Afghanistan, the troops called them ghost detainees. So many men were captured that the military had to turn to contractors to help keep track of all of them. Even after the Abu Ghraib scandal, the field detention sites in Afghanistan remained disorganized thoroughfares for detainees. Adham stopped, stared at his ghosts, and paused, a football coach conjuring the right words at halftime. He had come a long way from the night he'd been captured.

First, the two men discussed his fate outside of the container. They clearly knew who he was and were not telling the lieutenant in charge of the small base camp. Adham could see that the lieutenant left them alone and was tending to his troops across the base camp.

"This is the effing American Taliban that everyone has been talking about," the voice said. He remembered the voice and placed it with the man who wore the goatee and earring.

"So, what are you thinking?" the man with the Afghan accent said. He was the interpreter, Adham concluded, but he found it odd that the man had such gravitas with the military contractor, almost as if they were equals. They were whispering in conspiratorial tones. Then again, if they were both private citizens being paid by the military, they were both contractors.

"I don't know, man. It seems too easy. I mean, this is the dude. It shows up in Identi-Kit. There's his fingerprints right there. Adam effing Wilhoyt."

"That transmitting anywhere?" the interpreter asked.

"Chikatilo, I'm not a dumbass. This is all on the hard drive. It's only when you connect it to the secure wireless system does it upload."

"Speaking of using names, Vinny."

Adham heard the tension in their voices. They were trying to decide whether to put him in the system officially or make him a ghost. He knew about the ghosts. Good Taliban and al-Qaeda fighters disappeared every day from the battlefield and were never logged into the system. He knew this because a network of terrorists was inside Bagram Prison on the airfield where the

Americans had their main base. Every day they got an update on who was admitted and they matched that to who was missing. There was always a delta.

The other voice, the one "Vinny" called "Chikatilo" broke the silence.

"Copperhead's in deep shit with the DoD. The Army Inspector General is all over you, how do you say, like white on rice. You're going to lose contracts faster than you can say you are broke, and this may be your last chance to do something big. This is about as big as it gets. All of my people, here in Afghanistan, they listen to this guy on the radio and television. He taunts you Americans like you are idiots. No, he is not the top dog, but he is an important target with connections. I say we ghost him and take him home."

"We? You coming with us?"

"This is the opportunity of a lifetime. The possibilities are endless."

"Such as?"

"We ghost him. No one will know. We put him in a container, drive it to Karachi, put it on a ship, and get his ass to Fujaira. Throw him a few MREs and bottles of water and he'll be able to suck it up."

"Then what?"

"Then we get him on your airplane back to North Carolina and hide him. Use him for information. Sell it to the government. It's all about competitive advantage. Your boss, Nix, is making all these big bucks and we're out here dodging RPGs."

"Come on. You ain't broke."

"I'm not rich either. And neither are you. Why should we take all of the risk and let Nix make all of the money?"

Adham pressed his eye to a crack in the container,

*his temporary prison cell, and peered at the two men.
They were about twenty feet away and trying to whisper.*

"It's risky, but I like it. It's innovative. Only down-
side is that he probably has intel the Army could use
here," *the man called Vinny said.*

"And we can sell it back in your country. I am a
business major from university. I know supply and demand. They will think we are geniuses. We can invent
some name, call it TerrorFinder, or something like that
and say it's all proprietary technology when all we're
doing is ripping off his fingernails and giving the government tips in exchange for contracts. We produce
some high-value target within the first few months, we
are, as you say, golden."

*Adham banged on the thin metal wall of the con-
tainer with his hand.*

"Water."

*The two men stopped talking and looked at him, re-
alizing their mistake. They walked to the front, opened
the container, and tossed a bottle of water to him.*

"You hear all that?"

"Don't like the idea of you guys pulling off my
fingernails."

Vinny looked at Chikatilo.

"Now we either kill him or ghost him."

Adham decided to share his idea.

"Ghost me. But I have a better idea. Ghost some
others, too. You guys want business? I can increase
your market share. Sure, I can give you high-value targets. But even what I know will perish in weeks. You
need a sustainable business model. I can give you that."

Since that day, Chikatilo, the interpreter, had become Adham's most valuable partner in conducting
jihad in America.

The Fort Brackett and Suffolk attacks were already bringing offers into Copperhead for security contracts worth millions of dollars. Adham's idea was to attack military compounds initially and then branch out to corporations. The chief executive officers of corporate giants would have no choice but to increase security the same way the 9/11 attacks had led to the creation of the Transportation Security Administration, which doled out millions of taxpayer dollars to private security contractors. Now the American public was going to make them all rich. Cause and effect.

Back in the basement below the Buffalo City compound, with each step Adham heard the crunch of his Doc Marten boots crushing the fine gravel of the floor, making him think about the sound of crushed lives to come. He observed his charges, and then eyed the prisoner. Should he behead the captive now to motivate his troops? Or should he delay, to frighten the Americans as much as possible? It was a fifty-one to forty-nine percent decision for him.

On either side of him were his two most trustworthy lieutenants: Hamasa and Uday. They were standing on opposite sides of the room, facing each other with the ten recruits sitting cross-legged on the gravel flooring. Well, *trustworthy* was a relative word. The last shipment had brought him eight men, but only these two seemed worthy of leadership in battle. The others were pawns, puppets.

"Men, tomorrow morning we will attack the Americans. Not far from this location is a United States Naval fleet in port."

He stroked his beard for effect, attempting to project an image of Muhammad for his Muslim charges.

"You have trained in close-quarters combat. You have fired your weapons at targets and at mannequins.

You have prepared yourselves for this day and you have traveled far."

He eyed a nervous young man looking at his feet, pulling at his camouflage pants with a twitching hand.

"Do not be scared, men. You were all prisoners once, remember? You had been captured and now you are free. Your freedom comes with a price, does it not? But I demand that you fear no one. Some of you will travel by land and some of you will travel by water, but all of you will reach your intended targets tonight."

He paused for effect.

"Men, you have but one path to your freedom. You began it in Afghanistan or Iraq, and it is a warrior's trail that leads to the freedom of your spirit and your soul. If you are killed in battle, you will die with the highest dignity. And if you live, you will have served the cause you hold most dear with the greatest honor."

Adham raised his arms, lifting them upward, and his men stood.

"Steel your nerves, grab your weapons, and go fight!"

"Fight!" the men shouted back in unison.

Hamasa and Uday led the men through a small doorway and into the arms room, where each fighter secured an M4 carbine, ammunition, grenades, pistols, night-vision goggles, and rucksacks in which to secure all of the equipment.

In the cool night outside, two vans were waiting.

Chikatilo was standing by one and Vinnie Falco was next to the other.

Mullah Adham grabbed Lindy Locklear from their grasp, dragging her by the armpit, and pulled her into the tunnel system that led to Milltail Creek.

Chapter 47

Mahegan followed the tunnel system until he found signs of life at a T-bone intersection: lightly shaded footprints in the sand beneath a manhole cover, food wrappers carelessly discarded, and water bottles left behind. He could not detect any alarm system or monitoring devices. There were motion-activated spotlights every fifty meters or so. At the first one, he inspected it for a fiber-optic camera or transmitting device. He found neither, but he did detect a power line running in serial between the lights. He removed his knife from its sheath on his leg, wrapped rubber medical gauze from his first-aid kit around the handle, slid the blade between the rubberized grommet, and peeled away the insulation to determine what types of wires were encased. To Mahegan the wires looked strictly electrical. There were no fiber optics that he could see, which surprised him. He figured their security would be tighter, but wasn't complaining.

He reached another T-intersection and moved away from what appeared to be the primary opening. He wanted to attack with surprise, not be surrounded when he entered.

His first goal was to find Lindy Locklear. No matter
how badly the government had treated him lately, she
was a federal agent in captivity. He couldn't ignore that,
and he hoped that the text message he sent would bear
fruit.

He hooked a left, away from the obvious route that
had the most debris, and followed a long tube of concrete until he stopped at a dead end and a ladder. There
was mud on the concrete and the ladder rungs were
wet. He looked up and could make out a circular design not unlike the manhole cover through which he
had entered this labyrinth. He climbed the ladder and
pushed on the cover, which gave. Mahegan pushed so
that his night-vision monocle could perch on the rim of
the casement. With his infrared light, he studied the
immediate surroundings. He saw what looked like pine
straw, mud, and footprints. Farther out, he could make
out some tall trees that he assumed were pines and a
creek bed. It looked broad enough even to be a major
terrain feature, such as a river.

He circled back in his mind and recalled the maps
he had studied. He had to be looking at Milltail Creek.
It connected Boat Bay on the interior of Dare County
Mainland with East Bay, which was, ironically, west of
the Mainland and a major brackish body of water that
led to sea.

Another tumbler clicked into place.

He pushed the cover up slightly more and continued
to expand his field of vision . . . and fire.

Exiting the tunnel, he propped the lid up using a
small branch in case it auto-locked when closed. He
moved swiftly to the nearest cover, which was a sturdy
oak tree about ten meters toward the creek. Through
his goggles he saw a small pier that looked as though it
was in fairly good repair. The pier went about twenty

meters into the middle of the wide creek. He presumed this was for fully loaded boats to dock in the deepest portion of the waterway to allow for their drafts. He moved toward the pier and stopped when he saw the *Lucky Lindy* tied to the end.

There it was, sitting still in the motionless ebb of the stream like a statue. It was silhouetted against the wide creek with the waxing moon bouncing off the water's surface. As far as he could tell there were no personnel on board, but it had some space belowdecks that he could not account for through simple visual inspection.

He moved swiftly to the pier, his M4 at the ready with his thumb on the detent button of the Maglite fastened to the rail. As Mahegan crossed the pier, he picked up an anomaly in his peripheral vision. It was on the west side of the pier and appeared oblong as it protruded ever so slightly from the water. Not wanting to break his momentum or be caught flat-footed in the middle of an ambush area, he kept moving to the *Lucky Lindy*. He wondered by how much time it had escaped the dragnet that the Coast Guard had placed. It made some sense, in a tortured way, that the *Lucky Lindy* crew had heard the Coast Guard transmissions and when presented with the dilemma either to return back for their fallen comrade or beat the blockade, they hauled ass.

He swept through the fishing vessel quickly, finding only the unwashed blood from where the crewman had murdered one of the prisoners before Mahegan had killed that man and cut the line on the Bombard. Belowdecks, he found what he figured to be a piss bucket, the usual fishing gear, expended water bottles, and MRE wrappers. Ghosts.

Someone had moved quickly from this boat into the tunnel, and up into the "village." He also saw a toolbox with some basic boat tools and a three-foot length of heavy gauge chain, probably cut from the anchor line. He secured the chain in his rucksack and stopped. He remained motionless for a full minute, sure he was not alone. His senses were hyperalert, yet he was unable to pinpoint an adversary.

Remaining on guard, he moved up to the bridge and checked the waypoints of the boat's GPS, waiting as it powered up. He saw that the Galaxy location was loaded as well as many others. He scrolled through and saw one destination loaded after the "Return Home" label in the destinations menu. He clicked on "Continue to Destination" and saw the route light up that would take the boat out of Milltail Creek into East Bay, north of Roanoke Island, into Albemarle Sound, into Currituck Sound, up the intracoastal waterway into the Elizabeth River, and into port at the Norfolk Naval Base. He zoomed in on the destination point and saw a street name.

Admirals Way.

He visualized the plan. Take the Arab and Pashtun prisoners by boat into the heart of the US Navy and let them loose on the senior-ranking officials who lived on the naval base. Asymmetric attack. Indirect approach. Brilliant, truly.

An endless pipeline of ghosts made for infinite possibilities of attack.

He powered down the GPS. He was wasting precious time. There was always that balance between gathering actionable intelligence and acting on what he already knew. Mahegan now knew enough to stop the larger plan, but not enough to find Locklear. He was going to have to barrel his way through the urban village if he was going to find her . . . and save her.

He stepped from the gunwale of the boat to the pier and carefully scanned the horizon. Still no activity.

He knelt on the pier next to one of the oblong shapes protruding from the water. It was about six feet long and looked like the cockpit of a fighter jet. He slipped his night-vision device on and switched on the infrared light, which illuminated the outline of what was precisely that: a fighter jet, but underwater.

Mahegan had little experience with submersibles, but had seen some used in Iraq in the Tigris and Euphrates rivers. He slid across the pier to the other side and saw exactly the same thing. Two underwater fighter jets, essentially.

These would explain how Copperhead intended to escort the personnel carrier, the *Lucky Lindy*, to the objective, Admirals Way. He ventured that these devices probably could pump out some decent kinetic activity as well. They could shoot.

He moved back to the *Lindy*, quickly worked his Leatherman to remove the transom brackets, opened the engine compartment, and ripped the spark plug wires loose. He cut two with the wire cutter function of the Leatherman. He replaced everything else as he had found it, and then turned to head back to the manhole cover.

As he approached the tunnel entrance, he heard a voice.

"Who the hell propped this thing open?"

Mahegan moved quickly to the bank of the creek where the concealment was best. He flipped the safety off his M4 and tightened the night-vision goggle around his head. Making sure the infrared light was turned off, he conducted a quick pulse check on his PAQ-4C infrared aiming light. It worked.

He watched a man slowly emerge from the hatch of the tunnel. Quickly, two more men with backpacks and weapons followed and assumed firing positions, securing their positions against unwelcome intruders, or him. Next, a line of men with backpacks and rifles came pouring through the hole and ran onto the pier toward the *Lucky Lindy*. In all, he counted ten including the first three.

He remained motionless because they appeared to have good equipment and it wasn't a stretch that they could have night-vision goggles. If he was detected, Locklear would be dead and it would take an average boat mechanic ten minutes to repair the spark plug wires and have the *Lucky Lindy* operational.

His mission at the moment was to avoid detection and to stay alive. He had to ignore the movement he felt across his leg. He was certain it was a snake, but he remained focused and did not look down. Mahegan's knees were pressing into the mud and silt of the creek and he was surrounded by tall reeds and thick undergrowth.

"Maybe Falco or one of them dickheads did it."

He had heard the voice before, when he had first seen the exchange at the *Teach's Pet*. It was the captain of the *Lucky Lindy*.

"Aye. We've got to get moving if we're going to make our time on target."

"Let's load the cargo and get rolling. You've got to drive the boat. I'll lead in the jet—"

After a pause, the other voice said, "What's wrong?"

"There's two Vaders here. Just supposed to be one," he whispered, more to himself than to his partner.

After another silent moment, the man continued as if there wasn't an issue.

"Anyway. The radar will help us make up time. We want to hit those pukes just before sunup."

Mahegan watched as the soldiers loaded the boat and one man lifted the windscreen of the submersible jet and stepped into the cockpit like a pilot of a fighter jet. He logged in the back of his mind that someone else was supposed to have already taken the first Vader. Interesting. He thought he might know whom.

Regardless, he couldn't think about that now. The jet would get rolling and he assumed they could communicate between vessels, so his window was going to be very small to get back into the tunnel. Time was ticking and he knew that Lindy Locklear was bound and gagged and about to have her head severed with millions of people watching on the Internet.

The jet engine made a slight whirring noise under the water and Mahegan felt some vibration through the mud. Deerflies were biting his neck, but swatting them was not an option.

"Not working," said a voice from the boat.

The jet had moved off the pier and was aimed west in the creek. Mahegan had seen wild dogs in Africa once on a mission to Tanzania in the Serengeti. He had studied how the alpha male owned the pack and if he was missing, the pack would wander aimlessly. He needed to create that kind of disarray.

He moved slightly and leveled his M4 at the boat thirty meters away at the end of the pier. Shots would be heard and would provide early warning to the enemy, but the initial confusion would be an advantage to him. Those at Copperhead would first think that the captain had just wasted another ghost or two. No biggie.

Mahegan heard the voice mutter something and saw

the man begin to come down the ladder from the bridge. He thumbed the infrared aiming light, set it steady on the man's torso, and fired a double tap, scoring on both hits. The man tumbled to the deck of the boat. Mahegan moved to the pier and crawled onto it, leveling the weapon at the jet, which was drifting slowly away.

Stay and wait, or go? The jet was probably bullet-proof or at least had some kind of reactive armor. So why waste the shot or the time? He decided to leave the tough decision to the man driving the jet and get moving.

Mahegan was up and out of the reeds like the monster from the Black Lagoon, only sleeker and faster. He covered the twenty meters in five seconds and slid toward the manhole cover as if he were stealing third base against a catcher with a rifle arm. In one fluid motion, he had the cover up and was coming through the hole and down the steps. He ran the chain through the bottom handle of the manhole cover and secured it from reentry from above.

Checking the map in his mind, he moved quickly along the tunnel until he reached the original T intersection where he had taken a left instead of a right. So far, it seemed like the right move.

Only if Locklear were still alive.

Mahegan pushed forward, knowing the clock was moving fast, giving him a quick image of the basketball arena clocks where the seconds and tenths of seconds fall like sand pouring through a funnel. Ten minutes turned into fifteen after trying several different manhole covers, none of which gave him the access to Buffalo City.

Finally, whispering to himself, "Slow is smooth, smooth is fast," his heartbeat remained steady as he climbed the next ladder and pushed up on the heavy metal lid.

In the middle of a street staring at him were the headlights from two vans that were loading more prisoners. They were all fully armed with rifles and backpacks.

Like an apparition, the high beam headlights cast the goatee man's shadow on the road, stretching from the van to the manhole cover.

Chapter 48

Vinny Falco stared at the dark street, wondering about the two gunshots. The urban village was a five-block-by-five-block square. There were stores, homes, apartments, and traffic circles looking just as they did in Afghanistan and Iraq.

Not a tactical genius, but a determined criminal, Falco had a bad feeling. The gunshots could have been his friend, Dan Rogers, killing a ghost and dumping him overboard.

But the double tap. *Bang-bang*. That wasn't Rogers, he didn't think. It definitely sounded like the same weapon, so he didn't think it was a gunfight. Double tap. *Bang-bang*.

Delta Force. Mahegan.

He turned around to speak to Chikatilo, subconsciously edging closer to his vehicle for protection, and said, "Better call Rogers. Haven't heard anything from them for ten minutes. They were supposed to give us the cue that they are on the way."

"Don't like the sound of those shots," Chikatilo replied.

Falco looked at the vans and saw five fighters huddled around his van and another five near Chikatilo's.

"My motto has always been, 'Live to Fight Another Day,'" said Falco.

"What are you saying? Hold up?"

"I'm thinking to live, we might need to circle the wagons here. If Mahegan is back, those shots could have been from him."

There was a soft chirping from Falco's cell phone.

"Go," Falco said as he picked it off the seat of the van.

"This is Rogers," said the voice coming from the speaker. "We were pulling out and I think one of the ghosts shot O'Leary. They are swearing it was someone else, but I'm not so sure. I was in Vader, but I turned around and boarded the *Lindy* to check it out. I checked their weapons and none appear to have been fired. Still. O'Leary's dead."

"Okay. That confirms it. We have a problem," Falco said. "Here's the decision. We're on an official delay for twenty-four hours, except for Lars and the submarine, which is already near the Chesapeake Bay. I will tell Golden Boy. Bring those fighters back through the tunnel and come up on the west end. Set up a base of fire for anyone trying to move back toward the boats. We need them to defend the village tonight and then we can resume the rest of our attacks tomorrow."

"Got it. Mahegan?"

"That's what we're thinking."

Once he was off the phone, Chikatilo turned to Falco.

"Let me take these ghosts up to Norfolk," Chikatilo said. "We can still execute. All those admirals and generals are in one spot. Their meeting is over tomorrow. This is a target of opportunity, my friend."

Falco chewed on his lip and tugged on his earring.

"How you getting in there?"

"Got a Navy sticker and Navy ID. Hit it during rush hour. They always feel pressure."

"How about the other problem?" Falco asked.

"Thought I'd leave that for you."

Falco thought about it. If he was going to come out of this with any amount of fortune intact, he needed just a few more people dead.

"I can do it. But you know Rainbow, the gold, is probably gone, so our hand is forced into this bullshit here," Falco said, waving his hand as if to indicate a future of military contracting.

"Don't forget that there's still about a million in gold in the river that we haven't pulled up."

"I get that. Not anywhere near what it was."

"Remember, pigs make money, hogs get slaughtered."

Falco smiled.

"Speaking of slaughtering, we need to get this show on the road. Okay, take your ghosts up to Norfolk and we'll deal with Mahegan. Once he's out of the way, we're golden."

"I will wait on the word. If I don't hear from you by oh-eight-hundred, I'm going in with rush hour. Their meeting starts at oh-nine-hundred at the officers' club. We've rehearsed it and are ready."

"Then go."

Falco watched Chikatilo step into the panel van along with the rest of his ghosts. He noticed the Navy sticker on the front windshield. It was a blue officer's sticker. Chikatilo was smart. Officers received less scrutiny.

With Chikatilo moving toward Norfolk, Adham about

to conduct some beheadings, and Mahegan most likely moving toward him, Falco did the only thing he knew to do.

He punched a remote control that switched on all of the MVX-90s he had placed throughout the urban village. The MVX-90s were connected to passive infrared switches at key locations. Falco stepped inside his van, opened a laptop, and typed in the code to have the MVX-90s at strategic choke points activate the remote sensors, bypassing the need for a radio signal. The transmitter/receiver did its job and Falco could see that seventeen infrared switches had been armed. Should anything cross one of those beams, the infrared switch would send an electrical impulse to a blasting cap embedded in an explosive found on the Dare County Bombing Range. One-stop shopping. The MVX-90s were in the warehouse. The bombs were on the bombing range. The gold was in the river. This little shit job of clearing some bombs had turned into a literal gold mine.

But it was all being threatened at the moment. Adham's plan had always been a risk. But if they could keep him untraceable to Copperhead and "overseas," then the obvious benefactors would be those companies that could immediately provide security. Of course, Falco had to keep the Adam Wilhoyt/Mullah Adham plan a secret from Nix, whom Falco suspected wasn't quite willing to go as far as he was. Only Falco and his combat interpreter, Chikatilo, were there to interrogate Wilhoyt after watching Sergeant Colgate's vehicle explode, and they would be the ones to benefit. Falco shivered at the thought of how close he and Chikatilo had come to death that morning a year ago, riding in the second Humvee behind Colgate's vehicle.

In the end, Falco had only provided half of the Ghost

Mission to Nix, who had begrudgingly accepted the idea
of using ghost prisoners as slave labor in the marshes of
Dare County Mainland. The other half they were training for combat, which would funnel even more money
in security contracts from the government—money
Falco and Chikatilo would keep for themselves. It was
a double win, free labor plus government dollars funneled through ghost accounts. According to the Copperhead ledger, there were dozens of mine-clearing
personnel being paid. In reality, the Copperhead team
needed only eleven people, now going on seven after
the last few days of Mahegan's madness.

With seventeen bombs rigged to explode and maim,
and his eight-man ghost detail dispersed in defensive
positions in the city, Vinny Falco moved from his
empty van to the inside of a concrete storefront in Buffalo City and headed for the stairwell that led down to
Adham's hideout.

As he descended the stairwell, it occurred to him
that Chikatilo was gone, Rogers should be a few minutes away with his ten ghosts, and that Adham had already moved to a secure location. It was his ass that
was hanging out right now. He had a creeping feeling
that someone was watching him, the same kind of eerie
sixth sense he would have after watching a horror film
and returning home. He would turn on all of the lights,
grab a knife, and walk around opening closets, expecting a vicious maniac to leap from the dark corner
wielding a chain saw.

Mahegan was now that nightmare.

Chapter 49

Mahegan watched the van pass over his lowered man-hole cover, and then he raised it again so that he could watch and listen to Falco. He heard the discussion about the admirals and generals and while he couldn't give a rat's ass about a bunch of soft armchair warriors, he had an obligation to get the attack information to someone who could do something about it.

But timing was everything and the attacks and bombings were hours away. Locklear's death could be only seconds away, if she was even still alive. Now was his best chance to confront Falco and find Locklear. He watched Falco punch a button on a transmitter and remembered the MVX-90s he had seen around the compound. He assumed they were now armed and connected to trigger devices that would be connected to large explosives. Certain that Falco had bypassed the need for a radio signal, Mahegan knew that simply passing through an infrared beam would detonate the bombs.

He figured his one advantage was that Falco did not suspect him to be so close so fast, if at all. If he followed Falco's path, he would also be staying out of the line of fire of the rigged explosives unless Falco was switching new ones on as he progressed into the bowels of the urban village.

Quickly, he was moving down the steps inside the storefront, chasing the echoes of Falco's footsteps. He heard a door open and caught it before it slammed. He saw Falco glance over his shoulder briefly and turn left into a dimly lit hallway. Pulling the door open and leading with his M4 as if he were clearing a building, Mahegan walked quickly along the middle of the hallway. He slid to the left and leaned against the wall, listening. He heard fading footsteps as if they were beyond yet another door.

And he heard voices.

Mahegan moved around the corner, leading with his weapon, and then closed on the door. There were voices on the other side.

"Things are moving fast," Falco said.

"Then, we shall move faster." It was the manic voice of Mullah Adham. There had been so many raids and missions where the goal was to capture the media sensation that was taunting America and leading to the deaths of so many Americans. And now, Mahegan thought, he was in America. And here he was, about to break through the door and put an end to the number-one security threat to America.

He heard the door near the street open above him and the sound of footsteps beating along the hallway. Rogers had to have deviated from the plan to support by fire from the edge of the urban village. No one else was left to respond to his intrusion unless they were random Copperhead employees, but he didn't believe that this part of the operation was fully disclosed to all Copperhead members.

With no time to waste, he kicked the metal door

open and saw a camera, a large green backdrop like they use in television studios, two thugs who could pass for Arabic or Pashtun, both of whom were holding large swords, and a kneeling prisoner. He didn't see Falco or Adham.

His eye caught the glint of steel as one of the thugs raised his sword in an attempt to sever the head of the prisoner, whom he was certain was Lindy Locklear.

He shouted, "Stop!" and fired a double tap into the chest of the guard on the left, leaving time for the guard on the right to flick his sword under the neck of the prisoner, severing the head at the same time two of Mahegan's M4 bullets stopped his momentum.

All of the action, from time of entry into the chamber until Mahegan's final double tap and the concluding roll of the sandbagged head toward Mahegan's feet, took less than three seconds.

Still, he was too late. The prisoner's jugulars were spewing blood until the heart quit pumping. She was dead, so there was no sense in wasting time. He needed to find Falco and Adham.

The footsteps drew near and he turned toward the door, not fully understanding the layout of the complex behind him. He knew Falco was back there somewhere and he moved across the door to be adjacent to its opening.

The first man through was an Arabic man wearing a black jumpsuit and carrying a long rifle. Mahegan felled him with a single shot to the head from ten meters away. Three more men came stumbling through the kill zone and met similar fates.

He didn't see Rogers or anyone who could be Rogers. This was a diversionary tactic and told him that Rogers had seen him enter the building when he'd left the manhole cover and had moved to the stairwell.

He heard a voice behind him. It was Adham.

"Mahegan, so nice to finally meet you. Too bad you could not save the prisoner. But it just so happens that I have another one."

He turned and looked at the fifty-five-inch large-screen HDTV. Adham's face was filling most of the screen. The camera panned away and showed another prisoner, slight and feminine, at Adham's feet.

Snatching the blood-soaked sandbag, Mahegan dumped the head of Sam Nix onto the concrete floor. The man had died knowing what was coming and the grimace on his face showed the fate that he had anticipated.

"Such a good man, don't you think, Mahegan? I think Vinny's got something for you there."

He saw Adham's television image nod and Mahegan immediately ducked and rolled as a pistol exploded in the cavernous hideout.

Mahegan shot out the one lightbulb, figuring he was up against a Navy man in a dark room and that close-quarters combat would not be his forte. With his night-vision goggle he saw Falco scamper behind a wall that Mahegan had not seen. Mahegan flipped on the infrared flashlight on his device and began moving slowly toward Falco. He knew Rogers was still out there and he figured that Falco and Adham would have communications with Chikatilo, who could easily turn around and deploy his ten fighters into this fray.

Falco came lunging from the darkness wearing his own night-vision goggles. He had cued on Mahegan's infrared light, and with his pistol firing rapidly, Falco ran headlong toward the distant beam, putting him in Mahegan's crosshairs.

Mahegan shot the pistol out of Falco's hand and closed the gap between them. He grabbed Falco from behind, putting his neck in a vise. He pressed hard on the carotid artery until Falco went limp in his arms.

The only safe way out that he knew was the way in which he had come in. Undoubtedly, Rogers would be waiting with a decent sniper shot on him as he emerged. He could risk the tunnels, but knew that they would be rigged for explosions.

He knew where he believed Adham and Locklear to be, but had to extract himself from this tightly knit web first.

As he dragged Falco from the dungeon littered with bodies, he heard Adham's disembodied voice.

"Remember a year ago, Mahegan? I was in Hoxha's tunnel, you idiot. I triggered the bomb that killed your man, Colgate. And now I will kill your woman."

Falco began to struggle, awakening from the sleeper hold. Moving into the hallway, Mahegan dragged a now resistant Falco over the dead bodies that lay strewn about. He slapped Falco once in the face, drawing a protest.

"Two questions. Either you answer or you die."

Falco opened his eyes, blinking, realizing what was happening.

"Where are Locklear and Adham?" Mahegan pulled his knife from its sheath.

"You'll never find them in time."

"Answer the question or I will slit your throat."

"Go fuck yourself."

Mahegan said nothing. He raked the blade across Falco's neck. It was a close, personal kill. It felt better than it should have.

He dumped Falco's dying body amid the dead ghosts and moved along the hallway until he reached the stairwell. He opened the door to a burst of automatic fire. Stupid move on Rogers's part, Mahegan thought. He just gave away his position. Mahegan had him at about two o'clock, so he could move to the right side and be protected. Keeping the door open, Mahegan withstood the hail of bullets chipping away at the opposite end of the stairwell. He moved silently along a culvert that ran perpendicular to the stairway along the frontage to the street, like an Arabic open sewer.

Soon, Rogers was in his sights. Mahegan aimed his M4 on the prone body of an American male about fifty meters from his location and pumped two rounds into his torso. Certain the man was dead, he picked up and began moving quickly to the west, back toward the pier.

He tripped two explosives, but they were delayed and behind him. Returning to the pier, he could see the *Lindy* was unguarded and that the remaining underwater anomaly was where he had left it less than an hour ago. Stenciled on the side of the underwater fighter jet, just beneath the cockpit, was the inscription: *Vader 2.*

He lowered himself into the cockpit of the Vader, closed the hatch, and spent a few minutes figuring out how to make it go. With "autopilot," it appeared simple enough. He charted a course out of Milltail Creek, into Alligator River, and over to the northern tip of Roanoke Island.

Where Adham, Lindy, and the *Teach's Pet* awaited him.

Chapter 50

As he navigated the shallow waters of Milltail Creek, he used the slow pace to learn and adjust the controls as best he could. The heads-up display had a variety of instruments representing speed, water depth, and thrust capacity, which was showing ninety-five percent thrust available. He took that to mean once he was in the open water, this thing could move.

On the dash of the cockpit was a thermal and infrared radar system that constantly scanned to the front and sides, alerting him to potential hazards with beeps. The visual was constantly updated in three-dimensional, grid-mapped relief. He saw a fallen tree through the system and tried to turn the "steering wheel," similar to one in a video arcade game, but it turned without his assistance.

The machine had been programmed to avoid hazards.

This feature gave him more time to learn how the machine operated. It was fairly intuitive. Having flown in the cockpit of airplanes and helicopters, Mahegan was familiar with the fundamentals of flying, though he hadn't flown himself before and would have to depend on what he had observed. This machine was made to fly underwater.

The alarm sounded again and he felt the Vader turn sharply. On the grid, he saw the elongated forms of alligators swimming in the widening creek. One appeared to have an animal, probably a deer, in the clutches of its jaws, and a free-for-all for possession was taking place. The Vader made a wide swing around the melee and then reset its course to find the deepest part of the creek.

The alligators made him think back to three days before, when he had bumped into the mutilated body of Miller Royes. He wondered what had happened to J.J.'s body and guessed he now knew. He had probably been Adham's first beheading and then was promptly fed to the alligators. Why hadn't they been as careful with Royes's corpse?

He dialed out the view so that he could see the panorama that included the tip of Dare County Mainland and the northern section of Roanoke Island. Using his index finger, he plotted a course along the touch screen that took him into East Bay, north into Croatan Sound, and directly toward Locklear's cottage, near where the *Teach's Pet* was anchored.

The onboard computer immediately charted a path around known underwater obstacles, beneath bridges, and through the deepest portions of the bodies of water. The display showed him it would be thirty-point-four miles, even though straight-line distance was probably less than half of that. The bulk of the effort was in getting out of the creek and around the northern tip of Dare Mainland.

Soon he felt the vessel pick up speed and he noticed the depth finder was showing him traveling at seven feet below the surface of the water in a fourteen-foot channel. Mahegan calculated that the craft itself had to be at least four feet deep, top to bottom.

Not much margin for error.

Through the windscreen he could see the broadening expanse of the Alligator River. The vessel continued to the middle of the river, where he imagined it was deepest, then banked to the right and suddenly shot like a rocket to the north. The gauges showed him moving at forty mph. At this rate he would be at his destination in forty-five minutes.

Images flashed by in his heads-up display as well as the thermal dash display. To Mahegan, the sensation was a cross between playing a video game and what it might be like flying through outer space. The Vader was now in eighteen feet of water and traveling at the mid-depth point of nine feet. Mahegan figured the basic algorithm most likely calculated the deepest part of the channel of any body of water and then split the difference. The controls turned slightly every few seconds without his urging. Studying the dashboard, he saw that the autopilot light was glowing a deep orange. Next to it was a protected toggle switch that would allow him, he presumed, to go to manual override.

His hand reached out as he noticed on the thermal display a flashing warning indicating they were approaching bridge pylons. Of its own accord, the Vader slowed, adjusted its depth, centered on a gap, and cruised through it. Once on the far side of the bridge, it adjusted its depth again and increased speed as it began to bank to the right. On the GPS map they were rounding the northern tip of Dare County Mainland; they had covered nearly half the distance toward his objective.

Suddenly, he began to receive a series of signals indicating some type of radar activity coming from his target destination. The visual display showed semi-circles bounding outward from what he believed to be his target destination in dim purple light. The heads-up display began to slowly flash, RAM, RAM, RAM.

Having lived a life of deciphering military acronyms, Mahegan guessed that "RAM" stood for Radar Avoidance Mode. Key to his success would be at least getting inside his destination undetected, if that was even possible.

As the Vader pierced the bounding semicircles on the GPS display, a female voice erupted in the cockpit, "Undetected." The farther Vader probed into the radar field, the more frequently the mechanical voice said, "Undetected."

To Mahegan, she sounded like "Bitchin' Betty," the mechanical female voice that warned fighter pilots of impending disaster.

Suddenly, the target destination loomed large in the thermal display. He was three hundred meters away and coming at it broadside. He saw no point in abandoning a winning strategy thus far with the Vader, so he continued to plow ahead, though he did flip from autopilot to manual.

"Manual," the voice said. Then added, "Meshlink active."

Mahegan did not know what "Meshlink" was, but so far everything else was advantageous to his advance. He did notice that he had been able to discern the front nose cone of the Vader up until now. The entire craft had now blended perfectly with its environment, as if it were a chameleon.

Undetectable to radar and to the naked eye, Mahegan thought. Perfect.

Just like the MVX-90s and other radars, the radar he faced, Mahegan presumed, must have a minimum range as well, typically around the fifty-meter zone. This information guided Mahegan's decision to get to within twenty meters. He suspected that there were audible alarms built into the defenses as well.

When the thermal image showed his target less than forty meters away, Mahegan slowed the Vader to a crawl and stopped it at twenty meters.

He surfaced the vessel slowly, the hatch even with the meniscus of the sound. Silently, he eased the hatch open, grabbed his rucksack full of weapons, and began to exit the Vader, when he heard the voice.

"Vader One at twelve o'clock," the female voice said. "Vader One. Twelve o'clock. Current position acquired. Target lock. Defensive measures required. Mesh-link reactive.

"Missile fired."

Chapter 51

Adham looked down at the bound and gagged Locklear.

"A federal agent? Gotta love poetic justice. Did you know I had my entire life destroyed by a federal agent?"

Locklear shook her head. She must be wondering where Mahegan or her government might be. Why hadn't they rescued her? Well, Adham thought, there would be no rescue. Even though the incompetent Sam Nix and his faithful sidekicks had served their purpose of getting him a band of loyal fighters to spread throughout the countryside, Adham was now focused on this single entity.

The federal agent. Revenge. Finally.

Adham had watched from the forest when Mahegan had exited the manhole cover near Milltail Creek. Clasping his hand around Locklear's mouth, he moved as soon as Mahegan had gone back underground. Rogers had turned around Vader One and took control of the chaos aboard the *Lucky Lindy*. After a brief conversation, Rogers had agreed to Adham's plan, realizing Mahegan needed to be lured out of the urban village.

Moving at warp speed, Adham had made the trip in record time.

"A delicious woman like yourself working for the feebs?"

Locklear shook her head. Adham was unable to see the tears sliding down her face because of the burlap sandbag placed over her head.

Life's a Bitch!

And Then You Die!

Adham glanced over at the multiple computers, servers, and display monitors he had surrounding his makeshift office. He had never been that fond of boats but ultimately saw the genius in their employment to achieve his ends.

The *Lucky Lindy* had proven its ability to transport both gold and ghosts. The *Ocean Ranger*, as far as he knew, was doing its job of reversing the gold find so that he would be able to claim it with *Le Concord*. His terrorists on *Le Concord* should have by now attacked and overtaken the unsuspecting *Ocean Ranger*. It bothered him marginally that he had not heard yet from *Le Concord*, but it was only a matter of time, he was sure. Often it took a day or two for information to reach him given the layers of protection he required.

Now the Vader had served as his perfect logistical vehicle getting him to and from the *Teach's Pet* as necessary. Its stealth technology kept him undetected as he ferried back and forth between the empty ship that was really a communications relay station for all of the Outer Banks. Adham had figured out how to gain root on the operating systems within the satellite and Internet protocol devices. Once he was inside the firewalls, he had written some fairly simple code that bounced his video, e-mail, tweets, Facebook postings, and all social media around a set of satellites hovering above the Middle East. Keeping the Vader in defensive mode as he had dragged Locklear through the *Pet's* side hull compartment had been a brilliant move, because it would alert him to Mahegan's eventual approach.

Adham eyed the monitors. He could see the action that had unfolded in the urban warfare training complex. His two best ghosts, Uday and Hasama, lay dead on the floor. The multiple camera angles allowed him to see the disfigured form of Vinny Falco and the severed head of Sam Nix.

He guessed that there had to be a few of his trainees still alive, still ready to wreak more havoc than they already had. Adham's plan was as layered as Nix's product lines. The initial attacks were to strike fear into the American psyche. Now, Adham planned to kill the admirals and generals at Norfolk Navy Base. His ghost army would then spread into the surrounding area, going from house to house. Finally, he had the submersible that would explode a massive fuel air bomb at Fort McNair, in the nation's capital. Adham's notion was that bombs and large-scale explosions, while destructive, were not nearly as terrifying as facing someone mano a mano. But he could also rise to the physical challenge, as he had with the computer techie who had come to the *Teach's Pet* unexpectedly.

It was midnight and Falco docked the Vader behind the Pet, *to its north, so that no one could see them from the nearest land, which was Roanoke Island. The small side door on the* Pet *allowed them to walk along the "wing" of Vader and into the cargo hold of what had become a telecommunications bridge for the Outer Banks. Falco had already mentioned to him this nexus of computer networking gear. The* Teach's Pet *was the perfect digital island. Routers, switches, cell phone re-*

peaters, state, city, federal, county, all on top of one another. Voice Over Internet Protocol, K-band satellite shots, and basic wireless Internet fed by underwater fiber-optic cables. The masts were wrapped with antennae wire shrouded in silicon to defend against the salt water in exactly the same manner as the thousands of miles of underwater fiber-optic cables crisscrossing the oceans. Directional satellite antennae were perched atop the crossbeams, relaying terabytes of data daily around the world.

"We let you do this, you kill that virus and forget about the gold, right?"

"Of course, Mr. Falco," Adham said, eyeing the equipment ensconced in the hold of the Teach's Pet.

"What assurances are you giving me?"

Adham held up a flash drive and said, "Right here. This is the antivenin, so to speak. This flash drive holds the key that will remove the virus from your server and you can have your gold. No one will be the wiser."

"How do I know that's real?" Falco asked.

"How do you know the virus is real?" Adham countered.

"Maybe we should just kill you anyway," Falco said, anger rising in his voice. To Adham it sounded like fear. While Falco had seized on Adham's scheme, the Navy man had never fully trusted him.

"I assure you. The virus is real and the minute I don't update my computer at my preprogrammed time, signifying my presence, my Facebook site will announce to the world the latitude and longitude of your gold find in the Long Shoal River, as well as your subsequent reverse-find operation in the ocean." Adham opened his arms to Falco and finished. "So, have it your way."

Falco, feeling played but vulnerable, motioned for Adham to continue.

Adham turned back to the server farm. It was state of the art. He spent thirty minutes with his laptop hacking into the system and gaining access to the main drive so that he could control the data flow back and forth. He could hide in plain sight for all to see, establishing the perfect illusion.

The *Teach's Pet was Adham's lair; only, he was rarely physically present. He was mostly in Buffalo City, communicating through the elaborate Internet infrastructure J.J. had built.

As he finished, Falco was anxious. He heard a boat approaching.

"What the hell?" Falco asked. Leaning outside, Falco saw a white Boston Whaler center console Montauk twenty-one-foot motorboat approaching. He used the remote to submerge *Vader One* because there wasn't time for them to get out, remount *Vader One*, and depart without being seen.

"Get up on deck and lock the damn door from the outside and then let him board," Adham said, pulling Falco back and closing the cargo hold side door. Falco raced onto the deck to lock the side door. He climbed back through the hatch, locked it from below again, and joined Adham in the dark corner.

Soon, they heard the motor shut off and two men were arguing.

"Hey, Miller, why the hell we have to come out this late?"

"I need to download some data in a secure place, J.J. You run this joint out here for Dare County, so I figure this would be as good a spot as any. I'm already worried they're on to me."

"I need to know what it is, man. I can't be letting you upload some bullshit onto all these servers and *shit. We're a hub for the feds, state, county, everybody, man. I jack this up and I jack it all up."*

"You said you've got super-high-resolution display in here. I've got images from Copperhead. They found gold, I think, and they're trying to hide it."

"No shit?"

"No shit."

There was a long pause, as if they are thinking or looking. Maybe they noticed something?

"Do we get any if it's true?" J.J. asked.

"We can talk about it."

"Okay. Let's take a look."

Adham and Falco moved into the dark recesses of the room as one of them unlocked the door. The two men entered and paused.

"Over here," J.J. said.

J.J. powered up a computer and display monitor, and noticed an unhooked Ethernet cable.

"What the hell? This wasn't unhooked yesterday. You been out here, Miller?"

"Naw, man. I wouldn't come here without you."

"Huh."

J.J. loaded the flash drive Royes gave him into a small computer as he punched up the high-definition display screen.

His fingers worked the keyboard like a concert pianist as he pulled up the digital imaging that the Merlin optic ball had been recording.

Falco thought to himself, sonofabitch. He traded glances with Adham, who was holding a knife. Adham gave him the signal. He would kill the one called Miller, but they needed to keep J.J. alive. Falco nodded.

The two men stepped out of the dark corner before either man could react. Falco had J.J. in a hammerlock

while Adham drove the knife into the other man's kid-
ney and a few other places.

Falco used the butt of his pistol to knock out J.J. and
said, "Man, you're getting blood everywhere."

"Take the boat and do something with this guy,"
Adham directed Falco, who suddenly realized that they
had flipped from prisoner-warden to the other way
around. Adham tossed Falco the knife and now he had
him for blood, prints, and motive. Adham owned him.

"You can drive it. Just push autopilot. It'll do the
rest," Falco said, handing Adham the Vader One re-
mote.

In the rush, Adham connected the Ethernet cable he
had forgotten and removed the flash drive, pocketing it.
Another piece of ownership with the antivenom and the
virus.

Falco took the dead man and dumped him in the
boat, fired it up, and sped away.

Adham then spent another two hours in the Teach's
Pet *doing exactly what he needed to do. He built a back*
door into the Pet*'s communications network that was*
reachable from any Internet Protocol address. He was
golden.

He snapped out of the recent memory and leaned
over to remove the burlap bag from Lindy Locklear's
face. He could see she had been crying. She was certainly quite beautiful and appeared to be more of a
beach queen than a federal agent with the Treasury Department. "I'm removing the gag from your mouth,
sweet Lindy. You are in a place where no one can hear
you and there's nobody left to save you."

Adham pulled the rag from her mouth, eyeing her
small form as he did so.

"The Army combat uniform becomes you, Special
Agent Locklear."

"What the hell do you want from me?"

"Actually, nothing. You are of no value to me. I am taking revenge against the greater establishment that screwed me when I was just a mere child. But—"

Thinking he'd heard a noise, Adham stopped, and tilted his head.

"Probably just the wind," he muttered. The ship was small and creaked frequently with the shifting tides and swirling winds.

"You, an American, *killed* American soldiers," Locklear said. "American citizens!"

Adham cocked his head toward her.

"That, too. Most importantly, I killed our hero's best friend, Sergeant Colgate."

Locklear spat at Adham because, he assumed, she couldn't do anything else. Ha, he thought. For all of her marksmanship training, kickboxing regimen, and endurance running, she was rendered helpless at his hands. If a teenager could invent Facebook and rule the world, he thought, there was no limit to what he could do with a few men, a few hundred ghosts, and the wires of the Internet.

"How is Colgate different from the others?" she asked. "He was Mahegan's friend. So what?"

"Ms. Locklear, you are simply stalling for time, I know. But I will humor you for a moment because I would do the same. Perhaps we are more similar than you think. Al-Qaeda and Taliban forces called Mahegan's team the *Shebah Jeesh*. Ghost Army. They were raiding all of our hideouts. Their intelligence was uncanny and they were getting closer every day—until I hacked the secret Internet used at Bagram Air Base. Once we got through the encryption and code, we learned more than even you would want to know. We learned the details of the missions, which were not as pristine or noble as you might like to think, and we picked them off a man at a time. Just as the US military's goal was to kill Osama, my goal became to kill Mahegan. The al-Qaeda fighter doesn't fear the generals. We fight the warriors, the captains, and their sergeants. Somehow *they* got inside our heads. They were defeating us. So—do you play chess, Miss Locklear?— we began offering our pawns in exchange for their bishops. Hoxha the bomb maker was really just another pawn. Once we changed our strategy, mission after mission Mahegan began to lose one man here, two there, and suddenly he was down to a few *Shebahs*. Ghosts." He laughed. "It's funny, that's what Copperhead calls us now. We are ghost prisoners. No one recorded our capture and no one knows we were on the battlefield. We don't exist, except of course, here in the U. S. of A."

Adham paused. Purging himself of this information had not been part of his plan, but it felt good to communicate his feats to at least one person, a federal agent, whom he thought would at least appreciate his genius.

"But you never got Mahegan."

"Not yet. Our goal was never just to punish America. It was also to kill Mahegan, and we won't stop until we do. Not that you'll live to see it. When the opportunity presented itself to get him, knowing the corruption of the Copperhead team, we took a risk. Our best chance of smuggling fighters into the US became via the private military contractors who had their own airplanes flying in and out daily. They, by definition, were motivated by financial gain and so we played to our enemy's weakness."

"Brilliant," Locklear whispered, unintentionally.

"Yes, I know. Thank you."

"So now you take your gold and live in some palace in the Middle East somewhere?"

"It seems that would be a good plan. But I've grown fond of being a powerful player on the world stage. Would Gates step down from Microsoft in his prime? Would Zuckerberg walk away from Facebook? Bezos from Amazon? I don't think so."

"So you're the Internet genius of terror? You've got that market cornered?"

Adham regarded her a moment, his head tilted again to the side, his adrenaline pumping. She was simply stalling, feeding his youthful ego in an attempt to better her situation, because it certainly couldn't get any worse.

"Yes," he said before snapping himself out of his reverie. "Well, this chat has been useful, but now I must get on with the business of killing you, a federal agent, on live video streaming. You are a symbol of what set me on this course. In many respects you can say this is your entire fault. I was just a kid developing a web game. Some other dude got rich off it. Now it's my turn."

Adham replaced the burlap sandbag on top of her head and picked up a remote.

"Please don't do this," she said, her voice muffled through the sack.

Adham paused, mustering the courage to perform one more horrible task. He thought of himself cowering in his basement as the FBI stormed his home. Then he visualized himself huddled in the tunnel beneath Hoxha's home. Was he feeling courage or fear?

His hands trembling, he felt the whoosh of the blade lifting into the air as he prepared to behead her.

Then the ship rocked from an explosion.

Chapter 52

Mahegan stopped his exit from Vader Two as he heard the repetitive female voice saying, "Vader One has radar lock. Missile fired. Meshlink Reactive."

He quickly locked the cockpit lid in place as he noticed a line forming just beneath the surface of the water, looking like a shark coming in for an attack from his one o'clock. Having spent more time than he cared to admit in tanks and other armored fighting vehicles, Mahegan understood the term "reactive" in its present context. He had been inside an Israeli Merkava tank that had layers of reactive armor protecting it. The Syrians had mastered the art of the penetrating rocket-propelled grenades and in a defensive countermove the Israelis had hung a series of armor belts on their tanks that exploded upon contact. When a rocket hit the reactive armor, the explosives ignited and caused the rocket to detonate early, diffusing its capability to penetrate beyond the outer layer.

In short, all the explosions happened outside the tank, a lesson not lost on Mahegan.

As sophisticated as this underwater machine appeared to be, with "Bitching Betty" calmly telling him that Meshlink had gone "reactive," his first thought was to put the Israeli Merkava lesson to use.

Be inside when it hits.

His Vader rocked upward as a bright orange fireball flashed and then quickly dissipated. The sound was like that of a padded sledgehammer hitting a concrete wall. The flash was brilliant, then gone. Certainly, if he had been outside of the Vader, he would have, at the minimum, been shredded by shrapnel.

Bitching Betty came alive and warned, "Vader One assessing damage. Preparing."

Mahegan quickly programmed a new route into Vader Two, opened the hatch, and then closed it as securely as possible. Pushing away, he heard the muffled voice of Betty saying, "Vader One target acquired. Vader One has launched missile."

He dove deep, the backpack laden with weapons helping him get lower. The second missile was a muffled blast, as if he were wearing headphones. Vader Two was moving away as he had reprogrammed it to do. He felt the heat from the explosives and the shock wave from the reactive armor. He got caught in the turbulence as the sound absorbed the kinetic energy. Tumbling as if he were caught in a Hawaiian twenty-foot bone-crushing wave, he bounced off the bottom of the shallow sound and ricocheted upward. His packful of weapons was tugged hard in one direction as his body was pulled in another, but his grip on the pack was firm.

He had been blown toward the *Teach's Pet*, the only helpful by-product of the blast.

Surfacing, Mahegan quickly found the cargo door, which was amidships and which he presumed was used for uploading the communications equipment. This was not the area to enter, he surmised, as it was most likely locked and proximate to where Adham was hold-ing Locklear. He quietly guided himself to the aft end of the *Teach's Pet*. Scaling the hull and climbing over the gunwale, he slipped quietly onto the deck of the ship, noticing a locked hatch near the ship's wheel.

Kneeling next to the hatch, Mahegan first removed the Beretta pistol Sheriff Johnson had given him. Ma-hegan had taped a Maglite beneath the barrel and now tested the light and chambered a round after ensuring the safety was off.

Doubtful that Adham would be without a bodyguard or sentry of some sort, Mahegan proceeded with cau-tion. He handled the heavy gauge padlock, removed a small pair of bolt cutters from his backpack, and snapped the lock. Sliding into the darkened space below on his belly, he used one hand to brace against each descend-ing step while the other held his pistol. The flashlight highlighted a small circle of flooring where he acrobat-ically reversed his position and was suddenly standing.

Moving swiftly to the rear corner, he began to clear the large area belowdecks. He saw sleeping bunks lin-ing the walls of the ship and a small galley to his front. Mahegan stepped quietly along the wooden flooring wondering how many compartments were on this ves-sel.

His mind was churning through all of the variables. Locklear was in imminent danger. Ghost detainees were roaming, armed and dangerous. He was unfamiliar with the layout of the ship. Adham was elusive. Was he even onboard?

Remembering that this was a communications hub, he began searching the crevices of the deck for wiring. His search was quickly rewarded as he found bunched wires held together by plastic ties every five feet or so. They were running along the floorboard where it met the side of the ship and along the ceiling as well. He followed them until they all bunched together at a far wall and poured through a circular cutout into another room.

He saw a dim light surrounding the wires, like a halo. Dust motes floated in the light, which flickered.

As if it was cast by a television.

Mahegan placed his ear against the wall and heard a soft cry.

"Please don't. Please don't. Please don't."

Locklear was begging for her life and it was too much for him to bear. He frantically ran his hand along the wall searching for a seam, a door, anything.

"Please don't. Please don't. Please don't."

As if it were a recording, the voice continued.

As if it was misdirection.

As if he was he in the wrong place.

Mahegan stopped and stood still, listening. After the fight at the urban training village, he was certain he was in the right place. Bitching Betty had confirmed that Vader One was out there. Adham had to have taken it to here.

"Please don't. Please don't. Please don't."

Had Adham already killed her and was now trapping him inside the ship?

Moving to his left, he found black canvas covering a gun port, which blocked any moonlight from seeping in. Along the hull of the ship, he found the other ports as well, all covered with canvas that hung like drapes. There were mock cannons at each of the gun ports, perched atop carriages that were slammed up against the bulwark as if they were ready to fire on a passing vessel.

Was the only way into the server room through the padlocked door? Mahegan remembered Locklear telling him that they used this ship for the *Lost Colony* production as well as visits for schoolchildren to see pirate reenactments. It would make sense that they sealed off the highly sensitive equipment. However, they would want some type of airflow, he considered.

He moved to the nearest gun port and inspected it quickly. He pushed the cannon away from the hull along the firing platform and it actually rolled. The gun was light, a replica. It made a slight noise as he rolled it back so that he could fit through the gun port. Sliding through, he found a rope hanging over the gunwale running along the length of the ship. He pulled on it and it held firm. As if he were rappelling a rock wall, he moved hand over hand toward the bow, where he suspected Locklear to be.

He passed above one gun port and then paused.

"Please don't. Please don't. Please don't."

It had to be a recording. Every minute or so it would repeat.

"Please don't. Please don't. Please don't."

It was unmistakably Locklear's voice. Digital quality.

Suspecting a trap, Mahegan continued to the next gun port, where he heard nothing.

Then he heard a boat silently approach the north side, opposite of his position, of the *Teach's Pet*.

"Sounds like dear old Dad is right on time," Adham said loud enough for Mahegan to hear.

Chapter 53

Mahegan held on to the rope on the port side of the ship as he heard locks being unlocked and doors being opened on the starboard side.

He lowered himself along the hull until he could see the porthole through which he'd heard Adham's voice. A faint light escaped through whatever sealant the maintenance crews had put in place. He reached out and touched the material. It was rubberized, probably intended to protect the high-tech equipment inside and to minimize light escaping outward.

There was no cannon in this porthole and Mahegan thought about punching through it when he heard a noise from the deck above him.

"Boss is down below. Need to keep a lookout for Mahegan, and then we're out of here."

It was Bream's guy, Paslowski. And probably his sidekick.

"Wouldn't mind taking a shot at Mahegan myself," said Paslowski's blond-haired counterpart.

Mahegan's choices were to either go up on deck and fight through the two thugs or push through the porthole while attention down below was focused in the opposite direction. He pushed at the rubberized material, which had a mesh netting woven into it. The material covering the porthole was surprisingly loose. Using his knife, he cut around the edges and removed the twenty-four-inch by twenty-four-inch cover. He peered inside and saw that it led to a ledge above a chamber about fifteen feet below. He pushed the cover into the porthole, laid it on the firing runway, and slid through. He then placed the cover back into place behind him, forming the flexible material just enough to make it stay.

Once inside, he paused, letting his eyes adjust to the light.

"Mahegan said the *Concord* got away with all of the gold," General Bream said. His voice was harsh, scolding.

"That's good to hear," Adham said.

Mahegan saw Bream shake with rage. "How could you let this happen?!"

"This was never about the gold for me, *Dad*. Actually, it was mostly about you."

"Wait a minute," Locklear shrieked, struggling to listen more closely to the voices around her. "You're his dad?"

Mahegan watched the odd scene unfold below him as if he were watching from a box seat in the theater. The tall general squared off against his bearded son, who bore a resemblance to the father. Locklear was handcuffed with hands behind her back and the sandbag on her head. Adham held the sword in his hands. Bream held a Beretta service pistol.

"I know everything about you, Dad. I've been tracking your e-mail and your every move. I'm on your home computer, your work computer, and your classified computer. I've even sent your team some e-mails on your behalf. Told your two goons upstairs to back off Mahegan a bit. Couldn't run the risk of you locking him up. I wanted him.

"And it's how you received the e-mails offering the gold deal, because I knew that was your only motivation."

Bream dropped his head. He looked lost.

"So, what do we do?" Bream asked.

"You need to kill me, right? You can't be Chief of Staff with a son who is The American Taliban."

Bream shook his head.

"No. You're my son. You were two years old when your mother decided she wanted nothing to do with the Army. She left me. Changed her name. Whole nine yards. I couldn't find her anywhere. It was like she was in witness protection. It wasn't until your Internet tricks that I pursued you and learned who you are."

"So here I am," Adham said, holding his arms out wide.

"There was not much I could do about it when your mother left. But when you went off and I discovered *you* were this American Taliban and—"

"I was going to hurt your chances of being Chief of Staff."

"Something like that. I protected you as long as I could. But this little charade is over." Bream had sounded contrite, but not for long. "It's too late now. Locklear knows too much and we have to do something with you. You're obviously about to execute a federal agent. The scenario we're going to tell people is one where I got here a fraction too late to save the day, Locklear's head was toppling on the floor, and I killed you for the threat you are to the American people."

Bream lifted the pistol.

Through the sandbag, Locklear said, "I'm just expendable? So you can get promoted?"

"The Pentagon is tough duty, trust me," Bream said.

Mahegan was running several calculations through his mind. Foremost, who was the villain here? Adham had killed hundreds of Americans. Bream had as well, his instincts told him.

Mahegan watched the drama unfold, waiting for the right moment to move. Bream was an unexpected arrival, but not unmanageable.

From his perch, Mahegan saw the action begin to unfold. Adham spun with the nimble agility of a samurai and flicked the blade of his sword into Bream's midsection.

Bream was wearing body armor beneath his Army combat uniform and Mahegan heard the clang of metal on ceramic. Bream fired his pistol toward Adham, who was moving. And having lost balance, Bream's aim was wide. With precise aim, The American Taliban slammed the sword into General Bream's unprotected left arm, which fell onto the floor. The general's eyes followed his limb's descent, as if he were an aghast spectator. Just as so many troops in bomb blasts had watched their extremities severed, Mahegan thought. He would never wish it on anyone, but if anyone deserved a taste of his own medicine, it was Bream.

"You son of a bitch," Bream stammered. He stumbled backwards into the hull of the ship.

"I guess that's pretty accurate phrasing, Dad."

Bream still had the pistol, but it was hanging loose in his hand.

Mahegan moved quickly, knowing that Paslowski would be coming belowdecks after hearing the gunshot. He needed to keep Adham alive. He leapt from his perch on the firing platform at the same time that

Paslowski came barreling through the door into the high-tech computer room of the ship.

Using Paslowski's momentum, Mahegan grabbed the outstretched arm of the Inspector General's security guard and propelled him forward into the arcing blade of Adham's sword. Unsure if Adham had been aiming for him or Paslowski, Mahegan drew his pistol and focused on Adham's face.

Paslowski was doubled over, holding in his intestines. It would not be long before he bled out, Mahegan figured. Pentagon is indeed tough duty.

"You're a smart guy, Wilhoyt. Drop the sword and take a knee," Mahegan said.

The American Taliban stared at him. His eyes had the look of a feral animal. First they darted toward the slumping General Bream and then toward the dying Paslowski. He was calculating his odds.

"There's one more upstairs," Mahegan said. "I've wired the ship with some of your favorite explosives and I activated an MVX-90 when I came onboard. The next radio call blows us up. Sheriff, police, Coast Guard, you name it. Even if Bream over here uses his whisper mike to contact Paslowski's buddy up above, we're toast. You only live if you do what I say."

"Mahegan, you son of a bitch," Bream muttered. He held up his pistol, but Mahegan kicked it from his weakening grip.

He was telling Adham the truth. His text message had been to Major General Savage, who had sent his Delta Force comrade, Patch, on a solo mission to rig the ship with an improvised explosive device gathered from Copperhead's unexploded ordnance dump he had spotted on his ride through the compound two days ago.

"Save it, Bream. You've been played from the start,"

Mahegan said. "You lost an arm? Tough shit. Your little scam here cost thousands of American soldiers and Marines their lives and limbs."

"Get me a medic, Mahegan. For God's sake, I'm bleeding to death!"

Adham seemed to perk up, finding dark humor in the situation.

"Brilliant, Mahegan. We make the call, we blow up. I bet you even programmed the MVX to include the cell phone bandwidth?"

Mahegan gave Adham a slight nod. "Put down the sword. You're going to make one last television appearance."

"I said call some medics, captain! That's an order!" Bream shouted.

By now, Mahegan had picked up Bream's general officer Beretta pistol. He looked at Bream and said, "Order this."

Then shot the general twice in the forehead.

"Think I'm joking, Adham? You want one last chance to live? See if you can outsmart me."

Adham dropped the blade, lifted his hands as if to push Mahegan away, and said, "Okay, I'm game."

Mahegan kicked the sword to the side, drew his knife, walked over to Locklear to cut her ties, and then removed the sandbag. As she was trying to say, "Thank you," he took a strip of cloth from the sandbag and gagged her.

"Bitch talks too much," he said.

As she struggled and looked at him with wild eyes, Paslowski's partner came barreling in, shouting, "Freeze! Federal agent."

Mahegan spun and performed a textbook double tap to the man's heart.

"Damn. I like your style, Mahegan," said Adham.

Knowing that there was constant communications traffic funneled through the hold of the *Teach's Pet*, Mahegan had actually told Patch to program the MVX-90 to one constrained bandwidth.

"You're going to like it even more," Mahegan said. "You get to go on TV again. Tell America we are partners. That I killed an Army general. You think I give a rat's ass about this country after what they did to me? As far as I'm concerned, we are partners."

A slow smile crept onto Adham's face.

"You can't be serious?"

"I just killed a three-star general who was supposed to be the next Chief of Staff, and I killed his security guards. That gets me Leavenworth and then the juice. You think I'm on *his* side?" He nodded at the dead general.

"He was dirty. It was a righteous kill."

"There's that," Mahegan admitted.

"So I go on TV and rat you out? What's this do for you?"

"You're kidding, right? You've been ratting me out from the beginning. You just didn't know you were right. I've got Homeland Security, all the three-letter agencies, everyone looking for me. They know I'm close. You're going to tell them what happened here and that I've taken your gold and am living on the high seas."

"The high seas?"

"Yeah. Sounds mysterious. You should like that."

"Okay. I do. Kind of. The high seas. Could be anywhere. Like me."

"Like you," Mahegan said.

After a pause, Adham said, "What *about* me?"

"You? Shave, take a bath, cut your hair, and hide for a while. Keep your Facebook page. I'll be in touch.

Camera's right there. If you don't make the call, I blow the boat. If you do, you're on your own. Pretty simple." He held up a small rocker switch to demonstrate his firm control of the situation. "I need five minutes."

"What about her?"

"Fine piece of ass like that? She's coming with me."

With that comment, he tossed Adham Bream's pistol and said, "Be in touch, dude." He grabbed Locklear, pulled himself up on the firing platform and they dove over the side into Croatan Sound. He pulled her deep, removed her gag, and dug about twenty meters through the water toward the northern tip of Roanoke Island before surfacing.

She tried to scream, but he dunked her after she had enough time to take a breath. After another twenty meters they resurfaced and he clamped his hand over her mouth. Mahegan figured that even the best pistol shooter would have a problem at a range of forty meters in darkness. And he didn't think Adham was much good with a pistol.

"Shut up and swim, Lindy."

She bit at his hand and coughed, trying to breathe.

He took her down again and they swam another chunk toward land, surfacing twice more before they were near enough to stand in the shallow water. He walked her over to the shore. They were about two hundred yards from her bungalow. He sat her down on some riprap. Let her breathe. Put his arm over her shoulder.

"Get off of me. You. You. Murderer!"

She almost got the sentence out before the night sky lit to their front.

Mullah Adham arranged his scene quickly. He made sure that there were no signs of any of the activity that had taken place in the background of his camera shot. The image had to appear as if he was in a cave in Afghanistan or a village in Iraq. There could be no identifying material . . . or bodies to give away the fact that he had been in America all this time.

He considered what he would say. Mahegan had given him five minutes. Were those five minutes for him to get away or five minutes before he blew up the ship if there was no communication from him?

He wasn't going to risk it. He was ready. He aimed the camera at his tarp with the Iraqi flag, grabbed the saber and put it in his lap.

Clutching the remote control for the camera that would begin the satellite uplink, it occurred to him a fraction too late that the MVX-90 could be programmed for any frequency, including Ka Band satellite in the 2.75 Ghz to 3 Ghz range.

His thumb already had the momentum, propelled by the urgency in Mahegan's voice only minutes ago.

His last thought as the satellite transmission began and ignited the explosives planted by Patch was *Mahegan lied*.

Mahegan felt the heat from the blast lick his face. Locklear instinctively closed in on him, seeking protection. He held her as the *Teach's Pet* ignited and crumbled in Croatan Sound.

"You tricked him." It wasn't a question.

"I tricked him."

"But you killed an Army general."

"Who killed a bunch of soldiers. I should have let him suffer, but I was overcome with a need for justice, shall we say."

"What about the other two?"

Mahegan heard footsteps behind them. He didn't turn. He knew who it was.

"They were dirty as well," General Savage said. "And, my guess is, they were armed and threatening his life. Self-defense."

Locklear jumped.

"It's okay," Mahegan said. "He's my boss."

"Savage?"

"Nice to meet you, Miss Locklear. Now if you'll both excuse me, we have a helicopter to catch."

Savage escorted them to a black helicopter with blades spinning as it waited in the parking lot of the Lost Colony Theater parking lot. They ducked as they jogged below the whipping rotors and into the yawning cargo compartment. The crew chief closed the door and the pilot lifted the Black Hawk straight up before nosing over and flying low and fast over Croatan Sound, leaving the remnants of the *Teach's Pet* burning in the background.

Pulling on the headset to talk, Mahegan looked at Savage's set jaw and focused eyes. They weren't done yet.

"Sir, what's up?"

"You asked Sheriff Johnson to look at Copperhead's expenses. They bought a submarine from the DEA and they've got a missing van."

"What about the *Lucky Lindy*?"

"Disabled near Buffalo City and not moving," Savage said over the microphone.

"The van is going to Norfolk Navy Base."

"Okay. The submarine? What they called Vader Three."

"No clue. They've been attacking vulnerable military bases on the East Coast."

"There must be a hundred bases within submarine distance of the Outer Banks," Savage said.

Locklear had slipped on a headset also. She fumbled with the microphone and push-to-talk button, and said, "Where does General Bream live? Or . . . where did he live, I guess?"

"McNair. Fort McNair in Washington, DC. Why?" Savage asked.

"The Navy guys in Copperhead hated senior officers. My money says that submarine is going to park next to Fort McNair and explode near his house with the added benefit of destroying parts of DC," Locklear said.

Savage and Mahegan looked at her, a few seconds passing. It was obvious. Bream would have been a huge loose end for Copperhead.

"They would have had to send it a day or two ago," said Mahegan. "Can we get a P3 or P8 out there to sweep from the capital south along the Potomac and into the Chesapeake Bay?" P3 and P8 airplanes and jets were sub finders. The P8 was new and would be faster, if any were available.

"On it," Savage said. He barked directions into his headset.

The Black Hawk helicopter landed at Fort Bragg. Mahegan and Locklear hurried into a small office while Savage received an operations update elsewhere.

Mahegan watched the Common Operating Picture Display that the special operations command piped throughout the secure headquarters. Navy SEALS had scrambled in MH-6 Little Bird helicopters from Damneck, Virginia Beach, and seized Chikatilo's van and his ghosts.

The report, like a crawl at the bottom of a newscast, indicated that Chikatilo had evaded capture.

The P-8 sub hunter found Vader Three, the submarine, on the bottom of the Chesapeake Bay. The dive
team had retrieved three bodies, two ghosts and Lars
Olsen. Evidently, Copperhead had not conducted an
enduring test run of the submarine.

Satisfied that his job was done, Mahegan turned to
Locklear. He handed her the smartphone Johnson had
given him. He held out his hand and produced a small
square stone the size of a sugar cube. On it was a hand-
etched "D." "Here," he said, giving her the phone. "On
this phone I marked the spot where I found this."

Locklear looked at the cube, and then looked up at
Mahegan.

"The necklace?"

"Could be."

"Virginia Dare," Locklear said wistfully.

"Could be."

"Will you come look with me?"

After a long, noncommittal pause, General Savage
came into the room.

"Here's the deal. Chikatilo is on the run. We have
every first responder possible looking for him. We believe he is heading to central North Carolina or Virginia."

"We have to move fast," Mahegan said, standing up,
ready to go.

Savage nodded, pushing him gently by the shoulder
back into his seat. "We are." Then Savage looked at Locklear. "Locklear, Treasury is asking what you're doing,
where you are, where's the gold, all that happy horseshit."

"I've got a boss, too," Locklear said, adding a subtle
smile. Her blond hair was unkempt. She undoubtedly
appeared tired and stressed. But her countenance was
one of tenacity, of not having been defeated, of surviv-
ing. He watched her hand squeeze the cube tightly.

"You were involved in the deepest black operation we have inside the continental United States. You have to sign this piece of paper which basically says that if you ever talk about this with anyone we will find you and . . ." Savage paused, looked at Mahegan.

"You will have to deal with me. And you saw what I do to people who betray their country."

Locklear grabbed the piece of paper and picked up the pen. But she didn't sign. She tilted her head toward Savage.

"If I'm signing, I need to know. Were they 'righteous kills,' to use a term I just heard?"

"As righteous as they come," Savage said. "We've got e-mail and voice data showing a link between Bream and Nix. We had that a year ago, which is why I floated Jake's name to Bream. To my surprise, Bream bit. He didn't want Mahegan out there knowing about those MVX-90s."

Locklear shook her head. "Man."

Savage continued. "Paslowski and Wilkins, the blond-haired partner, did a spot check on Copperhead after Royes had called the Inspector General hotline. He reported waste, fraud, and abuse as well as something about gold. Bream sent his trusted agents down to Dare County Bombing Range when he heard the word 'gold,' and they blackmailed Nix. Cut the Inspector General in on the gold or they get revealed. Nix said he needed the *Ocean Ranger* to do it right. So Bream started working the contracting angle and got more money dumped into the operation. In all, Copperhead got a deep-sea fishing boat, the *Ocean Ranger*, a semi-submersible, the state-of-the-art tunnel system under Buffalo City, and all the money Bream funneled their way. Nix and Falco had thought of the reverse find on the gold, but it was Bream who funded the operation with government money. He may not have known it, but he was funding the transfer of MVX-90s and unexploded warheads to the enemy as Nix was working the trade with ghost prisoners. Those MVX-90s and bombs killed hundreds of American servicemen and women overseas and at home. Like I said, that kill was as righteous as they come."

"Let me guess," Mahegan said. "The first shipment happened about a year ago? It killed Colgate?"

"About fifteen months ago, it killed Colgate and a lot of other good men and women. That's how we first got clued into Bream's connection with Copperhead."

Savage paused, then said, "And, Lindy, I'm sorry to report it, but Wilhoyt beheaded J.J. We found him."

Locklear dropped her head, stifling a sob. Squaring her shoulders, she let the moment pass, steeled her nerves and said, "Righteous."

She scrawled her signature across the nondisclosure statement.

"Again, I'm sorry about J.J.," Savage said. "Now I need to talk with Mahegan alone."

"Roger. I made a deal with the devil," Mahegan said.

"And thanks to that deal, I have my own personal private military contractor working black ops on the home front. Lucky for you, the National Guard rounded up the ghost prisoners that you didn't kill. They were huddled in the basement of the mock village on the bombing range."

"Gotta be illegal," Locklear said.

"Probably is," Savage replied. "But necessary."

"Then we better not say anything about it," Locklear said.

"My kind of woman," Savage said. Then to Mahegan, "Let's go."

Mahegan nodded at the cube Locklear was holding. "Start digging at that grid coordinate. I'd like to know what happened to the colonists."

He left Locklear sitting in the gray metal chair and followed Savage into his office.

"I need you to spend some time in Raleigh," said Savage. "Get there, get lost, and I'll be in touch."

"Roger. I've got some unfinished family business to take care of."

"And, Jake, it is an honorable discharge."

Mahegan thought of his weapon firing just hours before.

"Well, they were righteous kills."

"No, I'm not talking about them. I've gotten your discharge changed." Savage slipped him a piece of paper. It read "Honorable Discharge" and had his name on it. While he had known all along the character of his service, it was good, he guessed, to have bureaucratic confirmation. He thought of Colgate and all of his men. He had done this for them. And he would keep doing it.

Mahegan shook his boss's hand. He stepped into the hallway and thought about Locklear. He nodded silently to her through the office window and walked out of the building, ready for what was next.

Epilogue

The following morning, Mahegan had one last mission to complete before heading to Raleigh. He returned his gear to Sheriff Johnson in Manteo, had a brief exchange of conversation, then drove across the Virginia Dare Bridge and parked his nondescript Army truck in a sand pullout on Dare County Mainland.

Removing his shirt, he entered Croatan Sound and swam parallel to the shore for about a mile, coming to the small beach where he expected to find them. Mahegan waded onto the shore in between two sand dunes. He sat and waited, looking east toward Roanoke Island and Kitty Hawk. The sky was slate, painted orange in areas where the rising sun seeped through the low clouds in the distance. He could smell the musty scent of fish going to bed in the brackish water.

His muscles that had been ripped by the shrapnel from Colgate's vehicle twitched. Closing his eyes, he felt them moving, pulling through the pain. He visualized the red wolves behind him and to his flanks. With justice delivered to those that had killed Colgate, his attention momentarily slipped to his viper in the cage. He couldn't keep the repressed memories of his mother's brutal murder at bay much longer. This was a moment of peace, though, and as he remembered his father's mantra, *The Spirit lives*, he opened his eyes to find himself surrounded by the predators. There were too many to count. There were mature males and females with pups nuzzling their fur. Dozens of watchful eyes locked onto him.

Mahegan met their steady gaze. They were close, within ten feet of him. He imagined they were congratulating him on a job well done, or comforting him for all he had lost: Colgate . . . and his mother. Like the wolves, he was backed into a corner, scratching to stay alive. Or perhaps they had felt the evil that had emanated from this place. He didn't know.

What he did know was that he had somehow been called to this specific piece of land the way a sea turtle finds her nest after long migrations at sea.

In a world where a homemade bomb could kill his best friend despite all the technology known to man to prevent it; a world that could whittle these red wolves to near extinction, while his own species looked the other way; a world that so needed the hard-won wisdom of the Croatan Indian tribe, but chose to destroy it, it made sense to Mahegan that these wolves were his kin.

And it seemed right that those buried among the Moline crosses were his ancestors. And that perhaps he was indeed a Croatan.

The defender.

ACKNOWLEDGMENTS

Many thanks to the incredible Scott Miller of Trident Media Group. Scott is the best agent an author could ask for: professional, patient, and determined. His steady guidance landed me in a wonderful place: Kensington Publishing. Thanks also to Gary Goldstein, my editor at Kensington, for his encouragement and insights. Both Scott and Gary go above and beyond the call of duty for their authors.

Kensington's editing and marketing teams have been tremendously helpful. Thanks to Arthur Maisel, Karen Auerbach, Maggie Valeri, Vida Engstrand, Alexandra Nicolajsen, and Michelle Forde, who all helped make *Foreign and Domestic* possible. Thanks as well to the amazing Kaitlin Murphy, who continues to make me a better writer. Also, many thanks to Scott Manning and Associates, and their high-octane public-relations strategies. Thanks as well to Judy Peppler, who reads my work and gives me straightforward feedback.

Special thanks to my in-laws, Harry and Janet Washburn, who introduced me to one of the lead bomb-clearing contractors on Vieques Island, Puerto Rico. Over a beer at the bar of Tradewinds restaurant we discussed the time-consuming and dangerous process of clearing unexploded ordnance from a bombing range. Of course, *Foreign and Domestic* is a work of fiction and the contractors in my story are elements of my imagination. Thanks also go to my brother, Bob Tata, now managing partner of the Hunton and Williams lawfirm in Norfolk, Virginia. He was an associate working with the Columbus-America Discovery Group twenty-five years ago, and our later conversations about the discovery of the SS *Central America* and its gold provided ample grist for the plot.

Most of all, many thanks go to my family, Jodi, Brooke, and Zach, for their support and love. Jodi is always the first reader and my most ardent supporter. Brooke and Zach, busy being college kids, still find time to cheer me on and provide fresh ideas.

Lastly, thanks to my parents, Bob and Jerri Tata, both lifelong educators, who taught me a love for reading and writing. They will forever be my mentors.